BALLOON TOP

BALLOON TOP

A *novel by* NOBUKO ALBERY

Pantheon Books
New York

To DONALD

All rights reserved under International and Pan-American Copyright Conventions. Published in the United States by Pantheon Books, a division of Random House, Inc., New York. Originally published in Great Britain by Andre Deutsch Limited, London.

Library of Congress Cataloging in Publication Data
Albery, Nobuko.
 Balloon Top.
 I. Title
PZ4.A335Bal 1978   [PR9515.9.A5]   823'.9'14
ISBN 0-394-50146-2   77-17652

Manufactured in the United States of America

FIRST AMERICAN EDITION

I

'You were born dead. But, merciful Buddha, outside the mosquito net.' Kana's maternal grandmother was a compelling story-teller. 'It's an old saying: a summer baby keeps a doctor in the house; weak, petulant, and crying without a stop. Imagine, what an evil start for a baby if, on top of this, you had been born under the mosquito net's shadow! Your mother took no chances, that stifling humid summer she slept without it. She was nineteen and you were her first baby. Then, you came out dead. Silence. Not a squeak of life. The midwife held you by the wrists and the ankles and slapped you on the little baby-green bottom. One, two, three times! Then came the first *Woo-gyat*! The baby was alive. Your mother fainted.'

Poor Grandmother. She never recovered from the shock of seeing the enemy B-29 bombers fill the Emperor's 'inviolable and sacred' sky. 'Twice did the Divine Winds save this land from the Mongol invaders. This time, I'm not quite so sure. . . .'

She died in the underground shelter down in the garden. In the dim light of a whale-oil lamp, her shrivelled tiny face, life gone, was already a mound of white ashes.

Her grandmother's death left Kana free to knead the story of her birth into a melodrama as spectacular as she liked. In her version her mother, panic-stricken by the silence that followed the delivery, staggers to her feet, snatches the baby from the hands of the midwife and, hoisting up the red limp object, slaps not just three times but seven times, recalling life in it. At the first peal of the baby's cry, she faints. A sinuous, liquid, feminine fall. The midwife snatches the baby just before it drops to the floor and washes it in a wooden pail. It is Grandmother who goes to the next room and reports, to everyone's grave, irrevocable disappointment:

'Well, it's a . . . girl.'

6

'I was born dead. But Mother, she slapped me seven times on the bottom and I came to life.'

When it rained or after playing outdoors long enough, Kana sat with her neighbourhood friends along the edge of the covered terrace, their legs dangling and their heads close together, and she told them stories of her wonder-working mother.

'Electric current cannot kill my mother. Whenever a fuse blows and the house is in tar-black, Mother climbs up the ladder and I hold up the candle, standing on a chair.' Mrs Toda's large sleeves blocked Kana's view and only now and then could she catch a glimpse of her mother's fingers deftly at work. The clutter of her tools, a waft of her camphor sachet mixed with the odour of burnt metal.

'Mother . . . ?'

'Yes?'

'You have no gloves on. Won't you be burnt to death?'

'Not I. Bring your candle closer. You see the positive current running here? There, the negative. Now, watch this. *Sss-park*!'

She flipped at the scraggy ends of the electric wires with her bare fingers. Kana shrieked, screwing up her entire face. When she reopened her eyes to the familiar soft chuckling, her mother was still alive. Light was back in the house. Coming down the ladder, Mrs Toda whispered dramatically:

'Careful, don't touch me now. Two hundred volts, exploding and sparking inside me. Mmmm, itchy!'

And how was Kana to know that her mother had turned off the mains switch in advance?

'And Mother made my tooth plop out by itself. It did. Off its roots!' Kana doubled the size of her eyes and nodded to each of the entranced faces round her. 'And what did Mother do? She just blew at my loose tooth. *Hoop*, like this.'

Kana's memory of the decisive moment when her mother uprooted her tooth was not clear. Or factual. But she went on telling the story, adding this and subtracting that, till it became the one and only truth.

'Wobbly, is it?'

Mrs Toda seemed not at all interested in Kana's loose tooth

when Kana first told her, but a little later, half yawning, she asked Kana, 'Do you want me to have a look at it?'

'Oh, please!' Kana ran to her mother, who then opened her own mouth wide, saying, 'Ah-a-a-n,' nodding to Kana to do the same.

'A rabbit's tooth grows about one centimetre a day, did you know that?' Mrs Toda went on talking idly as her fingers, alert and cautious, felt the gum. Then most casually she asked, 'What if I blew at it?' Without waiting for Kana's reply, she covered Kana's eyes with her left hand.

A warm, soft blackout!

Kana screamed and shoved aside her mother's blindfolding hand. Then, level with the tip of her nose, she saw in her mother's palm a pool of foamy blood with a tiny white tooth shining at its centre.

'Imagine!' Mrs Toda was staring at it incredulously. 'It dropped out at one blow of my breath.'

By then Kana's mouth was brimming with salty hot blood. Both dashed to the bathroom where Kana washed her mouth and Mrs Toda cleaned the fallen tooth.

'Let's see now. It's a lower tooth, so you toss it up to the rat in the eaves. An upper tooth ought to be sent down to the rat under the floor.' She then taught Kana, whose face was still a slush of tears, how to chant a song for her fallen tooth.

'Rat on the eaves. Rat on the eaves. Run quick, bring me a new tooth. My old tooth I let you have. Here!'

How enviously Kana's friends listened. After a long sullen pause, they sighed that it was no fun to have a mother who could not blow a wobbly tooth off its roots but sent a child to a dentist. Kana could tell that they were thinking little of their mothers, their ordinary mothers.

'Mrs Toda, you couldn't put back into the tube the toothpaste that you've once pushed out, could you?' spoke up one of Kana's friends, the only spectacled girl among them. Kana saw her thin neck twitch like a worm, trying to show off with as much impudence as she dared. Because of her spectacles the girl was considered sharp-witted. But Kana was not a bit worried for her mother, who looked particularly beautiful when she said, 'Oh, I couldn't? Come, girls!' her voice crackling with fun.

Mrs Toda walked straight to the bathroom and in one excited scrimmage, giggling, pinching and hugging each other, the girls ran after her. With or without a cunning design, Mrs Toda stood with the four-o'clock September sun behind her back. A furious orange blaze blinded the girls' eyes: only after much squinting under the awnings of their hands could they begin to see what was happening.

Mrs Toda pressed out nearly half an inch of the toothpaste, held the tube upright, primmed her lips and, gently shaking it, started to squeeze the thinned mid-waist part of the tube from various angles between her thumb and index finger. Not to push more out, but to make the vacuum spot inside swallow back what had been pressed out. With her resilient smile intact, she kept on shaking and squeezing. After some reluctant wriggles, the mound of paste began a slow but inward movement. When it stopped squirming downwards or sideways and stayed sulkily rigid, Mrs Toda gave a cautious press from a different angle to cause a new cavity. Someone gulped saliva loudly and at once the rest of them hissed, 'Shhh!'

When more than three-quarters of what had been pressed out had jiggled inside, Mrs Toda asked the girls: 'There, is that enough?'

The girls nodded in unison. Mrs Toda put the cap back on the tube and slipped out of the bathroom.

They stood stock still with their mouths agape, and their palms hot and sweaty. The challenger who was goggling her eyes wider than the frames of her glasses later became Kana's best friend. She often said, 'Your mother is a witch, but if she weren't so beautiful, we couldn't call her a witch. Not quite. Could we?'

Ah, but she was, and that was half of her witchery. Whenever Kana heard her mother opening and closing her chest of drawers, she skidded to the dressing room and sat in a corner making herself as small as possible. Her mother stood erect before the narrow tall mirror. She held five silk strings between her not yet

9

painted lips, their ten ends dangling down to the tatami* floor like festive streamers. Mrs Toda, slightly myopic, squinted her eyes in such a savage, anxious way that she appeared like a tiger about to leap on its prey. There was nothing demure or gentle about her when she was dressing up.

Kana would wince as her mother's long square sleeves slapped and sliced the air as if to whet it; she feared that her mother's head might come off as she fastened her collars and stretched her neck as far out of them as it could go. Meanwhile her lips deftly released one string at a time to tie her waist and to flatten her rising breasts, which, after having breast-fed two babies, had swollen a little too full to be proper under a kimono.

Now Mrs Toda was putting on a kimono which was pale blue, lined with even paler blue silk, with flocks of white cranes embroidered all along the hem and across the sleeves. The strings she had spat out of her mouth were working like extra arms, scooping up the copious slippery mass of silk and tucking it into place. When the last string, squeezing her waist, raised a taut silky shrill, pain was visible on her bitten lips and from the flush that spread from her forehead down to her throat.

She then began juggling with her twelve-foot-long obi.† Tossing its entire length up in a huge billow, she briskly swung her hips. The heavily lined silk reluctantly circled her waist once and thudded, crawled and jerked on a tatami like a boa in its death throes. The second time the obi whistled across the room, Kana ducked her head, goose-fleshed and shivering all over. An acrid camphor scent filled the room. The rustling of silk had grown so intense that it was now a tearing shriek. By the time the rampaging obi was tamed in a butterfly bow at her mother's back, Kana was reduced to a heap of breathless delirium. For there in front of her eyes stood the witch-mother who had slapped life into her baby bottom, a vision of savage violence, beauty and mercy, all inseparable in one burst of life.

*Modular floor mats made of fine reed straw.

†A long wide sash of silk, lined and stiffened, wound twice round the waist and tied at the back with a decorative flourish.

Kana's childhood coincided with the very tail-end of that era when the older generation were still vociferous and confident in their opinions about everything. They filled her gullible brain with superstitions and old wives' tales, mostly about death.

When they talked about life they meant not only the present life but those before and after. And deaths that preceded or followed a life were given as much friendly and daily attention as life itself.

They told Kana that death was everywhere, playful and watchful, and that she had to cover both her thumbs completely air-tight whenever she chanced upon a funeral procession. Otherwise, her elders warned her, her parents would be the next to fill a coffin.*

Catching sight of a procession of black shiny cars or even passers-by in mourning, she dropped everything she was carrying and squeezed both thumbs into the palms of her hands with such concentration that after a while she felt faint in the head. The right thumb was the symbol of the father, the left, the mother. And there was always the disquieting thought in the back of her mind: is my left grip tighter than the right? Not that she loved her father less, he was like anyone else's father, the head of the family, who made all important decisions, took his bath first and was served first at meals, receiving the best and the largest portion of everything. His bowl of rice was twice as big as her mother's and his lacquered chopsticks were the longest with mother-of-pearl inlay. But he was just a father; he could never inflict on Kana half as much pain and terror as her mother could. After the hearse had passed, Kana rubbed her hands to let the blood run again and somehow her left thumb always felt number and seemed to stay pale purple longer.

'Life, death, life, death and life ... you see, it keeps turning like a string of beads. It starts nowhere and ends nowhere.' Mrs Toda was polishing her string of beads before the family altar one morning. 'What were you in the life before, Kana?'

*'Thumb' in Japanese is composed of two Chinese ideographs: 'parents' and 'finger'.

'A rabbit!' No need to reflect; Kana had chosen it long before.

'In the life to come?' asked Mrs Toda.

'A chimney.'

'Or,' winking at Kana, 'an eggshell if you're a bad girl.'

Whether Kana would be reborn as a chimney, watching the life below from high above, cool in summer and snug in winter, or an eggshell doomed to be smashed and thrown into a dustbin, depended entirely on her behaviour in *this* life. Kana believed this firmly.

In each season there was a specific day on which the dead ancestors' spirits made a mass visit to the living. Such days were numerous in the calendar, but these were official and not intimate enough; private visits were necessary between those who had once shared living moments with special affection. Many made their reappearance in the form of insects: grasshoppers, ants, moths, butterflies, beetles and so on. Some slipped into objects in the house where they had lived, such as an old blurred mirror, a stone lantern under a swaying willow, or perhaps a squeaky door that sobbed in the night. Those visitors were so numerous and ubiquitous that the living could hardly move without disturbing them. Thank goodness, Kana often thought, they're invisible.

The altar was in the family's sitting room. Since it was the family altar, Chiyo was not allowed to touch it. Each morning it was Kana's duty to fetch fresh water for the flowers and see to the cleaning of the altar, while her mother set out new candles, incense sticks, arranged flowers, rang the bells and turned a page in the Book of the Dead. This book had thirty-one pages and on each page were the names of the family's ancestors who had died on that particular day.

'Already eight years ago today . . .' sighed Mrs Toda, after perusing a newly turned page. 'This favourite uncle of mine used to say that he would come back to see me as a typhoon every autumn: "I'll smash your enemies' houses and ruin their gardens." How he used to make me laugh.'

One morning Kana took the plunge: 'Mother, what will you be when you come back to see me?'

'A dandelion.' Her answer was swift. 'A dandelion that's turned into a white fuzzball. That'll be me. You'll watch out for it, won't you?'

After her mother left the room with an armful of wizened flowers and the half-burnt candles, Kana sat by the altar thinking about her mother and the dandelion fuzzball.

She did not like the idea: Mother, a dandelion fuzz? She used to love imagining who would be reborn as what. Now it was no longer amusing: it was frightening. Mother into dandelion fuzz! A sinister trick. For the first time she hated and feared death: only once, just once, during this short lease of life could she be her mother's daughter. Just one encounter, just one chance. Death was dreadful.

Kana moped about the house, feeling rancorous against everything. The late spring afternoon was listless, slimy, altogether cheerless. She felt very much like doing something outrageous. A raid on the family altar, the forbidden spot, seemed suitable. Mother was out for her weekly samisen* lesson and Chiyo was washing clothes at the other end of the house.

Kana ransacked the heap of ceremonial effects stored in the back of the altar steps; prayer books, packets of incense, strings of beads, sealed letters, feather dusters, and the chipped but ornate china and so on. Becoming bolder, her hands dug deeper till they pulled out two identical oblong boxes of pale, luminous paulownia wood. They were labelled with a thin paper mounted on a surface of silk brocade. One bore Kana's name and her date of birth, the other, her sister Yoko's.

The top lifted to release a cloud of crinkled rice paper. As her fingers whisked open layer after layer, a harsh smell of incense stung her eyes and throat. What finally emerged looked like a cinnamon stick. No, it was more animal than vegetable: rather like a shrivelled slice of meat.

Kana shut the box, shoved everything back under the altar steps and fled. She found her knees wildly shaking as she came

*A mandolin-like musical instrument with three strings, plucked by an ivory plectrum or a finger.

to the bottom of the stairs and could not go up to her room. Instead she locked herself in the bathroom and washed and scrubbed her hands, but the insidious smell did not quite go away. The question gnawed at her mind: what could that grotesque object be?

I can't be shaking for ever in the bathroom. She went out and heard Chiyo humming her usual silly tune in the kitchen. Kana prowled round the maid, watching her rinse the rice for dinner for a while, then casually questioned her about the two boxes.

'Do you know what's inside?'

Chiyo wrung her wet hands in her apron and hurried after Kana to the altar room.

'Why, this is yours, Miss Kana. Your navel cord.'

'My what?'

'You were tied to your mother down there with this bit of tube before you were born. That's what it is. Everything starts from the navel cord. Here!'

Chuckling, Chiyo applied her index finger lightly to Kana's skirt. The slight touch of the finger on her tummy was the last thing Kana could remember. She fainted. Chiyo, thoroughly alarmed, ran to the telephone.

When Kana recovered her senses, old Dr Togo was holding her wrist. Mrs Toda with her spring shawl still round her shoulders sat close behind him and Chiyo, by the sliding doors.

'Little one, can you tell me what made you feel strange at the very beginning?'

Kana was speechless.

Dr Togo was willing to wait but Mrs Toda quickly came forward on her knees to Kana's pillow side.

'Kana, you heard the doctor's question. Now, answer.'

'I was scared.' Kana managed this much, Chiyo nodded understandingly, but her mother sighed. 'What a difficult child. A summer baby, you see?'

'Indeed,' Dr Togo responded with sympathy.

'I was scared.' Kana could not have said more. The stark facts were that she had been born out of her mother and that both would soon be back to nothing, after only one brief life, just one life together. And if this wasn't unbearably sad, grotesque and terrifying, then what else could be?

From that day on she loved her witch-mother with such pity and passion as never before.

The Todas' house squatted like a sunken steamer way behind a dense grove of fir trees. No part of the house was visible from the street. A wall of coarsely chiselled stone and mortar, roofed with black baked tiles, stood nine feet high all round the garden. There were two entrances: the main gate in the auspicious south and the service entrance in the north-east.

Except on festive days the main gate was opened only for Mr Toda and his guests; normally the women used the north gate – a humble low wooden sliding door set in the wall – in common with fishmongers, kitchen-knife sharpeners, pilgrims with herb medicine, straw-mat menders and kimono merchants from Kyoto. All day long there was the ringing of the doorbell and the gay hubbub of a market-place. Yet, what to Kana made the house *inside* and the world *outside* was the seldom-used main gate. Every night she lay tense, keeping her ears pricked to the sound of Chiyo's footsteps down the pebbled path to the main gate. The iron bolt and the lock had to be re-examined for the night. When the wooden sandals tapped their way back into the house, Kana sighed and dropped her head to the pillow. Without a main gate, Kana thought, this isn't our house. She pitied all little children with no high walls and iron-bolted gates. How could they sleep, left afloat in the vast swallowing black of the night?

'Lock her out of the main gate, Chiyo!' was the first thing Mrs Toda said after the guest had left. What had Kana done to deserve this punishment? She had merely contradicted an elderly relative at the lunch table.

Kana raised a long beast-like howl and threw herself on the terrace floor, coiled her arms round the pillar, and hugged it like a monkey sliding down a palm tree, crying, 'Don't throw me out! I'll never do it again!'

By then Mrs Toda had finished packing a toothbrush, paper

tissues, a towel and two 10-yen coins in a furoshiki.* She then let the parcel drop in between Kana's arms which clung round the pillar.

'Chiyo!' Her voice was louder than necessary, her enunciation was razor-sharp. 'Make sure you bolt the bar across the gate.' Chiyo gazed at her mistress. Mrs Toda bent over Kana and said clearly, 'You heard what I said? I disown you. Dis-own. You're no longer my daughter; nor your father's.' She turned, her kimono sleeves fanning her camphor scent into Kana's tearful eyes, and walked away. All in such a final manner. 'Disown' was not yet in Kana's vocabulary, but the sense of doom conveyed in 'bolt her out of the main gate' with only a small parcel and 20 yen was lethally clear.

'Let's go,' Chiyo said in a purposely blunt tone. Kana dropped her arms from the pillar but would not move an inch further; whereupon Chiyo not only thrust her hands under Kana's armpits and shoved her up in one swoop, but dared make Kana pick up her parcel herself. Taken aback by the servant's insolence, Kana had to conclude: This is how things are when I'm disowned and no longer of this house.

'Stop crying, Miss Kana, stop crying.' Chiyo yanked Kana's wrist to punctuate her reprimand. Kana went on crying while Chiyo got more and more contemptuous and even hostile. She pulled Kana's hand higher and strode faster till Kana's heels were hardly hitting the ground but were flying and skidding like a kite.

Chiyo threw her scraggy body against the huge gate and pushed. She did not hustle the child out of the narrow opening but sternly waited for Kana to step out. She began humming her pet tune, 'Tennessee Waltz', looking away from Kana's wet clinging eyes. The gate was closed behind her and she heard the hinges creak, the wooden bar reluctantly slide through the rusted iron loops, and the terrible finality of the bolts being pushed home. Chiyo, still humming, walked away. After that fell an

*A large silk or cotton square used by men and women to wrap and carry almost anything.

absolute silence.

There on the steps, howling and snivelling, Kana sat with her only belongings in this world squashed between her thighs and her chest. A train whistled down the hill. Tears streaked down her face. As she examined and re-examined the items with which she was left, she noticed her mother had forgotten toothpaste. No soap either. What about fresh underwear? And what if Koreans kidnapped her? Kana sprang to her feet, banged on the gate, apologized, promised and pleaded at the top of her lungs.

'Mother, please take me back! Let me in!'

The wind rustled in the bamboo foliage, dry and brittle. But everywhere else, a dead silence and refusal. At regular intervals Kana made frenzied pleas but the house behind the fir grove remained deaf-mute. Exhausted, she hugged her kneecaps and squatted motionless in the same spot.

When the sun was starting to hide behind the Rokko mountains she heard Chiyo's wooden sandals on the pebbled path. On opening the gate, finding Kana exactly as she had left her hours before, Chiyo hissed through her teeth with undisguised scorn, 'Just sat there. Just sat there!'

Kana dived under Chiyo's arm and ran up the winding path at a desperate speed. So fearful of being locked out again, the back of her neck felt as if it were on fire. When she reached the top of the gentle ascent, she stopped and listened.

Pts-tsng-tsng. Yun. Yun. Tsng.

It was her mother with an ivory plectrum plucking the three tautly spanned strings of her samisen.

Why, it's six o'clock already! Kana said to herself. Just like any other day at home, her mother was practising. She took a deep breath – I am taken back! No doubt about that. I am back in the family!

Tsng. Tsng. Yun. Yun. Tsng-tsng-tsng.

Kana heard Chiyo behind her but she did not run; she was the young mistress again. She timed her steps to the beat of her mother's music. On each crystalline sound Kana stepped. On her blissful toes and ears fell her mother's mercy. On the *tsng*'s and *yun*'s Kana rushed up to her mother's room.

17

2

The miseries of war for Kana were her continual diarrhoea and her witch-mother rapidly dilapidating.

Late in 1944 Mrs Toda with Kana and Yoko, Kana's baby sister, were evacuated from the city. With a cartful of belongings they moved into a shack they had rented in a village called Shitsukawa, lost in the depths of a sunless valley. The rocky soil bore no rice and a farmer without rice was an embittered man. The villagers had to manage on their scarce wheat mixed with millet, mock barley and root yam. Men were either wood-cutters or charcoal-burners. Women tended their pocket-sized vegetable gardens, plaited straw into sandals or rain capes, and sent their children into the woods and to the riverside to hunt for herbs, nuts and edible roots.

Once Kana saw a woman holding her son upside-down, shaking him to make him sick up a poisonous mushroom. Other boys made a circle round the mother and son, shouting, 'We told him that the mushroom umbrella had red spots. But he said he didn't care and ate it!'

As long as it was tender, Kana thought, I too wouldn't have minded the red spots. Her famished stomach had been fed with such tough-fibred plants as clod burr, bog rhubarb, fern brake and yam roots. They grated her intestines like wire sponges.

The villagers took advantage of the evacuees from the city. Having no confidence in the currency, they insisted on bartering food and then only in exchange for silk, jewellery or something of lasting value. In exorbitantly one-sided deals and with malicious joy they stripped the Todas of their family possessions. For a few small fish, mostly carp from the muddy brook near by, or some nuts and vegetables they demanded one single-layered silk kimono; for a chicken and a dozen quail eggs, a lined kimono with hand-painted or embroidered designs.

18

From time to time the landlord slid open the doors to let in a villager who would thrust forward a still jerking fish, some nuts or an armful of greens. In squint-eyed silence they waited for Mrs Toda to go to her wicker kimono chest. Black despair on her face, her cheeks hollower, she studied the fish and the farmer's face, looked down at Kana and her baby sister – too under-nourished to wake or cry – then, slowly, she crawled over to the chest. Clasping a kimono against her thinning breasts, she made her way back on her knees. Until the farmer's knobbly hands grabbed it from her, she buried her face obstinately in the kimono.

After they had eaten the fish a hungry cat would not have bothered to stop at the plate. The last drop of marrow had been sucked. The bone had lost all lustre. Mrs Toda sewed with her tearful face stubbornly turned to the rain-stained wall and Kana hummed a lullaby and patted her baby sister as gently as she would have a dying kitten.

Kana had no one to play with: the village children were just as malicious and vindictive as the grown-ups – if anything, more unashamedly so. They could not bear the sight of the four-year-old girl 'from the city' dressed in 'inexcusable Western clothes' and spoiled by such luxury as leather shoes.

A gang of noiseless barefooted children were constantly on the watch for a chance to attack her. They laid ambushes, sometimes squatting in the dried ditches and at other times in the bamboo forest behind the shack, immobile and silent for hours on end.

Twice they succeeded. The first time they took Kana's leather shoes and threw them into a manure pond. Another time, they dropped a thin green snake down the back of her clothes. As she shook and wrung herself frantically to get rid of the snake, they rolled on the dusty ground, rocking with fits of rapturous laughter.

At night, listening to the raucous winds that stirred the bamboo forest just beyond the thin wall, Mrs Toda stroked and warmed her daughter's greenish swollen stomach with her hands. When the child's sobbing rose to a pained shrill, she picked Kana up in her arms and dashed outside to the toilet in the courtyard, a

19

mere box with a hole in the raised floor. No roof above, just a huge oak tree towering over it.

'I have a feeling ... perhaps tonight or tomorrow ...' Several times a day Mrs Toda let out the same languid sigh and Kana, alertly picking up her cue, responded, 'Oh, Father, Father!' If she felt strong enough, she might clap her hands or jump up and down to cheer her mother up. But then it was always Mrs Toda who instantly sank back to a grim despondent mood, muttering, 'Perhaps. It's just a feeling ...'

Mrs Toda sewed and mended clothes for the villagers who owned vegetable gardens. Kana went on rocking Yoko, as light as a cotton puff. Every night the same thing. Waiting for the father to come. Kana never knew of his arrival till Mrs Toda stopped her needle quietly, stretching the focus of her eyes to a far-away point.

Bamboo leaves would be rustling and the winds meandering round the courtyard just like on any night. But soon there would come the sound of footsteps crackling on dry fallen leaves. A knock on the sliding door and a harsh whisper through a slit in the planks:

'It's me!'

Mrs Toda threw aside whatever was in her hand, jumped down barefoot to the mud floor, unlocked the door and, flying back to the raised tatami floor, she bowed to her husband. Behind the low opening of the door stood a pair of gaitered legs in dust-covered soldier's boots. A reserve officer, Mr Toda was in uniform. Mrs Toda kept her forehead on the tatami till Mr Toda threw off his haversack. Then Mrs Toda, shyly at first but with increasing alacrity, helped her husband to take off his cap and greatcoat. She unwound his moss-green gaiters, a white puff of dust blowing into her face each time she loosened one more round.

There was not much conversation. Mr Toda took a handful of rock sugar from his satchel, smiling at Kana. Kana recoiled from it with utter disbelief. Mr Toda went on holding out his hand to her. Kana, flushed red in the face, shrank back further. Her father in the end put the sugar in her lap. The parents watched eagerly as the child, her eyes flashing with excitement, timidly put one lump on her tongue. The dense clinging sweetness of real sugar. With the first gulp she choked. She coughed and squealed fitfully. Mrs Toda could not help being furious with Kana: how dare she spoil the happy moment? She slapped Kana on the back, weeping and scolding alternately.

Soon Kana fell asleep and her parents' whispering undulated on and off like a deep river under her pillow. In what a warm glow did she sleep on such nights, beside both her parents, with her lips and tongue still savouring the luscious rock sugar.

But quickly it was dawn and her father had to wrap his legs in gaiters again, for his journey involved a twelve-mile walk to the nearest station and three changes of trains. Kana sat watching her mother help him turn into the green-uniformed soldier. Before he put on his haversack he whisked Kana up in his arms.

'What's the matter with this child? She doesn't smile; her wrists are like pine needles!'

He then hauled her on to his shoulders and skipped about, tilting her to right and to left. The vertigo and terror almost sickened her empty sleepy stomach, but she clung to her father's neck trying to understand what he expected of her. Before the war to be carried pick-a-back had been an unsurpassed treat. And he wouldn't be doing this for nothing, would he? Kana was frantic: what was she expected to do?

Somewhere Kana heard her mother laugh. A strange laugh, more like a breathy gurgle. Kana turned around and saw her mother's tear-filled eyes wide open and her lips paler than her teeth, contorted by her efforts to force a 'laugh'. Still laughing Mrs Toda nodded to Kana. Ah, she was to laugh: Laugh, Kana, laugh for your father's sake! Kana filled her lungs and did her best. It sounded more like an asthmatic cough but her father stopped hopping and shouted with delight.

'How she laughs! How she laughs!'

By the time she was let down from her father's shoulders she had vomited a small milky bile of terror on his green soldier's cap. He took up his satchel. Ready for departure, he made a stiff military salute. Mistaking it for another of his pranks, Kana forced herself to giggle, but to her amazement, she found her parents gruesomely serious this time. They stared at each other. Finally it was Mr Toda who briskly turned on his heel and closed the sliding door behind him.

Another waiting.

By the summer of 1945 there was nothing left in Mrs Toda's wicker chest except for her magnificent set of wedding gowns. She often spread them on her lap and felt them with her eyes closed. She told Kana that these gowns were as valuable as gold of the same weight.

During the monsoon season the baby Yoko had a serious case of food poisoning and a doctor had to be sent for from the town. Kana overheard her mother hiss through her teeth, 'Never! Not these! Not as long as my eyes are black and moist!' But in the end they were taken away.

With all her kimonos gone, Mrs Toda dwindled and looked twenty years older. Unkempt, her hair dangled in wisps round the shoulders of her grimy cotton kimono. She made no effort any longer to keep her knees properly closed when she sat on a chair husking wheat. She who before the war used to tie Kana's legs with a crêpe-de-Chine sash so that even in sleep the child would discipline herself against vulgar postures

For Kana her mother looking like a weather-worn scarecrow was an even more terrible and frightening sight than the mountain ridges flushed in lurid pink under an intense enemy air raid, even though she knew that beyond the mountains lay Osaka where her father kept his business in operation throughout the war.

Came the 15th of August, 1945.

The village chief's garden was jam-packed with villagers right up to the hedge. The entire population, including Kana and her mother with Yoko strapped on her back, had gathered and jostled against each other in order to get closer to the terrace, in the centre of which sat importantly on a soiled and tattered silk cushion of royal purple the only radio still functioning in Shitsukawa.

The Emperor was announced and the jostling and chattering villagers immediately bowed their heads in silent reverence. A reedy irresolute voice from the radio went on and the sun scorched relentlessly their exposed napes. Kana felt her head boil and her limbs on fire.

'Mother, I'm hot! I'm thirsty. I'm dizzy. Mother, I'm . . .'

A quick unrestrained hand struck across her face. Pure astonishment, she did not even feel the pain at first, only a bitter numbness on her left cheek. She looked up at her mother who had immediately resumed a warped posture. How hideously ugly she was: her washed-out cotton kimono tucked inside a monpe,* her hair dishevelled, her face glistening with the perspiration and tears that rolled down her hollow cheeks, and the strings that held Yoko on to her back biting deeply into her pitifully thin shoulders.

Finally the Emperor's speech came to an end. Without a second of reflection the entire congregation burst into throttled, bitter sobs, which rose quickly to a convulsive wailing and howling. There in the torrid bright sun men and women were wiping away their tears with the sides of their bare arms, gasping for air, snivelling and trying not to look at each other.

Kana's consternation was almost panic. She had never seen grown-ups behave like this. She clung to her mother's thigh, as if otherwise her mother would break in pieces.

After what to Kana seemed an eternity the village chief went inside his house; the villagers began dispersing. Mrs Toda and Kana trotted back on the path that made a short cut across the fields. Mrs Toda walked fast, heedless of Kana; she pulled and jerked Kana's arm so mercilessly that Kana feared it would be wrenched out of its socket. She whimpered; her mother took no notice. Kana screamed; still her mother did not slow down. Kana had to jog all the way home. At each step she took, her face, her skull and her teeth jangled with pain.

Back in the shack Mrs Toda, having no one else to talk to,

*Baggy trousers that were considered the appropriate clothes for women in wartime.

told her five-year-old child about the Emperor's speech. The war is over; the Emperor is no longer a god and from now on the enemy is going to be called the Allied Army of Occupation.

Kana kept on patting her feverish cheek, her eyes sulking on the old discoloured tatami floor. What about my swollen cheek? What if my left eardrum's broken? That night with the pain thumping her head, she cried herself to sleep, still not finding the justification for such a ferocious slap from her mother.

At home and the family together again, the first thing Kana begged for was the box of toys that had been buried somewhere in the garden. Many boxes had been buried underground to protect them against B-29 raids.

'Which box? Toys? Later, later.' First things first, Mr Toda said, such as the boxes of porcelain, lacquer plates, scrolls and screens of painting. And when it finally came round to digging up the toy boxes, no one could remember the exact spot. Kana whimpered loudly but in those days it did not sound like much of a grievance.

'There, there. Stop crying. We'll get you 'modan' nice toys very soon.' Another empty promise, just like the earlier one: 'Kindergarten? But, Kana, where do we find one? Of course, we'd send you to one if there were any in operation. Besides, people would say "What an extravagance!" or "How dishonourable at a time like this!"' Later Kana learned that a number of kindergartens had been in fact open, to which many honourable parents had sent their children.

The long winter was without much to eat and almost every night the lights went out. To economize on candles and fuel the family sat in one room, round a single charcoal brazier, and shared a common worry: 'How much longer can our black-market woman avoid arrest? What then?'

She was the widow of a sergeant and had a daughter working as a housemaid in the Army of Occupation barracks. The daughter was given American food, which the mother stowed away in two large brown velveteen bags and paid clandestine visits to her select customers, selling it to them at exorbitant prices. 'With me, you don't worry. I'm a soldier's widow. My lips are sealed,' she told them.

In early December she was arrested. She slipped on the frozen snow and spread her entire stock on the pavement. She was indeed a soldier's widow: none of her fearful clients were summoned by the police.

With tins of K-ration and Hershey bars no longer available, the Todas began a dreary regimen of what the authorities called 'substitute food': yams, taro, barley gruel, corn dumplings, and so on. In other words anything else but rice.

'I just can't feel I am Japanese without silver-white rice!' It was Chiyo who complained most about life without rice. She had stayed in Osaka to look after Mr Toda throughout the war and when Kana returned from Shitsukawa, she was astonished to find Chiyo so manifestly stricken by the onset of old age: morose and full of ineffectual grumblings. 'In my village my family had no gas or electricity, never saw a chocolate, never heard of peanut butter, but rice, rice they had in plenty!'

When at last 1945 came to an end, the Todas thanked merciful Buddha. To think that they had somehow survived such a turbulent year!

Towards the end of February came the requisition order from the Prefectural Office. The Todas were forced to move into the detached house in the garden, built originally to accommodate servants. And a family by the name of Bridgewater was to 'occupy' the main house: Colonel Bridgewater of the United State Army, his corpulent pink wife with golden fuzz all over, and their two sons.

Inevitably, a fleet of their own vetted Japanese domestic staff moved in: the maids in starched white uniforms and the house-boys with GI haircuts and an addiction to chewing gum. In addition two American military policemen with bayonets were stationed at the main gate with cigarettes drooping wet in the corners of their mouths. They did not bother to shake the ash off: once lit, a cigarette stayed till it died out between their wet fleshy lips. After the first few weeks they were replaced by two young Japanese guards, exact replicas of their US predecessors from head to toe, even in their manner of smoking.

The Japanese 'hosts' were allowed to use only a small area, the boundaries of which were marked in red pencil on a map which Mr Toda posted on the wall for his family to observe.

Mr and Mrs Toda reluctantly acknowledged the rights and the privileges of the victors and silently obeyed when Mrs Bridgewater required that the Todas and Chiyo, the 'natives', be vaccinated by an American Army Hospital intern before she and her family entered the house. But Mrs Toda could not stomach the strutting Japanese domestics. She said she could not live under the same sky with those gutter mice in their rented tiger furs. 'What are they?' she fumed. 'Traitors! Sluts dressed in *American* cotton. Spineless morons propped up by the guns and boots of the enemy. I should never have let them cross the threshold!'

'No use complaining,' said Mr Toda and he sought to make the best he could out of the humiliating situation. Whenever he was summoned by Colonel Bridgewater to the main house he returned with an armful of K-rations, sugar and oil. Mrs Toda, although with a faint flush of embarrassment, quickly carried the glorious food away and did not refuse to eat it either. It was Chiyo alone who refused to put any of this foreign muck on her tongue.

Kana and Yoko sometimes stepped out of their safe red-pencil area but they did not dare tell their mother.

Once they trespassed the limit line purely out of habit, and were caught by the patrolling guards. They pointed their odious bayonets at Yoko's breast and ordered Kana to turn three times and bark like a dog.

'Then, we'll let you and your sister free. OK?' The one with the square nose imitated an American accent with his 'OK'. So proud of it that he repeated it many times.

Watching their Japanese faces under the deep MP helmets, Kana did her act. The moment she finished barking, Yoko tumbled into Kana's arms. As they ran away, the men's guffaw hit their backs like a shower of bullets.

And then there were Persimmon and Dumpling.

At half-past three a shiny Lincoln station wagon, driven by a middle-aged Japanese butler who was dressed at all times of the day in a tuxedo with grease spots on the front, brought back the young Bridgewater boys from the American School in Itami. From then on, the garden, both inside and outside the red-pencil line, turned into a hunting ground, for the boys recognized no territorial restriction on their side. Persimmon and Dumpling had a copious collection of toy weapons. What terrified the Toda girls particularly was their home-made sling with the pebble bullets, made for them by their Japanese houseboys.

That May, after a gentle moist spring, the garden was aflame with azaleas. Kana and Yoko went from one plant to another, eating the honey stored generously in the mouth of the petals where the floral flesh, paler in colour, slimmed into a French-horn shape. The hungry children nibbled and sucked the cool sweet juice and swam in waves of violet, crimson and purple, but as soon as they heard the car down at the main gate they returned to the house.

One day after a lunch of sweet-potato leaves and a few K-ration biscuits Kana was still hungry. She went out alone into the garden. The azaleas were just beyond the dividing line. But with the sun so warm and crisp on her cheeks and the sweet scent filling her nostrils, a mere red line on the map seemed silly. Kana went on sipping the azalea syrup . . . .

The trumpet-shaped azalea dropped from her mouth! Kana turned deathly white and her thoughts raced wildly. But it's not yet three-thirty, surely! The movement at the edge of the bush did not stop. Three-thirty or not, there they were, Persimmon and Dumpling. Their heads, like emerging submarines, were sailing up to her fast. What is it today? A sling-shot? A water pistol? Or like the last time, the broken long-necked rifle?

Pzht!

A shot missed Kana, pierced the air like a whip. It's a sling-shot! Kana felt her blood curdle.

The red head made its way much more nimbly and faster than the darker one. Having had no friendly discourse with the occupying family, the Toda girls did not know their real names. They had nicknamed the older boy Persimmon: he was about twelve, slim and restless with radiant orange hair. The other, Dumpling, although not more than eight, was already bloated with lazy fat. He thudded along behind Persimmon with his neck bent forward.

Kana ducked low and scrambled through the azaleas and bushes. Staggering out of the bushes, she looked up.

Oh, no! She had come out on the wrong side. The only chance now was for her to reach the Todas' cottage by going deeper into the forbidden area and over the pond across the narrow wooden bridge. But if the Japanese MPs caught her? Kana, petrified, hesitated, but the boys were closing in on her, imitating the wild yoo-hoo-hooing of savages. Kana ran forward. She would have done anything, would have jumped into a volcano crater, just to delay the moment when their hands would grab her pigtails. Dumpling saw her and shrieked a warning to his brother. Kana reached the pond, looked back once and dashed on to the bridge, only to stumble less than half-way across where a rotten plank had caved in. She fell spread-eagled like a jellyfish over the width of the bridge.

Persimmon saw his chance, ran swiftly to the other side of the pond and with a falsetto cry gesticulated to his slowly waddling brother to trap Kana between them on the bridge.

'Pam-pah-pah. Dah-dat-dat!'

Persimmon sang a triumphant marching song as he approached his prey. Dumpling swung his arms round and round to balance himself as he gingerly stepped forward. He whistled and raised a bestial shriek, giddy with the excitement.

Slowly Kana rose to her feet. Persimmon stopped within arm's length. She could see the fiery red hair on his bare arms and hear his heart pounding. At the final moment, without fear or pity for herself, she stared straight into Persimmon's eyes. A look of hesitation and shame spread over his freckled face. He stood stock still, appalled.

Dumpling arrived on the other side of Kana, steaming out sour bad breath into her face, stuck out his chin and eyed his brother.

'What now?' He was not at all put off by this obscenely one-sided triumph.

Kana, now brazenly calm and almost indifferent, watched Persimmon's eyes, their pupils like two drops of pale aqua ink. She could see that he was in trouble. He could not finish the game. He lacked something that could sweep him into a mindless act of violence.

'Ehn? Ehn?' Dumpling kept on. Poor Persimmon, egged on by his brother, stretched out his arm and pushed Kana off the bridge. The shove on her shoulder had no speed or attack. He averted his eyes as Kana swayed and fell. She sank with her pointed toes first, neatly cutting through the thick mesh of water lilies. Little air bubbles rose. As soon as her feet touched the cement bottom with the water barely up to her shoulders, she looked up at the boys. Now that Kana no longer stood between them, Persimmon and Dumpling stared at each other. What went wrong? Why did it fizzle out like this?

Their glassy blue eyes blinked at each other, then looked down at Kana. They shrugged their shoulders, turned on their heels, and walked away. Dumpling picked up a few pebbles and threw them at Kana from a distance, grudging the sorry end of the game. But it was not a whole-hearted assault. The pebbles fell wide, splashing into the water or piercing the leaves of the water lilies that the sun had cooked soft, leaving big silly holes.

I'll catch cold. Kana was a born finikin. I'll develop pneumonia or pleurisy, then the doctor, needle, death and all the rest. . . . After she had mentally conjured up the worst possibilities, she felt much better. I – am – getting – out! I – am – going – to – be – all – right.

After a long struggle through the water jungle Kana clambered out of the water and rolled on to the grassy bank. She walked home slowly, slimy and dripping.

Chiyo squealed at the sight of the muddy child. Mrs Toda clutched at her throat, speechless for a while, then mumbled to herself that she would punish the boys even if it meant setting fire to the main house. But the mud was drying fast and starting to stink. The child had to be washed at once.

Kana sat on the sunny terrace, propped up inside layers of towels. Over her poured a torrent of questions. Kana thought it fitting that she should pump up some teardrops in response to their touching concern. She tried, but it was not easy. What few she could manage had dried away before she began telling them the basic facts of the attack.

'Then? But that's all. Really it was nothing . . .' Kana repeated. The lack of dramatics disappointed her avid questioners. 'Poor child, you're worn out.' Mrs Toda finally gave up and told Chiyo to spread the sleeping mats.

Kana lay down and chuckled softly into her pillow. What's all the fuss for? I never felt so all right in my life as I did then. So beautiful, just standing and facing them. I wasn't counting on anyone or anything. As Grandmother always said, 'It's *you* in the end. *You*, alone.'

3

In the spring Colonel Bridgewater was promoted and sent to the Tachikawa base in the north; the Todas moved back to the main house and Kana entered the Takaha Primary School in Rokko Hills. Everything was in short supply, even exercise books. Mr Toda brought back old business letters with one side unused from his office and Mrs Toda cut them down to the same size and stitched them together. The first pencil box Kana owned was a thin oblong metal box with a picture of the Alps, meadows with a herd of black and white cows. This had contained chocolate when Dr Togo had brought it back from Germany before the war. 'Don't you complain,' Kana was reprimanded when she scratched her hand with the nasty sharp edge of the chocolate box and cried. 'You're luckier than many others. You have your own pencil box, pencils and eraser. Your house is still standing and your parents both alive.'

One day at school Kana met a boy who had some live baby

crabs. 'Where?' asked Kana. 'Where did you get them?'

'From Ken.'

'Ken? Ken . . . Ken.' Kana rolled the name in her mouth. It had been grim without playthings. To have her own crabs! She held her breath and bent closer over the boy's lunch box, filled with sand, pebbles and some water. Two pink and orange crabs, no bigger than her nail in size, were waddling about, their tiny protruding eyes goggling and goggling. The owner frowned, squared his arms to ward off Kana, and with mean delight put the cover on his lunch box.

'All right,' Kana fumed. 'If you're so mean I'll ask him to catch me some too!' The boy grinned and enunciated each word like a drop of poison. 'Ken will not! It's a secret place and only for his best friends. Not for girls.'

She glared at him and with decreasing vehemence repeated, 'I'll ask Ken . . . I'll ask him in any case.'

Kana had never spoken to Ken, although they were in the same class. His family were refugees from Manchuria who had only recently settled in this town. During the long and hazardous journey from the Continent his two small sisters had died, making him an only child. His father worked as a clerk in Hyogo Prefectural Office and from time to time contributed poems and short essays to the local paper.

Everyone at the Takaha knew Ken by reputation; he was the unruly new boy with the long bushy hair. Till General Mac-Arthur's reforms, a boy had to shave his head clean and smooth like a dusty grey onion; to let one's hair grow long had been considered vain and 'unpatriotic'. Although it was now more or less left for the mothers to choose, in the spring of 1946 there were still only very few boys with long hair at the Takaha. Seniors teased and derided Ken, and one of them tried to teach him a lesson by shearing off his insolent mop of hair. Ken seized the older bully, scissored off a large clump of hair right from the middle of his head, and went on carrying his own bushy head as high as ever.

At this open challenge five senior boys got a pair of professional barber's scissors and planned an ambush on Ken.

31

Fortunately for Ken, he was walking home with five other boys. Five against six. They fought and tore at each other till a truckful of road-construction workers passed by and intervened. Ken's notoriety was further established. He was a bad boy.

Whenever Ken stormed across the playground, leading a gang of rough boys from one end to the other, the girls, giggling and shrieking, ran to the side and let the wild horde pass. Their lips quivered, their eyes sparkled with fright, their skipping ropes lay abandoned on the ground. After the storm passed the hopscotch lines on the sandy earth had to be drawn all over again. Yet they never protested. The girls were quick to sense that a whimpering appeal to good manners and sense would be sheer waste with Ken. He was too unpredictable, incomprehensible, and what made it more hopeless, without a trace of sentimentality. So as the time-tested Confucian maxim had it, 'After the age of seven a boy and a girl should be kept apart,' best to avoid a too heterogeneous proximity.

Kana considered these unwelcome facts. But still she wanted those little crabs and she wanted them beyond reason.

The following morning began with a silk-sieved rain filling the entire sky. Everyone had to stay indoors during the first break. When the second period began, Ken, all his limbs jittering with boredom, pulled a chair from under the boy in front of him who had stood up to answer the form master's question. The hapless boy dropped with a thud to the floor. Ordinarily this would have ended with a light punishment and a good laugh. But it happened to be one of Mr Ikeda's arthritis days. He was looking particularly sour and mud-yellow. He sentenced Ken to a punishment that so far no one had ever been put through. Ken was to stand on the platform facing the class holding a small wooden stool above his head for the whole lesson.

'No resting the stool on top of your head. Both arms straight up. And no break for you even if it stops raining,' said Mr Ikeda.

'Sir, am I – ' began Ken courteously – 'am I allowed to be excused, sir?' So inordinately courteous was his tone that everyone burst into gales of laughter. Mr Ikeda's eyes screwed up into furious tiny dots behind the lenses as thick as mushroom umbrellas. Someone swore Mr Ikeda's knees actually shook inside his baggy trousers.

'Qui-et!' squawked Mr Ikeda and the laughing stopped. 'You'd try the patience of Buddha. Yes, but you will ask my permission every time you wish to leave the room.'

'Thank you, I will, sir.' Ken cheerfully hoisted up the stool. It was late in May and he wore over his khaki shorts a blue polo shirt, faded almost to white and shrunk unevenly. As he raised the stool in a vigorous sweep, the polo shirt lifted, exposing a strip of the sorrel gleamy skin that undulated over his lean stomach. No one laughed at this point. But Ken, in a fluster of embarrassment, pulled in his stomach as tight as a whip and with his free hand tried to pull up his loose-fitting shorts, which now dropped still lower round his hips. His navel button peeped out like a surprised big eye. Everyone guffawed at this. Except Mr Ikeda. 'This clowning is a calculated insult,' he screamed. For this additional offence Ken would have a longer period of punishment. The class stopped laughing; murmured it was too harsh. Ken smiled appreciatively at his friends who in sympathy raised a long and loud grumble.

Towards the end of the third period, in Japanese history, Mr Ikeda's voice was rising to a dramatic shrill: 'The cruel brother Yoritomo said to Yoshitsune . . .' There fell a solemn pause. The class heard Mr Ikeda as he took in a full breath before continuing, and it was while his protruding Adam's apple was still lifted mid-high and rotating that Ken bellowed, 'Please, sir, may I be excused, sir?'

What blatant cheek! What cunning timing! Everyone jumped in his chair. The effect was electrifying. A throttled squeak from Mr Ikeda. Consternation had almost choked him. His eyes crossed and his face bloated like a purplish red balloon. Poor Mr Ikeda, in addition to arthritis, had chronic asthma. The class had already seen him in one of his violent fits, when he had gasped and rattled, his scrawny body writhing and his complexion alternating from red to cucumber-green. It had been a ghastly sight. Now to see Mr Ikeda again beating at his chest and

33

clutching at his jumping abdomen made Ken uneasy and scared. Taking one of Mr Ikeda's spasmodic jolts as a nod of consent, he dashed out of the room. When he returned, Mr Ikeda was drying his tear-misted glasses. His anger had turned to vengeance. He ordered Ken to stand for the rest of the day.

'And my lunch, Mr Ikeda?'

'Right there on the platform.'

Ken stared at the stool for a while, then with one nod to himself he lifted it up and kept both his arms straight till the lunch bell. The rain had stopped and the grey skies were lifting. Soon a rainbow would span the blue sky. After Mr Ikeda left, someone took Ken's lunch box from his desk and gave it to him. Ken took advantage of his punishment not to wash his hands before eating and immediately unwrapped the furoshiki. The others, all but Kana, dutifully filed out to the washroom. When the room became empty except for the lunch boxes waiting on the desk tops, Kana dashed to Ken, stopping only when she banged her foot hard against the platform. Ouch! Blood rushed to her head, boiled and thumped against her skull. She heard nothing but only felt the stinging urgency of the words on her lips: 'I – I want some baby crabs!'

He did not look up but went on eating greedily, occasionally smacking his lips. Standing on the floor one step below, Kana's face was level with his lunch box. Rice mixed with twice as much wheat and just a sprinkle of beet pickles.

'Mmmm! Wasn't I hungry!'

An ecstatic breath reeking with pickle swirled to her face. Kana quickly held her breath: Ken raised his dense dark eyelashes, fixed his eyes on Kana, and went on masticating. The whites of his eyes gleamed near-blue and the pupils, like a dragonfly's, shifted in a dozen different shades of black with such a faraway look on his face, like an owl listening to the night wind. He doesn't hear me Kana thought. She asked again, 'Will you catch me some baby crabs?'

'Ahn?'

Ken opened his mouth, shoved in the last big morsel of rice and wheat, and froze with a stunned look. The rice got stuck. He gave himself a whack on the chest. After the third whack he said casually, 'I will, if you give me your lunch box.'

Before he looked up to see her reaction, Kana had reached her desk. Others were coming back; she had to be quick. She flew back to the platform with her heavy lunch box. He snatched it, handing her his empty one.

It was touching how his face lit up as he saw the white rice with very little wheat mixed in, eggplant in soy sauce and a generous portion of seaweed relish. His happy sigh was smothered by the first large mouthful. Kana still stood before him hugging his tin lunch box against her empty tummy. She had done her part. Now it was his turn. But he was eating. Eating with a white-hot ardour. She coughed, swayed and scratched her knee-caps. He looked up and knitted his brows suspiciously as if to ask, 'What are you standing there for?'

'Crabs,' Kana whispered softly. 'Crabs?'

'Ah!' He opened his full mouth. 'After the class. After . . .' Kana walked away thinking: I've been rather clever. He's eaten my lunch and the greedy pig in him must feel obligated.

The afternoon passed rapidly. Kana witnessed Ken silently belching a few times. He withstood his punishment admirably for the rest of the day. Just as the last bell began ringing, Ken let go of the stool from above his head. It hit the edge of the platform, bounced on Kana's lunch box and crashed against the wall, two legs breaking loose. Ken flung himself into the cheering boys and led them out of the room like the eye of a tornado. Not a bow did he bother to make to Mr Ikeda. Not a glance at Kana, who was now left with both the empty lunch boxes, one inside her desk and the other lying on the floor.

Mrs Toda shuttled her detective eyes between her daughter and the two empty lunch boxes.

'He did not take it. I gave it to him!' Kana insisted, snivelling. The misery of having to defend her lunch thief on top of having fasted and no sign yet of the promised crabs!

'I'm afraid I was right about the co-educational system after all,' Mrs Toda said and clapped her hands twice. Instantly the

35

paper screens slid open and Chiyo poked her head in. Her eaves-dropping was no longer a surprise. Mrs Toda told her to fill both lunch boxes the next morning.

'And what was the name of this boy – Huh?' She had to bend very low to catch Kana's murmur.

'Ken . . . Otani.'

The next day, Wednesday, Kana observed him eating the lunch she had left on his desk earlier in the morning. But no sign of acknowledgement. Did he think it had fallen from the sky? But at least he's eating with gusto. Kana consoled herself; she had a profound admiration for a sound appetite.

On Thursday morning just as Mr Ikeda stepped on the plat-form and the class made a stiff bow, shouting in unison, 'Good morning, Mr Ikeda,' something solid but soft-edged hit Kana on the back of the neck and dropped to the floor. The cotton furoshiki with which Chiyo had wrapped Ken's lunch box.

Hot tears trickled down her face at his crude and ungrateful behaviour. Don't pick it up, leave it. Just leave it! Kana tightened her fists and refrained from feeling her nape.

The Saturday noon siren did not announce lunch but serenaded the end of the week. On Saturday 'Goodbye, Mr Ikeda. Thank you, Mr Ikeda!' was three times as robust as on weekdays and in anticipatory hush everyone listened to the teacher's receding steps. The moment they began pattering down the stairs bedlam broke out. Some crawled under desks to trip up girls, who shrieked but loved it; some let frogs out of their lunch boxes; paper aeroplanes flew; some grappled and slapped each other with affectionate yells; there was a timid squint-eyed boy who picked at his nose industriously and flipped the muck from his finger at his neighbour who was gloating over the screeches from the girl whose skirt he had pinned to her desk. All this, because it was Saturday noon.

Someone pulled the end of Kana's plait. She spun round.

Ken! It was Ken, glum and huffish, looking not at all a part of the Saturday revel. His hands were sulking deep in his khaki shorts pockets. 'Let's go,' he whispered, his eyes furtively darting about the room.

He had good reason to be jittery: a boy who yakked away with girls became a sorry outcast. 'Here comes a stinking "girlie creep".' The other boys pinched their noses and fled.

She tilted her head slowly to one side with a look of total bewilderment, which made Ken goose-fleshed with irritation. Just the sort of feminine coyness he could not stand.

'The crabs!' He stamped his foot and shouted, beside himself, 'The crabs, the crabs!'

He meant it! Turning crimson red, Kana managed to say about four thank you's in one hot breath. Thoroughly put off, Ken spat out, 'Monkey's red ass!' and stalked out of the room.

In a language that had no provision whatsoever for swear words this was about the worst one could find to say. Kana was sobered at once. Now what have I done wrong? Will I ever get my crabs? She hoisted her satchel on her back and sped after him.

Ken timed his pace so as to keep her at least half a block behind him. The annoying short-legged creature, however, jogged pit-a-pat, her satchel shaking to a clacking rhythm, which to him never fell quite far enough behind.

They soon reached the foot of Crow's Pillow, one of many hills that bridged the north end of the town and the steep rise of the Rokko mountain ranges. The narrow path along the creek was wet and shimmering like a black velvet ribbon. The bamboo forest on the other side grew so lushly that the air round it seemed solid with a dark green stain. The sunless valley smelled cool and pungent with dead leaves and decaying roots. Where the creek narrowed Ken stopped and, while waiting for Kana, idly pitched a handful of stones into the shallow but rapid stream.

'Take off your shoes. We cross *here*!'

On saying 'here', he threw his last stone, took off his dirty shoes and socks and squeezed them into his satchel. Kana imagined the smell and the mud all over his books and felt quite repelled.

'What are you going to do with yours?' He hadn't missed her reaction. 'Hang them on your tongue?'

At once Kana pushed her shoes and socks into her satchel. For her baby crabs she would gladly have swallowed them! She did everything Ken told her to do: hopped from one rock to another; climbed the friable pebbly hill on all fours. But she really was no good at climbing; sometimes the step she took brought her right back to where she had started.

'Come on! You're sliding down more than coming up.' Ken climbed back, took her by the wrist and pulled. Her hand in his grip became bloodless, ice-cold and soon numb. Just when she decided to cry out, 'Let go of my hand,' she felt her feet resting on a sandy secure level.

Halfway up the hill there suddenly opened up a plateau where a shallow placid pool reflected the blue of the sky. On the far side of the pool, Crow's Pillow was emblazoned with forsythia in full bloom. Like furious tongues of fire thousands of flame-shaped forsythia petals swept upward in dazzling array.

Ken dropped her hand and ran into the water, kicking and splashing. Reaching the far end of the pool, wrapped in an orange halo of forsythia, Ken squatted with his kneecaps in water and began lifting large black stones. Kana dipped her toes into the water without causing so much as a gentle ripple, but Ken turned his head sharply and hissed:

'Ssh! You're scaring them away!'

Oh, you brute! What about the loud splashes *you* were making? Kana wondered how much longer she could put up with his bullying. Suddenly she covered her mouth. Scaring *them* away! *Them* away! They are there! My crabs! Feeling her eager thoughts miles ahead of her tiptoeing feet, Kana stole up to Ken.

Yes, they were there. Under the cool shade of the stones the quadruple-cornered crabs, streaked with various pastel colours: orange, green, pale blue, grey and hushed pink. When a stone was lifted, they halted dead still, not daring even to roll their pinhead eyeballs. Then, with nervous diffidence, almost apologetically, they began sliding sideways. As they swaggered on faster, their thin legs scratched at the slate pebbles. But poor wretches, no matter how fast they ran, they were not getting under their familiar roofs; Ken was juggling the stones with a magician's cunning.

For a good five minutes the two children squatted in the lazy warm water, studying the pale ones and the gaudy ones, a red one with a fierce grimace sculptured on its shell and a pink citrine one with vivid emerald rings round its eyes. One with a leg short waddled with pathetic gait. Did he himself or his greedy stepfather eat the missing leg? Kana, although intimidated by Ken's silence, couldn't help sighing, cooing, giggling and hissing. She panted out her exultation in small whispered snatches, but Ken, vexed by this female nonsense, vowed that he would never again bring a girl to his crab pond.

'How many do you want?' asked Ken.

'As many as you can put in my lunch box. Some big ones and some tiny ones, please.'

'Stupid!' he replied, 'The big ones will gobble up the small ones in half a second.'

Kana primmed her lips and pouted. All right, whatever you say. Just give me my crabs. He scooped a handful of sand and water into Kana's lunch box and picked five tiny ones of more or less equal size. Before closing the lunch box he looked her in the eyes:

'Now promise you won't tell anyone where my crab pond is.'

'I promise I won't tell anybody.'

'Right!' He nodded.

She stretched out her arms. Her fingers tingled with excitement, anticipating the weight of her crabs. She leaned still closer to Ken who smelled like a puppy that had frolicked all day out in the scorching sun.

I'm drowning! Kana shut her eyes. Such a dull, rich, excruciatingly sweet pain was filling her up and up and up! Warm and unbearably lovely all over, as if she were being strangled by cotton candy.

'Let's go.' Ken's voice gave her a jolt. 'I'll carry it till we climb down.'

Kana opened her eyes and saw Ken's tanned legs planted in

the water. Have I gone mad? Kana still felt numb and strange as she tried to rise.

Ken was waiting for her at the end of the pond. She ran and the wild splashes leapt up to her face. He carried her crabs till they got to the creek from where the houses of Rokko Hills could be seen beyond the fields abandoned since the start of the war.

'Here,' Ken handed the lunch box to Kana. 'Don't change the water too often. Every other day, that's enough.'

Before Kana could say a word, he hurried away.

4

Times were changing. General MacArthur's compulsory educational system was in full force and parents no longer blinked their eyes in puzzlement at such abbreviations as PTA or '6-3-3' (six years in primary school; three years each in junior and senior high school) and co-educational schooling worried few parents now. No more substitute food. Rice no longer adulterated with wheat. No more electricity cuts. Kana and Yoko no longer had to have their hair sprayed with DDT every week.

And Chiyo retired.

'Retire!' Mrs Toda was profoundly shocked and hurt. 'No maid gives notice and retires of her own will. It is up to her mistress at a convenient moment to arrange a marriage for her; or, if after working for the family all her life she remains single, to bury her.'

At the age of forty-five Chiyo had gone back to her native village to live with her old aunt. 'What a world . . . everyone insists on independence these days and look how unhappy they are.'

At twenty-nine, a little plumper and once again with a pearl glow on her skin, Mrs Toda was the best dressed and most admired mother to visit the school on the monthly PTA day.

Many heads turned when she entered the room and the girls gossiped about and guessed at what country her perfume had come from.

Later, at home, looking over Kana's homework, Mrs Toda held her head in her hands. 'Dear, dear. So many changes everywhere. Just look at these New Chinese characters. Simplified, yes, but ugly, bare and without image. However, I'd better be quiet. General MacArthur probably knows best what is good for you young people. . . .'

And soon the day came when Mrs Toda abjectly surrendered to the new brat generation. Yoko, now six years old, stripped her mother of her magic power. Right under Kana's gaze.

Yoko, during one of her illicit 'explorations' in her mother's dressing room, smashed a bottle of Guerlain's Vol de Nuit, a two-ounce bottle. It was the first real French scent Mrs Toda had bought since the war. She choked with anger and the effluvium of her spilt perfume.

'Put her outside the main gate, Miki, and bolt it top and bottom,' Mrs Toda commanded Chiyo's successor. And she did not forget that odious parcel of toothbrush, toothpaste, paper tissues, towel and one large coin with a hole in the middle – 50 yen this time, due to the post-war inflation.

Kana's heart bled for her sister. After Miki, a perpetually giggling teenager, took Yoko down the path, Kana sat on the terrace and anxiously watched the sun stoop towards the mountains in the west.

Within less than two hours Mrs Toda told Miki to let Yoko in, and as she waited for her sister to run back to the house a cynical thought crossed Kana's mind: only just over an hour . . . is it because of the PTA meetings? Are mothers fearful of their children reporting too harsh a punishment at home to their teachers?

'Miss Yoko's gone!' Miki's raw piercing voice came from behind the azalea bush. 'She's nowhere. Nowhere!'

Mrs Toda ran down to the main gate in her white tabi* with-

*A pair of tightly clinging white socks.

41

out bothering to put on her wooden sandals. Kana followed her. At the wide-open gate, not a sign of Yoko.

The search was taken up by the police station in Rokko Hills. At seven o'clock Kana was told to eat her supper alone. Her mother was shuffling around the telephone. Till there was some more definite news she would not worry Mr Toda who was in Tokyo on a business trip. At eight the three of them were still hovering over the silent telephone in the draughty hallway where the night's chill rising between the floorboards nipped at the backs of their feet.

When the clock in the kitchen chimed half-past eight, the bell at the north gate rang. Mrs Toda gave a quick nod to Miki, who darted out, her young acne-covered face glowing with excitement. Mrs Toda and Kana stood at the edge of the entrance hall and soon heard her yell.

'Miss Yoko! Miss Yoko's with a policeman!'

Back to her normal self, Miki was giggling agitatedly as she heralded the policeman. Yoko's homecoming, to her mother and sister who had been through hours of anxiety, was flabbergasting.

Yoko was mounted on the policeman's shoulder, her legs swinging merrily against his broad chest. Hoop-la! Hoop-la! She was having great fun, swaying like a festive banner and now and then even venturing to stretch herself to touch the camellia buds.

The policeman stopped at the threshold and swung the furoshiki parcel in his hand. 'Not to worry. She's here and all's well!'

Mrs Toda stood mesmerized for a while, then with a short cooing rattle in her throat she opened her arms wide with a burst of smile. Yoko slipped down into her embrace matter-of-factly. The policeman sat on the hall step, sipped hot green tea with guttural sighs of appreciation, munched ginger wafers and told the story: Yoko had walked to the nearest loop-line tramcar station right after she was pushed out of the house. She bought a short-distance child's fare ticket and spent the rest of her fifty yen on her favourite nougat. Without going near the ticket gate she jumped on and off the trams, riding everywhere within the loop line, free of charge and unquestioned. It was a long while before the conductresses became suspicious. By the time they took her to the police Yoko had made five complete rounds.

Mrs Toda listened to the entire story with a benign, amused smile. 'I may sound like a doting mother but I've always found her to be a resourceful, independent, bold child. A "modan" child, you know?'

The policeman readily agreed. He bowed and left with a box of dried fruit that Mrs Toda asked him to take home to his children. It was long past bedtime when Yoko and her mother started to dine. Miki served. Kana watched.

Watched with lethal envy. There was something so extra-delicious about dining when one should have been asleep. Why let a criminal brat enjoy such a privilege? Why not me? Kana could not take her eyes from Yoko who ate with a voracious appetite and talked about her adventures: the elevated tracks, the unknown streets and towns, the harbour, the tunnels and the zoo and the park watched from the tram windows.

Kana who had not even ventured beyond the lower steps outside the main gate, listened to her sister and could no longer shut her mind's ears to this dreadful question: why didn't I, why? I could have, too. Yes, she could have watched the strange faces, streets and shop windows with her mouth full of milky nougat. And to crown the rich new experiences she too could have buried her wonderfully tired head in her mother's welcoming breast and without a breath of reproach! All of this, Kana had not dared. To break Mother's law? It had been unthinkable. Un-imaginable. Because her mother was no ordinary mother . . . Kana turned her puzzled dark eyes to Mrs Toda.

The defeat she had to admit then was not her mother's alone but hers as well. In front of Kana's dumbfounded eyes sat a mother, an ordinary, good-natured, easy, fickle, accommodating mother, vulnerable to a child's threat. This mother chewed, nodded and beamed while Yoko with barefaced impudence was complaining how little nougat one could buy for thirty-five yen!

Kana was walking by the deserted kitchen.

Half-past four; an awkward in-between moment of a long summer afternoon. The clock was ticking away loudly. The shafts of light that dropped in from the high windows illuminated the room in a lattice pattern of gold and amber. The half-wet cutting board, the glistening edges of knives and some washed glasses diffused the sunlight in prisms all over the room. How lovely it was to take the kitchen by surprise and find it at its most beautiful. Kana curtsied, skipped inside and flitted about in an improvised dance.

Oup! She slipped and quickly grabbed the doorknob of the old-fashioned ice-box. As she regained her balance, it occurred to her that now that her hand was there on the door, she might as well pull it open. She did.

At her eye-level sat a bowl, full of eggs.

Ever since she could remember she had been forbidden to eat eggs. An acute case of allergy: an egg turned to poison the moment she ate it and the agony that followed was such that she had never even missed having them. But now there they were, strange and beautiful. Her mind was still a limpid vacuum as she watched them raptly. Then it seemed to her only natural that she should touch, feel and weigh one in her hand. Kana took one out.

The egg sat in her hand, just as dear, wicked, mysteriously compact and fragile as she had always imagined it to be. The chill from it gently traversed the thickness of her hand. The indolent weight of its liquidy substance made her palm curve respectfully round it. The gloss on the shell was milky and muted; the pores stood out more lucent in soft pinpoints. Not even an intimation of harshness in all its opaque oval entity.

Suddenly Kana was aware of the tiny red tongue of temptation licking somewhere deep inside her brain! At once she stood on the defensive: she began reliving mentally the infernal sequences of egg poisoning. Not once, but at least three times, back and forth, she made herself go over the full revolting details. She went further and thought about the family's not-too-fertile hens in the back yard and the inexcusable waste of *her* consuming an egg only to vomit it out a minute later, and the doctor and his cold wet fingers and the long painful squatting in the toilet. And above everything else her mother, her mother, her mother.

At first it was not more than a diffident temptation. The more she tried to ignore its seductive voice, the more power and speed it collected. Now it was galloping at full tilt, jeering 'Bah!' to reason's protest. Kana knew it was too late. It had taken full control of her and now was rolling its own defiant way straight to madness. She grabbed an empty bowl from the shelf.

'Knock the egg, stupid,' Kana heard the voice say, 'knock it against the edge of the sink.' Kana followed the instruction timidly. She banged her hand against the sink top. Her fingers, petrified round the egg like a cast-iron grille, kept the egg intact with its top still chastely cold and its bottom warm in her hot grip. Biting her lips at the pain in her knuckles, Kana tried a second swing. This time, before her hand reached the sink edge, her over-anxious thumb had squeezed its way into the slimy white. She felt the oozing out of the egg white against her thumb, then heard the heavy thud of the yolk in the ceramic bowl. Stunned, disgusted and fascinated, she opened the ice-box, grabbed a second, then another. As she broke them and watched the translucent dribbling, Kana knew she could not stop. She broke two more.

'This couldn't be real!' Kana mumbled when she finally counted five vivid yellow eyes staring up at her. Witch-mother's yellow eyes. Kana plunged a pair of chopsticks right into them. Her blood churned and pounded at her eardrums. It's got to stop. This is squalid, I could still stop and walk out. I still could.

She stared at the dull yellowish sludge; five distinct eyes, no more. She crouched lower, poured in some soya sauce and a few drops of water as she had seen Chiyo and Miki do.

Hell must be like this. All out of control. Just tumbling head-long down down down. Yet one goes on!

Kana worked briskly now. Turned on the gas, heated oil in the thick square egg pan, poured the eggs in and stirred. Bubbling and grunting, the eggs turned opaque orange-gold. It was done. Kana turned off the gas, sat on the stool, already feeling sick and satiated, opened her mouth. Gulping down the first mouthful, she burnt her tongue. After that, except for the resilient texture of egg that stroked her gorge, she tasted absolutely nothing. Shove in and down. Again, shove in and down. Only the pain of her burnt tongue was wrathfully alive and Kana was almost grateful for it. When the last mouthful, cold and rubbery, went down Kana was very glad. She studied the empty plate on which the grease perspired and turned to the door, gazed at it hoping that someone - ideally, her witch-mother in a fit of demonic anger - would barge in. No, no one. Silence was solid everywhere in the house.

Kana washed up the dishes, the pan, the chopsticks and the bowl. Still, no one stirred the thick idle silence. With her stomach gradually sickening and her tongue twingeing with pain, she trotted round the kitchen, feeling hopelessly adrift. Her 'resourceful, independent and bold' sister, Yoko, would have swiftly cleared out of the place of crime. But Kana stayed. She made a few more rounds. At long last, Miki caught the cooking odour, poked her head in, snorted first, then screamed: 'Oh, no, you've eaten eggs!'

Miki was thudding and yelling up the stairs. Kana looked for the spot to face her mother's entrance. She walked over to the sink and stood in front of it. She was not steeped in the water-lily-meshed pond nor was she facing Persimmon and Dumpling. But she felt that she possessed exactly the same cold strength that had filled her then.

Mrs Toda appeared in one of her best summer kimonos; thin-bladed reeds were hand-painted in silver and deep purple on the mauve silk crêpe. Her left arm held the coil of the obi.

'Eggs!' she said to herself, then again, 'Eggs!'

Miki had nimbly stationed herself at the best viewing spot between the mother and the egg-allergic daughter. Kana looked straight in her mother's eyes and did not flinch. Mrs Toda threw a quick glance at the clock. A quarter to four. She made a grimace and flung out her left arm, dropping the entire length of the obi to the floor, took out two silk strings from one sleeve and bit them between her teeth. Too vexed to speak right away, she busied herself with folding of her obi. Miki went behind her and attempted to be helpful. Mrs Toda solemnly brushed aside Miki's banana-fingered hands and tried to say something to the effect, 'Thank you, but I can manage,' but with the silk strings between her lips it only came out as a long fierce groan. Miki shrank back.

Mrs Toda finished knotting the obi; the rustling and squeaking of silk suddenly stopped and the three heard only the winds outside. Mrs Toda and Miki glared at the unrepentant child and Kana calmly watched how her mother frowned, trying to find words dripping with venom; words that would pain and shame Kana as long as she lived; but she could not find any. Defeated, she turned with one sharp squeak of her heels against the floor, and walked out fast.

There was a lapse of only a few moments before Kana held her head down and shaking, vomited straight into the white sink.

As late as 1949 it was compulsory that schoolchildren be vermifuged, for during the years immediately after the war when food was scarce and prices rampageously inflated, people had to survive on vegetables, home-grown and sewage-manured, which made it imperative that every child's intestines should be flushed out twice a month by the abominable makuri.*

On the day of makuri Kana would wake up with her mouth running with the sour bile of dread. Handkerchiefs were no use. She brought a dish cloth to school into which she would spit till it was her class's turn for the hateful mixture.

'I'm afraid she is responsible for it herself,' Mr Tanabe, Kana's teacher, told Mrs Toda. 'She works herself up to such a pathological state of fear, you understand, it's no surprise that she should be foaming at the mouth, fainting, running a high temperature and God knows what.'

It was the second makuri day in June.

The night before, the school janitor and his wife lined up three huge iron kettles in the open space before their cottage. They started boiling the makuri at six in the morning, and by the

*Infusion made from seaweed and rhubarb to expel round-worm.

time the children arrived, the atmosphere for blocks round the school was reeking with the sickening odour.

During the third period there was a knock on the door and the messenger cried, 'Tanabe class, please follow Maki class!'

Kana quickly took out a clean dish cloth and stood up first. Having achieved the top grades in the last semester, she was the head girl in her class. She lined them up in double rows and led them downstairs. The first fresh makuri vapour slapped into her face like a foul sodden mop before she got near the janitor's cottage. She pressed the dish cloth tighter against her face, looked for the end of the Maki class's queue and saw Ken.

Kana had not been in the same class with him since her first year. She had never thanked him for he crabs nor had she reported on their gradual disappearance and death. The co-educational system had existed for only three years, while the Confucian teachings on the benefits of separatism for boys and girls were centuries old: Kana had therefore considered it her gracious discretion not to address herself to him in public.

Kana watched him curiously. At the age when growing in height outstripped growing soldier in flesh, Ken stood like an image of himself in a warped mirror, elongated out of proportion. To come down level with the boys round him, he had to curve his back. Having shed his child's fat, his jaw angled out squarely from his neck. When he threw his head back and laughed, Kana noticed on his exposed throat the faint projection of the Adam's apple. A blush rose on her pallid cheeks, she looked away and spat into her dish cloth again.

The line before her edged steadily forward; Kana's stomach cringed and cringed till it was a peach stone. Next to each fuming kettle stood a nurse from the Health and Education Department, with a square of white cotton gauze covering her mouth and nose. Above this white mask, two hawkish eyes peered. Each child had to stand in front of her and exhibit his emptied cup and report his name and his class.

'Go on, drink it up, all of it!' she would shout, if there were but a few drops of the gluey rust-green liquid left.

'Tanabe class, step forward and fall in behind Maki class.'

With her nostrils clogged up Kana was breathing entirely through her mouth. Gasping like a steam engine, she stood behind Ken, who, being the tallest, was the last in the line.

The janitor, a scrawny old man, hovered over the kettle like an enormous spider. He stirred, poured, distributed the cups, and in between times, washed the soiled cups in a pail of luke-warm water. Presently he was holding out two cups filled to the brim. Ken took one. Kana removed the dish cloth from her mouth but made no other move. The janitor tutted in his toothless mouth and stretched out the cup towards Kana. A swirl of makuri steam rose right up her nostrils.

'Ugh!' Kana recoiled, letting out a belch-like groan. At this weird noise Ken turned his head and saw a pasty white face. The janitor turned to the nurse, bellowing for her assistance. 'This girl, here, is holding up the line!'

In pure reflex, like blinking against a bee, Ken's left hand sprang out of itself and grabbed the second full cup. The janitor looked up. A split second too late; Ken had turned his back with the two cups held close to his chest. As he stepped aside, the next two pupils advanced to the kettle, shoving Kana out of the way.

Ken downed one cup of the makuri in one gulp, then, screwing up his face and groaning with distaste, he looked round: Now where's that girl?

There she was right on his heels, her hands obstinately tucked behind her skirt and with a look of complete helplessness.

The nurse grumbled louder behind her gauze mask. Ken thrust the second cup at Kana, hissing, 'Drink, it's yours.' But the dumb clod, her eyes bulging with huge teardrops, just stared motionless at the cup of makuri. He stood aghast; *he* was in trouble.

The nurse finally snatched off her mask and shouted, 'Hurry, you two there – name, class!'

With a furious growl, Ken dropped his face on to the warm stinking cup and by gradually arching his body backward managed to drink it up. With the dire gluey stink inside his mouth he hissed, 'Take this. Monkey's red ass!'

He slapped the empty cup into Kana's hand, dashed up to the

49

nurse and held the other cup right up to her chin. The nurse quickly averted her face and blared at him, 'I can see it's empty. Thank you!'

Kana stepped forward, not daring to look up, and waved her impeccably empty cup towards the towering white uniform.

The makuri day had followed too close on her disastrous egg raid on the kitchen; Kana, although she had not imbibed the makuri, was very sick all through the evening and was absent from school for two days. On the day she returned to school she bumped into Ken. He came hopping down the steps by twos, counting, 'Two, four, six!' When he noticed Kana cowering on the lower landing he stopped at once. His eyes flashed and a wild confusion spread on his face. He even looked frightened. 'Stupid monkey's red ass!' He said each word as if to verbally purge Kana, then jumped down the rest of the steps and ran out to the playground.

Still cowering, Kana stayed on the landing. Gradually a smile glowed on her face. She said very tenderly to herself, 'Stupid monkey's red ass . . .' Each word with a mellow cajoling fullness.

By the time Kana advanced to the fifth grade the makuri had been replaced by neatly sugar-coated tablets. Every time a mouthful of cold water and the pills went down her throat, the words 'Stupid monkey's red ass' flashed across her mind, leaving her strangely disturbed.

5

Kana was not a boy: a simple, irrevocable and unwelcome fact. No one dared in so many words to blame Kana for being the eldest and not a boy therefore quite useless as an heir for the family. Whatever discontent there was amongst the relatives on her father's side had mercifully been kept hidden from her, and those on her mother's side, feeling guilty about the situation, avoided the subject as much as possible.

But as for Mrs Toda, no one quite forgave her and the poor woman had to bear the brunt of everyone's criticism. Her mother-in-law, the elder Mrs Toda of Kamakura, had been positively vicious about it: 'What's the use of a wife, may I ask, if she is barren-wombed for a boy? A cartful of girls won't do. We need an heir in this family.' And when the fierce Toda matriarch turned eighty years old, her voice got more strident and pressing: 'Now that I'm at the age when to wake up and find myself still alive comes as a surprise, I am more chagrined as each day passes. How am I to break the news to my late husband when death joins me to him on the Other Side? Am I to come straight out, "Husband, we've relinquished your Toda & Son Company to a stranger"?'

'Stranger' meant Kana's future husband, who would be adopted through an arranged marriage and made to take the Toda family name and subsequently to become the head of the firm her great-grandfather had founded.

Soon after her eightieth birthday Mr Toda of Kamakura telephoned Rokko Hills to say that she had made an appointment for her daughter-in-law with a well-known gynaecologist at the Tokyo University Hospital.

'But, Mother . . .', the younger Mrs Toda whimpered.

'Nothing risked, nothing gained, isn't that true? Don't argue with me; between eighty and death, I can't afford the time to procrastinate. Be sure to get on the ten o'clock express tomorrow morning. I'll have you met at Kamakura station.'

'Thank you, Mother. Very thoughtful of you.'

'If I were you, I wouldn't mention this to your husband.' The matriarch hung up. Mrs Toda, murmuring 'Thank you,' bowed to the receiver. She then walked into the bathroom, ran the water and cried.

'I'm afraid . . .', the specialist in Tokyo said, 'I'm afraid it is most unlikely that Mrs Toda will bear another child successfully. She can't expect to have come out undamaged from the privations she suffered in the war and four subsequent miscarriages. I am so sorry.'

After this verdict the growl in Kamakura got even louder and more openly unkind.

On the 5th of May, National holiday for Boys, every family blessed with a son flaunted atop a pole in the garden two cloth pennants, shaped and painted to represent a black and red carp, symbols of male courage and virility. These fish pennants of the families so blessed swam jauntily above the roofs all day long. At night the proud mother would throw bundles of iris and fragrant herbs into the bathtub and let her boy take an iris-scented bath before anyone else in the family.

At the Todas' it was naturally a quiet unfestive day. But this year, early in the afternoon, a large parcel addressed to Kana was delivered from the Mitsukoshi Department Store in Tokyo.

'For me? It's for me! From the Mitsukoshi in Tokyo.' Kana, after handing her mother the accompanying card, tore apart the multi-coloured wrapping paper and opened the box. Inside was a complete set of medieval warrior's attire for a boy. At an increasingly wilder pace Kana pulled out a helmet, bow and arrows, white silk underwear, kimonos and hakama,* a brocade battle-field mantle, a pair of sandals and tabi. In a flat wood box was a commanding metal shield with a crest of arms. Staggering to her feet, Kana held out her thin arms warped under the weight of luminous silk, leather and steel.

'Look, Mother! Look!'

One glance at her mother, and all the bubbles of joy fizzled out. Her arms fell limp and the heavy load of presents slid down to the tatami floor. Kana could not believe her eyes. Never had she seen her mother so black and magenta all over, like a fire-gutted house.

Think quick! What's wrong? What am I to do? Kana stood petrified. Mrs Toda fumbled with her right sleeve and dropped the card. Kana held her breath but did not pick it up till her mother nodded to her to do so.

Happy Boys' Day! Ask your mother to send me some photographs of you, dressed up in my May the Fifth gift.

*Amply pleated culottes worn over kimono.

52

A photographer was sent for. The prattling clown went from room to room looking for the right background for Kana's portrait. Coming into Mrs Toda's dressing room, he clapped his hands.

'Perfect! See that bamboo-and-young-deer pattern on the sliding screens? Perfect!'

Mrs Toda, stone-faced, did not protest and merely told him not to damage the tatami with his photographic equipment. She then retreated to a corner where she stayed immobile with her eyes focused on nothing and her hands clasped. She offered no assistance, just let Miki and the photographer fuss. Yoko and several of her girl friends, allowed to watch only from outside the room, knelt on the corridor floor.

Kana blinked her eyes miserably in the strong lights. She could hardly stand erect, not because of the weight of her costume but because of her mother. The photographer, popping his head in and out of the black cloth spread over his camera, did everything he could to make Kana smile. While Miki was rolling with fits of laughter and the jostling girls outside the room hee-hawed, Kana did not crack a smile. She was determined to communicate her silent message to her mother: 'See, Mother? I'm with you. I'm on your side. Look at me.'

On her side against what? She did not know. It mattered little what issue, what side, excepting that Kana felt the pain in her mother.

In a Japanese-style house it was virtually impossible not to eavesdrop. With such flimsy devices as paper-and-wood latticed sliding doors, panels, paper screens, thin walls of mud-and-hay mixture, and the total absence of locks, to possess normal hearing was already to eavesdrop. Especially so in summer when the partitions were replaced by gossamer curtains and shades, and the house became a structure mainly of divided air that would echo the faintest breath of a secret to its farthest corner.

One night, too stifling hot to sleep, Kana heard somewhere downstairs her mother hiss and Miki sob.

'Shh! Miki, listen,' gently said Mrs Toda. 'Come to me any

time and I'll put your disjointed jaw back into place. It's not that tragic or rare. So, stop crying and just be careful when you laugh or yawn.'

A bit of information such as this was fun; it helped make Miki a more exciting figure. But sometimes by eavesdropping Kana learned too much and suffered agonies as a consequence.

Shirato, the kimono merchant from Kyoto, came to Rokko Hills twice a month with his two young apprentices, who carried on their bent backs rolls of silk, dyes and patterns. Shirato, at the age of seventy-four, was in brisk good health and spirits which he attributed to his smoking and drinking a great deal and eating nothing much but raw fish. He looked more like a crane than a man. In all seasons of the year he wore Scottish cashmere combinations and over them a kimono of the finest quality and taste. Contemporary with a generation unfamiliar even to Mrs Toda, he could still remember in exact detail the colour, dye, weave, patterns of a kimono he had made for Kana's great-grandmother on such an occasion in which year of Meiji,* and he never tired of comparing the two sisters in his kimono language:

'You think it's too sombre, Miss Sadako? No. If *you* wear it you'll inflame it with life; naturally, till then it looks dull. Now your sister, Miss Sachi, she's a difficult customer all right. She disappears if I put on her a strong design, and dies if I pour bright colour on her. Yet, without them she's even more invisible. So I have to cajole her gently and deviously to come to life.'

His visit would last from one to two hours. He sat on the edge of the raised floor of the entrance hall, reminisced unhurriedly about this and that, sipped tea, nibbled some sweets with the few teeth left in his mouth, rolled and unrolled the bolts of kimono fabric, and all the while his fingers tirelessly caressed and savoured the various textures of silk.

'Shirato, today I'm going to tell you exactly what I think of you.' Kana caught her mother's voice as she was tiptoeing over to her customary eavesdropping spot. Whenever Shirato was

*The reign of the Emperor Meiji, 1868–1912.

54

her partner in conversation Mrs Toda's voice rose higher and a girlish lisp crept into her speech. Today there was something more in her tone: a tremor of danger. Kana quickly installed her bottom on the floor and her ear against the paper panel.

'What you think of me? I hope I have done nothing to . . .'

'Scum! Traitor! Disloyal schemer! That's what I think of you, Shirato.'

Kana heard only a guttural squeak from Shirato.

'You not only made a kimono for that woman in Kyoto but used the arrow-and-iris pattern in silver on antique purple. That pattern, you remember, you designed for me, for me alone. Of all women, to use it for her! Traitor! And to think you've known my sister Sachi and me ever since we were born.'

'Well, you see, Miss Sadako . . . Mr Itoh himself brought her to my shop and I couldn't quite . . .'

'You couldn't quite what? Money-grubber, charlatan, liar! You thought I'd never find out, didn't you? Silly man. I told you that woman and I happen to go to the same samisen teacher in Kyoto. When I saw her arrive for her lesson in the self-same kimono I said nothing to sister Sachi. But if she finds out, and she probably will, she'll kill you.'

The relentless witch was spitting fire. Kana felt the fuzz on her bare arms stand on end. What was it all about? Aunt Sachi and 'that woman'? Who is she?

A long heavy sigh; Mrs Toda exhaled all her raging steam. When she began speaking again, Kana learned what had been kept from the children: her Aunt Sachi, three years older than Mrs Toda, had borne two daughters but no son within the first five years of her marriage. Mr Itoh, a wealthy ship-owner, then told his wife that under the circumstances she must consent to his keeping a mistress. Aunt Sachi had no choice but to agree. The girl he chose, a geisha called Yuki, whose existence in Mr Itoh's life had been gossiped about even before this, she not being of a very high rank in her profession, gladly quit Kyoto's gay Gion district and became Mr Itoh's 'second wife'. The following year Yuki gave birth to a boy, who was legally registered as the Itoh heir.

55

'All because sister Sachi bore her first son too late . . . What an ironical turn of fate! Have you ever heard of a case like this, Shirato?'

'No, not really . . . Was it two years or three years later?'

'One and a half. Just one and a half years after the birth of the bastard. When I heard the first scream and the midwife announcing that sister Sachi had borne a son, I didn't know whether to cheer or weep. And what a sturdy big boy Shozo was, kicking his plump red legs and crying like a fire engine.'

'Ah, but you must be fair, Miss Sadako. There's no telling in advance.' Shirato started on one of his irrefutable clichés.

'No one is really to blame. Just bad luck. That's all there is to it.' Mrs Toda's voice cracked and tapered off. Shirato was wisely silent.

'Tell me, Miki, what is a mistress?' asked Kana. Miki, speechless, began quivering her jaws. Kana grabbed the maid by the wrist and shot another question at her. 'Do you think my father too will find a mistress to get a son for our family?' This time Miki dilated her eyes to such a width that her pupils floated like two black flies lost in the white centres. Kana let go of her hand, saying gently, 'Don't be sorry for me, Miki. You've got your loose jaws to worry about.'

Kana had no intention of being unkind. On the contrary she spoke with an immense affection which only two convicts or two lepers might share. Miki did not interpret it so. Then and there her jaw came off its hinges. Kana screamed for her mother as she dragged Miki upstairs, where Mrs Toda put Miki's jaws back in position with one quick twist of her wrist.

If the mere mention of a word could strike Miki dumb, knocking her jaw off its hinges, the situation the Todas were in must be bad. Very bad. Kana took it all extremely personally. Fearing perhaps she was the cause, she could not even bring herself to consult the dictionary to find out exactly what threat 'mistress' or 'bastard' could pose to her family.

Kana had always disliked her uncle: greasy-pored, loud, hoity-toity and gushy. Either guffawing like an old accordion with a hole in the bottom or raging in a tantrum; nothing moderate in between. But now she hated him, hated him with determination, for this man had been capable not only of making a brutal decision but of carrying it out; bang, wallop, he had done it. Kana longed for some disaster to strike him. If she heard on the radio about an earthquake in Shikoku, she prayed that her uncle had been there. What about a streak of lightning splitting him in half, she wondered, or what about blow-fish poisoning? Well, Kana did see some real possibility in that.

'It's not just liking, you understand? It's a passion,' Uncle Itoh often said. 'I'll eat blow-fish as long as I'm alive and can afford it.'

He certainly could afford it. Ever since the outbreak of the Korean War, he had been sailing on the crest of the war boom, wallowing in easy and stupendous profits.

'What a time to be a ship-owner!' he would chuckle, and slap at his bouncy belly, shake his double chin and play with the tips of his moustache.

'I tell you it's like coating both hands with glue and plunging them into a pail of gold coins.' Rocked by laughter, his bloated body seemed to disintegrate into a more and more slovenly mess. With her icy dissecting eyes on her uncle's nose, a ripe strawberry from heavy sake drinking, Kana could not help wondering, how could Aunt Sachi, so delicate, so elegant, share the same roof with such a gross character?

Aunt Sachi was the type of beauty much idolized in the Ukiyoe school of painting. A smooth cucumber-shaped face with beautifully elongated ears; eyes shaped like sleek flames slanting radically upward and a tiny mouth which was just an intimation of its purpose. Her neck, her famous neck, was 'a white magnolia petal rolled tightly,' as one of her suitors – not Mr Itoh – had once written to her. She also possessed the exemplary 'Mount Fuji' forehead, a criterion of beauty in the old Japan: the way her hair grew formed the sharp peak of Fuji upon her demure high forehead.

Kana's mother had the same Mount Fuji forehead and the same elegant cucumber-shaped face, but otherwise they had nothing in common. Mrs Toda was taller and a little more amply fleshed, with eyes twice as large and expressive as her sister's. Her lashes went boldly curling upward, unlike Mrs Itoh's drooping canopy-like ones. Her lips were full and sensuous. Altogether, Kana found in her mother more bite, more life, more devil and more woman.

In the autumn of 1951 Mr Itoh announced the launching of his new tanker at the port of Kobe.

'Kana, Aunt Sachi is coming to stay tomorrow night.'

'Is Uncle Itoh staying in Kyoto then?'

'What do you know about Kyoto?' Mrs Toda sharply struck back.

Kana turned pale. Too much eavesdropping; she shouldn't know about the woman in Kyoto!

'It's not for you to question what your elders do.' After a slight pause Mrs Toda continued in a milder tone. 'It's just that your uncle is a funny man. He is funny, isn't he?'

'He is! He is funny!' Kana said as her mother walked away mumbling to herself, 'That man loves making things difficult, very difficult. . . .'

The night before the launching ceremony Mrs Itoh left her newly air-conditioned house in Tokyo for Rokko Hills, riding for the first time in the huge squat Mercedes Benz 3000 which Mr Itoh had ordered from Hamburg, Germany. The interior of the car was upholstered in glossy red leather and stank so aggressively of hide that Mrs Itoh had been sick in it. She was unsure on her feet and looked pallid as she walked into the entrance hall.

'Auntie, what's that you're wearing?' Kana said out loud, pointing at a cape which sat incongruously on her aunt's delicate pale blue kimono. Her parents frowned but it was too late.

'It's mink . . .' murmured Mrs Itoh almost inaudibly, looking uncomfortably hot and embarassed under their gaze.

There was a long awkward silence. Even Miki could tell that so much animal hair on Mrs Itoh looked a bad joke. It was Mr Toda who urged his sister-in-law, 'Take it off and be more comfortable, please.' As Mrs Itoh shed her mink the two rings on her hands shot harsh sparkles to all corners of the hall. Kana thought Aunt Sachi blushed when she saw Kana looking at them.

Mr Toda, longing for his evening hot bath, excused himself and told Miki to throw three more logs into the boiler. Taking after his mother, Mr Toda was a cleanliness fiend; in the evening he sniffed at every garment he had worn during the day and with a horrified grimace threw them into a wicker basket. 'You'll be a pumice-stone soon,' he was warned. But no use. He insisted that the bath water should be hot to the point of torture and that he should scrub every square inch of his body with a coarse fibre loofah till he was chafed scarlet with his eyes blurred and his brain in a simmering coma. Very good for one, he maintained.

While Mrs Toda hurried after him to the bathroom to help him undress, Kana and Yoko made tea for their aunt, who sat rubbing her temples. Mrs Toda returned and said she would telephone for a blind masseur for her sister. 'He's very good, he will help you relax after the long journey.'

'Oh, thank you,' said Mrs Itoh, pulling off both new rings and putting them next to her untouched cake on the lacquer plate. 'I can't wear jewels.'

'Neither can I,' said Mrs Toda. 'Nor could Mother. Remember?'

'And I'm just like Mother. That little extra weight gives me such a dreadful shoulder ache and migraine after a while.'

Aunt Sachi played with her rings, rolling them idly in the pastry crumbs, and said, raising her soppy beautiful eyes at the girls, 'Isn't it time for the little ones to go to bed?'

'Yes, it is!' said Mrs Toda and looked at Kana and Yoko.

As soon as Yoko started her gentle snuffling Kana sneaked back to the top of the stairs, where she heard: 'I think she'll be there tomorrow. I think . . .'

'But, big sister, how dare she?'

'He asked her.'

'Oh, no!'

'I'm afraid he did.' A pause. 'Can you come with me to-morrow? Please.'

'Of course I will,' said Mrs Toda.

There was another long silence. Then: 'What are they?' asked Mrs Toda with little interest.

'This one, a star sapphire. And this, diamond and emerald. She has exactly the same rings . . . I found out . . .' Mrs Itoh tried but could not laugh.

'Isn't he late! He usually comes right away,' said Mrs Toda. She meant the blind masseur. No response from her sister and the conversation came to a halt. Kana tiptoed back to her sleeping mat.

The following morning Aunt Sachi was up early and, although still unable to eat, she sat with Kana at the breakfast table, gently rubbing her temples. 'That blind giant had knuckles as big as cabbage heads. Oh dear, I'm aching all over. Maybe I shouldn't go to the hairdresser. Just to think of a drier . . .'

After putting the satchel on her back Kana stirred up her courage. 'Aunt Sachi, could you tell me . . .' There she stopped and could not go on. She had intended to ask about 'mistress' and 'bastard'.

'Yes? What is it?' Mrs Itoh stood stroking Kana's hair with her five fingers evenly apart like a coarse-toothed comb.

'I wanted to ask you . . .' Kana halted again. 'Nothing, Aunt Sachi, it is all right.'

Suddenly one of the rings on Mrs Itoh's hand caught in Kana's hair. During the manoeuvre to untangle the ring Kana asked, 'You like them? You think they're beautiful?'

'What dear?' Mrs Itoh was trying hard not to pull Kana's hair.

'Your rings.'

'No. Not really.' Her concentration on her finger operation made her speak with absent-minded candour.

'Why do you wear them, then? Why don't you throw them away?'

'I will.' Her ring came out of Kana's hair at last. 'Now, run. You'll be late for school.'

Kana ran. After she joined the streams of children walking to school, she began wondering if she had in fact heard the two words 'I will'.

When Shirato came to Rokko Hills for his second visit in November Kana overheard that Yuki had not come to the launching ceremony after all. She had caught flu. True or false, it was clear that for some reason Yuki had backed out.

60

'She intended to come, that I know. I had an order from her specially for the occasion.'

'Did you now, Shirato?' A quick sardonic response was shot by Mrs Toda.

'Oh please, Miss Sadako. I'm a merchant. A client is a client.'

Aunt Sachi lost her rings, both of them.

On her way home to Tokyo she had left them, she said, in the train lavatory. Outside the station Mr Itoh slapped her on both cheeks in front of his chauffeur.

'But you know –' Mrs Itoh spoke slightly out of breath but coolly, leaning against the wing of the Mercedes Benz – 'I never wash my hands with my rings on.'

Mr and Mrs Itoh, the chauffeur and the platform inspector searched the carriage in vain.

'It's one of your feline revenges. You must've thrown them out of the train window or flushed them down the toilet!' her husband shouted and ordered her to make inquiries the next morning at the Lost Property Office. She obeyed, but without success. He continued to nag and nag till by the grace of a poisonous blow-fish his tongue became paralysed.

The blow-fish season was short, the few coldest months of the year. No one dared eat them outside the season. Government inspection was frequent and strict. The licensed specialist restaurants were therefore open only from late November till early March. It was in late March and an unseasonably warm March that Mr Itoh entertained his clients, four oil company executives, at a centuries-old blow-fish house in Kyoto. Naturally he ate the greatest quantity and *raw*, as serious blow-fish lovers prefer them. He was deriding the others, who squeamishly watched him devour huge quantities of the pale translucent slices of uncooked fish, till suddenly his speech failed. The poison worked fast; in no time he was in a coma. An ambulance rushed him to hospital in Kyoto at eleven o'clock at night. Mrs Itoh immediately called her sister in Rokko Hills.

'Please, Sada-chan, come with me. I couldn't face that woman alone.'

Mrs Toda agreed to meet her sister on the Kyoto station platform the following morning. Kana had hardly fallen asleep when her mother slipped into her room.

'Tomorrow you won't go to school but come with me to Kyoto.' Kana nodded gravely and asked no question. And all Mrs Toda said by way of explanation was: 'Uncle Itoh is very ill. He's eaten bad fish.'

Blow-fish poisoning, just what she had prayed for! To think that her hard and long prayer had finally rid Aunt Sachi of the monster! Kana had not slept a wink when her mother, fully dressed and made up, turned on the light. 'Kana, get up, it's past five.'

During their fifty-minute train journey to Kyoto, Mrs Toda sat up as straight as an arrow, but Kana was soon sound asleep. In her mind there was no doubt whatsoever that Uncle Itoh would die. Still in the dim of the dawn they arrived at Kyoto and walked up and down the platform waiting for the night train from Tokyo. At six the kiosk opened and Mrs Toda bought the morning paper, which carried a story on the first blow-fish poisoning case of the year. When her sister's train arrived she quickly threw the paper in a trash can.

Kana skipped up to Mrs Itoh, clung to her sleeve, and in a congratulatory bright voice repeated, 'Oh, Auntie, Auntie.'

Aunt Sachi was far from jubilant. Mrs Toda, helping with her sister's hand baggage, quickly silenced Kana. The sisters talked in whispers throughout the taxi ride to the hospital. Kana bitterly ruminated on adult behaviour: will I ever get to understand them, such ungrateful turncoats.

As they drew up to the main entrance, a swarm of blue bottles, men in dark suits wringing their hands, burst out of the waiting-room door and darted down the steps to meet their employer's wife. Bowing frantically in the direction of the slowing taxi, they chorused at the top of their lungs that owing to the quick injection of an antidote Mr Itoh was going to live. As he had done so often in his devil-may-care life, he had dodged death again. Kana was so disappointed that she glared at the large white hospital with raw hatred.

The most alert member of the buzzing, bowing and hand-wringing group held the door open for his employer's wife and led the way to Mr Itoh's room.

The air inside the small ante-room, furnished only with a wooden bench and a hat stand, hinted at the fresh stench of human struggle for survival. A woman was standing like a cut-out billboard in a posture of calculated humility, self-debasing but consciously sinuous. Despite having been at the hospital all night, her hair was neatly coiffed with not a single hair astray. Her plump dimpled hands, one on top of the other, were placed over her kneecaps to which level she also lowered her forehead. This low bow was directed not exactly at Mrs Itoh but generally towards the door by which the three had entered. Towering behind the half-bent woman stood a boy aged about sixteen with arrows of hostility shooting out of his dark eyes. A very handsome, nervous, bitter-acid-looking boy. Kana understood: they were 'mistress' and 'bastard'.

With her head still at the height of her upper thighs, Yuki spoke with a coy little-girl's precipitation.

'I am Yuki Kashima. This unfortunate accident has brought me at last to meet you. Would you please . . .'

The incredible scene that followed saw Mrs Itoh with much panache leaping into a dramatic performance. She made a bow almost as low as Yuki's, and not letting Yuki finish her ceremonial blah-blah, she exclaimed: 'Oh, Yuki-san!' Yuki-san! – even Mrs Toda was startled at this – 'would you please accept my most sincere and heart-felt gratitude for all you've done for him and for the courtesy you've extended to me at this time. . . .'

Now it was Yuki's turn. With an expression of genuine alarm she stretched out her right arm as if to halt Mrs Itoh's aggression of kindness. 'Please!' She then gave a vigorous shake to her artfully puffed hair. 'Please! Whatever I've done couldn't possibly deserve such kind words from you. It is I who must . . .'

I'll vomit in a second, Kana thought, spitefully watching the two heads popping up and down with nonsensical murmurs.

Mrs Toda surveyed the scene from above with her back defiantly arched. When she judged enough rites had been performed, she pulled the end of her sister's sleeve.

'Sister Sachi, shall we?'

At this Yuki twisted her hips in one curve with such spry coquetry to face Mrs Toda, that the two sisters had to groan inside: 'Once a geisha, always a geisha!' She looked up at Mrs Toda with a ravishing smile pouring from the corners of her upturned eyelids. 'Mrs Toda of Rokko Hills!' The agile creature began bowing. Mrs Toda did not bend her back at all; she merely dropped her head. Kana could have cried out: 'Bravo!' Doesn't Mother put Yuki in her right place? Mistress! A former geisha!

'Yes indeed, I am Mrs Itoh's sister,' Mrs Toda said politely and quickly shifted her attention to her sister. 'Sister Sachi, *you* go in. Kana and I had better wait here.'

Mrs Itoh took one breath and gazed at the sign on the door that read: ABSOLUTE SILENCE. NO VISITORS. Yuki made a move to lead Mrs Itoh inside.

'Miss Kashima!' Mrs Toda's voice shot at Yuki's feet and nailed them fast to the floor; it could have stopped a bird in mid-flight. Yuki turned back and her stunned expression changed to one of bewilderment. Mrs Toda was smiling with toasting warmth and friendliness this time. 'You must be worn out. Have you slept at all? Have you eaten anything?' she asked.

Yuki's worldly sagacious face betrayed her acute perplexity at this unexpected gush of affability. Never minding, Mrs Toda went on chirping merrily about their samisen teacher and Shirato, making sure that Mrs Itoh had slipped inside the patient's room and had closed the door behind her. She went on prattling till Mrs Itoh came out. As abruptly as she had begun, she stopped her sentence halfway through, begged Yuki's pardon and went up to her sister.

Some more bowing and murmuring and they all left the room excepting the bastard who did not even say goodbye. Just as they reached the end of the corridor where the stairs went down to the exit, without warning Mrs Toda bent towards Kana and in a clear loud voice enunciated: 'Who is she? She's your uncle's housekeeper.'

'Oh, aren't you childish!' Mrs Itoh hissed. Blushing down to her nape, she was too embarrassed to look at her wicked sister. Mrs Toda rolled her happy chuckle for a long while inside her throat. Kana took a stealthy glance backward before she descended the steps and saw Yuki still bowing correctly at a ninety-degree angle.

As soon as Mr Itoh was released from the hospital, he began counting how many more weeks he had to wait till the next blow-fish season.

6

The Korean War boom also shone down on those who did not own ships.

Six years after the end of the Second World War it was the time for rebuilding and new construction. The Toda & Son Company, founded by Mr Toda's grandfather, was thriving briskly in the production and sales of cement, asbestos and other building materials. Relations no longer muttered behind Mr Toda's back, 'Wait and see. Success never survives three generations. What his grandfather built and his father kept, he'll wreck.'

His mother, the formidable matriarch, had passed away in the winter of 1950 and Mr Toda, the eldest son, was now the patriarch of the Todas. No longer necessary to make a hurried trip to Kamakura to obtain his mother's seal of consent every time he wanted to sell some stocks or even a patch of family land.

As for the young Mrs Toda, she had just turned thirty-one. Generously sprayed with *Vol de Nuit* and rustling in layers of the best silk, she illuminated the atmosphere for miles around her with the bliss of being bereft of her mother-in-law. That she would no longer hear 'You have not borne us a son!' was such

65

a heaven-lifting relief that as soon as the period of mourning was over every pore of her skin shone lustily with a new sap of life.

For Mr and Mrs Toda the immediate post-war struggle was also over. The eyes that used to scavenge for the means of day-to-day survival could be lifted to a prosperous future, and now with a flourishing business to pass on, it was their turn to sigh: 'If only Kana were a boy!'

The first Monday in April, 1951, Kana advanced to the sixth year at Takaha Primary School.

In a country so intensely over-populated and education-conscious, every child's life had to be punctuated by one severe sifting-out competition after another if he or she was to gain a place in a higher educational institution.

'Of course, you will sign up for the intensive entrance-exam class, Kana,' Mr Toda said firmly. 'Which school? It doesn't matter as long as it's a private school and not co-educational. We can decide later which.'

So, suddenly, Kana found herself in an 'entrance-exam hell'.

'Hell, it really was a hell,' everyone who had been through it had told her. 'What's so dreadful is that it's not you alone who's in it. For, if you fail, the shame falls on everyone in your family, who will avoid old friends in the streets, and whose accusatory eyes will rub it in that you've let them down. No wonder so many failed students commit suicide. It's really this family pride and expectation that's so hellish.'

By June one could not mistake the children in the 'entrance-exam hell' for the rest. Those in the intensive classes had turned dull green and lethargic. They bit their nails and ungratefully squinted at the generous summer sun while the others turned a healthy copper-red in it. During a break they took shelter in the wisteria shade and stood immobile, excepting their lips which were set in perpetual movement: '1274, the first Mongol Invasion. The second, the second... 1280? No, 1281! Mongol invaders numbered some 100,000. Both times they were overcome by the Divine Winds.'

So much had to be memorized before next March: dates,

places and names of historic importance; mathematical formulae; how to convert centigrade into fahrenheit; the spelling of some one thousand Chinese characters; how to calculate the distance of thunder by the difference between the speed of light and of sound, or where and when two ships, one sailing downstream and one upstream at different speeds, will meet; and so on. In the entrance-exam classes the seating order was rearranged every Monday according to the pupils' achievements in the previous week. Kana never lost her place at the top of the class; she stuck to her seat in the first row on the centre aisle; and naturally this meant gruelling hours of extra work. She was at school from eight-thirty in the morning till three in the afternoon, then took a short nap before her private tutor arrived at five, and studied till one or two every morning.

Masticating and digesting became too much of a chore: she lived solely on dried Hiroshima persimmons, bean curd and apple. Not any kind of apple, it had to be an India apple, sweet and mushy. At midnight she drank tea and nibbled biscuits. Her eyes became bloodshot and watery; every evening she dashed to an oculist for an eye-wash.

Kana did not resent the drudgery of it all, as long as on PTA day her mother, in one of her best kimonos and perfumed and rouged slightly more than at home, could hear on her first step into the classroom the envious whisper: 'That's the mother of the top girl,' she was more than amply rewarded.

A cloying hot July night. After midnight Kana began wilting. Creeping into her frayed brain was the thought of all those lovely things outside her window: sky, moon, stars, pines, bougainvillaeas, sweet daphnes and scentless hydrangeas nodding head-heavy. . . Stop!

Kana kicked her chair back and went downstairs to fetch the cold tea Miki prepared for her every night. Before she got to the kitchen she heard her mother's voice from her parents' room.

'Mr Tanabe told me after the PTA meeting today that Kana's been getting the highest grades in all five major subjects. If we wanted, or rather had no objections, he'd like to have her try for

Faith College. Last year their admission rate was 1 out of 7.5, the highest standard for a girls' school in the country. Of course it'll be to his credit if Kana passes.'

'Faith College? But that's a Catholic school!'

'*It is?*' cooed Mrs Toda, in a gravely shocked tone. Kana heard her father burst out laughing. Who could have helped it? 'Disarming' would be too tepid, too ineffectual a word for her mother's '*It is?*' Ringing with that wicked delicious innocence; a sheer witchery of charm, timing, guile, and once more charm. Pure honesty would have sounded like a silly crow after this. Mrs Toda was well aware that Faith College taught a heathen religion. Every PTA-going mother knew this and felt somewhat uneasy, but their emulous vanity always got the better of them. What mother could resist the honour of having her child accepted at Faith?

Now with renewed vehemence Mrs Toda was saying: 'But where else can we find a school with central heating? Flush toilets? Marble and granite floors? And it is not only the best but the hardest school to get into. The hardest.'

Mr Toda laughed, totally undone. If his side of the family, all pious dogged Buddhists, growled, well, too bad, let them! Kana, too, was melting all over.

'If Kana were a boy, she'd be striding ahead on the Nada-to-Tokyo-University route, you know?' said Mr Toda wistfully without realizing what a blunder he was committing.

From then on it was no longer a conversation, but a soliloquy. Mrs Toda was now aplogizing and now lamenting their heir-less state, dropping here and there some acid remarks about the late Mrs Toda and other vociferous Toda relations. It went on and on, interrupted only by sniffling. Desperate to end her drizzly whine, Mr Toda hurried to say with a cheering lift to his voice: 'Listen, we could look at it this way: luckier to have the best of girls than a scum of boys. After all, a good-for-nothing son will be good for nothing. Don't you agree?'

While listening to the exchange, Kana's front teeth had dug right through the wooden flesh of a pencil and had crushed the lead. Gritty bits of wood and lead spread in her mouth. She spat them out noiselessly. With so much hurt inside she could not stay still. She thrust her tongue as far out as possible, crumpled her face to a hideous mess and screamed inwardly.

'Bah, bah, bah! Smiting her tight belly with her fist she went on making faces in the dark. I'm good for anything, good for everything. Monsters. Why don't they understand? What would I care for my own sake, if I were a half-wit, failed in the entrance-exam, became a pickpocket, got thrown into a reformatory or got hanged? I wouldn't be up and studying at this hour, if it were only for my sake. Ogres! Heartless monsters!

She went back upstairs without getting the cold tea, gargled and brushed her teeth. She was drying her tears when her thoughts made a sudden leap: it'll hurt me terribly, but I'll have to leave them. Leave home. Not yet, but one day when I'm ready.

Soon it was August and Kana became twelve.

First it was merely a drop of blood in a maple-leaf shape.

Did I swallow a fish-bone last night? Kana was still in her pyjamas late on Sunday morning. It went on gently draining out of her for hours and hours and for the rest of the day. She had to admit something was wrong, very wrong. If it were a bloody nose, a bleeding between the teeth or a scratch on the kneecap, she would have cried out for attention immediately. But it was a bleeding – from such an unmentionable sordid shameful place of her body. Why, why must it be there? Why me? The question never stopped ringing in her ears. Every ten minutes Kana checked. Each time she opened the toilet door her hope throbbed new and whole. Perhaps it has stopped? She looked down. No, it went on.

When the vivid crimson tarnished to copper-red Kana began smelling it herself and such disgust and fear as she had never imagined possible came over her that she felt it necessary to keep on testing her sanity by the multiplications: $11 \times 11 = 121$; 12×12, 120 plus another 24, 144! On and on she mumbled to herself.

I must keep all my wits ready and sharp. I need them to survive.

No pampering, you hear me? Kana told herself time after time. You can't afford to be sensitive or maudlin about this. Just look at it as a blood leakage. It won't last more than a day!

Kana checked all the closets in the house and stole from each drawer a just-unnoticeable amount of towels, paper tissues, waxed wrapping paper, cotton gauze and first-aid bandages.

The night came. Kana diapered herself as best she could and lay on top of waxed paper. Behind the paper-and-wood screens Yoko slept. Even under the eiderdown the waxed paper made wild crackling noises every time Kana moved. The dark that enveloped her stiff sleepless body was a blackboard on which she drew and redrew the plans of how to manage the next day.

As soon as the eastern sky whitened and the first rooster was heard Kana stole to the bathroom with a pair of scissors, a pile of cotton gauze and other needed materials. A fervent quick prayer, then she looked down. No use. It had not stopped during the night. So she started the operation she had planned during the night. She cut up the gauze into some small pads and wrapped them neatly with paper tissues to take to school. She worked fast and deftly as if she had done this for years, spying on the sounds of the new day that were rapidly coming to life outside the window. Garbage collectors were calling to one another; Miki was opening the shutters; newspaper boys rang their bicycle bells. The world, so alive, so astute, how could she possibly fool it? And how much longer?

She pushed several fresh gauze pads into the bottom of her Walt Disney felt bag, which had a Dumbo appliquéd on each side. Then she laid a handkerchiefed parcel, containing the soiled pads and panties of the night before, on top of her still-warm lunch box. She left the house half an hour earlier than usual: she had to hunt for an unobserved garbage box to get rid of her secret.

Kana roamed from one unfrequented back alley to another, watching out for the sudden appearance of a passer-by, avoiding any wall with the sign BITING DOG! and keeping away from kitchen windows that too closely overlooked the street. In this residential part of the town each house was equipped with a fairly large garbage box with a cement body and a wooden flap-door with the owners' name elaborately painted on. Kana had taken it for granted that all the garbage boxes in the world looked exactly alike. Not any longer. Now she could tell that some were too intimidatingly clean and shallow-bottomed and some too prominently located. Finding one with the family name of a friend Kana fled like a criminal. Not a single garbage box fit to swallow her parcel? She was getting late for school. Her despair was beginning to numb her brain as she scurried on through the streets. All she needed was one inconspicuous garbage box.

When she noticed a pot-bellied bin with a tin top, a very humble one, she said to herself aloud: 'Drop it. Just drop it!' She raised the top, into the acrid stench she let go of her secret, and only after she heard a dull thud on the recently emptied bottom did she remember she had forgotten to remove the handkerchief, but a thousand linen handkerchiefs could not have kept her there. She jogged away fast but as smoothly as she could manage, for the cotton gauze was too precariously diapered. Before she walked into the streams of schoolchildren on the main avenue, she steadied herself and coughed for the sake of morale.

Kana watched the girls in short skirts with white stockings, how they strode and spread their legs nonchalantly, how some kicked at the pebbles or made frolicsome jumps for no purpose. Oh, those unappreciative privileged brats! Kana bit her lips and walked on stiffly. Inside the school building she made sure she kept her upper thighs tightly closed as she climbed the stairs. When she stood up at the teacher's bidding, her pulse beat faster and she felt her blood stir down there; she forgot the answer and stood petrified. And the fifteen-minute break was far too short for her. She had so much work to do.

'Yes, yes! I'm coming out in a minute. Just one minute!' Shouting back at the persistent knocking on the toilet door, Kana worked at frenzied speed. When she finished the re-diapering she was flushed, perspiring and breathless as if she had just robbed a bank. How could she face the rows of girls outside? She stayed inside the cubicle in spite of the angry banging on the door till the bell rang.

'Whoever it is inside this toilet must be smoking,' Kana heard the naive whisper as she stood on the toilet bowl so that no one outside could identify her from her shoes and socks seen under the swing door.

Silence returned, except for the staccato dripping from a leaky water tap. Kana stayed inside a few minutes longer, even after the bell. Then she came out with the soiled pads squeezed small and wrapped in newspaper.

Kana counted her survival not by days or weeks but by minutes. After the second night any hope that it might stop as stealthily and mysteriously as it had begun evaporated as soon as she woke up on the waxed paper. No need to go down to the bathroom and examine in the pale dawn light. That furtive spilling of blood was only too familiar. She found herself too weary to feel the sharp-edged disappointment any longer. The world and the people who occupied it had proved themselves surprisingly unwatchful and obtuse so far: perhaps it would not be totally impossible to guard her secret from them for some time to come. But then there was the rapidly decreasing supply of cotton and waxed paper and this exhaustion! No, she thought, I can't possibly hold out much longer. It was too constant and too inside a disaster to live with.

When Kana came home at three, Mrs Toda hurriedly came out to the entrance hall. A quick smile and a short greeting. Kana sat down to take off her shoes and felt on her back her mother's intent gaze. Mrs Toda followed Kana to the dining-room. Biscuits and a tangerine were ready on the table as on any other afternoon but two cushions were laid, instead of the usual one. They sat down face to face. Kana took the fruit and peeled the skin. Her mother fidgeted, picking up invisible dust here and there, and rubbed the perfectly clean surface of the table, over and over again.

When Mrs Toda caught Kana's questioning eyes, her hand halted and lay flat on the table like a starfish left on the sand. Kana looked away and went on chewing and sucking and gulping in the tangerine flesh and the hard bitter seeds indiscriminately.

'There's ... there's something that you haven't told me about ... ?' her mother began.

Kana dropped the rest of the tangerine. She held her fingers spread apart like a begging dog's paws, not thinking, not feeling, not even seeing. She stayed in a trance till a moan sluiced itself out of her:

'Mo-o-oth-er ... Ah-ah-ah ...'

'Miki came to me. She found a small wrapped thing ... this morning in your Dumbo lunch bag.'

Kana cried. A deluge of a cry. It rolled down in torrents, ripping the shrouded secret, now three and a half days old. It flooded to all the sore ends of her wounds, licking them with wondrous healing tongues. Thankful for the relief this out-pouring of tears had brought, Kana cried more. Mrs Toda spoke, but Kana went on wailing and howling.

Then came the moment when Kana had to stop.

She let out a frightful gasp and stayed in a death stupor as Mrs Toda glibly explained, taught and assured her that this happened to each and every healthy girl of her age. And that this would now occur every month.

'But, of course, it's over quickly. Within a week. Just one week.'

Her hands, moulded stiff in the drying tangerine juice, dropped on the table. She took a straight look at her mother.

Mrs Toda flushed, giggled nervously, then started introducing a collection of objects that Kana was to be familiar with every month from then on. Mrs Toda fondled this and fussed with that. Busy, busy! It was some time therefore before she took notice of Kana's savage silence and the flinty way she was glaring at her. When she did, Mrs Toda erased her forced gaiety at once. She sighed wistfully.

'Honestly, I wish I had some idea how other mothers cope with daughters of your age. Don't you agree that it is the school, not mothers, that ought to warn girls about such a matter? I couldn't bring myself to. ... I'm your mother. How could I start a discussion with you, my daughter, on such a ... such a ...'

She made a disapproving grimace without spoiling her lovely features. 'Still, I am sorry. I am sorry that you had to be taken by surprise. Things happen so quickly with the eldest child that it's hard to catch up.' Another sigh.

Her mother, beautiful, almost virginal, only nineteen years senior to Kana, had to deliver her monologue to an insoluble wall of silence, all her charm and vehemence wasted.

Kana stretched her back tautly, looked at her mother and wondered why she had been so in awe of this woman. What had made her think this woman a wonder-working witch, 'inviolable and sacred'? Bah!

Kana had shed blood, her own blood. In three and a half little days she had borne so much needless shame and torture alone. Her mother who had slapped life into Kana's baby-green bottom had now unwittingly given Kana a new life, Kana's own, to live. The blood darkened, lessened and soon stopped.

Kana was skipping and hopping again on the wide sunny avenue heading the group of her friends.

The witch-mother was finally no more.

7

'You mean' – Mrs Toda seemed astounded – 'Amen every morning?'

'Yes, Mother. From eight to eight-thirty, five days a week. And there's a voluntary early-morning service at seven for the pious sort of girls. And of course we are expected to go to the full-length service in church on Sundays.'

'Oh, Kana, why didn't you tell me this before? You must have become half Catholic by now.'

'Not Catholic, Mother, Faith College is Protestant Episcopal. The two are quite different.'

'Don't argue with me. Wait for Father and tell him.'

At dinner Yoko eyed her father's plate holding twice as many strawberries as anyone else's and grumbled, 'Scientifically, the younger you are the more vitamins and fructose you need.'

'But it is Father who deserves the bonus of longevity, not you,' said Mrs Toda firmly and sent Yoko upstairs to finish her homework. A centuries-old legend had it that the first-picked fruit of the season brought bonus years to one's normal life expectancy. As Yoko went upstairs with ill grace, Mrs Toda nodded to Kana, who began like a radio with a run-down battery.

'Lessons are read from the Bible, we sing hymns, listen to a sermon, then comes what we call "greedy bucket", a collection, I give twenty yen.'

'Who washed the strawberries?' asked Mr Toda abruptly. 'Did you? Or ... or what's her name again, the new one?'

'I did. I haven't yet trusted Yoshi to wash fruit or vegetables,' Mrs Toda spoke softly in case Yoshi should overhear.

'Well, in that case ...' He pitched a large glistening strawberry into his gaping mouth as if afraid of contaminating it by contact with his lips. At the age of forty-one, of medium height and lean build, with his bouncy excitable manners, Mr Toda had retained a remarkably young, almost boyish, air about him.

'The Japan of 1952 should have abolished the use of sewage manure.' He sniffed at his fingers for no reason but from habit. He in fact sniffed at everything. The hot-bath fiend was free of any recognizable odour himself and would ask his wife, 'Tell me, is it your scent or a cooking smell?' To Mr Toda's sharp olfactory sense a day-old perfume was a reeking stink.

Meanwhile Kana was playing 'Für Elise' on her lap, waiting for her listeners' attention.

'Kana tells me that her American teachers live on chemically fertilized greens,' Mr Toda continued as he scrutinized the last and largest strawberry from all angles. 'I find that civilized. Mind you, I am not saying they are more hygiene-conscious than we. Not at all. For instance their abominable custom of shaking hands and rubbing their cheeks and kissing with no matter whom they chance upon. Their insensitivity, barging into the house with their filthy outdoor shoes on! And their toilet bowls, what an idiotic invention! Think of hundreds of bottoms coming in direct contact with . . .'

'Please!' cut in Mrs Toda.

'Ah, sorry. Nothing excels the first-picked fruit. Soon we'll be having bamboo shoots and loquat seeds. Well, that was a good dinner.' He smacked his lips noisily, a polite gesture to please his wife, and dipped his ivory toothpick in hot green tea to clean it.

'Why your mother worries so much about the influence of the Catholic Church, I can't understand.'

'I'm not worried at all. I just wanted you to know *in case* –' here Mrs Toda threw a wicked smile at her husband – 'in case *your* relations . . .'

'Here we go again! My relations never raised a squeak unless prodded by one person, my mother. And where's she now? Oh, women *are* vindictive! Let me tell you this, Kana: all religions are worth getting acquainted with. In my life I have worshipped Buddha and our ancestors, and I have been acquainted with about half a dozen after-the-war religious movements – some people called them spiritual quackery or a sorry substitute for Emperor, but they were helpful at the time for many. And now my daughter goes outside to a wider world than I have known and comes home to tell me she is learning a foreign god's way. Fine! No harm done. I have found that unless you yourself accept or let them, gods cannot do a thing for you or against you. In the end it is entirely up to you. Anyhow who am I to judge the Catholic Church? Ach, broken again! I must get a more durable kind. Ivory toothpicks are ridiculous. Stainless steel might be the answer.'

'Do you think there's such a thing on the market?' Mrs Toda winced, for she, personally, found the idea of a metal toothpick unappetizing.

Kana's immediate desire to correct him – 'Father, Faith College is Protestant, not Catholic, and teaches us to worship a one and only God' – turned to a suppressed chuckle somewhere down her throat.

'Anyhow, you can't have it both ways. For the central heating, the pure mountain air, the haikara* environment, and above all the best education, we must be prepared to be a little broad-minded.' Signalling the end of the conversation, Mr Toda retreated behind the evening paper, having first put on a pair of freshly laundered white cotton gloves to protect his hands from any smudge of printers' ink.

'Well, what about a toothpick made of the finest bamboo?' Mrs Toda pursued the earlier subject of conversation.

'Hmmm!' Mr Toda groaned not at his wife's suggestion but at the newspaper article on the Japan – USA security treaty that had just been signed. 'It seems Okinawa will never be returned to us, and since our constitution provides that Japan shall never be armed, America-san will protect us from all enemies – what enemies, I don't know. I guess you can't discuss international politics without having an enemy. We give Okinawa to our Big Brother America, have a hundred Colonel Bridgewaters on our four islands, but materially we'll flourish, for we shan't be spending a penny on armament. I can see all of us turning into diligent, gutless and middling-rich men. Hmmm. . . .'

'As long as there's no war . . .' Mrs Toda sipped her hot tea thoughtfully.

There was a feigned cough outside the sliding door, then a timid little voice announced: 'The master's bath is ready.'

'Hoop-la!' With his usual bath-time alacrity Mr Toda pulled off the gloves and sprang to his feet. 'Thank you, Miki!'

'Yoshi!' hissed Mrs Toda, picking up the gloves.

'Honestly, you can't expect me to keep track of all their names. Every few weeks there's a new servant greeting me at the entrance and as like as not a wedding for her a month later as a result of your match-making.'

'Shh! Please –' Mrs Toda hurried after him to the bathroom – 'a "household help". She'll quit if you call her a servant.'

*Derived from either 'high collar' or 'high colour', the mongrel adjective means sophisticated, urbane, elegant in a Western style. Therefore a Japanese gentleman who travelled abroad and came home in a suit tailored in Savile Row, London, with a blue Basque peasant beret, would be a most distinguished *haikara* gentleman.

'What's the matter with people? Nowadays we can't simply ...' Water began splashing and purling down the drain pipe. The breezy conversation from the bathroom was now drowned and inaudible.

'I – am – happy.' Kana tried aloud the sentence she had learned in Miss Cobb's English class. She then tried to change it to fit her mood:

'We – family – am – happy'.

The history of Faith College goes way back to the 1890s when in the port town of Kobe two American missionary ladies hung a hand-painted wooden sign outside their lodging: Bible and English classes for young unmarried ladies.

By the time the First World War broke out, the school had been firmly established and was known throughout the country for its advanced educational system and its haikaraness, its reluctance to accept more than fifty new girls a year and its outrageously high fees. The higher the fees soared, the more applications poured in.

When Miss Jo Ann Hale, the fifth Dean, heard that the Hankyu Express Company was planning to construct a new branch line from Nishinomiya to Takarazuka where high-quality sulphur springs had just been discovered, she hurried to see the Hankyu directors.

'You give me lovely site Takarazuka, I build school. School flourish. Many many extra passengers students staff parents relatives all ride longest distance to Takarazuka terminal station. You more money. How nice. Yes?'

The spectacular outcome of the baby-talk bargain was that the whole of Mount Okada, near the third stop from Nishinomiya junction, was given to the school. It took Miss Hale four years to raise enough funds. When the school finally stood on Mount Okada she christened it Faith College, a college which embraced both a six-year high-school and a two-year college course.

Miss Hale's paradise on earth consisted of beautiful grounds and gardens, a chapel, a gymnasium, an auditorium, classroom buildings, dormitories, Santa Monica Cottage, a residence for foreign instructresses, with every window and door double-screened against the native insects for which they seemed to have such unChristian hatred, and a music school isolated far out on the sloping edge of the mountain.

'What, to waste a dozen buildings on a mere five hundred females in this over-populated land!' It seemed exceedingly offensive to the space-stingy Japanese that so few human bodies, let alone young and female ones, should be floating about with so much unutilized air, green and space around them.

Three gardeners mowed the lawns all day long during the green seasons and shrouded all the tree trunks with straw mats before winter. There were fountains and marble benches; yards and yards of crimson velvet dangling from the celestial height of the chapel dome. . . . No wonder that during the school holidays local families came to experience this haikara paradise. Whenever they caught sight of the blond-haired and blue-eyed instructresses, they clicked their cameras, and they came near to swooning with excitement if suddenly the chapel bells pealed or someone practised a thundering scale on the pipe organ inside. 'Just like in a Hollywood film!' they would sigh raptly.

Soon after the school moved to Mount Okada, the Hankyu Express officials came to congratulate Miss Hale and at the same time to negotiate the operation of a bus service between Faith College and the station, like those they had arranged for the Sacred Heart and other private schools along the Hankyu line. Miss Hale waved her meaty pink hand. 'Girls walk. Good for them.'

Ever since the Faith girls walked. The walk from the station to Mount Okada took at least thirty minutes. The mud track was hardly wide enough for two persons to walk abreast, weedy on the sides and deeply grooved at the centre where on rainy days gushed a gruelly torrent of bucolic horrors, which made life hazardous for everyone concerned – not least village commuters hurrying to catch their trains. Those, overwhelmed by the onslaught of bouncy young female bodies, often faltered and side-stepped into a ditch or – worse still – into one of the manure ponds whose odious mouths gaped at almost every crossing. The local residents' representatives came to see Miss Crowe, the eleventh Dean of the Faith, to suggest that perhaps the traditional blue serge uniforms might help discipline the giddy young girls. Many parents promptly supported the restore-the-uniform campaign, but Miss Crowe opposed it firmly:

'No uniforms not no discipline. Can't teach our school motto, "Bi-Chi-Shin"* without respecting freedom of their young souls.'

Amongst the many friends Kana made at Faith, she got on best with Emiko, whose infectious, almost exhausting, vivacity and outrageous sense of humour Kana found irresistible. Emiko's family were the fifth generation proprietors of Mikasa, a traditional restaurant with the highest reputation in Osaka, one of the few remaining establishments in the country where clients had first to be introduced and fully vetted before they could even make a reservation and where no menu or bill was presented to avoid spoiling the aesthetic experience of eating there. Emiko had lived in an atmosphere of mature sophistication all her life. 'Full of magazine knowledge and tea-house chit-chat,' she said shrugging her round shoulders, undervaluing herself as usual so as to be free of envy and competition; but behind her indefatigable efforts to become the centre of attention by clowning rather than by shining, there lurked a rich understanding of life and people.

When they moved up to the third-year class, both Emiko and Kana were elected to the Arts Committee and together they organized Arts Day performances twice a year and presented a Nativity play for Christmas. On each such occasion Emiko was immensely popular in a comic part, while Kana played the male lead, pinning up her long hair in plaits.

With the success of her stage appearances Kana began receiving a large number of letters which were pushed under her locker door. Written timorously on pastel-coloured paper, scented, with dried flowers glued on them, they read something like this:

*Beauty, Intelligence and Love of God.

Please, if you would become my Eternal Sister, touch your forehead three times as you come into the chapel tomorrow morning. . . .

Kana never complied with such requests; she was utterly uninterested in entering into such a queer bondage. Hardly had she finished reading such a missive before she had flushed it down an impeccably functioning Faith toilet.

Sometimes knotted letters from boys were dropped in her school bag during the jam-packed train ride from Nishinomiya junction to Mount Okada. Since the boys wrote much more flamboyantly, their letters made more exciting reading.

> As your cheeks blush there bloom tea roses
> your bright double-lidded eyes lift dawn's gloom
> your giddy small steps up and down the station bridge
> tap at my heart like drum beats of joy.

If I were a bee I'd rather court your nectareous dimple than the sweetest flower in the field. Please do not miss the 7.25 semi-express. Please do not deny me the morning delight of watching you! Yours ever.

'I bet he has sticky wet hands and volcanic acne,' was Emiko's succinct comment on this knotted letter.

When Kana showed this letter to her mother, she said, 'Tea-rose complexion? Sun-tanned like a road-mender is more like it,' and plastered Kana's face with her home-made egg yolk, cucumber and lemon bleach for an hour. 'You have become a different girl, Kana. I can hardly recognize you. . . .'

And she was right: Kana had changed. No more queasiness or egg poisoning. She had long forgotten what it was like to be sick. Nothing reminiscent of that touchy scrawny child of Shitsukawa. Round what her father had once called a skeleton of pine needles gathered a thin layer of flesh like that of kumquat with the same tight-pored sheen and resilience. Expressions such as 'mimosa gaiety' or 'spunky as a winter apple' which her anonymous admirers now used would not have been appropriate for the Kana of some years ago.

'But why must I always be a flower or fruit?' Kana groaned.

'Why not "supple as a tiger" or "saucy as a boiled egg" or something exciting like that?'

'You can't expect them to say what you aren't. You are hardly animal yet,' said Emiko knowingly.

'Animal? What are you talking about, Emiko? You know, I do sometimes find you obscene.'

'Obscene! Me obscene just because I fail to see you as a tiger or an egg?'

'I am an egg, and an egg is from a chicken!' shouted Kana.

'A chicken's from an egg, imbecile!' There they stopped making sense and started chasing each other about.

Two years younger than Kana, Yoko was now in her entrance-exam hell. With an ampler and better-quality after-the-war diet, she stood taller than Kana by almost two centimeters and weighed seven kilos more, and her teeth were larger and sturdier.

'After reading such drivel I'm determined to go to a co-ed public school,' said Yoko, her throat rattling with contemptuous laughter, when Kana showed her one of the perfumed letters left in her locker, requesting a paper tissue or a handkerchief stained with Kana's tears or even snivel. 'There is clearly something very unhealthy about an all-girl school.'

Yoko did not alter her anti-girls'-school atittude till as late as February, when under her mother's last-spurt pressure she finally succumbed, but on her own terms: 'I might put up with a hot-house of girls, if you'd let me go to Konan and join their famous volleyball team.'

'First, you must pass the examination,' said Mrs Toda sternly. 'Konan College is by no means an easy one, in fact the second hardest to enter. They admit only one out of five, you know.'

'I'm not going to turn into a measly bean-sprout by cramming day and night as sister Kana did. I'll be happy if I can scrape in just slightly above the minimum passing grade.' Yoko slept nine hours nightly, ate with healthy constant appetite, never worried, studied little, and to everyone's surprise passed. Just as she had planned, at about the lowest passing level. A week before the official start of classes she was already attending volleyball practice in her brand-new Konan uniform.

After her entry to Konan Yoko's monthly allowance was raised to 500 yen, part of which she secretly spent on judo lessons and the rest on 'stamina food': chocolate, nuts, ice cream and cheese. Kana, on the other hand, spent all her 900 yen pocket money and an additional 8,000 yen a month from her parents on what Yoko sneered at as 'good-for-nothing' lessons.

'What sissy arty-crafty lessons will you be starting next, Amen! They won't turn into flesh and blood. What a waste,' Yoko snarled.

'Never mind, you brute. I'm curious, wildly curious.'

'With an average duration of three to four weeks, your wild curiosity doesn't last long, does it, eh?'

'Long enough, thank you!' Kana tried a smooth uppercut jab into Yoko's jaw. But she was no match in athletics. Yoko instantly twisted her sister's arm, and hoisting up Kana over her shoulder, threw her down on the tatami floor with a terrifying thud.

'That is called the "butterfly-drop",' Yoko announced, clasping her hands above her head in a gesture of victory, as Kana rolled on the floor with laughter.

'Watch out, watch out, your days are numbered. I won't tell. But Mother will find out sooner or later about your judo lessons.'

'What about your modern dance classes, huh?' Yoko flopped down on the floor next to Kana.

'Stopped weeks ago. I couldn't stand all those filthy bare feet and bodies squirming on the studio floor.'

'Would you like me to try a "seagull-shoot" on you?' Yoko rubbed her hands as a professional fighter would.

'Oh, do!'

They jumped to their feet at once and Yoko seized Kana by the collar and flung her round and down in a huge circle.

'No match-maker will arrange a marriage for a tomboy like you!' groaned Kana, flattened on the floor.

'Who wants that anyhow?' Yoko, gloating over her progress

in the art of judo, arrogantly placed a conqueror's foot on Kana's tummy.

Although in short bursts, Kana had tackled practically every learnable art that had been in fashion amongst the Faith girls. With the exception of her piano lessons which had now lasted for four and a half years, she had spent periods ranging from two to four months on batik wax dying, water-colour and oil painting, French and Swedish embroidery. Typing and steno-graphy lessons at the YWCA in Kobe lasted exactly one week: the teacher had bad breath.

Mrs Toda, like all mothers keenly aware of the importance to their daughters' marriage prospects of an impressively long list of accomplishments – or even the attempt – in the arts and crafts and other practical skills, was all for Kana's flirting with each season's fad at Faith College.

One winter a French cookery class was the craze. One would have felt quite *démodé* without knowing the difference between hollandaise and béchamel. No longer did one simply talk about so many eggs, but in terms of so many whites and so many yolks.

'Beat five whites first and add five beaten yolks! Why not beat five eggs from the start?' Emiko argued with the instructress but got nowhere. The first seven classes, unfortunately for Emiko, concentrated on sauces. After four weeks she dropped out. 'Week after week of rich sauce after rich sauce!' Her skin had turned into a lunar landscape of pimples. Kana persevered and after her fifth lesson, which was fish in sauce Mornay, she volunteered to cook the family dinner. Mrs Toda was delighted; Shirato, her old kimono merchant, had died a month before and by the irrefutable power of a death-bed wish had bestowed his old maid, Shima, on the Todas: and this Shima, aged fifty-three, asthmatic and with low blood pressure, was not only a hopeless cook but such a slow worker that she had to start shuffling about in the kitchen at least three hours before a meal. To risk one exotic meal prepared by Kana seemed a better proposition than Shima's guaranteed disaster.

'I had Shima shop for everything you asked for,' Mrs Toda

reported to Kana cheerfully in the late afternoon. 'The red snapper is as fresh as alive.'

Her euphoric mood, however, ended abruptly when Kana explained her French recipe.

'Cream! On red snapper? Cream? But Kana, how *could* you?' The idea of defiling the proudest and most delicate of all fish in a mire of cream, egg yolks, butter, flour and so on offended her so deeply that Mrs Toda told Kana to clear out of the kitchen immediately. 'None of your haikara cooking here.'

Kana left the kitchen crestfallen and her mother herself prepared the fish according to the traditional manner: raw, leaving the fish as fishy as it could be. Kana was not allowed to go back to the next class; instead Mrs Toda took her to her own tea-ceremony class where Kana sat on her squarely folded legs for over an hour, watching the other ladies perform.

By the time it was her turn to go and sit opposite the teacher her legs had become so severely paralysed that they could have been sawn off without her noticing it. With great difficulty Kana rose halfway but fell back, knocking over a vase of tall flowers against a mid-Edo period scroll. Mrs Toda apologized to everyone present, and took the damaged scroll to an expert in Kyoto, who charged her 67,000 yen for repairing it.

'I think we had better wait.' She sighed. 'You're still too – how shall I say? – too raw.'

To speed the mellowing process Mrs Toda decided to send Kana to Miss Hanayagi of the Hanayagi classic Japanese dance school.

'All I ask is that you are able to sit on your legs like a decent Japanese. Nothing more.' Mrs Toda laughed cheerfully as she packed a yukata,* an obi, a fan, a pair of tabi and strings in a furoshiki.

It was a heavy opaque Tuesday afternoon in the monsoon month of June. Kana sat in the train to Okamoto, three stops from Rokko Hills, with all her features sulking downward.

'How can I stop my legs getting more bowed, if I have to sit

---

*Cotton kimono worn in summer or after bath.

for hours on my legs folded like hairpins?'

When she arrived at Miss Hanayagi's, a maid with flushed patches on her face, sniffling and sneezing in turns, came to say that Miss Hanayagi was in bed with flu. Kana smiled and was about to turn on her heel when the maid informed her that the lesson was to be given by Miss Hanayagi's disciple.

Kana took off her shoes, went inside the house, undid the furoshiki and at a sullen slow pace changed into the yukata. As she opened the sliding door to the large twelve tatami-mat-sized room, a crystal-sharp voice commanded: 'Kneel down as you open the sliding door.'

As if shot in the knees, Kana flopped down on the tatami and looked into the room.

'Saint Misa!' Kana screamed.

'Shh. . . .'

It was Saint Misa smiling like a pompon dahlia with her head too big for her scrawny body.

Misako Takano was nicknamed 'Saint Misa', and no one was being sarcastic or poking fun at her. Since the majority of the Faith girls were either downright indifferent or only intellectually curious about Christianity, a staunch believer like Misa, baptized early in childhood, with a pious stoop and a self-humbling blink, would normally have fallen easy prey to teasing. But this was not the case with Misa. Everyone looked up to her and liked her. When she was elected head of the Religious Council at the beginning of her second year, other candidates for the post, all of them her seniors, far from being jealous or offended, were only too glad to work under her leadership.

Emiko, who professed to have a 'goose-flesh aversion' to anyone set up on a pedestal, once nudged Kana while Misako was praying during the morning service.

'Look at that "I-am-a-saint" stoop and those pigeon-toes. Ugh!'

'Sh!'

'She's not my type at all. But just the same I like her.'

'What?' Kana thrust her ear right up to Emiko's mouth. 'What did you say?'

'I said I like her. Is that so strange? She touches me as if she had a "faint shadow". I don't think she'll live long.'

'What a terrible thing to say! She's only sixteen.'

'Just a hunch. No one of our age should be so touching.' Emiko held her whispering tongue a while to make her next remark more provocative: 'She's a *menopause* child.'

'What is that?' Kana hissed, almost abandoning her pretence of prayer.

'You're re-tar-ded,' said Emiko and joined the congregation just in time for 'A-m-me-nn!'

The following morning, having looked up the word in the dictionary, Kana poked Emiko in her fat-pleated waist with a wry smile. 'I'm not retarded; you're just obscenely precocious! Tell me then, is Misa's mother very old?'

'Very. And her eyes – look at me, Kana!' shouted Emiko. Kana looked but with a scared gasp quickly turned away. Emiko presented a hideous portrait of Mrs Takano: her pupils were turned inward, so close together as to climb up the bridge of her nose.

And now the menopause child was pointing her closed fan at Kana. 'Your first lesson, how to curtsey to your fan. A self-deprecating ritual you must observe each time you begin dancing. Is that understood?' Kana snarled inside – oh, you, saintly faint shadow – but obediently followed Misa's instructions, the correct three paces behind her.

Eventually with a deep bow to the fan and to Misa, the lesson came to an end. Kana being the last student of the afternoon they both changed in the ante-room and only then did Misa allow herself a personal comment. 'What a coincidence. I was so surprised to see you.' Then timidly, almost apologetically, 'Toda-san, would you like to come to tea? We live just a few minutes away.'

'How kind. Yes, I'd like to.' After accepting the invitation, Kana in a flashback saw Emiko with her eyes criss-crossed over her nose. But it was too late to change her mind, for Misa's small face had flared up with joy like a firework, and there appeared a 'peach stone' in prominent relief on her shy pointed chin. She *is* touching, after all, Kana thought and said warmly: 'I've never known anyone of sixteen with the Hanayagi dancing title. My mother took something like ten years to get the title for Utazawa singing. I am impressed. I am, Saint Misa.'

On this first visit to Misa's house, what Kana remembered most vividly were Mrs Takano's tiny narrow feet neatly clad in white tabi, sailing soundlessly on the dark shining floor like a couple of pale fish. And as to her eyes, Kana avoided meeting them by constantly bowing or scratching her forehead.

Misa's father, the late Dr Takano, had studied for many years in Munich and founded the School of Dentistry at Osaka University. He was a devout Protestant all his life and in his youth an ardent xenophile. Although towards the end of his life he had turned more and more nationalistic and wrote many books on the spirit of Yamato,* he staunchly stuck to some Western principles and customs, such as a European-style breakfast of coffee and bread, butter and jam instead of the usual bean soup, fish and dried seaweed with rice, and above all the pursuit of personal privacy. To this end he had installed thick wooden doors with locks in his otherwise purely Japanese-style house.

The following Tuesday Misa suggested that Kana should leave her lesson attire at her home. And so from then on Kana came every Tuesday to have tea in Misa's room with its lockable door.

'Mother, could we put a lock on my door?' soon Kana was pestering her mother.

'How are we going to put an iron lock on a paper door?' Mrs Toda did not bother to look up from her calligraphy practice. 'Why?'

'Why? Because, Mother, pri-va-cy!'

'Privacy!' Contrary to the alarm expressed in her voice, Mrs Toda's hand holding a long writing brush swept serenely over the paper. 'It's not good for you at your age.'

Before long Kana got used to Mrs Takano, a shy, emaciated lady

*Ancient name for Japan.

88

warped like an elegant fish fork. Her perpetual effort not to let anyone look at her eyes had become second nature. She came in holding the tray of tea and sweets high up to shield her eyes and laid cups, plates and utensils in a pure symmetry with fanatical fastidiousness of which Kana tried not to take notice overtly, not so much for Mrs Takano's as for Misa's sake. Then she bowed to no one in particular and slid out of the room, still bowing from her waist. Misa counted up to ten before she went to lock the door. A delicious moment was when the key had finished turning with a slight clinking noise. For no reason the girls sought each other's eyes and smiled. They could never get over the joy of being alone behind a locked door in a world of their own.

During the winter months Kana had to leave Misa's house almost immediately after a quick cup of tea and nibbled biscuits as she hurried to the station through the rapidly darkening streets, but as the days grew longer after the spring equinox, they were able to spend hours together in the library where Misa's father had left an extensive collection of foreign literature both translated into Japanese and in the original German, English and French, in addition to copious medical books and a wallful of Japanese classics.

Having had no one to guide her, Kana had read haphazardly. One day she would be reading *Anne of Green Gables*, then the following day, Storm's short stories, then for months the Arsene Lupin novels, interrupted by *Le Bal du Comte d'Orgel* which she had chosen because someone at school had mentioned that the author had died at the age of twenty.

Misa on the other hand had been brought up on a well-balanced diet of Eastern and Western literature. At a time when Kana was still raving about Walt Disney's Dumbo and Bambi, Misa's father had been reading aloud to her *Le Petit Prince* or Oscar Wilde's tales. There was a wide gulf between their reading, which Kana was now determined to bridge.

The first book Kana borrowed was *Mayerling*. A day later, almost at midnight, Kana telephoned Misa and sobbed for a whole minute, then promised to show Misa an ode she had composed for the star-crossed lovers.

'You might say it's a sickly sweet uck,' Kana blushed. 'But Misa, I had to do it. To keep a record. In case in ten years' time I shan't be able to feel so deeply about anyone or anything any more.'

Misa was saintly indeed about Kana's unrestrained after-reading reactions. She would listen for hours on end with goat-like patience, nodding and blinking, clasping Kana's hand between her cool palms.

Soon Kana was reading Herman Hesse, but this time Misa heard no ecstatic sighs from her.

'Can it be . . .' Kana asked after four volumes of Hesse, 'that he is untranslatable?'

'You're bored with him, aren't you?' With her question-mark chin full of mercy, Misa walked over to the bookshelf.

'I've just thought of a beautiful poet for you.'

It was Rainer Maria Rilke. Kana laboured through his works with head-aching concentration but quickly gave up. 'If he hadn't died of that rose thorn stuck in his finger, no one would be torturing himself with the precious nonsense he left behind. No more poems for me, please, Misa.'

A few weeks later, as soon as Miss Hanayagi dismissed her two Amen girls – she called any student from a Christian school, an 'Amen' girl – Misa took Kana by the wrist.

'I found, found a . . .' Her stringy neck seemed convulsed with the urgency of the news.

'What? What did you find?'

'A fantastic poem.'

'Oh, no . . .' Kana staggered one step back.

'Wait, Kana. Wait till you read it yourself.' It was so rare to see Misa run in the street that Kana sped after her laughing and yelling, 'Wait for me. What on earth is the matter with you?'

As soon as Mrs Takano left the room, Misa pulled out her desk drawer and nodded to Kana to lock the door.

'Here, "Excelsior". It's in English.'

Misa opened the book. On the left of the poem was a starkly unromantic line drawing, almost a cartoon. A rather common-looking bald man with a blunt ugly nose like a door-to-door insurance salesman, lay half buried in snow. A sleepy-eyed dog was sniffing at the hapless man's frozen right arm which held a flag with *Excelsior* written across it. Three monks knelt near by, their stupid faces raised vacuously to the sky. Jagged mountains soared in the background. That was all. Totally uninspiring. The cartoonist's name was James Thurber.

'So . . . ?' Kana looked at Misa and the book in turn. 'Is he dead or something?'

'Read the poem, just read it!'

' "Excelsior" by Henry Wadsworth Long . . . fellow, what a name!'

'Never mind, Kana. Read!'

Kana read aloud. Each time she faltered at an unfamiliar English word Misa without a moment's delay interjected its Japanese equivalent. When she had finished reading Kana did not look up, but holding the book within reach of her eyelashes, read it again in silence.

'See?'

Kana nodded emphatically, biting her lips together to stem the tears welling up in her eyes. The girls brooded like mother hens at the wonder and excitement the poem, or rather the word, 'Excelsior', held for them. The English-Japanese dictionary gave:

> *Excelsior*, int., higher, still higher. Latin=higher; the motto for the State of New York, USA: 'as dry as excelsior' means 'parched dry'.

This perfunctory prosaicism did not daunt the girls. Indeed every one of the seven syllables of its weighty Japanese equivalent, '*e-ku-se-ru-shi-o-ru*', seemed to cast a magic spell on them, plucking strings of their hearts that had never rung out before. Higher, still higher! Excelsior!

'My piano teacher told me about Mozart's letter to his father in which he says that before he actually writes down a single note he can see the whole of the music inside his head like a painting spread before his eyes. The entire music! How it starts, rolls on, and ends.'

'Yes . . . ?' Misa squinted her eyes in the densening dark of the room, trying to understand what Kana was leading up to.

'Ever since, I've wanted to see the entire blueprint of my life as Mozart did with his compositions. But I'm not a genius; I can see only blurry patches here and there. Supposing I earnestly followed the banner of Excelsior, could I bring these blurred bits and pieces into focus? Will I one day be able to see the whole picture?'

'I don't think you can expect the whole picture,' answered Misa thoughtfully. 'But at least you'll find the direction.'

'Don't you always pick the right word, Misa! Direction, that's it. Exactly, direction!'

From then on they kept their own Excelsior diaries, which they exchanged in order to save themselves writing a daily missive and signed each page with '*e-ku-se-ru-shi-o-ru*' instead of 'Yours sincerely' and the like.

'I am convinced,' Misa wrote, 'that you will soon come to God. For, if you keep your vision on Excelsior, higher and higher still, you will eventually reach the point where you will not be able to go any higher.'

'I'm not at all confident myself,' wrote back Kana:

Forgive me if I sound pedantic, but Excelsior to me is higher and still higher, never the ultimate. I'm not fascinated by absolutes as you are. To tell you the truth, I actually prefer containing within me both the fresh spring and the cesspool. If my life was only one of pure goodness, I'd somehow feel cheated. I don't want to miss anything, anything at all, splendid or sordid. So, the day after the Judgement Day, look for me and if you don't find me amongst the chosen, give me up and drop me a letter to Excelsior, c/o the Devil.

Misa, although amused by such a reply, could not help regretting her friend's flippancy and arrogance. She wrote, c/o Excelsior,

With your acute lucid mind how can you allow yourself this shallow thinking? You never pursue a subject in depth to its logical conclusion. You stop halfway, exclaiming 'Enough, I shan't think further, it will be too great an involvement.

All is well, I am in love with life just as it is!' Kana, don't be complacent; you must be involved; you must be concerned; you must want change. Don't start out by steering an easy middle course between God and the Devil. And I'm not criticizing you for your religious sloppiness alone, but for your political, social and moral attitudes as well. Your conscience blows its fuse as soon as it starts to threaten your own selfish comfort. You may cry your heart out and may even compose an ode after reading *Les Miserables*, and for a Bazaar day's entertainment you and Emiko put on *Uncle Tom's Cabin* and playing little Eliza you may shed hot tears, but if I ask you to come with me on Sundays to visit old people's homes and orphanages you tell me you are going to the Takarazuka Girl's Revue. Every weekend you and Emiko marinate your brains with cheap soppy musical extravaganzas. I think too highly of you not to protest with all the strength I have in me.

Kana read this and was moved, copied it in her own Excelsior diary, prayed to her ancestors, incantating 'Nam-myo-ho-ren-ge-kyo', then quickly mumbled 'Our Father Who Art in Heaven . . .' ending it with a nasal, impassioned Amen and fell asleep. The following morning she whispered to Emiko, 'Guess what. Saint Misa is jealous and angry that I go every Sunday to the Takarazuka Revue with you!'

The next Sunday saw Misa standing outside Osaka station with a collection box, shouting all afternoon through her cardboard megaphone, 'Help Mr Kuboyama and his family! Please help the victims of the H-bomb tests!' while Emiko and Kana were raptly gazing at their idol, Miss Sakura Minato (meaning literally Miss Cherry-Blossom Harbour) in high black boots, with her man-like bobbed hair glossily pomaded, singing and groaning about love in her baritone voice in the new musical revue titled *When the Desert Sings Blue*.

A few weeks later, both Kana and Emiko were horrified to discover that Misa had joined a protest march against the H-bomb tests on the Bikini Islands.

'Now, Misa, do be sensible,' they scolded her in turns. 'You'll end up by getting clubbed and kicked by the riot police.'

'But what about Mr Kuboyama,' said Misa, 'and his family, what about them?'

'But, Misa, he was a fisherman.' Emiko stamped her foot impatiently. 'He could have fished somewhere else in the vast Pacific. Too bad his boat was covered by radio-active fall-out. But then he didn't own the Pacific or the sky.'

'After all, it was just an experiment, not war. I think it's brazen bad manners that you should protest against American policy. After all, without them who'd protect us?' said Kana.

'All right, stop sulking, Misa,' said Emiko. 'If you're really so serious, the three of us will write a play and present it on our next Performing Arts Day. A young fisherman, Kana's part, falls in love with a mermaid, but before he can get her a pair of legs to walk on the shore, the underwater explosion of a hydrogen bomb kills her. . . . We can add a funny part for me. Octopus or sea dragon or something. How's that, Miss Saint?'

'You think that'll change anything, do any good to anyone?' With a dimple registered on her sad pointed chin, Misa looked Emiko sternly in the eye.

'Oh, stop it, Misa. You do go on.'

'If I may say so, you haven't the slightest clue about life as it really is.' Misa said each word clear and sharp. 'As long as pain and misery are portrayed in a book, film or on stage, you pay attention and may even be moved to tears. Just as you lose your head over the male impersonators like Sakura Minato in the Girls' Revue rather than over real live men!'

'Oh, Misa, Misa.' Emiko and Kana hugged her till she squealed with pain. 'You, Saint Misa, you telling us about real live men! Oh, Misa, you're adorable!'

There is more in Misa than just a saintly faint shadow. . . . Kana could not get to sleep that night. What Misa had said kept echoing in her mind. Do I substitute fantasy for reality? More specifically speaking, do I substitute Sakura Minato for a real man? A real man, well, say, for instance, someone like . . . like Ken?

There she curled up like a shrimp under the eiderdown. She had not seen Ken for over four years now, but her inner memory still held the crisp burnt animal-fat scent of his body. That strange and somehow disgusting boy. Why does the mere thought of him disturb her and why does she go all taut at the slightest mention of his name?

Kana often walked home from her piano lesson with her childhood friend with the spectacles who now attended Sacred Heart and saw Ken every Sunday at the Catholic church in Ashiya.

'Kana, you'd walk right past Ken, if you met him. He looks like a black lizard, now that his hair is shaved off. No, it's not only how he looks, he's a different person. He went to the Jesuit boys' school only because their basketball team had wangled him a scholarship. But guess what happened then, you'll never guess!' The girl pushed up her rimless spectacles and fixed her beady eyes on Kana.

'Why bother to ask, if you're so sure I won't guess?' retaliated Kana, pretending to be half asleep with boredom.

'He never knew when to stop, remember?' With breathless over-eagerness, the Sacred Heart chatterbox went on. 'He's become *religious*. And as he always goes too far, he's a *fanatic*.'

'I thought you once told me that he's the star player of the Ashiya Jesuit team.'

'He is! Can't you be both?'

Kana heard much about the fabulous leaps and dashes of the Ashiya star player. She thought of going to watch a game but somehow never did. In the early spring of 1957 Mrs Toda raised her eyes from the morning paper and asked: 'Wasn't Ken Otani the name of the boy who ate your lunch box at Takaha?'

'Yes! What's he done? What does the paper say, Mother?'

'I thought the name was familiar. He was the only high-school student among the twenty-six anti-US-base demonstrators who were arrested after violent scenes outside the Tachikawa US Air Force base.'

Later Kana asked a member of the Faith basketball team,

95

'What happened to the Ashiya captain, Otani?'

'Ah, him, he moved with his family to Tokyo. When? Quite some time ago; the Ashiya team hasn't been doing so well since.'

'I see . . .'

Friday morning, the 21st of April.

Mr Oyama, the calligraphy instructor and deputy headmaster, suddenly cut the last silent prayer short.

'Girls, you remember Misa Takano.' He stopped abruptly, visibly at a loss as to how to continue. 'Of course – you all know Miss Takano – Misako Takano. If anyone has seen her since yesterday afternoon, or hears any news of her, even the slightest detail, please report to a member of the staff immediately.'

The girls raised hisses and gasps of vivid agitation, knocking their heads together, sniffing and salivating for some sort of scandal. Kana ground her teeth, crushing her contempt and rage against those who took a sadistic delight in fabricating wilder and wilder theories to account for Misa's disappearance. Herself faint with foreboding, Kana bent down till her forehead rested on the edge of the bench in front and stayed immobile till Emiko tapped her gently on the shoulder, standing like a huge black cloud with the empty chapel behind her.

'Come on, Kana, the bell just rang for the first period.'

'You should never have said that.'

'What? What did I say?'

'You brought this on Misa with your "faint shadow" stuff!' Kana screamed at Emiko.

Early in the afternoon Kana was sent for during her mathematics class. She was not surprised when Mr Oyama introduced her to a police detective, a ruddy, keen-eyed man who perpetually tapped his right foot. As soon as Mr Oyama left the room, he began: 'I am informed that yesterday, like any other Thursday, Misako Takano presided over the weekly Religious Council meeting, which broke up shortly after five. But Misako Takano stayed on –' he looked up from his notebook to make sure Kana's concentration was on him – 'telling the others that she had to write some letters enclosing contributions to various charities. I'm told that she generally did such unpopular chores herself. So, with "Goodbye, don't work too late", etc, the girls left her behind. That's the last any of them saw of her. Now, did you see or hear from her after that?'

'No. I went home early.'

'Now, listen, strictly between us, you understand?' He pulled his chair closer to Kana and began jiggling his right foot faster than ever. 'Has she – don't forget this is strictly between us – ever talked to you about suicide?'

'No, never.'

'No . . . ?'

'It wasn't possible for her. Not Misa.'

'Why is that? You sound very positive.'

'Her mother, for one thing, and . . .'

'And?' Here the detective stopped tapping his foot. 'And?'

'Misa would never, never go against God's will!'

'Ah ha! Are you a Christian too?'

'No, not really.'

'Good! Now we can talk like two decent Japanese. Has it occurred to you that when there was no other way to save your dignity, or shall I say, honour, that's right, your honour, you would probably choose self-extinction?'

'Mr Policeman!' said Kana brusquely, too upset to use the appropriate honorifics in her address. 'What are you trying to tell me? If you know something. . . .'

'Thank you, Miss, thank you for your. . . .' He opened the door with unexpected agility and ushered her out before she had time to say another word.

Kana telephoned Mrs Takano the moment she got home. Ohama-san, the Takanos' maid, answered and hearing Kana's voice, let out a bird-like screech: '*Phee*! Little miss!' She went away and immediately Mrs Takano came on the 'phone.

'No, no, this is Kana, Kana, Mrs Takano!'

'Ah . . . yes, it's you.' Kana could almost see the dear old lady and her hope being deflated; it was not Misa, just her friend.

'Have been on the 'phone continually since. . . .' she spoke in a tired disjointed way. 'No, no news, no trace. . . . Kana-san, you pray too, please. God will not forsake my Misa.'

The following morning, Kana combed through all the three newspapers her father subscribed to, but none of them carried an article on the missing seventeen-year old girl. Not a line.

Mrs Toda said Mrs Takano might have paid or persuaded the press to remain silent.

'Why silent? The more people know, the better!'

'No, Kana. When a young girl disappears, the less said, the better.'

On Sunday Emiko and Kana cancelled their seats for *White Lilies of Versailles* at Takarazuka, went to church together, and put the largest sum either of them had ever offered to the passing 'greedy bucket', 100 yen.

'What about. . . .' began Emiko as they passed through the church door, but suddenly thought better of it and finished her sentence only when the church fell behind out of their sight. 'What about offering some incense sticks and prayer to our family altar tonight?'

'Better stick to one god at a time. They might clash with each other; that's why I pray only Amen now.' Kana stopped and began rapping her head with her fist. 'But, having said that, Emiko, I must confess I can't help putting my last hope in the teachings of Buddha – you're the cause, you're the effect – I mean then, how could anything really bad happen to Misa?'

In the early afternoon Kana telephoned Mrs Takano, no reply. She tried later, still no reply. Now Kana sat with the telephone in her lap, dialled five, ten times. Each time, it rang and rang with the harrowing metallic rejection.

God will not forsake my Misa, Kana had to repeat to herself, feeling clammy hands of horror round her throat. She went to Okamoto and, turning the familiar corner and seeing Misa's house, ran faster. She rang the gate bell, waited, then rang again, but no one came out. A determined, stiff-shouldered hush of a house with people in it, not of a deserted house, with the shutters opened as usual. Kana wanted to scream, don't keep me out of what you're going through, but stunned by the silence of the house with a dozen lockable doors, turned and walked back to Okamoto station.

Monday, immediately after the service came to an end, Mr Oyama stepped forward; the whole school held their breath. Kana grabbed hold of Emiko's hand, shutting her eyes in prayer.

'Girls, from today onwards committee meetings are to be held during the lunch hour and every one of you must leave the school buildings by three forty-five at the latest. The bell will be rung . . .' Mr Oyama went on, wooden and level. 'When you reach the bottom of the hill, be sure to take the road by the chicken farm, *not* the short-cut through the wheat field and past the Fox shrine where the road works are going on. I also suggest that in no circumstance you go down to the station in a group of less than four.' Mr Oyama shoved his small memo pad and reading glasses in his jacket pocket and as if terrified by the possibility of a barrage of awkward questions, disappeared on noiseless flying tiptoes.

Only a moment to wet their lips, then a miasma of surmises, hunches, interpretations and opinions exploded on all sides. Kana, without saying a word, flew to the door. When Emiko caught her up, she turned on her, aggressive, like a cornered beast.

'So, where does Misa come into all that drivel?'

Emiko, a verbal acrobat, always so ready and swift with her wisecrack replies, opened her mouth wide with a long slow exhalation.

'Emiko!' Kana shuddered, growing cold inside. 'Tell me, how bad? Something gruesome, isn't it?'

Emiko, still wordless, came very close to Kana, wound her heavy right arm round Kana's neck – a rough, clumsy way small boys often do – and pushing her head against Kana's made her walk slowly and aimlessly forward.

'Come on, out with it, Emiko, I am ready.'

'Don't brag, Kana, you're not. I don't think you can take it, that is, *if* what I think is correct. . . .' Emiko said gently.

'What is your filthy vicious mind cooking up?' Kana articulated fiercely. To Misa, of all people, to Misa of Excelsior!

'Sh! No need to be rude.' Emiko gave Kana's neck a nudge. 'I live amongst grown-ups and I hear things when they say hush. I see things when they tell me not to look. So, you could say I have a filthy vicious mind, which mind tells me, Kana, that Misa is alive. I'm sure of it. If she'd been dead, it would have been out in the open. When it's hushed up like this, she's alive and it's worse for everyone, much worse.' Emiko dropped her arm from Kana's neck and stared at the ground before her feet. 'I think she and her mother will go away, somewhere very far where no one knows them. I've known a case like that. I knew the girl too. And I am not cooking that up.'

Kana put her cold limp hand on Emiko's arm, hot in the sun.

'Sex,' she uttered the word for the first time in her life, a word of which she knew in fact nothing. An admission on her part of the existence of an unknown hell. 'Sex, was it?'

'I'm guessing, of course. . . .'

'Right!' Kana cut Emiko short in a harsh, dry voice. 'Right, if you're right, there's no god, not even for Misa.'

Tuesday, Mrs Toda said nothing when Kana came home earlier without going to her dance lesson. In the evening Miss Hanayagi rang. 'I have your furoshiki parcel here,' she said. Kana, dry-eyed, dry-mouthed, said very quietly: 'Are they going away?'

'Tomorrow,' replied Miss Hanayagi, much relieved by what she mistook for Kana's composure and strength of knowledge.

'Did she come home on Saturday night?' asked Kana, even more quietly.

'Yes, she. . . .' here, Miss Hanayagi's voice broke, 'the poor child was hungry, got caught, stealing some biscuits from a shop display shelf. She'd been roaming . . . ever since the men. . . .'

Kana saw in a flash MEN AT WORK signs by the Fox shrine. Men laying sewage pipes, and Misa was a saint!

'No more questions, please, for Misa's sake. Let's forget. You know nothing. . . .' Miss Hanayagi was saying; but Kana heard nothing any more. She mumbled to herself: 'If she hadn't been a Christian, she could have jumped under any one of the fast Hankyu express trains.'

Miss Hanayagi softly hung up.

Mrs Toda who had been standing behind her daughter took the receiver from her hand and was ready when Kana burst out crying.

The moon on the fifteenth night of the eighth lunar-calendar month – this year it fell on the 3rd of October in the solar calendar-month – is said to be the most beautiful of all full moons. Ever since the Manyo* period 'the moon' in songs and verses had always meant the full moon on this particular night.

Mrs Toda observed the traditional moon-viewing evening at home with her haiku teacher and ten fellow students. While the moon lay low they dined. As the moon sailed mid-sky they sat on the terraced corridor making up impromptu haiku. In front of the haiku master, a gaunt priest in exquisite sepia robes, round white moon cakes were piled up in a pyramid on a wooden dais and tall vases stood at either end of the long corridor with dried susuki reeds shooting upward like fountains, voluminous but weightless. Kana and Yoko sat on the thick silk-covered cushions at the extreme end of the terrace, while their father, his arms crossed inside his kimono sleeves, sat at the other end of the terrace as still as if he were asleep.

At half-past nine the haiku master rose to catch the ten o' clock train for Kyoto and the guests left after him, vociferously admiring the way the hostess had arranged the evening. Kana and Yoko, although demurely bowing goodbye to the ladies, chuckled and poked each other in the side at their hair-raisingly quaint expressions till their 'navels could have boiled a tea kettle'. Mr Toda tried scowling at the giggling girls, but fearing he would himself burst into laughter, sneaked quietly away, his heart dancing at the thought of a steaming hot bath.

Mrs Toda and Shima cleared the terrace of tea cups, rolls of paper, charcoal ink bottles, brushes, cushions and so on, and upstairs Kana and Yoko nibbled the moon cakes they had pilfered; while Mr Toda sang heartily in the bathtub.

'Mother's right. The moon cake is a purely seasonal decora-

*The earliest surviving collection of poems dating from the 8th century.

tion.' Yoko threw the rest of the cakes one after another into a waste-paper basket with expert control.

'Little misses, please get ready for your bath!' Shima, nowadays as pithless as a salt-sprinkled slug, squeaked from the bottom of the staircase.

'All right, Shima!' the girls yelled back and began picking out freshly starched yukatas from the closet.

After their bath (like their father they too liked the water extremely hot), their blood churning fast under their hot skin, the girls stretched out on the terrace floor as long and flat as possible, to capture the chill of its wooden surface, and the pale moonlight covered everything as if after the first snow.

As they lay in pleasant silence, Kana felt like crying out of fondness for her sister, who did not utter an obvious 'Oh, how beautiful!' but stretched beside her like a calm deep river. Kana looked up at the black pine needles etched against the moon-lit sky till suddenly their acute points began shimmering and diffusing into many overlapping halos. Without her knowing, tears had flooded her eyes and now trickled down both her cheeks.

'Awful!' It was not premeditated, the word oozed out of her by itself. 'Awful, I'm seventeen!'

'Yep, you're getting on,' came Yoko's response. Yoko would never stoop to anything as predictable as 'Why awful? It's lovely to be seventeen.'

'What am I going to be?'

'An adult,' answered Yoko.

'How did you guess? You have a mind like a football!' Kana began laughing.

'Let's go mad!' Yoko sat up in one jolt and jumped into the garden, barefoot.

'Let's!' Kana rolled over and shot up to her feet and kicking up her long yukata skirt, hopped on to the dewy grass. Yoko was spinning round and round, her arms stretching up to the moon, her yukata loosened and flaring. So glorious and lofty was the moon, and they such paltry earth-bound worms that they had to writhe, twist and turn themselves and go mad, for how else

102

could they respond to so much beauty?

Tossing their heads back, scooping up the moonlight on their up-turned faces, they danced, hopped and stamped their feet. When their two hot breaths came close, the sisters squeezed each other for an instant, threw each other away and madly danced till they collided again. Yoko made a somersault, her body arched like a boomerang against the sky. Kana smashed into Yoko and they both collapsed on the lawn. Shima had closed all the sliding shutters and only here and there the paper-thin streaks of house light crept out. All the rest was overwhelming moonlight.

'Next year, eighteen ...' Kana moaned, out of breath. 'Suppose I live to sixty, I have forty-three years to go, and I don't have the faintest idea what to do with them. I must do something, spend my store of usefulness on something!'

Yoko's breasts rose and fell like a slow tide as she kept silent.

'But what? What do I want to do? What usefulness do I have? Oh, hell, hell, hell! I haven't touched my Excelsior diary for months now; I have no thought in my head these days. Not a milligram. Misa would have given me something I could hold on to. . . . You see I have nothing to hold on to. One day . . . I'm going to . . .' Kana began rolling away on the grass at a frightening speed.

'I'm going to . . .' Now she rolled back, till she bumped against Yoko. 'I'm going to get out! I'm going to leave home!'

'Gosh, you're mad tonight. All right, sister Kana. You leave home!'

'Oh, yes, I will! I shall go to. . . .'

'To where?'

'To Tokyo!' Kana yelled. How very far away and unreal the capital city was to the girls.

'Tokyo? Excellent. You'll go to Tokyo.' Yoko swung her right arm pompously.

'Waseda University, Tokyo, Japan.' Kana was chanting in an equally comic vein, when suddenly a ray of hideous yellow light shot at them, as artificial as a bucket of cheap paint. Blinking their eyes in a stupor, they slowly sat up and turned round. Mrs

Toda in black silhouette stood where the shutters were drawn open.

'Kana? Yoko? Have my rabbits gone mad?' She was laughing, her voice sweetly cooing at every interrogative. The girls in frightful disarray rose to their feet. Mrs Toda asked, still gently laughing, 'Why's my little rabbit crying?'

For, indeed a great quantity of tear and howl was coming out of Kana.

'Wow, wah, wah, wah . . . I'm going . . . going away. . . .'

'All right, all right. Where will you be going?'

'She says Tokyo, Mother,' cut in Yoko. 'She says she doesn't know what to do. Nothing to hold on to. Says she'll go to Waseda!' Kana wept harder, nodding at each item reported by Yoko.

'Yoko, fetch a pail of warm water and towels.'

For the first time as far as Kana could remember Mrs Toda herself washed Kana's feet and then gently wiped the mud, tears and grass from her face.

I

'The first victim of this year's entrance-exam hell! A model student and only son commits suicide after doing badly in a series of trial entrance exams.'

Reading this, Kana shivered as if a bucketful of cold water had been thrown over her and sat for a long while staring in front of her. It was not because of the gory messiness of a body crashing to earth from a department store's rooftop. It was the realization that to the dead boy entering the university of hi choice had meant so much.

Did it matter to her if she passed? Why Waseda, why not Keio? And for that matter why go to university at all? Why was she cramming? What for?

She had to admit that she had just gone in for it. Just gone in. It had begun quite unceremoniously, in fact, with her buying several exercise books and a box of rubber-ended pencils one afternoon, a sort of play-acting, but gradually since then she had become immersed in, and even mesmerized by, the rigours and slavery of the entrance-exam hell. Her parents had tried neither to stop nor to encourage her, subconsciously relying on the fact that Kana was up against odds of nearly fourteen to one. Out of pity and respect for someone fighting an uphill and probably losing battle, they never once grudged paying for Kana's books, her Sunday trial exams, and her extra evening classes. They even arranged a masseur's visit every other night to relieve her eye strain. Yoko who was then captain of the Konan volleyball team considered anyone in quest of higher education a decadent loony; as soon as Kana put up new charts of the conjugation of English verbs or of Chinese ideograph spellings on cupboard doors or in the toilet, Yoko's rude graffiti were on them.

So, Shima was probably the only person in the household who

cared about and believed in Kana's entrance-exam hell; she fussed over her with the alacrity and unctuous watchfulness of a race-horse trainer, constantly supplying her with hot tea and wrapping her legs in a blanket, after having placed a hot-water bottle at her feet, since Kana worked in an unheated room in order not to feel drowsy. She alone rushed to the gate to ask how she had fared in the latest trial exam, and if Kana had come out first she excitedly told the tradesmen the proud news.

At Faith College the girls were expected to go on to take its own two-year college course and those who dared go astray and cram for entrance exams to co-ed universities outside met with silent reproach and non-cooperation. Nevertheless each year a few girls decided to break away or follow medical or scientific courses which the Faith did not offer. These girls took great pride in being 'in hell', considered themselves alien to the rest of the 'hot-house grown' girls and played truant from all classes that had no direct bearing on their exams, such as music, gymnastics and the arts. Kana had joined this elite group and wore the same sunless, exhausted, arrogant look, but despite a most convincing and convinced enactment of hell's rituals she had no real understanding of why she was doing it.

And now someone had killed himself for it! Kana tore the newspaper to shreds and listened with alarm to her pounding heart, full of fierce yearning to achieve. But achieve what? Oh, well, achieve something, anything! What a fraud I am, she thought as she listened to her Excelsior wings flap vigorously with neither purpose nor direction.

In mid-March Kana was in Tokyo, taking written and oral tests at Waseda. A week later, a night-long vigil and at five o'clock in the morning in the snow-covered university square, she saw her number on the board and thought of the seventeen-year-old boy who had jumped from the department store roof.

At once the congratulatory telegrams began arriving from relatives, her father's former and present employees and her mother's friends, tradesmen, Kana's Faith friends, and even from some Takaha teachers. Gifts followed, either by post or presented in person with a lengthy eulogy.

'I'll have to go ... don't you think, Mother? Go to Waseda, now that so many people have congratulated me?'

'Of course! What do you mean you'll "have to go"? What's the point of having passed and not going? Don't be silly.'

Mrs Toda was exultant over her daughter's unexpected and up till then unwished-for triumph and spent all day in the entrance hall, sipping tea and chatting with a continuous flow of visitors bearing congratulatory gifts. Yoko gloated over the roomful of presents, collected ribbons and handsome empty boxes and when more than one alarm clock or fountain pen arrived, she claimed the second for herself.

It would not be an exaggeration to say that finally Kana went to Waseda because it seemed to make everyone happy. Once there, she felt lost, insignificant and morbidly lonely. She remembered how her mother had loathed Tokyo while Grandmother had been alive and reigned in Kamakura: 'I would not be seen dead in the place,' Mrs Toda had said. 'That unending sprawl of ugliness and indifference is made even more unbearable by the fact that it is flat. Without mountains and sea you never know which is north or south. You hobble about all day feeling groggy and cross-eyed. And as to Tokyo women, they are a flinty, bossy lot with no understanding of *mono no aware*.'*

Kana had thought her mother's decree too harsh at the time: for someone like Mrs Toda, who worshipped the world of haiku poetry, to lack *mono no aware* was to be less than human, a condemnation to end all condemnations. But now Kana entirely agreed with her mother's verdict on the capital: it was a charmless boom town.

There was, however, one nice thing about the city: her beautiful aunt lived there. And for Mrs Itoh too the arrival of her little niece was glad news. Fussing and worrying over Kana became one of her principal pastimes, now that her son Shozo was grown up and her daughter Sachiko had been parted with by an arranged marriage to a shipping family's heir in Kyushu Island. So it was Mrs Itoh who found for Kana a haikara boarding

*Vaguely translatable as 'awareness of the pathos of transient life'.

house on Nampei Hill in Shibuya, one of the best residential areas in Tokyo, where Prime Minister Kishi's residence assured a vigilant police watch, well-kept roads and efficient garbage collection. Film stars, foreign diplomats and emigré Chinese millionaires had in recent years flocked into the area, raising the real-estate value of the district to dizzy heights.

The boarding house was named Jardin-En, owned and run by a Miss Arashi, an ex-opera singer with a considerable fortune inherited from her wealthy merchant father. 'It is not a business, it's my hobby,' she insisted, 'to watch over ten girls from ten different universities and see how their dissimilar personalities develop in my Jardin.'

A snob, a phoney and a passionate skier, Miss Arashi, the Honorary President of the All-Japan Skiers Association, dressed almost permanently in ski trousers and a matching turtle-neck sweater, both stretched to breaking point over her copious proportions, kept a fastidious watch over her ten intimidated Jardin girls with the help of two young maids whom she recruited from a mountain village where she skied every winter.

Curfew was set at 7.30 p.m. on weekdays and at 10 p.m. on Saturdays; anyone who had a good reason to return later than this was expected to submit a late-return slip in the morning. With shrewd business instinct Miss Arashi believed in charging the highest fees in Tokyo and maintaining indisputably the most haikara establishment, in order to impress wealthy provincial parents: the two-storey white modan building had window sills painted in dark green, making the house look like an oversized ski chalet, and the spacious dining room was complete with a large television set and prints of Parisian street scenes covered the walls. And then there was the Steinway in the drawing room.

'Second hand, yes, but a Steinway. A Steinway will always be a Steinway, as we say "A red snapper is a red snapper even when it's dead",' Miss Arashi proudly told her visitors, fussing with the starched lace doilies located under every vase, ashtray and objet d'art. A mahogany banistered staircase wound its way upstairs where there were ten tatami-floored bedrooms and three toilets and three pink wash basins at the end of the long corridor. Downstairs there were blue and pink tiled bathrooms with constant hot water heated by gas. Clean modan gas.

For a monthly fee of 10,500 yen every girl was entitled to all these Jardin amenities and a skimpy but stylish breakfast and supper. Girls from the provinces, accustomed to their bulky rice and salt fish and bean soup breakfast, found the Jardin offering a joy for the eyes but not for the stomach: a dainty cup of English tea with a paper-thin slice of lemon, a tiny brioche and three sandy Nabisco biscuits, a pat of margarine and a teaspoonful of incredibly red jam. Some of the braver girls appealed to Miss Arashi to use cheaper native ingredients, thus increasing the quantity for the same cost, but she would not hear of surrendering to such plebeian tastes: 'Once you lose your style, you lose everything.'

Kana missed her old friends who had chosen to remain in the easy-going gentle Faith College world, all so effortless and congenial. Kana had no friends in Tokyo, or rather she would not make any. The Waseda girls she found rude, foul-mouthed, bookish and openly contemptuous of 'little misses' with provincial accents. Because of her father who had retained his native Tokyo accent, Kana had, for a Kansai-born person, an almost unnoticeable regional accent; but too vain to take any risk of being found out, she restricted herself to monosyllabic replies whenever she was with shrill, staccato Tokyoites, who as a result found her dull beyond words.

As for the opposite sex, for the whole of her first year at Waseda she kept clear of them. After six years at the Faith she had lost her natural ease with boys and was aware only of a heterogeneous unpleasantness. In a jam-packed lecture hall their distinct male odour, their bulky restless presence and their coarse sense of humour made her feel faint with disgust. Fearing that one might seek to make her acquaintance at the Student Union cafeteria, she lunched alone in a brightly lit, well-ventilated restaurant mostly patronized by professors and lecturers. As for the innumerable coffee houses which seemed to play such an important part in the Tokyo students' life, she never went near them. Her father had warned her: 'A high percentage of Tokyo taxi drivers and students suffer from stomach ulcers and I'll tell you why. Simple. Excessive absorption of coffee. It rots your guts. Now, promise me three things, Kana: that you will not imbibe coffee, nor be infected by the Zengakuren nonsense, and lastly that you will never attempt to be someone other than yourself, a great pitfall for the impressionable young. Content yourself with just being the eldest daughter of the Todas.'

The Zengakuren nonsense! Even after a year at Waseda, if asked what the initials ZGR actually stood for, Kana would have faltered for the right words: 'All-Japan . . . something students' . . . self-governing, or rather . . . movement?'

That all ZGR members were vicious Communists who, having tired of setting fire to rubbish dumps and throwing Molotov cocktails at police stations, now went in for anti-Americanism and for heaven knows what reason violently opposed the government's decision to negotiate a revised ANPO, the Japan-US security treaty – this much Kana did know and that was more than enough for her. In the last few months, however, it had become increasingly difficult not to be acutely aware of the ZGR presence, for there had been so many People's Movement's United Action or similar idiotic demonstrations with the entrances to the classrooms barricaded, the ringleaders of the Movement with red armbands bawling through microphones all day, a swarm of smelly, scruffy students yelling against this and against that, handing out abracadabra leaflets, and leaving the whole face of Waseda and the neighbouring streets covered with red paint and fly-posted propaganda posters.

Againsty, stand-uppy, show-offy, tiresome lot, all of them, Kana thought to herself; she who stood neither for nor against anything, she who for a whole year had been vegetating elaborately and expensively in Tokyo.

When the noon siren sounded, startling the syrup in the warm air, Kana was sitting on the cement balustrade outside the Literature Building in the shade of a fir tree. She yawned, scratching her left eyebrow where a streak of sunlight through the foliage was baking an itch, then began her letter home:

My honourable Mother, here I am, back in Tokyo, safe and intact. The train was on time and Shima's packed lunch was delicious. Please tell her so. What good luck, for the first time I saw Mount Fuji without its usual cloak of mist and cloud, its magnificent peak soaring heavenward in a single vigorous stroke, most moving. You remember how Grandma grumbled during the air raids: 'How they waste their bombs! If they bombed Mount Fuji, we'd surrender tomorrow. Without Fuji-san what's the good of saving Japan?' I thought then she was going ga-ga, but now I understand what she meant. I'm sure you watched the wedding ceremony of the Crown Prince and Miss Michiko Shoda on television yesterday. The fabulous weather still here today. They say it will last another week. I feel homesick and very far from you all. Humbly yours, Kana

A stupid weather-forecast of a letter; feeling more miserable each time she thought of home, Kana shut her eyes and dozed off till. . . .

'April the tenth, 1959! How many times have you lived and will you live this day?' suddenly blared out an urgent question. Kana almost fell from the balustrade, her eyes and tongue heavy with the mouldiness of interrupted sleep. In front of the School of Economics hawk-eyed recruiting seniors were on parade, trying to inveigle freshmen into their respective extra-curricular clubs, a familiar campus scene at the start of a new term. The particular cry that had woken Kana emanated from under a large floppy sombrero striped in pink and green. The crier continued with enough vehemence to burst his cardboard megaphone: 'Once and never again will you live this day. This day comes once, only once in your lifetime. So, today, join the Waseda Tango Lovers Association and give your life a new rhythm and the joy of new friends. Join, everyone, join today!'

Two girls set up a folding table, pinning to it a large poster proclaiming the merits of the Waseda Tea Ceremony Club: 'An oasis in the desert of modan life will bring beauty and serenity to you at the yearly fee of only 1,000 yen.' And next to them stood a gorilla of a man in a black serge Waseda uniform and a diamond-shaped black cap with a sparkling brass Waseda emblem. His banner trailing from a long pole read: 'The pride of Wasedanians, Waseda Karate Club, established in 1888!'

Intimidated by the line of recruiters, a handful of strolling students quickened their pace with their eyes carefully averted. The wind was rising, chilling the air. It was nearly four o'clock by the Okuma Theatre's clock. Her bottom feeling bloodless and concrete-hard, Kana decided to move on. As she limped her way slowly across the square, she was sniffling. . . . Why bother? What's the point of sticking it out here? Excelsior? Bah! Don't believe in it any more, not really. Trying to prove what to whom? And there at home, my family and friends, cake-walking a cosy effortless life. That's it, effortless! Non-endeavouring, non-accomplishing, non-over-existing. . . .

Someone yelled at her. She stopped and saw a freakish little creature halfway down the square. A miniature man. His stature, barely five feet, was gobbled up front and rear by two enormous placards, leaving in view only a blue beret rakishly tilted and a pair of twig-like ankles sticking out of dusty down-at-heel shoes. On the front billboard was a photograph in phosphorescent orange of a tortured-looking man clinging to a bamboo spear with his eyes desperately peering upwards at these words:

FREE STAGE presents KONMINTO
A new full-length play about Chichibu peasant uprising!
Performances: 10, 11 and 12, June.
Admission: 100 yen.

Squinting against the glare of the setting sun, Kana saw the apparition wink at her. A pair of hyperthyroid goggling eyes. She stopped, nailed to the ground. Suddenly he fluttered his huge cardboard wings, turned his back to her and began back-stepping at a St Vitus's dance gait, giving her now a full view of the other side of his sandwich board.

Suffering from homesickness, from big-city alienation, or

113

feeling rejected in the maze of a university life?
Then, join FREE STAGE!
Experience the bliss of togetherness.
We create theatre and its total environment.
To join, apply to FREE STAGE sandwichman.

The sandwichman now faced Kana and was making a final spurt towards her. She took a few quick steps sideways.

'Don't go, you slug!' he bellowed in a voice that was alarmingly out of proportion to his size. 'I saw you sitting there, wasting your youthfulity, going to seed before the bloom. Inexcusable. Broody or constipated or whatever. No excuse. Hate to see anyone of your age looking so futile. Tell me, are you all right?'

These last words of his, washed suddenly clean of stagy jargon, held Kana where she was.

'You're sure you're OK?' The dwarfish character sidled up to her.

She nodded.

'Just imagine yourself straddled on top of a spiked fence,' he began as if he had known her for years. 'Only two alternatives for you: either to jump off or to keep your juicy bottom permanently skewered. Right? Well, then, what have you to lose, come on, jump. Join us, join Free Stage! We'll give you the bliss of being useful, together and creative. What more can you expect in this difficult world? OK? Right!' He nodded to himself, immensely satisfied. 'I'll slough off these bloody impedimenta and take you up to our Headquarters.'

'Er . . . Excuse me, but I have a seven o'clock curfew.'

'Wha-at? Curfew?' He screwed up his hyperthyroid features to a kabuki demon's physiognomy. 'What sort of a dump are you cooped up in?'

'Jardin-En. We dine at seven-thirty sharp. I didn't make out a late-return slip this morning.'

'Jardin-En? Did I hear what I heard? Jardin-Jardin, *Jardin des salopes!*'

'En' meaning 'garden', Beret was not the first to remark on

the ridiculousness of the name Miss Arashi had concocted, but, it was the way he delivered it, with so much fire and thunder in his condemnatory rage. Kana gawked at him.

'All the more reason to join Free Stage, twerp. Believe me it'll do you a hell of a lot of good. We'll find something to stuff into your empty bourgeois balloon of a head.' He stepped out of his sandwich boards, just a husk of a man, baggily sheathed in a drab serge Waseda uniform with his head surmounted by the greasy old beret and his jutting Adam's apple squashed under a high white celluloid collar.

'My name is Nakabori, known to all as Beret, majoring in French history.' Abruptly handing Kana the sandwich boards, he snatched off his beret and turned it inside-out to display a grimy label which read 'Made in France'. He then pulled out a folded newspaper from his pocket.

'*Le Monde* . . .' he whispered, 'and only a month old.'

Fascinated by the whole droll proceedings, Kana politely groaned with admiration, and he let out a shrill chuckle and with a choppy lilting gait began walking up the square. Stuck with his 'impedimenta', Kana felt she had no alternative but to follow. Presently they were climbing up the steep concrete steps that connected the square with the new Graduate School compound.

'Mind not to drag the boards. Your name?'

'Kanako Toda. English Literature.'

'Might have guessed. All the nit-wit daughters from the provinces flock to the Literature Department. Female invasion knocked the ivory tower to pieces. It's a cackling hen party everywhere now. Mind you, long before that the university had degenerated into a mass-production factory of men *manqués*.' He gabbled on without pausing for breath. 'That's why I've paid no fees nor attended those blasted mass-pro lectures for four years now and I have every intention of prolonging the lease of my carefree days with student discounts and other fringe benefits till I'm literally yanked back onto the shitty Waseda conveyor belt. Till then, *vive ma vie!*'

Relieving Kana of the sandwich boards, Beret led her to the top of the winding steps, from where they had a panoramic view of the university, a huddle of square grey concrete boxes in the midst of the bustling city.

'Steel and concrete buildings do not a wise man make.' Beret grimaced scornfully at the new Graduate School building that soared five storeys above them. 'It's only benefit to humanity are its WCs with mirrors and toilet paper galore. Our girls practically live in them.'

Reaching an iron grill fence that marked the limits of the university grounds, he raised his voice half an octave: 'Through there, that's the Warehouse, the seat of true learning and creative inspiration!'

Kana blinked. Surrounded by shabby old houses, shops and small family workshops, a piece of flat dusty yellow earth, encircled by a wooden fence, gaped unexpectedly. Not a tree, not a blade of grass; and in the centre of this dismal enclosure stood a wooden and asbestos building with a gabled tin roof and narrow uniform windows. Two wash basins under a wooden shelter by the entrance seemed an incongruous luxury, set beside the peeling paintwork and the sagging window frames with their broken panes.

'And over there, the shrine of Fox Deity to keep little ones like you out of mischief.' Beret pointed to a red-painted torii* gate from which a mud path led into a lush grove of beech and ever-green.

As they walked into the Warehouse Kana quickly held her breath against a sour biting odour.

'Oh, that, that's the Chat Bleu drying their papier mâché props. For your information they're just a bunch of capitalistic dilettantes, presenting season after season the same old lousy French boulevard farces. Haven't tickled one giggle out of me yet.'

On either side of the passage stood ten doors; the occupants' activities were spelled out in the posters and pennants that adorned them: INTER Theatre Company, Stamp Collectors' Society, Waseda Naleo Hawaiians Democratic Riding Club,

*A Shinto shrine archway.

Japan Alpinist Association Waseda Branch, Judo Friends and so on. From a singularly clean uncluttered door with the words Waseda High Society Jazz Orchestra engraved on a chrome-plated sign, crooned out a stop-and-start-again trumpet solo of 'Smoke Gets in Your Eyes'. Beret gave a contemptuous rap on their door. 'How do you think they can afford a door like that? They're pimps. Where there's easy money, there they'll be, playing at posh clubs, downtown hotels, and, don't puke, at US bases!'

Just then the Chat Bleu door which boasted an extravagant four-colour poster of *Jean de la lune* flew open and a handsome young man, a burgundy-red silk scarf sprouting out of his dark brown shirt, dashed out and barged straight into Beret and his boards.

'*Merde!*' the young man growled, without stopping to apologize.

'See, didn't I tell you?' shouted Beret. 'They're not only shit-brained xenophilic dilettantes but bad-mannered lice to boot!'

'You bloody Commie!' the Chat Bleu dandy spat back as he pranced out of the Warehouse.

'Are you?' Kana had to ask.

'Am I what?'

'A Communist!'

'My dear adorable Balloon Head!' Beret roared with laughter. Pirouetting with a midget's agility and laughing still louder, he yanked open a door with *Konminto* posters glued all over it.

It took no great imagination to see it was indeed a cesspool of scum and vermin and all of them Communists. The air inside, smouldering with nicotine tar, hair grease, damp rotting canvas, and above all the steam rising from the densely packed young bodies, was as muggy, gooey and sour as stale blue cheese. An electric bulb, painted yellow, dangled at the end of a long cord, casting eerie uneven stains everywhere. The ceiling was a fish-scale montage of posters from past Free Stage productions, mostly faded sepia from age and cigarette smoke. A rusty stove, standing adjacent to an old wooden filing cabinet, stretched its tortuous pipe out of a broken window. The remaining floor space was cluttered with wardrobe skips, dimmer boxes, lighting equipment and countless sacks bursting with old newspapers. The walls were just as overcrowded: notices and work schedules dominated the centre, while the peripheral space was a collage of cartoons, newspaper clippings and an incredible collection of pin-up photos which included earless Van Gogh, an Egon Schiele nude, a Honda motorcycle and Audrey Hepburn as a nun.

'Come on in, Soap Bubble,' Beret urged Kana and those seated round an oblong table at the centre of the room fell silent, while in the murky corners some squatting figures snickered simply out of astonishment at the sight of Beret's latest recruit, dressed in a salmon-pink tweed suit with an embroidered blouse and a large felt bag with butterflies and wisteria clusters appliquéd on it.

'You'll never believe this, but. . .' Beret triumphantly addressed the roomful of Commies whom Kana estimated at about two dozen. 'Miss Kanako Toda, alias Balloon Top, boarding at a certain Jardin *des jeunes filles bien élevées et complètes* with curfew chastity belt, wants to join Free Stage!'

'No, please! Excuse me, I am not quite. . . .' Kana protested amidst a peal of cheers and clapping.

'Yes, love, 300 yen, thank you. Membership fee 200 plus monthly fee 100, in total, 300 yen!'

Flustered and overawed, before she knew what she was doing Kana was holding her purse in her hand. Beret drummed on his large account book like a magician before his climactic act.

'She's paying up! Unlike most of you, *she pays*! No fuss, no question of instalments, she pays!'

'Er . . . but I really don't know if . . .' Kana went on even after her 300 yen had been put into Beret's money box, but was not heeded.

'Home address? Address here? Telephone?' Busily jotting them down in the book, Beret called out like an auctioneer and the whole room listened.

'High School?'

'Faith College,' Kana replied.

'You mean "the Faith" near Takarazuka?' He looked up at her.

'My dear girl, you've been messed about. Freshman?'

'No, not exactly . . . I'm starting my second year. . . .'

Beret gave a long mournful look at her, shaking his head.

At once a general discussion began as to what to do with her, as she had apparently been enlisted too late in the season to be cast in either of their two productions, *Konminto* or *The Good Woman of Setzuan*.

'Normally we'd have put you in the freshman try-out, *The Good Woman*, but you see, it's a bit late; it's been in rehearsal for a week now and all the parts are cast,' the stage manager silenced a dozen voices, his shy donkey eyes convulsively blinking. He was so emaciated that his shoulder blades were traceable from outside his uniform. His pointed sad chin reminded Kana of Misa and she immediately decided to like him.

'Roppa,' Beret turned to a chain-smoking mound of sallow fat with thick-lensed spectacles. 'Can't you and Octopus-Eight give her a line or two in that fourth-act mob scene at the silk-worm factory?'

'Otani's just forced us to cut that scene. Too many sets.'

'Then, something else. You see, I'd like to give Bubble Brain a promise, sort of a mortgage on expectation, however small or remote, of the glamour and excitement of the thee-ay-terr.' He drew a rainbow in the air with his short arm.

'Steady, Beret, steady!' a womanish high-pitched interjection came from a thin, bespectacled man who all the while never withdrew his attention from the Chinese chess board. 'Why use bait to catch Miss Bourgeois Empty-Upstairs? She won't last a day.'

Who said I wanted to last? Kana wished she had the courage to say so, but lacking it, she resigned herself to watching the slave auction.

'OK, Yamada, OK,' Beret held up both his arms in mock surrender. 'She's only too eager to be useful, that's all. Now come on, who'll use Balloon Top?'

'I will, if no one else will.' The voice came from outside the window and almost immediately a tall, thick-set, sunburnt Tarzan was sitting astride the window sill, wearing a white cotton towel horizontally round his head and a hammer, screwdriver, pilers and a folding ruler slotted into loops in his wide leather belt.

'Don't be silly, Asano. She couldn't tell a nail from a hammer.'

'That's all right, Yamada. You leave her to me. She can just sit pretty in the back yard and make us feel good.' Asano's bold black brows, meaty jowl and large flashing teeth jostled with each other in hearty laughter. His boys, thronging at the window behind him, cheered and yelled in agreement. Beret wrung his beret and said, 'All right, go ahead.'

'Back to work! And you, too, Balloon Top,' Asano said. A quick swivel and a flick of his legs, he was back in the yard amongst his boys. Beret added to the staff list on the wall: Balloon Top.

'Excuse me. . . .' Kana shuffled behind him. 'Will I always be called by . . . that?'

'Don't you like it? It's very you,' he said.

'Well, not that I. . . .'

'Balloon Top! What the hell's keeping you, there's work to do out here!' Asano yelled outside.

'Sorry, Balloon, it's too late now. Once Asano has adopted the name, you haven't a chance. Run along, little one.'

There is a saying, very Confucian, very equivocal: 'Once you have swallowed poison, why not the cup as well?' And it was precisely this sort of desperate resignation that prevented Kana from picking up her bag and running away. Besides, whether a Commie or not, she found her recruiter, Beret, kind and rather endearing, and it would have required a much harder heart than hers to walk out on him.

Tucking up her sleeves she went into the back yard where Asano's boys hammered at the sets they were making for the new plays; all the while humming a wordless chorus of moos, waw-waws and groans, since their lips were firmly closed round rows of nails. As soon as someone had used up his mouthful, he would burst into a rapt solo:

> Flow gently Mother Volga
> Over our rich green land of Ro-ssi-ah. . . .

Meanwhile Asano kept on barking his orders at Kana from the

top of a stepladder: 'Make a fire in that perforated drum, Balloon!'
'With what? Not with your skirt and hair, you twit. Pick up
shavings, bits of wood and anything else that will burn off the
ground. Give her ladyship matches and newspapers, boys!'

Her eyes watering in the smoke and her pink tweed jacket
smeared by flying black ash, Kana mumbled to herself – I can't
believe it's happening to me, the Commie boys singing about
Russia and me making a fire like a Robinson Crusoe – and she
thought of the lunch she had missed and the cool and quiet of
her room at the Jardin.

But no time for rumination; Asano kept a close watch over her
now from the rooftop of the scenery store which he and his boys
called the 'Butterfly'; four pillars, a cement base and a corrugated
tin roof flaring upward like butterfly wings.

'You're supposed to make paste, not dumplings, clot. Mix in
more water!'

For nearly two hours in the gathering dark Kana shifted from
one brush stroke to another, till her right hand was stiffly
moulded in paste.

'Don't forget, Balloon Top –' Beret came up behind her –
'there is ennobling spirituality in hard labour. Here, give your
blood sugar a lift.' A caramel flew into her lap. She could just
manage a thank you and a bow in the direction of his receding
steps, before tears welled up and flowed down her cheeks. The
hot salt of her tears mixed with the caramel was good, crying in
the open was refreshing, and after the cry, she felt happier than
she had been for a long time.

At seven o'clock the stage manager with Saint Misa's chin
shouted through the HQ window: 'Asano-san, both companies
have broken. Get ready for Circle, please!'

'Pack it up, boys. They've let the actors loose,' yelled Asano.
The ladders were folded, tools collected and the work in progress stacked away under the Butterfly. A single naked working
light was left suspended in the moist starless night. A rumble
like a huge boiling kettle was approaching from the direction
of the Fox Shrine and soon what seemed to Kana's eyes a fast
moving black lava, a solid mass of a hundred or more young

bodies, poured in and brimmed over the place in a blink of time. Kana was now in the midst of them, the yak-yakking, wig-wagging, air-stropping mob.

'Quiet! Quiet! Make Circle, please!' the stage manager shouted. Simmering down to silence, the crowd strung themselves into a large circle. Two tall boys scooped up Kana by the arms and swayed her in suspension like a kimono on a washing line. She kicked the air, squeaking till they had laughed enough and returned her to earth.

'Beggars-on-river-bank!'* Kana hissed and the boys laughed even more.

'First, a word from Abe-san,' a keen green girl's voice screamed.

'I know it is asking a lot from freshmen to open *The Good Woman* with only three weeks' rehearsal,' a morose, desperately sincere voice spoke up – a typical Commie voice, Kana thought. 'But no use going *kaput* as some members of the cast came very near doing this afternoon. And it's most unfair to accuse me of being gratuitously sadistic. Please remember I'm only trying to get the play on in an impossibly short time.'

'Who went *kaput*?' whispered the boy on Kana's right.

'*Der gute Mensch* herself,' hissed back the voice on her left.

'Next!' Again the green keen voice bounced out of the darkness. 'Myshkin-san!'

And it was the stage manager with Misa's chin. Why he had to have such a stupid name, like a dog's, Kana could not fathom.

'I'd like to ask for everyone's sober reflection. *The Good Woman* is after all a getting-to-know-each-other, a sort of family affair, but *Konminto* is a formidable challenge; not only the whole of Waseda but the professional theatre will keep a jealous eye on its outcome. We could have repeated the sell-out success we enjoyed last season with *The Government Inspector*. But rightly or wrongly, we decided to get out of the rut and put on an original

---

*The expression comes from the fact that in the early years of kabuki, then officially banned, vagabond actors roamed over the country, performing in dried-up river basins, and is still used in a derogatory sense for the acting profession in general.

play written by two of our own members. Having accepted the challenge, we must see it through. The Executive Committee met last night and reached the conclusion that *Konminto* in five acts and twenty-three scenes with its two most prolific authors rewriting, adding and cutting every day could not possibly be ready to open on June the tenth, unless we adopt the most Draconian measures. First, rehearsal. For the next two months we must rehearse on a continuous basis from ten a.m. till eight p.m.' Gasps like wind in the reeds rose from the circle.

'I will therefore need by tomorrow evening a detailed schedule, twenty-four hours, seven days a week, of both private and academic activities of every one of you, so that we can plan an efficient shift system and where necessary substitutes for lecture roll-calls. Finally,' he went on, 'Otani-san had to leave on his fund-raising visit to Chichibu immediately after the Executive Committee meeting and asked his co-producer, Beret-san, to make an urgent plea on his behalf.'

Here, Beret, droll and intense, raised a series of martial yells to make sure everyone located his diminutive presence in the Circle.

'It's plain that due to this ten-to-eight schedule many of you will be forced to see curtailed or entirely give up your remuneration from various *arbeit*. We won't object to your continuing with home tutoring of entrance-exam kids till we begin run-throughs, but from now on please don't take on late-night or all-night *arbeit* for the obvious reasons of voice and health. This will be very hard on some of you, therefore I appeal to all who can afford it to please bring an extra lunch box. Any kind of nourishment is welcome, solid or liquid, so long as it's energy. So, please, anyone who can offer or needs a free lunch, come to me, the comforter-general and the life, soul and conscience of the company!'

To end his speech Beret tried a can-can routine, to whistles and laughter from the Circle, which Myshkin's clear, clean voice cut short: 'Thanks, everyone, that is all for tonight.'

Kana saw no sign and heard no cue, but every chest in the circle filled with a soft hiss then released on one exact beat a vigorous note of music, as the entire Circle swayed from one side to the other. The chorus rolled on, some singing soprano, some alto, and some tenor, swelling lustily:

> Friends we are put on earth to
> Work together, help each other
> To make it a better fairer place
> Give us your hands, bring your hammer
> Brick by brick we'll build a society
> Yesterday unknown of peace
> And love and harmony.

Trite, hackneyed, how naive, and 'bring your hammer', really! I'd be ashamed to mouth such barmy lyrics, let alone sing them aloud, Kana thought to herself. But as she swayed with the Circle, her arms in hot and bumpy friction with theirs, hungry and worn out, her tear ducts loosened and hot lumps choked her throat. Dotty, absolutely, she thought. But, there she was, suddenly thinking of nothing else but the bucket of steaming paste, 'Mother Volga', and how to get back to the Warehouse at the first possible moment the next morning.

Kana took a taxi; it was long past dinner time. She pushed the gate buzzer and the first reaction from inside was the frantic yapping of Poti, Miss Arashi's neurotic white spitz, then heavy footsteps thumping up to the bolted gate.

'Late! Late! Naughty Miss Toda, late!'

As the door was flung open, Poti, yelping hysterically, bounded at Kana and Miss Arashi loomed, standing arms akimbo, her censorious narrow eyes inspecting her up and down. Oh, no, why do I have to come back to this phoney mawkish snob dump, *Jardin des salopes*! Kana eased away the dog's claws from her torn stockings.

Miss Arashi, her fat thighs amazingly like mutton legs, led Kana into the house, lecturing, 'Don't think for a moment that I am an old-fashioned disciplinarian. No, on the contrary, I am a modan liberal, but I do insist that the girls in my Jardin respect the house rules. I can't control what you do or where

124

you go or why during the day but I must have my girls back by seven, unless, of course, I have consented to your late return for a good reason. I am not picking on you, you understand, but I must for your parents' sake keep close watch on you. That's all. Take a bath. The blue bathroom is free. Ah, oh, yes!' Her amply oiled face suddenly melted into a sickly simper. 'Your aunt's chauffeur came this afternoon and left a parcel of books for you. I had it sent up to your room. Good night. Sleep well.'

Miss Arashi appreciated the value of having girls with relations who owned chauffeur-driven foreign cars or summer houses in Karuizawa or historical names; all of which helped her attract 'the right sort of girls' for her Jardin next spring.

Kana bowed, closed the door behind her, and rushed upstairs with her mouth watering. Kana had warned her aunt about Miss Arashi's phobic fear of mice and therefore of her girls' keeping food in their rooms; she guessed it was a food parcel in disguise that Hirano had brought. Praying to Buddha for Aunt Sachi's longevity, Kana opened the furoshiki parcel. There it was, under four glossy ladies' magazines, a flat lacquer box, orange inside and black outside, containing chicken and fish teriyaki,* omelette, prawns and quail eggs, each neatly wrapped in nanten leaves from her aunt's garden. An unpainted wooden box at the bottom was filled with Kana's great favourite, dried Hiroshima persimmons.

Kana was lustily tucking in some teriyaki fish when a coy 'Excuse me' came from outside. 'It's Usami, Toda-san. Please, could you lend me a pair of nylon stockings?'

Kana gobbled down the unmasticated lump of fish and spread her tweed jacket over the banquet, while Reiko Usami of Keio University in her effete breathy voice cooed again, 'So silly of me, completely forgot. I've been so terribly excited. It's the first time I'm to have an arranged marriage luncheon . . . it's at Prunier's. He's a Tokyo University graduate. . . . Isn't that grand?'

Snatching a new cellophane-wrapped pair, Kana slid open the door the minimum necessary and thrust it at Miss Usami.

*Fish or chicken broiled in soy sauce and sake.

The moment her muttering of gratitude began, Kana shut the door and pounced again on her aunt's heavenly cold collation.

The stale old routine world of Prunier's, arranged marriages, ubiquitous doilies, Steinways, dainty breakfasts, 'my girls must have style' and other such blah-blahs! Kana raged inwardly. How can I stay in it, whilst there at the Warehouse a world exists where my 'youthfulity', whatever that might be, is questioned and I am offered the bliss of being useful, together and creative?

As she lay on her sleeping mat that night, Misa and Excelsior seeped back into her mind as gently and naturally as drowsiness. Such a day I've had, Misa. So exciting. So brutal and new! You'd have approved of it. Good Night, Misa and Excelsior. . . .

The next morning Kana changed into jeans and shirt in the Graduate School lavatory and with her heart as light as a breeze walked into the HQ at ten a.m. sharp. The place was in a tearing chaos: the door slammed continually; orders, reprimands and private jokes flowed round the room and through the open window; actors darted in, jotted down their schedules, and were out of the room in a flash.

'Here comes my little nit-wit who's only too anxious to be useful!' Beret greeted her and she could not think why, but heard herself respond: 'Oh . . . thank you!'

'How's your youthfulity holding up, eh?'

'Oh, thank you, not bad, I hope. . . .' Kana mumbled, getting more and more confused.

'Have you read any Brecht?' Beret asked.

'No.'

'You'd better read a few. Start with *The Good Woman*. And Chekhov. Chekhov, you must read everything, plays, letters, short stories, everything! You know Stanislavsky, of course?'

'Sta . . . sorry, *sta*-what?'

'Never heard of Konstantin Sergeyevitch! My child, this is a grotesque offence!' The irrepressible clown clutched at his heart and lurched as if he had been stabbed. Naturally the whole room shook with neighing laughter.

'Quiet!' Beret yelled. 'Now, who'll nip down to Bunmei Second-hand Bookshop and get her *An Actor Prepares* and *Creating a Role*? No doubt Miss Empty-Upstairs would be glad to pay you commission, say half of the reduction you get on the two volumes.'

'Me, me, me,' everyone clamoured for the job.

'Ozawa, you go.' Beret singled out a spindly dark boy clad in an olive-green US Army surplus jacket, whose hair hung in uniform lengths over his narrow close-eyed face in the shape of a half-opened umbrella. He sped off, having extracted two 100-yen notes from Kana.

Myshkin had arranged with Asano to borrow Kana till noon. Her first assignment was to deputize for Miss Takashima who had rehearsals all day at Science Hill. With a copy of *Russian History Before 1917* and Miss Takashima's notebook Kana sat through an hour-long lecture on the Decembrists, trying to look as keenly interested as she could with occasional nods. And finally when Miss Takashima's name was called, grabbing the desk as if it were a life-raft, she screeched, 'Present!'

As soon as Kana returned, Myshkin gave her a sheet of paper filled with minute instructions. 'This time, Balloon, you sit in for three boys. Don't worry, an easy half-hour stint. Once you've filled in the attendance cards, you can sneak out.'

Room 677 in the Business School was huge and fan-shaped with a professor far down at the bottom, drivelling into a squeaky over-sensitive microphone. Following Myshkin's instructions Kana perched on the edge of a back-row bench, nearest to the exit. After what seemed a very long half hour a white-smocked assistant instructor placed a pile of attendance cards for the number of students seated on each bench. Kana pulled out three before anyone else, pretending to make notes, quickly filled them in, then, ducking low, stepped backwards with her bottom feeling its way out, put the completed forms noiselessly into the attendance box, and sped down the stairs, momentarily expecting the rough hand of pursuit at the scruff of her neck.

Once outside the building, she had to cling to a plane tree, perspiring copiously and gasping with relief. With a final glance back to see no one was following her, she ran diagonally across the main square. As she passed the bronze statue of Dr Okuma, the worthy founder of Waseda, Kana inwardly apologized: Sorry, Dr Okuma, but why suddenly today do professors seem such dull idiots, their lectures bogus, and the University a blinkered cart-horse?

Lunchtime. The HQ was empty except for Ozawa who had waited for Kana with the two Stanislavsky books and her change.

'You know Art Blakey? Thelonious Monk? The MJQ? No! Well, you're probably as dumb as everyone says you are.'

Snapping his fingers, kicking his US Army surplus boots one against the other, he suddenly broke into singing or rather ejaculating lengthy musical grunts and hiccups, gyrating his thin long body and crooning down the back of Kana's neck.

'Call me Oz, will you? That's funkier. Know what "funky" means? No. Told you, you're dumb. My old man is a station-master. Mother, a midwife. I was brought up in a highly pro-gressive sort of atmosphere and I believe in the fair distribution of the earth's wealth You have, I have not. Now, think what a poor life for both of us, if you don't give and I don't have the graciousness to accept what you give. By giving just as much as taking, believe you me, one enriches and ennobles oneself,' he went on glibly, still gyrating and snapping his fingers. 'I'm a genuine have-not. I live in and out of all-night coffee houses in Shinjuku. I reckon it knocks me back less than a third of the cost of a permanent dump.'

'What . . . do . . . you . . . want, really?' Kana said slowly.

'Oh, not much. Just anything, any old edibles will do at this particular moment.' He smacked his tongue about with a salivating grin. 'You feed me. I'll be loyal.' He clicked his heels, and Kana got herself a sponger.

At the University Co-op Ozawa made Kana buy two peanut cream buns and two choco-milks.

'See how far fifteen yen can go? Acquired taste, of course. It'll grow on you,' said Ozawa as Kana slapped at her chest in a panic when a dense starch ball got stuck midway down her gorge. The sponger went back to the Co-op to get a refund on the empty milk bottles and Kana to her sociology class, where, completely exhausted, she slept through the lecture.

When Kana reappeared at the back yard, Yamada, the go*-playing props chief, was kneading papier mâché into the shape of a life-sized Buddha.

'Gosh, so you're still with us, Balloon, are you?' he said with a friendly smile. 'Asano has stolen away to the Agony and Ecstacy Mah-jong Parlour to make up a foursome and his message to you was "Scavenge as best poss". Got that?'

The smile coming from the man who had pronounced less than twenty-four hours before that she would not last a day cheered her up no end. With renewed enthusiasm she began scavenging from fence to fence for odds and ends and shavings.

Asano returned early; having lost the game he looked glum. He told Kana to run to a grocer, buy two kilos of sweet potatoes, make a fire and roast them in its hot embers.

As Kana was struggling with the fire, Beret breezed in with a chubby pancake-faced girl in a sailor-collared high-school uniform, who carried a roll of *Konminto* posters.

'This is Single Cell, and this is Balloon Top. OK girls? Balloon you get a bucket of paste and flat brushes from the HQ and go with Single Cell. She'll show you what to do. Never mind Asano's sweet potatoes. Now off you go and don't get into trouble.'

'What did he mean, "Don't get into trouble"? What trouble?' Kana asked as they trotted together down the avenue.

Single Cell just shrugged her shoulders with a contemptuous little grin. 'Lurk in the dark,' she said bluntly. 'Avoid bright neon signs and lit-up shop fronts, 'cause we're not out for an evening stroll, you understand? We're fly-posting.'

Oh, Mother! Kana shut her eyes, but when she re-opened them, she took a faster grip on her bucket handle and peered aggressively into the dark; she was not going to be left behind

*A very popular Japanese chess game.

weeping in the hands of the police by this ruthless seventeen-year-old. Single Cell who had done this many a time before ferreted out suitable electricity or telephone poles, construction hoardings and even some private house walls which happened to command the public eye. Flinging back her long plaits, she darted from target to target, and tut-tutted impatiently till Kana caught her up with her heavy paste bucket. Although her nerves squirmed with dread, Kana bit her lips hard and pasted vigorously, she wasn't going to be a coward, not in front of Single Cell!

At the District Town Hall Single Cell stopped in front of the photograph of Crown Prince and Princess which dominated the notice board. 'Paste over the war criminal's brat,' she said chuckling. Kana gawked at her and at the newly-weds. Their Imperial Wedding had taken place only two days before.

'Go on, what's the matter with you? Paste it thoroughly and the police won't bother peeling it off too soon.'

Kana splashed down the flat wide brush on the forehead of the smiling Crown Prince, involuntarily closing her eyes. No sooner had she finished smearing the Imperial images with the lumpy thick paste than Single Cell spread over it a *Konminto* poster and her muffin-soft pink palms banged down all over it, massaging the air bubbles from under the paper.

'You must see the macabre side of the spectacle, Balloon,' the pancake-face said to Kana on their way back to the HQ. 'The poor little commoner girl is nothing but an instrument to inject healthy blood into the Imperial corpse that's gone half rotten after two hundred or more generations of incest, intermarriage and degeneration. See?'

What a splendid free country Japan must be, Kana thought to herself, if Single Cell could voice these thoughts and still remain outside prison. It was something of a shock to Kana to learn later that Single Cell was the only daughter of Shusaku Azuma, the famous painter and a fellow of the Academy.

Kana was becoming quite useful. In a matter of a few days she had learned how to mimeograph with an iron pen and a slate board, and how to operate a printing machine. She could make mock-canvas flats by pasting old newspapers one on top of the other over a three-by-six wooden frame, mend a fuse and hammer a nail in straight.

One evening Beret told her to wear a 'Balloon sort of dress' and when she appeared in a blue polka dotted frock the next morning he ordered her to solicit display advertisements from the shops round the University for the *Konminto* programme. By noon she had won ads of all sizes, ranging from 300 yen up to 1,500 yen from two pawn-shops, three booksellers, one plastic surgery clinic, six coffee houses and the restaurant she had frequented. The total proceeds added up on Beret's abacus produced a long whistle from him and an invitation to a cup of tea at the Eleven Potatoes.

Halfway through his coffee, Beret suddenly said: 'Ask me, Balloon, if I know how to get to Saint-Germain-des-Prés from the Etoile. Imbecile! Don't you know anything? They're underground stations in Paris!'

Kana dutifully asked him, 'How do you get to, Beret-san . . .'

'You change at Châtelet,' he answered and a broad grin of satisfaction spread on his tiny face. 'Ask me, then, Balloon, at which hotel you should *descendre*, if you wanted to be near the Louvre.'

Kana asked.

He screwed up his face as if this time he found the question a very tough one. 'Well, you could . . .' He scratched and wrung the point of his chin. 'You could try the Regina or the Saint James et d'Albany, the one where Felix Krull worked, you know, or be boring and stay at Hotel du Louvre right bang opposite the Museum entrance.'

Kana groaned and dilated her eyes as expressively as she could to show her astonishment at such erudition.

'You see, Balloon,' he said, 'I'm a man of innumerable pieces of useless information, which I like wearing all over me like protective fish-scales.'

'But it *is* useful, Beret-san, you'll never get lost in Paris.'

'Oh . . . I'll never get there,' said Beret bashfully and Kana almost wept. At that moment she would have given him everything she possessed, if he had asked her for the fare to Paris.

Perfect bliss, working and singing 'Mother Volga'. Kana was mixing the paste in a deep aluminium pot; Asano's boys were hammering and sawing away with small white kerchiefs round their heads to stop the perspiration from running into their eyes. A sunny, warm, yet crisp afternoon.

'Elder miss!' A croaky old voice took everybody in the yard by surprise; Kana stopped stirring and as she turned round, she knew her face was burning red with anger.

'Shh! Pouch, not here!'

Pouch, whose real name neither Kana nor Yoko had learnt, had served their grandfather by carrying his hand luggage, his Inverness cape, umbrella and so on like 'a pouch in Master's pocket'. He was now way past retiring age, but her father had kept him on and he now sat at a small desk in the office and received a salary and bonus for cat-napping most of his day. Whenever someone urged him to pension Pouch off, Mr Toda said, 'Ah, but Pouch enjoys obliging me by doing odd little chores when I am at the Tokyo office.'

Kana hustled the old man away to the far end of the yard.

'Is Father in town?'

'Yes, till tomorrow morning, miss. He wants you to dine with him tonight.' Pouch had a baying kabuki way of speech. The boys had stopped working in order to hear him.

'Not so loud, Pouch, please, when, where?'

'At seven at Prunier's in the Imperial Hotel.' Waiting for Kana to walk away, he bowed and held his head low. With so many eyes peering at them, the top of Pouch's head with its bald patch, the size of a 50-yen coin, made Kana all the more exasperated. She felt like crying.

'Please, Pouch, next time, just leave me a message at the Jardin. . . . But how did you know I was here?'

'Oh, just kept on trying, miss.' He bowed again. Kana was now literally in tears as she walked away.

At five o'clock Kana asked Asano for permission to leave early. 'My father is in town,' she said in a thin whisper.

'OK, OK, run!' He began pushing her out of the back yard. 'And change. You can't meet your dad looking like a shoe-shine boy.'

Hurrying to the Graduate School lavatory, however, Kana was accosted by Myshkin and the girl with the green keen voice, Wood Peck.

'Beret asked us to speak to you,' she said with a grave mis-sionary look on her well-scrubbed round face.

'I'm meeting ... someone downtown at seven.' Kana pro-tested.

'You've got plenty of time,' jauntily declared the bossy meddlesome lump of goodwill and hooking her arm in Kana's forcefully led the way to the raised terrace of the Fox Deity. Here, Wood Peck and Kana sat with their short legs dangling in the air, while Myshkin, as immaculate and thin as the innermost stalk of a head of celery, knocking off his wooden sandals, put his bare feet on the white pebbled ground and quietly began:

'Beret-san feels you suffer from the hallucinatory idea that we are all a bunch of rabid Communists. If you think we are carry-ing secret messages sewn inside our student uniforms or manu-facturing Molotov cocktails in our closets, you are out of date by a decade at least. In fact we not only condemn the infantile terrorism under the Japanese Communist Party leadership of the fifties, but despise the middle-aged JCP sops with their "sky-was-bluer-then" type of nostalgia. We find them pathetic. No, we are *not* going to dance to the JCP tune again, nor will we ape any other established political institution. We must prepare for our own original social revolution.'

Kana stopped swinging her feet, her mouth agape. She had never dreamed that a day would come when an actual protagonist would be talking to her face to face about REVOLUTION!

Wood Peck, who had been panting like a thirsty dog, so eager to take over the talking, jerked Kana by the arm.

'Balloon, Zengakuren, ZGR for short, is today an organiza-tion comprising at least 300,000 members from 177 universities throughout the country, which is roughly 44 per cent of the

133

nation's total student population. Pretty impressive, eh?' Here she gave Kana a poke in the ribs, being one of those people who had to punctuate their speech by nudges and slaps. 'When it was first established in 1948 by, guess who? the Occupation Army GHQ, it was meant purely for brotherhood of song and dance, picnics and pen-pals and some such polite pastimes, but in no time at all Communist students and their sympathizers took control of its central committee. Then in '56 came the Hungarian revolt. The impact was startling.' Another nudge. 'Anyone who had a thinking heart leapt out of the JCP and joined the independent revolutionary movement under the name of ZGR Mainstream, which left the remaining minority no alternative but to call themselves Anti-Mainstream, and ever since there has been a feud between the two factions that often reaches fratricidal intensity, but that's neither here nor there. . . .'

'Excuse me . . . which side are *you* on?'

'Which side? Mainstream, of course!' Wood Peck gave an impatient whack on Kana's back and wetting her lips amply, looked hard into Kana's eyes. 'It is all a matter of sincerity. Large sincerity. You follow me?'

Kana stared blankly back at Wood Peck. She had never, quite frankly, thought about sincerity being either large or small.

'Balloon, don't worry your little head too much.' Myshkin stood up on one leg, like a flamingo, one bare foot rubbing the other for warmth. 'You'll soon get the hang of it. Now you'd better go.'

Since it was already so late, Kana took a taxi straight to the Imperial and changed in the scented powder room there. Folding her jeans, it flashed across her mind: they're brainwashing me! But she was not frightened or annoyed; far from it, she felt waves of excitement and gratitude ripple all over her. They take a genuine interest in me and spend time on me, she thought, and could vividly see Wood Peck's lusty fat wet lips with Large Sincerity trumpeting out of them.

Mr Toda was always the same, flourishing on being overworked and ceaselessly on the go. When Kana arrived at Prunier's, more than half an hour late, he was sitting at a table where he had all the plates and cutlery pushed to one side, happily redesigning the hot-water system for the summer house. The first ten minutes he talked entirely about pipes, ducts, air locks and heat loss but seeing how Kana's attention was wandering, finished somewhat self-pityingly. 'Too bad you're not a boy.'

'A suicidally depressing place, isn't it, Father?' Kana said as they stirred green pea soup that was mis-spelled in the menu as 'Postage St Germany'.

'Maybe, maybe, but I'd rather be depressed than killed by an earthquake. I'll never forget the morning after the 1923 earthquake: everything razed to the ground with the Imperial Hotel alone standing proudly intact. A monument to the genius of Mr Frank Lloyd Wright.'

'I wish you'd stop blowing on your soup, Father. The waiters are all looking.'

'Let them. Unlike a hot bath, hot liquid is bad for your stomach. It destroys your intestinal flora. Incidentally, you really must read Dr Hauser's book. After reading it I bought an electric mixer for making health juice from carrots, celery, apples, water cress, oranges and anything that grows out of earth. Shima who makes it for me night and morning and four times on Sundays drinks it herself and loves it. Looks younger and fitter too.'

Hot plates with Lobster Thermidor descended from over their heads and Mr Toda put on his reading glasses and fell silent as he picked pieces of lobster out of the cream-sauced maze.

'Pouch tells me it took him all morning to find you and when he did you were carpentering, is that right?'

'Ye . . . yes.'

'Good. Honest hard work has done no one any harm. There's no greater joy in life in my opinion than making the best use of oneself. I employ some five hundred people and as long as they enjoy their work and give of their best, I reward them with a very generous bonus twice a year, help them with their houses, children's schooling and weddings, funerals of their parents and so on. A few years ago they suggested forming a union. I said, are you out of your tiny minds? No.'

'You said no?'

'That's right. Why should a man want shorter working hours if he enjoys his work? I assured them a union would turn them into an effete unhappy lot.'

'Didn't they go on strike?'

'Strike? You must be joking.' Kana's father chuckled and she stared at the honest untroubled grin on his face.

'As long as my eyes are black, there will be no union. When I go, it'll be another matter. I hope long before that we'll find you an able young man whom we'll adopt to carry on the family name and business.'

'Please, Father!' Kana pushed her dessert plate aside. 'No arranged marriage for me. I'd rather pass the eldest daughter's privilege to Yoko than. . . .'

'Now, now, don't make a rash statement. Drinking Dr Hauser's health juice I'll be around for quite a while yet, and you'll have more than enough time to change your mind. Ah, yes, take 5,000 yen before I forget.'

Since her father never touched money without washing his hands afterwards, he handed Kana his wallet and she pulled out 5,000 yen.

Father's will be one of the first capitalist heads to fall if my Free Stage comrades' revolution succeeds, Kana thought darkly as she was driven back to Jardin-En in an Imperial Hotel hire car.

2

It was the day when the Free Stage General Assembly was scheduled for three at the Sancho Noodle House. At noon Kana's sponger surfaced at the Warehouse with a studied look of hunger; Kana gave him 60 yen. 'Not a penny more, eh? You're learning, kid,' said the sponger with a big wink. When they settled down under the Butterfly with buns and milk, Ozawa asked: 'Heard about the crisis on Science Hill? The leading lady stalked out of the rehearsal last night, calling us Free Stagers a bunch of sadists.'

'No!'

'Yes, indeed she did, though I'd never have thought Ichikawa had the guts to do that. Unless they –' Ozawa pointed his chin at the HQ window – 'find a replacement quickly, I'll be an unemployed actor before even embarking on my career.'

Inside the HQ Beret was pacing the floor like an ostrich with its tail on fire, while Abe, the sadist director, and Myshkin, now a distraught stage manager, sat motionless on a bench against the wall.

'I could murder that scoundrel, Otani! I told him to be here at one and now it's a quarter past. He's been at it all night. Mahjong, what a game! O great China, the nation that could produce such a game will conquer the world, I bet my head on that. . . . Now, look, who lurks there, none but our willing dumb belle!' Beret stuck his head out of the window. 'Drink up your choco-milk, piglet, and go to the Agony and Ecstacy, and ask for Otani. Pay no attention to his protest, just drag him back here!'

In addition to feeling shamelessly well after the capitalistic meal with her father the night before, Kana felt herself so clean and well ventilated in the leafy green air of late spring that as she passed the Fox Shrine she threw 20 yen in the offering box, rang the heavy bell and quickly prayed for the health and happiness of everyone. Who's everyone? Never mind, everyone, it was a beautiful day.

The Agony and Ecstacy was a sooty old wooden house, cramped between a pawn shop and an abacus-maker, with a small Chinese lantern hanging from the porch. As Kana slid back the badly fitted door, it rattled open on to a scene not dissimilar to the Scroll of Purgatory where a multitude of sinners are seen immersed in a River of Blood, writhing and struggling with demons and phantoms of their own accursed desires. Some thirty students, their faces rigid as if in a trance or distorted with gambling passion, sat four at a table, either in deathly silence or emitting cries of joy and pain. The air was stifling, thick with a foul odour of feet, oily hair and nicotine. What a shame, with so much chlorophyl and ozone outdoors, Kana winced.

To the right of the door the madam of the house was surveying her domain from a sort of rostrum, nearly five feet high, a combination of desk, chair, and ladder. Her face, powder and rouge filling its deep flaccid wrinkles, loomed like a monster pink duster.

'You, what d'you want?' her cigarette-hoarse voice demanded.

'I'm looking for. . . .' Kana leaned forward awkwardly, her feet awash in a sea of men's footwear.

'Who?'

'Mr Otani, I have an urgent. . . .'

'Ken-san!' the painted witch shouted. 'An urgent message. From Beret-san, I bet.'

'Oh, hell, just when I'm winning!'

Kana stumbled back and grabbed the edge of the madam's throne, feeling as if she had been kicked in the pit of her stomach. Of course, looking back, it was unforgivably stupid of her not to have connected the Otani of Free Stage with the Ken Otani of Takaha Primary School, but somehow it just had not crossed her mind; besides, Otani was not a rare name, there were tens of thousands of Otanis in the country.

To steady herself, Kana focused her entire attention on the madam's sparkling gold front teeth, repeating to herself like a prayer, 'Who'll inherit the lump of gold after her cremation?' The commotion over Otani's collecting his due from his reluctant debtors took some time to subside. Kana heard the wailing squeak and rattle of the door being forced open, and saw a pair of long legs in navy blue uniform trousers outside the threshold.

'Damn it, overnight my feet have swollen to twice their size!' He hopped and skipped, trying to put on his shoes.

'I know you,' he said.

Kana looked up. Not having seen him for seven years, she was struck dumb by his hairlessness. That unruly wild black bush of hair she remembered from the Takaha days was now short, trimmed like a helmet of shiny dark moss, with a deep long indentation at the nape. His face had tautened and lost the puckish monkey that had once frolicked there and his skin, although as sorrel and gleamy as before, now fitted closely over his bone structure. There was about him the easy, cool ruthlessness of an animal.

'No comment?' Ken stepped backwards, studying Kana with friendly curiosity.

'Excuse me?'

'I said, I know you, any comment?'

'Comment. . . .'

'Oh, don't bother. So you're the new recruit they call Balloon Top. My, how the cap fits.' He turned and walked away fast. He's going! Kana was aghast at the abrupt bathos of the whole scene. After seven years! She stood stock still for an instant, then began madly running after him, swerving to right and left like a dog determined to overtake its master.

'Excuse me, how is your family, are they well?' She thought the question most appropriate, but he burst into laughter.

'My family! Are they well? Honestly, Balloon Top!' He smoothed down his short hair in apparent agitation. 'My family I haven't seen for over two years now.'

'You're . . . forgive my being inquisitive . . . have they disowned you?' Always possible with a Commie son, Kana thought.

'No, I did it.'

'Excuse me?' Kana shielded her eyes from the sun that blazed down between them. He swept the air with his mackintosh which smelt intensely of him and kept on walking.

'I don't understand,' Kana said.

'It's not difficult. *I* disowned *them*.'

'You can't. One can't disown one's own parents.'

'Who said so?'

'One just doesn't. Was it . . . er . . . ideo-political disagreement or a . . . .'

'Hell, no! Nothing of the sort. I just can't stand my father. He scribbles a load of muck, which happens to sell faster than he can churn it out. The kind of stuff you see in paperback on a station kiosk. When you knew me at Takaha my father was writing poems and essays after his work at the Prefectural Office, which nobody wanted to publish. Now, the famous Saburo Otani writes this noxious crap full-time except when he's playing golf or getting drunk in Ginza bars. At forty-eight he's contemplating suicide, which soon won't be necessary if he continues to lap up Scotch at his present rate. And you, Balloon Top, aren't you a bit of a mess yourself? Who are you trying to fool here? What's all this "ideo-political" crap? Take my advice, scram back to Rokko Hills.' His sensuous heavy lips moved gently, independent of his frowning brows.

'No! I'm staying here. I want to stay, Ken-chan!'

'Monkey's red ass!' he hissed. 'If you must stay, please don't call me . . . Ken-chan.' He turned on his heel and stalked away. As she could not stand for ever in the middle of a busy street, Kana went back to the Fox shrine, sat on the raised terrace with the palms of her hands against her eyes. Never before had she felt a such a jumble of sensations race inside her: full of hope, betrayed, sad, happy, pained, blessed, exulted, depressed, humiliated. . . . After what may have been either minutes or hours she got up to attend General Assembly.

Half-past four. The Sancho Noodle House, downstairs. Kana was telephoning her aunt. She loved her aunt dearly, but Aunt Sachi was a clinger and sometimes Kana wished she could love her by correspondence.

She told her that she could not dine at Azabu that evening.

'O-o-oh, but I've been looking forward to seeing you so much,' Aunt Sachi whined in that hopeless way of hers, and under any other circumstances Kana would have dropped everything and rushed to Azabu, but today she remained silent.

'Where on earth are you, Kana? Tokyo station?' Mrs Itoh's voice echoing in the deep silence of her large house sounded very suspicious, and rightly too: for behind Kana there raged the wildest cacophony of clanging plates and pots and pans; orders screeched by waitresses to the kitchen; television going at full blast; the entrance door continually sliding open and shut, causing the indigo-blue curtains, emblazoned with a huge trade symbol in white, to billow inwards, letting in the boom of the traffic from the avenue; and on top of it all Mrs Sancho greeting the arrival of every Free Stager with a deafening shout of 'Up the stairs!'

'No, I'm not at Tokyo station. I'm at a students' meeting place. Look, Auntie, I really must go back to the discussion.'

'I miss you, when will I see you next?'

Kana cleared her throat and said, 'Next time when Uncle is away. I'll get a special permission and stay overnight.'

Just as she hung up, in walked Beret and Myshkin, followed by Otani. Kana grabbed the telephone again, turned her back and pretended that she was still conversing.

'Here she is! Enough, Balloon, stop yak-yakking,' the unmistakable Beret screamed. Kana replaced the receiver and faced the three.

'You know Otani, our production chief, a rascal whom I had the pleasure of meeting for the first time in a prison cell back in '57 and undoubtedly the best thing to come out of that ghastly anti-US-base demo.' Beret swung his right arm towards Otani, who bowed slightly towards Kana, with his eyes obstinately fixed on the television.

'Now, look, Balloon, we've something very. . . .' Beret began.

'Let's move out of everyone's way.' Myshkin, blinking solicitously, shepherded them to the far end of the restaurant.

'To come quickly to the point –' Beret lowered his voice – 'we've had to accept the fact that you're the only recruit of the right type to replace Ichikawa as the Good Woman. You look horrified, Balloon, believe me, so are we all!'

Otani without ever glancing at Kana said to Myshkin: 'With an absolute beginner in the lead we'd better postpone the performance. We'll need at least three extra days.'

'Say the 30th then, provided of course the Okumo Theatre is free on that date,' said Myshkin. And that was that; settled. Kana who had started reading Stanislavsky only the night before was to play the female lead and was not even asked if she wanted to or thought she could do it. She who had never played a female role even at the Faith.

Upstairs, in a monkey-house hubbub a hundred human bodies jostled against each other in the space of a mere two ten-tatami-mat rooms. Those who had overflowed on to the verandah had to huddle as best they could under festoons of the Sancho family's laundry. As Kana sat down Ozawa shoved his way towards her, creating a frightful commotion amongst the squatting crowd. 'Pay for my noodle, OK, boss?' He literally poured himself into the space next to Kana that had looked too small even to spread a handkerchief.

In a raised alcove where normally a seasonal scroll of painting hung sat Minami, the President, and Bobchin, Chairman of the Executive Committee, flanked by the joint secretaries, Wood Peck and Sta-san. Minami was the man whose likeness had been used on the *Konminto* posters. Strikingly handsome, straight-nosed and thin-lipped, with a nervous twitching smile.

'A Tyrone Power, eh? But wait till you see him act, a ham, oh what a ham. So wooden that you'd think he'd swallowed a ladder,' Ozawa whispered to Kana. 'And a rabid Marxist too.'

Bobchin, so named from the part he had played in last season's *The Government Inspector*, was the director of *Konminto*: squat, jocular, hairy like an Ainu with thick eyebrows which jumped and almost collided when he laughed. Sta-san looked already middle-aged, with a gourd-shaped face, receding hair, drooping shoulders and weak jaws, but, considered the best Method actor in the company, had been allowed to use the honorary title of Sta-san after Stanislavsky.

'Silence! Silence, please!' Wood Peck screeched, rapping on a frail little tea table with a hammer. A compact parcel of energy, her thick straight hair was cut short like new thatch and her little pink nostrils flared and wriggled most expressively at the centre of her Pekingese-like face. She reminded Kana of the motto: Small is vital.

Announcing the start of the General Assembly to the slowly simmering down crowd, Wood Peck reverently handed the hammer to Bobchin, who then spoke: 'Before we begin, may I beseech every one of you to order a noodle dish, any kind, any price, when the order slip is passed round? We are given the use

142

of these rooms free of charge and we must keep the Sancho family happy. Even noodles in clear soup at 30 yen will do. Thank you.' Another tap of the hammer.

'I have an emergency announcement to make. *The Good Woman of Setzuan* lost its leading lady last night, but no undue alarm, please, for the Casting Committee has already chosen a replacement, Miss Toda, better known to you as Balloon Top. Due to this change of cast. . . .' His speech was cut short.

'Hip, hip, hurrah for Balloon Top!' It was Kana's dutiful sponger giving a cheer.

'Shame, they've pinched our Balloon!' Asano and his back-yard boys booed and growled in mock protest, and those who had not taken any notice of Kana before stretched on their knees to get a closer look at her. Kana felt fire in her ear lobes as she blushed and cowered as small as she could make herself.

'Next, some good news. Otani, accompanied by Kubo whose family breeds silkworms in the Chichibu region, has succeeded in raising 25,150 yen from various local unions and educational institutions.' Sta-san led the applause. Another tap of the hammer and at a nod from Bobchin, Minami took the floor.

'I speak on behalf of the Executive Committee. Up to now Free Stage has never joined a May Day demo nor the People's Movement's United Action as a whole group, but the Executive Committee believe that the time has come for us to take part and to manifest our identity as a progressive organization both politically and artistically.

'We all know that the revisions proposed for the New ANPO not only violate the principles of our so-called "Peace" constitution but will inevitably force Japan to come under the American nuclear umbrella. Having achieved a spectacular economic comeback under the original ANPO signed in '51 with Uncle Sam looking after our defence and not a penny being spent on rearmament, the capitalists of this country with no sense of moral or political perspective are naturally dead keen to renew ANPO on whatever terms, so that they may continue to suck the honey of its economic blessings for another ten-year period.

'And Kishi, we all know, is the embodiment of all the reactionary forces and the servile transistor-radio-salesman's mentality. This man who served in the Fascist Tojo government and was tried as a war criminal will stoop to any foul means to push the New ANPO through the Diet, and what weapons do we have in our hands but a dissenting voice so loud and unanimous that even this Fascist Prime Minister could not ignore?' Here Minami took a deep breath and his pale cheeks flushed in a tubercular access of red. 'Friends, the Committee urge every one of you to join the United Action May Day demo against the New ANPO!'

'Hear! Hear!' Enthusiastic applause and cheers boomed till a loud heckling punctuated it like a bullet.

'Infantile radicalism! Dilettantes, all of you!'

Kana held her breath in astonishment, it was none other than her sponger, raising his odd dark head like a dancing cobra out of its coiled body.

'I joined Free Stage, rather than INTER, after having been assured by many senior members now present at this meeting that here I could make up my own mind about political issues without fear of being ostracized or lynched. But now, what do I hear? The Executive Committee dictates to us what to think and what to do. Listening to you rant up there like a rabid self-righteous dog in a fake proletarian coat, drivelling nonsense out of your well-fed mouth, I can't help being struck by the uncanny resemblance between you and your Meiji forefathers, those good-for-nothing sons of landed gentry and ex-samurai lords who voyaged grandly to St Petersburg. When they came home they considered themselves proletarians and bragged about this new thing called Socialism for want of anything better to do. Let's face it, "comrades", you're suffering from the same sham dilettantism today. Those ridiculous *poseurs* of Meiji are the spit image of you! You are dividing this otherwise congenial society of Free Stage by . . . the pity of it all. . . .'

Ozawa ran out of steam and gave out a frivolous little giggle. 'Er . . . what point was I making?'

'You have no point to make, Ozawa. Sit down!' Minami banged down the hammer. 'You yourself are the prime example of muddled dilettantism, you in your US Army flea-market jacket and your Modern Jazz Quartet!'

'Leave my MJQ alone, you with your superior braggadocio Marxism!'

'Please, please, freedom of speech is defenceless against such abuse of its privilege. We are here to discuss our participation in the May Day demo,' Bobchin cut in.

'Anyone else?' Minami called out sullenly.

A dozen hands shot up, all fingers eagerly shaking. While several Free Stagers were speaking in favour of unconditional support for the ZGR Mainstream manifesto, a noodle list, a piece of torn loose-leaf paper, was passed round. Kana signed Ozawa's and her names under her favourite dish, Moon Viewing, an egg dropped over a cloud of diced chicken and vegetables.

'Defender of ivory tower!' someone heckled as a young woman with a delicate little head rose halfway on her knees to speak. It was Miss Takashima whom Kana had the honour to substitute for at lectures. She had been the Free Stage's leading lady for three years and was the only female member to whom the boys accorded the honorific 'san'.

'Am I daft to believe,' she began, 'that in a democratic society an individual's rights in the society must be rigorously reciprocated by his duty to the society? And am I very parochial to insist that the boundaries of my duty lie in my lecture rooms? Inside an ivory tower, if you like, but surely not out there on the streets arm in arm with professional demagogues, union leaders bloated with sake and bribes, or politicking politicians? They know and you and I know that we are not working-class. The sense of solidarity you boast of is an illusion. Yes, it is either blindness or delusory presumption to think that the workers feel any comradeship with us, the pampered, parasitic and half-fledged. The very composition of the Special Fourth Riot Task Force proves my point: these young policemen, recruited purposely to cope with riotous students, are all our own age and from poor families who cannot afford university education. They see our falseness and understandably hate us. If I were one of them, I would too. I am against the New ANPO, but that does not mean I should run amok all over town screaming my head off. I'll have my say later when I will have become a contributing member of the society.'

A polite sustained applause followed her speech.

'President!' A new speaker, it was Otani. He had come back into Kana's life; a strange drowning sensation of incredulity overcame her.

'At first sight, what Takashima-san said seems to make sense, may even seem unassailable in its neat, exclusive and defensive terms of Small Sincerity, dividing her own conscience into convenient little categories, concealing a lack of positive action behind the smoke screen of a self-applied timetable. But please, I beg of you, think *not* in terms of Small Sincerity, but in terms of Large Sincerity.

'While Small Sincerity fidgets over the details: students' duties and rights, workers' grudges, law and order or the evil of causing traffic jams, Large Sincerity holds you responsible to your own conscience which, after all, is the conscience of this world of ours. Yes, if we, young, able and alive today on earth, do not make the world a better place, who will? The complacent middle-aged? The people of our age who never bother to read any printed word other than traffic signs? No. We students owe it to this world to meddle, participate, serve, and above all to lead. We must show to the rest of the world that we are in the van-guard of progress, not only inside the wall of a theatre but in the streets with the people!'

A brief hush, then the floor was sagging with a roar of consent. Kana saw Bobchin, about to seize the chance to call for a vote, rise on his knees.

'Irresistible specialities of the house coming up!' The Sancho proprietor with a long tray hoisted on his shoulders stood on the landing, beaming like the sun. Behind him followed his wife and waitresses with tray after tray of noodle dishes.

'Damn noodles, what a moment to choose!' Bobchin collapsed on his haunches.

By the time a hot earthenware bowl with a set of fresh chop-sticks was passed to Kana and she paid 150 yen for two Moon

Viewing into a collection basket, the precipitant sipping noise and happy tongue-smacking had filled the place like an orchestra tuning up. Bobchin finished his noodles in a breathless hurry and cradling the empty bowl in the hollow of his lap, hissed fiercely to let the air clean between his teeth before he spoke.

'While you are still eating, let me tell you about the ZGR Mainstream arrangements. To date almost 50 per cent of the teaching staff have agreed to cancel lectures and some of them will even go so far as to stand with the ZGR members at the barricaded entrances to persuade the uncommitted to join the demo. The march itself will be along the customary Waseda-Akasaka-Tiger's Gate route, ending at Hibiya Park where the main rally is scheduled from three to five. Now –' Bobchin raised his right hand and looked challengingly over the steamy, jam-packed room –' those of you who will join us on May Day, please raise your hands!'

Either way Kana had to look silly: if she joined the demo, they would no doubt accuse her of following the crowd without conviction, and if she didn't, they would say, Ah, what did I tell you, she's a stinking bourgeoise. So, Kana cringed low and small, embarrassment and indecision and the knowledge of her being the village idiot literally warping her spine.

How interminably long it took Wood Peck to count the raised hands! Finally she whispered a word to Bobchin and he rose on his knees again.

'Eighty-two! Eighty-two will march on May Day. Now, those who will not, please!'

'Hoop-la!' Asano gave out a rousing yell. His faithfuls, Miss Takashima, Ozawa and others lifted their arms defiantly high.

'Sixteen will stay behind,' Bobchin announced. 'Wait a second, it doesn't add up. . . .'

'But she has every right not to vote till she knows what she's voting for or against.' It was Beret with a tinny jangle of vehemence in his voice. Bless Beret and all his descendants, Kana prayed inside, and felt her skin break out in a rash at the thought of Otani watching her in this ignominious scene.

'All right, it's Balloon, as long as we know. . . .'

147

Bobchin sat down. Just then, mercifully for Kana, Wood Peck cried out: 'Someone has short-changed the basket by 30 yen!'

'Sorry,' a timid voice came from the laundry verandah. 'I realized I didn't have enough money after having eaten. . . .'

The whole assembly burst out laughing. Several coins were tossed on to the President's raised seat. Bobchin, covering his head with both hands, shouted: 'Thanks, everyone, I declare this meeting closed!'

Mother would be furious with me, if she knew how I have aped and have almost *become* a typical left-wing Tokyo student, Kana admitted in her resurrected Excelsior diary. And with what ardour she aped. She gulped down, raw and unmasticated, everything her new colleagues offered her, above all else their determined xenophilism. Discovering that Myshkin was neither a dog's pet name nor a way of cooking vegetables and that she was, according to Beret, an indescribable wretch not to know the works of Fiodor Mikhailovitch (Beret would not deign to call him Dostoevsky), Kana waded into them, starting, of course, with *The Idiot*, till she felt she knew more about Ivan, Natasha, Masha, Misha or Aliosha than about her own sister Yoko.

Now she would not dream of quoting her favourite poets and philosophers such as Bashô, Buson or Soshi, and certainly would not dare opine that perhaps Zeami in the fourteenth century had developed a theatrical system which might have been in many ways superior to that of Stanislavsky. No. Instead, she went the whole hog with 'super objectives' and 'perspective' and 'commitment' and 'alienation'.

And the girls, what girls! They made Kana shrivel with every sort of inferiority complex available. What wouldn't she have given to be like them, to attain that cool, disdainful, maniacal style!

For a start, there was this saucy, perky thing nicknamed Denim, who lived in blue jeans day in and day out all year round. Her carroty sepia hair, bleached in beer, flew in all directions, smelling of rancid soap oil and cigarettes, which she chain-smoked, often scorching her own eyelashes. Being a Western

History major, her self-identification jolted back to George Sand and her scene was the era before 1848. She even had her salon, a 850-yen-a-month room in Shibuya where she kept an ample supply of beer, cheap cigarettes, rice-crackers and so on. Everyone just walked into it. 'Often I wake up to find my room full of Free Stagers who have missed their last train home,' she said. Kana's family would have called Denim a slut, a degenerate, or even a panpan*, but here in Tokyo she passed as a perfectly respectable modan young lady.

And there was Single Cell, the pancake-faced four-footer, whom even Beret found slightly frightening. 'Oh, the raw youth! What terrifies me about her is that she doggedly follows the basic rule of revolution: once you're involved in it, the easiest and surest way of survival is to ally yourself to the most radical extremes.'

But, of all the Free Stage girls Kana found Tamiko Fujino the most fascinating. A lawyer's daughter, she was in the crack Political Science Department (1 out of 21.8 was the last year's entrance-exam rate). She was liable suddenly to look up from her lunch box and snort: 'O château, O saison!' or some such wonder and Kana found it hard not to feel goose-fleshed all over with the sheer thrill of it. There was also something dashing about the way she mixed vile men's expressions with esoteric foreign words and never bothered to explain or reiterate. With her fierce memory she managed to quote right, left and centre from Rosa Luxemburg, Simone Weil, Aragon, Fournier and other such people whose names were mere sounds to Kana.

Tamiko was sparsely fleshed everywhere, especially her face, what Kana's mother would have called 'all furniture, no tatami', and looked uncannily like Louis Jouvet. Kana admired the way her veins came very near the surface and spread a blueish shadow round her eyes and how her meatless legs clamped into position like two hinges when she crossed them.

Above all else Kana was impressed that Tamiko never even

*A word coined during the American Occupation for a Japanese woman who dangled from a GI's arm, but now it means a prostitute in general.

tried to be discreet about her relationship with Minami; while the other members hid such personal emotion like a bad disease from the public notice, Tamiko and Minami carried on as if they were acting in a French film, hand in hand, calling each other by their first names.

When Kana had learned her lines and blocked her moves, her director, Abe, told her, 'Just be yourself, Balloon.'

'But, don't I have to act?' asked Kana.

'No, don't bother. We haven't the time for that. But just do this for me, will you? Before taking up your cue and I mean every cue you have, say "She said".'

' "She said"?' Kana asked. 'But, who's "she"?'

'Quiet! I'm not going to attempt to make you understand what "alienation" is in half a day. Just say "She said".'

So Kana rehearsed with 'She said' all day till seven-thirty and after the Circle took a taxi back to Jardin-En. It was 9.15 when she rang at the gate.

'Miss Toda, your aunt has just telephoned you. You did not dine with your aunt tonight, did you?' Miss Arashi stood akimbo in turquoise blue roll-neck sweater and matching ski trousers filling the entire frame of the opened gate. Hugging the large furoshiki parcel of her rehearsal clothes, Kana hung her head. On three previous occasions she had submitted a false late-return slip with 'dining with my aunt, Mrs Itoh in Azabu' as an excuse; sooner or later she had to be caught. Kana told Miss Arashi of her new life in the theatrical arts, making it sound as artistic, palatable and worthy as possible.

'Please, Miss Arashi, you don't know my parents or my aunt as well as I do. If they weren't so terribly Meiji in their attitude, of course, I'd have told you and them straight away. But my father is the kind of person who to this day calls an actor a "beggar-on-river-bank" and as to my mother and aunt, they consider any form of theatre except for kabuki and noh dangerous and subversive. I'm sure you realize they'll never understand why I joined. . . .' Kana listened to her own voice and thought it most effective.

150

'Quite right!' Miss Arashi slapped at her right thigh in agreement. 'Why should you worry them unnecessarily? I myself suffered my own family's Meiji mentality when I wanted to attend the Ueno Conservatoire, so I know what that is like. I'm glad you have confided in me. Don't worry, I have always been a supporter of arts and sports.'

She then granted Kana, to her astonishment, the special privilege of a nine o'clock curfew.

'Only please keep me informed. I want to be abreast of all that goes on in the young world. Will you?'

Kana was so completely overcome by the turn of events that she promised to invite Miss Arashi to *The Good Woman of Setzuan*.

Miss Arashi is really rather a pitiable pseudo-culture-cum-youth clinger, Kana thought, and with a heavy sigh picked up a phone. Mrs Itoh was obviously very suspicious of Kana's late return and her infrequent visits to Azabu. With the zest of a mother monkey hunting lice in a baby monkey's hair she cross-examined Kana.

'Have you made the acquaintance of many young people? Girls? And boys?' Kana did not like the way her aunt had said 'And boys?' When she finally hung up, her forehead was wet. I'm afraid she's going to meddle, Kana thought as she went upstairs, banging her furoshiki parcel against the polished mahogany balustrade.

For the first run-through Beret, Otani and Myshkin appeared at Science Hill. Their presence naturally made all the beginners fidgety. As for Kana she was so confounded by the sight of Otani's glossy black helmet head next to Abe that when Abe told her hurriedly, 'Balloon, take that out today, will you?' she remained dead blank for a minute.

'Take . . . *what* out, please?'

' "She said", you fool, "She said" !' Abe, being highly nervous himself in the presence of the three visitors, screamed and the whole company could not help laughing. Abe, scowling and laughing in turn, signalled to the cast that he was ready to start.

Kana stood alone at the centre of the room with a burning wet forehead. How she wanted to be good: she felt spent before she even started.

'Go!' Abe clapped his hands. Kana opened her mouth but quickly shut it before 'She said' automatically popped out of it. From that moment on, she spoke, sang and moved with her mind's eyes fearfully peering ahead to the next 'She said' hurdle.

One and a half hours later Abe clapped his hands. 'Ten minutes break before notes!' Kana crumpled down on the floor just where she had finished and stayed there pretending she was invisible. Were I a grasshopper or a pig in a field, I wouldn't have to be dragged through this humiliation, she thought as she squatted with her dry lips against her knee cap.

In the evening after the Circle Asano and his right-hand man, Tonton-the-steady-hammer, stopped Kana and gave her a roasted sweet potato with its singed black skin still very hot.

'I hear you had a run-through, Balloon.' Asano had a paternal concern for anyone who worked or had worked under him. 'Beret says you ran through your lines like a Tokyo-Osaka bullet train. The sign of a first-timer. But Otani thinks you've got something.'

'What? What is something?'

'You can keep still,' said Asano simply.

'Keep still? Is that all?'

'Repose. That's the important thing. Come on, eat your sweet potato while it's hot.'

Kana cogitated on 'repose' and asked Beret to the Eleven Potatoes.

'Repose? That's Otani's big thing. With him it's always this repose, the supreme criterion. But who, I ask you, ever meets or touches or shakes hands with repose nowadays in Japan! I suppose we must remember the chap was born in Manchuria, on the edge of the vastest continent on earth. . . . Trapped as he is in this frene-hecti-chaotic Oriental Lilliput of a country and sired by a Birth and Marriage registrar's clerk at Shibuya town hall, he dreams of big repose; and if the bloke says you've got it, that's praise indeed.'

'A Birth and Marriage registrar's clerk!' Kana could not help repeating in pure amazement: to think that Otani would go so far as to lie about his father's identity!

'Don't show the ugly face of your class snobbism, girl.'

'Isn't life dizzy with surprises, Beret-san!' Kana sighed, shaking her head.

'Now Balloon's talking like a Dostoevskian lady from Kiev.'

'From Kiev!' Kana laughed hilariously, savouring the full thrill of sharing Otani's secret, alone with him.

The freshman try-out production had only one performance, just one performance on a Saturday afternoon.

'Don't worry, everyone has a butterfly or two in the stomach, it often helps you to give a better performance,' Sta-san told Kana, but it did not help. After she had made up and put on her costume, she had to run back and forth to the toilet, purely from nerves. When the curtain finally rose, in fact nearly an hour later than scheduled, the small audience, consisting mainly of families and friends of the cast (and Miss Arashi lurking somewhere) warmly applauded.

The moment Kana was caught by the spotlight in the hushed and hawk-eyed darkness of the auditorium, the butterfly turned into a positive panic: her knees started to give and she could almost hear the nerves in her temples creak in recoil. Anything but prolonging this ordeal! Kana rushed her lines and moves as if she were on a hot frying pan. Everyone followed her example and the first act went at an hysterical speed and in what seemed no time at all, the actors on stage suddenly saw nothing before them but a mass of creased greyish cloth. The first act was over! They stood like zombies, till Asano hustled them out.

As Kana was groping her way down the corridor, she heard Otani's voice from behind the dressing-room door: 'Never mind the speed, Abe, a bit skittish, that's fine. But the make-up! She looks exactly like a dirty raccoon. Why the hell did you let Balloon go on looking like that, Dre-ma?'

Kana flew down the corridor into the toilet again. When she returned, Abe was still grumbling about his leading lady ruining the rhythmic perspectives of his direction. No sooner had Kana got to her dressing mirror than Dre-ma, the costume chief from the Dress-Making Institute, and Otani pounced on her.

'Get rid of those smudges under her eyes and that ghastly brown smear there.' Otani bent over the short, tub-shaped Dre-ma as she scrubbed Kana's face with a towel dipped in cleansing cream.

'Second act beginner, please!' Myshkin darted into the room and Kana jumped to her feet.

'Sit!' Otani pushed her back into the chair.

'For God's sake, do hurry up!' Myshkin and Abe stamped their feet behind them but Dre-Ma's quick, adroit index finger went on skipping over Kana's face. As she stepped back to examine the effect, Myshkin and Abe, braving the wrath of Otani, hoisted Kana out of the chair, shouting, 'Perfect! That's perfect! Thanks!'

As Kana was being shoved back on to the stage, her head was reeling. The delicious, narcissistic, addictive spell of acting was on fire under her skin. This make-believe world, the stage, tra-la-la, she thought. I'll never get over this!

In the second act she even had nerve enough to see and hear everything that was going on around her and no longer did 'She said' worry her. In the eerie overflow of stage light Kana noticed for the first time Miss Arashi sitting hugely in the first row centre. She felt like putting her tongue out at her, and this threw her into a confusion of panic and impudence.

Eventually the Gods departed, leaving the Good Woman pathetically imploring their help. The curtain tumbled down. That was the end. Abe took the curtain call next to Kana. In a state of great agitation, his hand was like hot gruel, but Kana squeezed it gratefully when he whispered to her, 'Well done, Balloon.'

The actors quickly took off their make-up, packed their costumes, tidied the dressing room, then joined everyone else in loading the scenery and electrical equipment on to the push-carts borrowed from a near-by lumber merchant. It was past seven o'clock, warm and star-lit. The students going to evening classes laughed and whistled at the Free Stagers pushing the barrows loaded with the painted rubbish into the main square. They didn't mind, for they felt themselves infinitely more interesting and original beings than those who jeered at them.

The Circle was later than usual. Otani, after a few generous words of praise for the good work done by Abe and the new recruits, led the applause. The cool sting of the evening air against scrubbed pink skin was delightful. A job has been done, I am empty again, give me more work, prayed Kana, more, more!

Aunt Sachi must be psychic, Kana had to conclude. Why else should she have chosen May Day to take Kana to a kabuki performance? The way she had cajoled, coaxed and dragooned Kana into finally saying yes had been quite a remarkable performance. Some sort of danger signal must have communicated itself to her solicitous aunt, for Kana had been more and more tempted to join the May Day demo, just to see what it was like.

Mrs Itoh, obviously mistrusting her niece, arrived at Jardin-En at three, though the performance did not start till five-thirty.

'Here I am, too early. But Hirano insisted that we should leave in plenty of time in view of the demo,' said Mrs Itoh, and Kana could see her aunt was actively disapproving the simple cotton dress she had put on. Mrs Itoh had telephoned her the night before to make sure that she would wear a kimono.

'I am sorry, Auntie, but if I'm parcelled up in a kimono and obi on top of having to sit in a stifling theatre for hours, I'll be sick. I swear I will. Dr Togo always warned me to leave my intestines unsqueezed,' Kana said, placatingly.

'Well, you see –' Mrs Itoh fussed with the back of her spiral coiffure –' both Mrs Masuda and Mrs Shinoda are very clothes-conscious.'

'Oh, never mind, Auntie. They know I'm just a student.'

Mrs Itoh would not give in, went on and on in her velvet-pawed, strangulating fashion, till finally Kana gave in and put on a pearl-yellow Thai silk ensemble as a compromise. Kana grumbled that she felt herself like a Siamese cat 'tarted up for auction'. Mrs Itoh laughed nervously but said nothing.

Hirano, square and neckless, who sincerely wanted Japan to be ruled by a right-wing religious group, accelerated the Mercedes to a murderous speed at every crossing on Ginza Street, gnashing his teeth as he made the jay-walking demonstrators scatter, and escorted the ladies up to the Kabuki-za main entrance with the bull-dog grimace of a protector of law and order.

'Just in time!' Mrs Masuda, wife of the president of the YNK Line, poured out of the milling crowd. 'Mrs Shinoda, poor thing, has gone down with flu, so rather than waste her ticket I persuaded my second son Akio to come along. Goodness, Miss Toda, in the short time since I last saw you you've become a pretty young lady. Tokyo water obviously agrees with your skin,' said the tall, buck-toothed lady, and with a typical Tokyo woman's aggressiveness pushed her son forward. 'This is my marine insurance boy. . . .'

A neat package of a young executive in a well-cut conservative suit with a white handkerchief squarely peeping out of his chest pocket. He bowed formally to Mrs Itoh, but to Kana gave a perfunctory nod.

When they were shown to a tatami-floored box, Mrs Masuda designated the seating arrangement. 'You two sit behind us so that you can chat to each other.'

Kana got it only then. What a confounded idiot; Kana could have kicked herself, to be so easily tricked into an arranged-marriage rendezvous! She could not help flushing furiously. She wriggled herself as far away as possible from the young Masuda, and shut up like a clam with her eyes fixed on the stage. The older women went on chattering at normal speech volume throughout the performance, gossiping about each and every actor; who had rheumatism; who had lost his looks; how inferior this one was compared to his great granduncle; remember Kichiemon in the role of. . . . And so on and so forth, like a running tap.

'Excuse me . . . I must, or I'll faint!' Midway through the first scene, Kana brusquely stretched both legs sideways sighing with relief.

'Thank goodness.' The young man promptly did the same

156

with an even louder hiss of relief. He was, to do him justice, quite pleasant, with an easy open manner. He would have been tolerable, she thought, in different circumstances.

'The tension's killing,' Kana said while the samisen music crescendoed. 'Have you any idea why we're gathered together tonight?'

'Well . . . .' He blinked his eyes bashfully.

'It's diss-guss-ting!' Kana said.

'What is?' he asked good-naturedly.

'This arrangement. Disgusting! They chose *you* because you are the second son, so that you could take over my father's business. A grubby capitalist's trick of self-preservation.' Kana stopped as she saw Mrs Masuda, noticing that the young ones were chatting, nudge Kana's aunt with a big knowing grin. Kana paused till the great Utaemon appeared on the hanamichi.*

'You won't take this seriously, will you?'

'Why not? You're nineteen, and I'm twenty-six. Seems like an eminently satisfactory match.'

'Oh, no! My functional age is way below my real age. Please believe me. It won't work.'

'Don't worry, I can see a baby-green mark on your bottom – speaking, of course, metaphorically,' he chuckled.

'Diss-guss-ting!' Kana felt silly repeating the same word as if it was the extent of her vocabulary, but it was, the whole thing was disgusting.

'I'll take you out in my Triumph sports car one day,' he said.

'Very kind of you,' Kana thanked him politely, but thinking: a useless, goofy son of a capitalist pig. A Triumph sports car, ugh!

During the long intermission the pre-ordered dinner was delivered, in a high pile of lacquer boxes, from a near-by restaurant. Eating dainty bits of delicious food in the gay bustle of the theatre was pleasant, but Kana was determined to cloak herself in a sullen black mood. Every time Mr Masuda junior

---

*A raised passage-way from the main stage area through the auditorium, used by actors for dramatic entrances and exits.

called her 'Kana-san' she felt her stomach turn, but the two ladies giggled with joy.

As the party drifted out of the brightly lit theatre foyer just after half-past ten, Hirano, wildly waving his cap, rushed up to them. 'They're still at it, ma'am. Why the police don't turn the water hoses on them, I'll never understand.'

'It's a non-violent demo, Hirano. The police shouldn't interfere with a peaceful demonstration,' Kana spoke up.

'It's violence all right, miss. Those Commies are occupying public streets and disrupting the traffic.'

Mrs Masuda's chauffeur, equally riled, joined in, while the audience from the Kabuki-za, mouths agape and eyes agog, watched the streetful of marchers as if it were another entertainment.

'Masuda-san,' Kana turned to the young businessman, 'you know I'm supposed to be in the demo myself. I am ...' she, paused to make sure he was listening ... 'I am one of them Zengakuren.'

'I'm sure you are,' he said. 'You'd be an unfeeling fool if you weren't one at the tender age of nineteen.'

'But a bigger fool,' Kana cut him short with an I've-heard-that-before irritation, 'if you are still one at forty. A rotten stale mouthful of a cliché.'

'It was our former Prime Minister Mr Yoshida –' he pronounced the name with reverence – 'who said that.'

'Yoshida the pig,' Kana hissed and was immensely pleased with herself for acting so like Tamiko and Wood Peck. 'He turned Japan into a brash American boom town.'

Masuda junior yawned and stretched with a relaxed smile. He won't even be provoked, so smug at twenty-six! Kana felt like stamping her feet and vowed that never again would she be left standing on the pavement while her friends marched arm in arm down the centre of the street.

It was a disastrous drama season for Waseda: the Waseda Playhouse gave two dull performances of *Death of a Salesman* with a total attendance of only 180. Kodama went bankrupt in the

158

middle of rehearsing *The Importance of Being Earnest* and could not refund the pre-sold tickets. INTER, the largest and the most radically left-wing company, fared better with Hauptmann's *The Weavers*, but it was only by dint of their intensively sought group bookings from factories and trade-union supporters.

Things were not going any better with Free Stage either. The advance-ticket sale had been sluggish. None of the members had time or energy left to ring up friends and relatives, besides with only three weeks to go before the opening, the authors were still adding extra scenes to the already four-hour-long play.

Finally, the exasperated director, Bobchin, threw his script on the floor and lashed out.

'For God's sake, Otani, it's your job as producer to stop their creative diarrhoea. If they had any sense, they should re-read all Shakespeare's and Chekhov's plays, take sleeping pills, go to bed, and never wake up. What more can they say, what else can they possibly add? Mediocre talents should learn that brevity and economy are their sole virtue. Now, Otani, go on, tell *them*!'

Otani, in his filthy worn-out mac, sat on a pile of old newspapers and listened, palming his head in continual circular movements like a cat before rain. When he stopped, he said, 'Right, I'll call a meeting with the authors.'

Bobchin stopped pacing the floor, horror-stricken.

'What, with Roppa-san and Octopus-Eight-san? Must I be there too?'

'Of course, we'll all have to be there,' said Otani, not without uneasiness.

Seniority. It was curious how seniority like a stone collecting moss gathered such privilege and deference in a community as militantly progressive as Free Stage. The complex rules on the use of the honorific 'san', for instance, governed entirely by the order of seniority according to length of membership, were observed by all members with scrupulous care.

The following morning, after much heated exchange, all the red pencils were out on Science Hill. Eight whole scenes were deleted and a great deal of dialogue was pruned, till the play was

159

reduced to just over three hours. As those who had their lines cut wailed and sulked in protest, Otani disclosed his intention of adding two new scenes, of rape and of torture.

Miss Takashima flatly refused to take part in the rape scene, even if it were only to be simulated and played in a darkened upstage corner. The scene had to be re-jigged for Denim, who had no such scruples. As for the torture scene, Minami, playing an idealist samurai who later joins the peasant uprising, was to be 'beaten with whips and burnt by a red hot iron rod'.

To the expected attack from some members, 'Nothing but cheap, heinous commercialism!', Otani laconically pointed out what an uphill struggle it was to sell an unfashionable commodity such as *Konminto*, a non-classic, non-Western, home-made play about silkworm breeders.

'But we could sell it and survive financially, if *you* would help us.' He paused, staring at every anxious face in the Circle. 'You may not like this, but this is what I'm going to enforce on every active member: a norm of selling twenty tickets each. Anyone who scores less will be fined a proportional penalty and disgraced at the Circle. A graph showing the sales result to date of every member will be put up on the HQ wall starting first thing tomorrow morning. In lurid orange ink.'

Kana, back at her frenetic routine of scavenging, deputizing, fly-posting and running errands, was told to put on her Sunday best and accost the university population with *Konminto* tickets on the main square. 'And at the performances we want you to be an usherette cum ice-cream seller cum first-aid nurse in charge of kids who might suddenly decide to have a bleeding nose or a fit of crying,' Beret told her. 'I'm afraid you'll only be able to snatch the odd moment to watch the performance.'

'Oh, Beret-san,' Kana pouted. 'I'm treated like a blinkered drudge. Where lurks the art?'

'Ah-uhm . . .' Kana's recruiter who had promised her a rainbow solemnly shut then re-opened his pop-eyes. 'When a man shaves his head and joins a monastery his day begins before sunrise with sweeping the pebbled garden. All day long he goes on cleaning lavatories and scrubbing floors. At night he helps the drunken monks to their cells. The celestial lesson is the rake and the floor cloth. Got that?'

No, not quite, but Kana had to admit that perhaps she too had derived as much spiritual fulfilment and stimulus from hard labour as from her nebulous proximity to art.

Otani's diktat worked a miracle. The four performances of *Konminto* grossed 81,540 yen, including the revenue from the programme ads and the sale of sweets, with the net profit of 40,220 yen. Beret said he saw stars every time he whispered the figure to himself in bed.

The *Waseda Sun*, normally a fence-sitting conservative paper, gave it a splash headline: 'FREE STAGE'S ORIGINAL PLAY BOTH MOVING AND ENTERTAINING', and the *Waseda Avant Garde's* critic praised the production as 'one of the most significant achievements of the left-wing theatre movement, student or professional'.

The morning after the last *Konminto* performance Kana woke up at seven from habit, then, realizing there was no urgent work waiting for her at the Warehouse, just an undefined vapid and pointless long day, she fell back on her sleeping mat with a groan of horror.

Kana had not been able to go to the party at the Twenty-Fifth Hour in Shinjuku with the company because of the Jardin curfew, and was the only person to emerge in the Warehouse back yard before noon. She sat lost in the huge clutter of scenery and props now waiting to be stripped and re-used for future productions. At about two Myshkin trotted in. The rest of the company, he said, were undoubtedly still wallowing in hangovers or morning-after-stupor. It was hot and bright, late June, summer almost. Kana could not help thinking of the long days and evenings of holidays at home, the boredom and languor oozing out of the walls and the floors of the house she had grown up in. . . .

'I want to work, Mysh-san. Want to act.' Kana blurted out. 'Scrub, paint, anything.'

'Try the mud road,' said Myshkin.

Senior members of Free Stage called their summer tour in the remote provinces 'the mud road' with infinite yearning and affection. Kana had heard Wood Peck declare – and she was not a gusher – 'I'd go even if I had to carry wardrobe baskets and walk on foot from village to village!' and Bobchin had been saying only a few days earlier: 'Graduating from Waseda has one heart-breaking disadvantage: no more mud road.'

'Oh, no, they'll never take me.' Kana said, but her pulse began beating faster. If only they would. The mud road!

'Why not? Nothing attempted, nothing done.' Myshkin sat up, his eyes on Kana. 'No harm in trying, anyhow, is there?'

Kana could feel every faculty in her that was capable of willing turn diamond hard.

The mud road repertory committee chose *The Fox and the Grapes* by a Brazilian playwright, Guilherme Figueiredo. Kana was mortified by the rumour that it did not call for a large cast. As with everything else, the order of seniority was strictly observed and Kana could not get to read a mimeographed copy of the play till everyone else had done so first.

On the 16th of June the staff for the mud road was announced:

Producer:	Beret with two assistants, Single Cell and Denim, working under him during the three-week rehearsal period in Tokyo
Director:	Otani, assisted by Minami during the Tokyo rehearsals
Company and Stage manager:	Myshkin
Scenery:	Asano and three assistants
Costume:	Dre-Ma
Props:	Yamada
Lighting:	Oka and one assistant

Kana hoped that this meant at least Single Cell and Denim were out of the running for the two female parts. Since Asano never took a girl in his crew on the road and Oka had his well-trained assistant, Takado, the only possibility left for Kana was

162

to get one or the other of the two female parts, but as she prayed to her ancestors that seemed beyond their most willing aid. . . .

Kana finally got to read the play. The time, the sixth century, BC; the place, the island of Samos. It was about Aesop.

Xantos, a bogus philosopher, buys Aesop to amuse his young wife, Clea, who, languishing from the boredom and futility of her sequestered life, spends all day listening to the gossip brought back from the market place by her slave, Melita. Aesop tells Clea his stories of freedom and of love, and she listens with her whole being suddenly stirred.

'Clea is me before Free Stage.' Kana snatched at this thought. 'I could play the part, I am the part!'

As she sat by her Jardin window, imagining herself clad in a sun-bleached white garment of a hundred pleats, she could not see why anyone should refuse her the part: I'll be so good in it, she thought. In the scene where Clea begs her ugly slave to love her and to take her away, Kana was determined that she could shed floods of real hot tears at every performance. And at the close of the play when Aesop chooses to die for freedom, Kana could already feel the hard dusty stage floor under her cheeks as she lay prostrate in lament.

So, there it was: it was either Clea or the oblivion and summer lassitude of Rokko Hills.

Kana chanced upon Myshkin outside Takadanobaba station. The end of *Konminto* had meant a break-up of the 'family life': since he had gone back to his home-tutoring *arbeit*, they had not lunched together.

'I want Clea!' Kana hauled him inside her umbrella.

'Can't blackmail me, I'm just one of many on the committee.' He laughed.

'I love the play. I love the part. I never wanted anything so badly in my life. Why is the casting announcement so delayed?'

'Otani-san's being troublesome, trying to ram down our throat something that is positively hair-raising. . . .' Myshkin suddenly stopped.

'Yes, go on.' Kana clinched up to him.

'No, I won't. I've said much too much already.' He then

looked Kana in the face, blinking fretfully, as if his eyelashes were coming off their roots. 'Tell me, Balloon, are you going to join the twenty-fifth of June demo? What have. . . .'

Kana had been waiting for this. Pressing his shoulder-blade with the handle of her umbrella, she cut him short.

'Joining, yes, I'll be there!'

'Oh, splendid, Balloon. Hope it won't pour like this.' He shot outside her umbrella and ran away in the pelting rain, his white celery-stalk ankles and feet dripping wet in his geta* sandals.

The alarm clock went off at seven. Kana rolled off her sleeping mat and opened the shutters. Rain. Black, glistening streets and burbling gutters of a sodden metropolis. She put on her oldest washed-out blue jeans, a white jersey, shrunken too small for her sister Yoko, two pairs of cotton socks one on top of the other against sore feet, and her geranium-pink raincoat. She plaited her hair and tied a kerchief round her head. She shoved a few 100 yen notes, a handkerchief and trolley bus season ticket into her trousers pocket.

Kana was the first down for breakfast. By the time Miss Arashi in her electric-blue satin dressing-gown with Poti perched on her hip bone strutted into the dining room with a strident order: 'Take off the raincoat and the kerchief at table, Miss Toda, where're your manners?' Kana had finished consuming every source of calories allocated to her. She shot to her feet, and bowing in the direction of the canine growl, said good morning and turned to leave the room.

'Don't forget your umbrella. The meteo-man says it'll pour all day.' The blue mountain followed Kana to the hall and made sure she took her nylon umbrella with pink raindrops printed all over it.

Waseda main square at 9 a.m. One umbrella to five bodies, several hundred umbrellas formed a roof from one end of the square to the other. A steady straight downpour tapped and tapped at the umbrellas, nylon kerchiefs and the tight cluster

*Wooden platform sandals raised on ridge heels.

of hydrangeas that bloomed round Dr Okuma's statue. Kana's plastic rain coat hardened in the rain and the colours of the hand-painted banners began running in rainbow-coloured streaks.

Before marching downtown to join the People's Movement's rally, the chairman of Waseda ZGR, a dishevelled scrawny young man, delivered his speech, an unbroken string of incoherent shouts and snarls. No one seemed to take much heed of the orator. A number of boys were either humming or whistling the current No. 1 hit song, 'You're so old and I'm so young, oh, please, Di-a-nah . . .' A Paul Anka.

'It always rains on a demo day, always, always rains . . .' grumbled Beret, looking important with a ZGR marshal's red armband and a whistle hung from his neck, as he pushed and pulled the rank-and-file into neat six-in-a-row lines.

'Who's that pink dotted nonsense!' he shouted through his soggy cardboard megaphone. Kana pulled in her neck like a rapped turtle.

'Damn it, it's Balloon. Don't you know that the riot police go for eye-catching females to break up the scrums? For goodness' sake, boys, put her right in the middle of the row and keep her there, will you?'

Otani and Abe, both with the ZGR executives' blue armbands, rushed up to Beret, whispered a few urgent words and rushed off again. Beret with a glassy-eyed, almost scared look bit his whistle between his teeth and blew it. Immediately, every red armband on the square followed suit.

One, two, one, two . . . three thousand Waseda marchers in orderly columns started to file out of the square. A ZGR car, a dilapidated Datsun, smothered with slogans and topped with a huge snail-shaped loudspeaker, crawled alongside the scrimmage line, inciting a *sprechchor*. 'Down with ANPO!' the raucous voice exploded into the microphone.

'Down with ANPO!' The rank-and-file shouted back as loud as their lungs allowed.

'Kishi out!' yelled the louspeaker.

'Kishi out!' returned the massive roar.

When the *sprechchor* slogans ran out of steam, the red armbands led the marchers in song. Mostly working men's songs with catchy tunes and heroic refrains, but now and again sentimental Russian folksongs in a minor key.

The rain turned finer and soon became only a convolution of mist. With puddles of water inside her shoes. Kana folded the umbrella, wrung the kerchief, and sang with greater elan.

As they neared the centre of the city, from almost every major avenue a group of demonstrators streamed out and fell neatly into line with the students, swaying their sodden banners in response to the welcoming cheers. Kana was mightily affected by this flamboyant show of brotherhood in dissent. To her it was as good as a scene from *The Battleship Potemkin*. Images passed flashing by: Odessa; wailing women in kerchiefs; and that black pram shooting down the white steps! Tears swelled in her eyes as she stepped bravely forward, kicking up water and her galoshes making funny squelchy noises.

'Easy, Balloon, easy, or you won't make it to the Hibiya Park,' Yamada on her right cautioned her.

'Oh, I'm all right. I'm fine.' Kana kicked up more muddy water.

The People's Movement's central rally, after such a jubilant march, turned out to be a dreadful disappointment. The General Secretary of the Socialist Party, flanked by the People's Movement organizers and a dozen executive officers of the almighty SOHYO, the Japanese Trade Union Council, sat on the podium, all looking exceedingly pleased with themselves, with yellow artificial chrysanthemums in their lapels, and took their allotted turns at the microphone 'boring the pants off everyone', as one ZGR red armband aptly put it. One extremely rubicund and gross SOHYO representative belched repeatedly and finally dozed off, undoubtedly suffering the after-effects of too good a lunch. This scene incensed the famished and thirsty demonstrators and they hissed and booed till the guilty gentleman had to be woken up by nudges from his colleagues.

Free Stagers soon turned their backs on the podium and either chatted or listened to the Afternoon Hit Parade on Rudo's transistor radio, and waited anxiously for a purveyor of any kind of nourishment to approach them. Eventually a sprightly little man in a white smock, chanting 'ANPO bun, sweet, soft ANPO bun, only ten yen, ANPO bun!' hove in sight but he was doing such a roaring trade that, most provokingly, he ran out of stock just before reaching the ZGR lines.

At 6 p.m. the police permit for the rally expired and in spite of the chilly, yawning reception the congregation had given them, the Socialist Party and SOHYO leaders burst into three banzai cheers, followed by a People's Movement official who crooned into the microphone, bending towards the students.

'We urge you, student friends, to be sensible and responsible. Disperse peacefully, please, and at once. The police permit expires in. . . .'

'Piss off, grandpa!' someone heckled and even Kana did not hesitate to join the rude jeering and hissing that followed.

As soon as the 'grandpas' and 'sensible and responsible' members of the Movement had drifted away to beer halls and coffee houses in light-hearted twos and threes, the ZGR red armbands got busy. They ran up and down along the lines.

'Scrum! Scrum! Six in a row!'

'ANPO hantai!*' the first *sprechchor* came from the ZGR loudspeaker. 'ANPO hantai!'

'No more US bases! No more US bases!'

They screamed with renewed vehemence and the one-two, one-two whistles jerked their tired legs into action. The clouded sky darkened early; by the time the head of the ZGR lines began pouring into the Tiger's Gate intersection, the famous neon signs of Max Factor, National Cash Register and North West Orient Airlines were aglow. The students quickly filled the vast square and for a few minutes stood still.

Kana was still gaping at the clever Max Factor twinkles, when an urgent whisper zoomed at her from the row behind:

'But, we are not going to "zigzag", are we?'

His voice was choking, and Kana felt her palms turn cold and clammy, suddenly aware of what was coming. I haven't come to

*'We are against!'

167

zigzag! Later perhaps, but not today, it's my first demo! Kana looked round. There was the Ministry of Education building right in front of her, the Self-Defence Army and the Police Headquarters on either side of the intersection, and the Foreign Ministry's new building was only a stone's throw away. If one had to zigzag, one would without hesitation choose *here*, it was the ideal spot.

The ZGR loudspeaker continued, ranting slogans, the voice cracking in hysteria. The traffic policemen's whistles became short-breathed and buses, cars, trolleys and trams honked and hooted in mounting irritation; the nerve centre of the metropolitan traffic at the height of the evening rush hour was now completely blocked.

'Look,' Yamada yelled. 'There're our friends, the Fourth Riot Task Force, with their armoured trucks behind them. Hundreds of the bastards, look!'

Kana could not look. She was much too frightened. She had seen the Fourth Riot Task Force at work in news films and that had been terrifying enough. It was unbelievable that she, Kana Toda, was about to zigzag there and then, surrounded by the Fourth Riot Task Force!

Beret hurriedly began collecting Free Stagers' purses, watches and anything else of value and shoved them into his large megaphone.

'Balloon! Where's Balloon? If she's still in the line, push her out at once!' In the deafening clamour of the square, Kana caught only her name but knew it was Otani. 'There, Yamada, let go of Balloon.' His voice was now directly behind her.

Once released from the stranglehold of the scrimmage, Kana felt herself like a skinned rabbit and turned towards Otani's voice. Snatching the megaphone now full of valuables from Beret, Otani grabbed Kana by the scruff of the neck and spun her round in the direction of the North West Orient neon sign.

'Come on, push, no argument, to the pavement. Push!' The mass of wet human bodies was so solid and resistant that when at last Kana was yanked out of it, she collapsed at the foot of the onlookers and gasped with her head between her knees. But

Otani quickly gathered her up in his arms and squeezed their way into a space in the doorway alcove of the Noritake China Shop which had its shutters down. He then unbuttoned the top of Kana's raincoat and shoved the bulging megaphone inside the yoke above the belt. Looking oddly top-heavy, like a kangaroo mother, Kana stood hugging herself and the megaphone.

'Listen carefully. Whatever you do, don't move from here till Wood Peck joins you. I want both of you to be out of the zigzag. And I mean *out*.' A tap on the megaphone and he plunged back into the mob. Kana's mouth was dry, her tongue felt like sandpaper, out of sheer fright she perspired in cold sweat.

For a time the students stood ominously still and silent; the armed police drew their truncheons; TV news crews bent low behind their cameras; the police chief was no longer sweetly caressing his microphone with his 'Dear students . . .', crowds of spectators stood expectantly on the pavement; impotent drivers had stopped their engines. A spiky uneasy silence hung over the square.

'Zeeg-zaag!' The first battle cry came from the ZGR loud-speaker. Heads dropped, knees bent, eyes dipped, they were ready.

'Go!'

Six shoulders and heads in each row pointing to the right, the whole square charged forward, four steps to the right and four steps to the left. The movement forward had an irreversible force, a will of its own. Waves of demonic frenzy accelerated at every sharp zigzag turn. No more *sprechchor*, no time for that. Mouths were open but rigid, capable only of short breaths, and eyes were glazed, oblivious of danger. Right, 2, 3, 4! Left, 2, 3, 4! Once in a zigzag, foaming at the mouth and pain distorting their faces, they could not stop. Kana felt her friends' choked lungs and clammy foreheads . . . and there she was, once more, an onlooker, safely on the pavement.

'Balloon, Balloon!'

Wood Peck, looking like a space monster in her transparent nylon rain jacket, thrashed her way up to Kana, heedless of the commotion she was causing amongst the crowd on the pavement. With a whining cry of relief Kana hugged the megaphone to her chest.

'Don't look so scared, Balloon. They'll soon stop. Can't go on for ever,' Wood Peck yelled. 'Besides, the Riot Police won't be provoked, not tonight. Last time the TV showed so much of their savagery in action, that tonight they've been told to play it cool. Come, follow me; I know every nook and cranny around here.'

Wood Peck had surmised correctly: the girls had sat on the station step hardly more than half an hour, before the marchers began trudging into the brightly lit tube station. Soon the Free Stagers, worn out and muddy and voiceless, lined up to receive their valuables back from Kana. In a foreign film, Kana thought, I'd be embracing each of them with hot kisses, sniffles and all the flowers of emotion, but being proper Japanese they only nodded to each other rather sheepishly.

'Hurrah, Balloon!' Yamada was at the end of the queue. 'Come to Kachusha for hot coffee.'

'I'm afraid she can't, Yamada-san,' Myshkin, who had been quietly standing behind Kana, cut in, pulling her aside. 'She's coming with me to the Twenty-fifth Hour.'

'Balloon? Twenty-fifth Hour?' Yamada stared at Kana, then at Myshkin, speechless. After an audible gulp of air he managed to say, 'OK. Well, so long. . . .'

'How sweet of you, Mysh-san, is this to celebrate my first demo?' Kana asked, but worrying inside: he shouldn't waste his hard-earned money on me. Twenty-fifth Hour sounds terribly decadent and expensive. . . .

'W-well, yes, it's a sort of celebration. . . .' Myshkin stammered, blinking faster and scratching behind his ear.

Throughout the underground ride he was the one who did the talking, gabbling his words, breathless almost, as if he were being whipped to keep on chattering. The Twenty-fifth Hour was, he said, like so many post-war bars and cafés, owned by one of those depraved ex-aristocrats, deplaced, decadent, if you like, good for nothing else now but for playing the flute of all things, with his concubine at the cash register who keeps the wretch on a tight string, and so on. . . .

The sky was washed clean of rain clouds as they stepped out of

Shinjuku tube station; the district of bargain-priced pleasures shimmered like an illuminated aquarium.

Kana was about to say, 'Why, Mysh-san, you're such a chatterbox tonight!', when he pulled open the bar's imitation log-cabin door, 'Here we are, Balloon,' and strode straight into the darkened, steamy atmosphere of alcohol and cigarette and whispers. Kana followed him with gingerly small steps. Round the corner and in front of an inanimate fireplace Myshkin stopped, turning to Kana with a mischievous grin, and there at a round table who else but Otani, Beret and Abe were knocking their heads together!

'*Un café au lait* for this ragamuffin, *s'il vous plait!*' Beret seemed to be in a state of happy jitters and fussed over Kana like a mother hen, bouncing up and down in his chair. Otani, as always hiding half of his face in his hand, did not betray any emotion, while Abe looked gruesomely preoccupied. As the minutes of excruciating uneasiness passed, Kana sat on the edge of her chair without daring to breathe.

'OK, it's all yours.' Otani nodded to Beret, who swayed delightedly and stretched his neck so as to place his Adam's apple above his collar.

'Balloon, we, the mud road Casting Committee, have come to accept an . . . an outrageous choice for our leading lady. Buddha help us, our director is a lunatic, Balloon, it's you.'

Kana slapped down her right hand on her abdomen where the warm milk and coffee curdled at once. It had been her sacred wish, to be given a part on the mud road, an obsession that had virtually distorted her every waking hour. She would not let anyone make a joke of it. She now hid behind a mask of disbelief and turned to Otani for his confirmation, but trust him at this crucial moment to down his drink with his head thrown back and his eyes wide open staring at the bottom of the tall glass.

'Balloon, you are to play Clea, understand? The most coveted role of all!' Beret edged forward, shriller at every word; but Kana sat there motionless, incapable of believing.

'Beret, you'd better make sure she gets her parents' consent.

We can't have a drama a minute before the train pulls out.'

Without looking up Otani swirled the ice cubes in his empty glass.

'Oh, yes, that's right, Balloon, you do just that. Your parents. You can persuade them, can't you?'

The question of her parents' consent blew a cold blast of reality into the fairy tale. Kana began nodding her head frantically as if her neck had been put on a coiled spring.

3

When Kana woke up the next morning it was quite unlike a thousand previous mornings she had known. She was someone springing up from the sleeping mat who had the part of Clea. She brushed her hair, waited for a bus, walked, looked, sat with the glorious knowledge that she had been chosen to go on the mud road.

'Didn't I tell you, you have repose, huh? And don't you worry about those eggheads. Once on the road, it's the practical chaps who run the show. We'll look after you, Balloon Top.'

Asano was overjoyed at the incredible news. To him honour awarded to a member of his crew was his.

'It was Otani-san who told you about my holding my head still, wasn't it?' Kana retorted ungraciously

'Never mind who said it. You've got it and what's more the part. I am delighted.' Asano patted Kana on the head. She laughed at this and could taste the sun pouring into her boldly open mouth.

The cast list had been pinned on the HQ wall since 10 a.m. Most of the senior members considered the casting of Clea the height of irresponsibility and one of them said to Kana with an anxious, condoling look: 'It's really not fair to you, is it? Such a demanding role and only three weeks' rehearsals. It's short enough time for anyone of us, let alone for . . . er . . . . Otani-san shouldn't have done this to you. It's not only mad, it's cruel.'

Go on, go on, say what you like. I don't give a damn, the part's mine! Kana ground her teeth under a fixed polite smile.

Another surprise in the casting was Ozawa, who had been given the part of a slave called Ethiopia.

'Big deal,' he grumbled but was quite unable to conceal his joy at being in the mud road company. 'I wanted Aesop, and what do I get instead but a part I could have played with a golf ball in my mouth!' The part called for not a single spoken line but pots of black body make-up and gold and silver chain round his ankles.

Bobchin, the *Konminto* director, who had postponed graduating next spring for the sake of being once more on the mud road, was to play Xantos. Rudo was Agnostos, the handsome captain from Athens. Melita, Clea's maid was to be played by Wood Peck, and as everyone had forecast Sta-san, who was also an expert at make-up, had been chosen for the hideously deformed slave, Aesop.

Now, Kana had to tackle her parents. After much oscilation she decided to write: 'My most honourable Father and Mother. I could not bear the thought of having an argument on the phone, so I am writing to tell you. . . .' She told them frankly about her new life with Free Stage and about the great honour bestowed on her of playing a leading role on the summer tour. 'I assure you, it is not a troupe of "beggars-on-river-bank". They are intelligent, idealistic, hard-working young people. I know I shall miss a large part of the summer holiday at home, but I promise I shan't be doing anything you will be ashamed of. Please don't be too angry with me.' She made sure she put much emphasis on the spiritual and ennobling side of the whole affair.

Mrs Toda telephoned Kana the very next evening.

'Kana-chan . . . Your letter, why so dramatic,' began Mrs Toda and Kana, detecting an amused little chuckle in her mother's voice, felt rivers of worry drain away.

'Oh, Mother. . . .'

'An irrevocable decision, in search of my *self*, commitment to Large Sincerity . . . Honestly, Kana-chan, you write such a dreadful Japanese. Anyhow, we are not going to disown you or send a band of strong armed men to fetch you home. I am worried, of course, but you won't alter your mind, I know. Your father? Oh, he's taken it very sensibly. He likes the idea that you're playing the lead. "Not a bit player, my daughter," he says. Since he goes to his Hiroshima office so frequently, you must write and let him know when you are going to be there, so that he can make a visit to coincide with yours. Ah, yes, I rang Aunt Sachi and asked her to give you the six thousand yen you asked for.'

'Was she horrified?'

'You know Aunt Sachi. Everything horrifies her. Life horrifies her. That you have to grow up horrifies her. Send her a postcard from every town you visit. Oh, yes, by the way, according to Auntie, the young man has told his mother that he'd like to wait.'

'What? Wait for what?' Kana said, bristling at once.

'Well, this is again what Auntie told me, he said till you stop being too young.'

'Please, Mother, don't let him do anything of the sort! How patronizing! Wait? How dare he?'

'Shh! You're hurting my ear. We'll see, we'll see. . . . But there is one thing you must understand, Kana: a match-maker gets just as worked up as the girl herself; that's the classic case during the overture to an arranged marriage. So, whatever you do, do be nice to Auntie. She means well. Incidentally, why don't you stay with her after Jardin-En closes for the summer?'

'Over my uncle's dead body!' Kana yelled, for effect.

Mrs Toda laughed and chuckled like a sensible adult who knows when not to press a point.

'All right, then, stay at an air-conditioned hotel. Heat doesn't agree with my summer baby.'

Before going to bed, Kana faced what she judged to be the direction of Rokko Hills and prayed to her ancestors for her parents' long life and serenity, but still her guilty conscience troubled her, especially in the light of her mother's most elastic and generous understanding. As she lay in twilight of sleep she felt mean and small that she had concealed from her mother that she had already accepted Wood Peck's invitation to share her room in the slum district of Ikebukuro.

The last day of spring term, Kana tidied her room, smothered the woollen clothes with moth balls, packed the basic summer necessities for the mud road in two large furoshiki bundles, said *au revoir* to Miss Arashi and the staff and was out of the place by midday.

'Why waste money? Come to my place. Spacious enough for three,' was how Wood Peck had described it to Kana, but it turned out to be just an eight-mat-sized room with a narrow wooden terrace opening on to a tiny mean patch of earth, fringed with pebbles, where Wood Peck grew tomatoes and scallions. The only flower in the house was a solitary carnation in a milk bottle in the toilet. This primitive toilet was shared with the proprietress, a war widow of fifty-five who worked as a life-insurance saleswoman. Kept fastidiously clean though it was, the combination of its intrinsic odour and the camphor deodorant was so strong that one minute inside it made Kana weep and sneeze. Kana searched everywhere in the tiny paper house, but no bath was in sight.

'What are we going to do? There's no bath!' Kana said, slightly hysterical.

'What do you think we do?' Wood Peck said blithely. 'There's a very decent public bath just two blocks down.'

Kana turned pale at this. To visualize herself being simmered in one huge kettle with strange bodies, their germs, skin and hair, and to scrub herself in the public gaze!

'Come on, don't be so Balloonish,' said Wood Peck. 'Just think that your mud road is starting right now.'

The Breath of Pine Bath House turned out to be perfectly decent, but Wood Peck, whose virtues did not include sensitivity, behaved quite atrociously with Kana. Right in the centre of the white tiled arena she would bark at Kana: 'Oh, stop it, Balloon, the more you hide, the more we want to look at you!' How Kana writhed and cringed in embarrassment, and Wood Peck never even noticed it.

175

But, Kana did not regret for a second that she had not gone to an air-conditioned box of a hotel room. Wood Peck herself was a remarkable experience for her. Kana followed her example in everything with something approaching educational reverence, spreading their pleated skirts underneath the sleeping mats every night, putting each pleat most meticulously in place and sleeping as still as coffins on them, thus doing away with ironing in the morning. Before breakfast they folded and put away their battered thin sleeping mats; swept and scrubbed the tatami floor on all fours with a tightly squeezed wet rag; and washed down the wooden terrace. Breakfast consisted of tea, slices of bread appetizingly burnt on the gas fire, margarine, and raw carrots. Kana paid half the cost of food, electricity, gas and rent. Wood Peck insisted on doing all the shopping and cooking herself, and ever since Kana's arrival she had produced nothing else but calf's liver, chicken gizzards and other irregular parts of fowl or animal, spiced with ginger and soy sauce, calling them 'stamina food'.

'You've got to last, Balloon. We can't afford to travel an understudy.'

Although her taste buds squirmed in revolt even to think of these innards wriggling down her gullet, Kana ate them, for the sake of surviving the rigours of the mud road.

The first two days of rehearsal concentrated on the background research. On the second day, while Ozawa, whom everyone now simply called Ethiopia, was reading his report on the historical and political situation of pre-Periclean Greece, Denim sneaked into the rehearsal room without any apparent mission from her chief, Beret, and at the end of the morning rehearsals came with Wood Peck and Kana to Mother's Apron for cold noodles served in a small bamboo basket.

'You know Tamiko didn't tell him? Went off and had it done all by herself?' Denim told Wood Peck with an air of conspiracy, ignoring Kana as if she were not there.

'No comment.' Wood Peck shot a hard warning glance across the table but Denim went on breathlessly.

'The last time Minami-san paid. He can afford it, my good-

176

ness, after all, his father's a Mitsui Chemical executive. But, this time, for some cuckoo reason, she has made a lone martyr of herself. Imagine, most men would be only too pleased to find the problem so neatly dealt with, but he's carrying on like a lunatic. Morally castrated, he moans. . . .'

'Enough, Denim!' Wood Peck cut in. 'I have no patience with those maladjusted intellectuals.' She flung up her hand and waved it, calling for more ice water. As Kana listened, sucking in the noodles as noiselessly as possible, everything became clear: only four days before, as the last Circle of the spring term broke up, Tamiko clutched at Kana's elbow and said, 'Proof of the pudding is in mal-digestion.' Cool and angular. Since she was prone to such irrelevant utterances, Kana waited for what she had to say next.

'Do you have money?' asked Tamiko.

'Money? How much?'

'Five thousand,' Tamiko said looking exquisitely bored.

'Five thousand? Yes, I do.'

'May I borrow it from you?'

'Of course. I'll bring it tomorrow. Will tomorrow do?'

'Fine.' Only then did Tamiko let go of Kana's elbow.

The following day Tamiko took the money without so much as a thank you but rather spleenfully as if it were Kana who was borrowing the money, and mentioned not a word about returning it. For the rest of the day Kana worried if she had in some way offended Tamiko.

Now I know what my 5,000 yen was for, Kana said to herself: sex and abortion and all that!

Kana had known her uncle would be at home on the Star Festival* evening; but the temptation of a leisurely hot bath in

*According to an ancient Chinese legend once a year on the seventh night of the seventh month the Shepherd from the east coast and the Weaver from the west coast of the Milky Way meet. To celebrate their annual rendezvous a tall shapely branch of bamboo is decorated with cut-out stars, pictures of seasonal flowers and fruits, which by custom is later thrown into a river in the hope that the paper-festooned bamboo will reach the Milky Way in a summer night's dream.

private had got the better of her. She accepted the invitation to dinner.

She arrived early, took a heavenly hot bath, and changed into a yukata. Just as she was coming downstairs, the 'arranged marriage cad' arrived with his parents and Kana went straight on to a pouting strike. Besides the three Masudas, there were Mr and Mrs Shinoda, Aunt Sachi's tea-ceremony friend, and her two giggling Sacred Heart daughters, aged thirteen and sixteen, whose prissiness in adding honorifics to everything, even to shoes, mustard and napkins ('O-napkin') irritated Kana to such a degree that she felt like pouring the soup over them, just to find out what then they would have to say.

To complete the dreariness of the evening, there was Kana's uncle in all his repulsive entirety, presiding over the dinner, an endless procession of dishes, each just a dainty mouthful or two, which in fact took far longer to wait for and then admire its rare or seasonal ingredients than to eat. Mrs Masuda and Mr Shinoda, a suave, plummy-voiced diplomat, did most of the talking in between dishes, while Mr Masuda senior, a taciturn, pale man, emptied cup after cup of sake, turning increasingly paler but remaining for ever sober.

The young man who had been made to sit next to Kana must have felt the full blast of her frosty rejection. Having tried one or two opening gambits, he concentrated his attention on the Sacred Heart girls, and Kana spent the rest of the evening watching her poor aunt who sat there like a masticating tombstone with her doe-eyes anxiously set on her husband, for Mr Itoh was making no effort whatsoever to be pleasant.

'How I envy you,' he said to Mr Masuda at one point, 'you have your own two sons to leave your business to.' Then, rudely pointing to his wife with a thrust of his chin, he went on, 'The son this woman produced turned out an unfilial ingrate. Even a dog obeys the master who feeds him.'

For a moment a stunned silence fell round the table, to be softly broken by Mrs Itoh herself: 'I am sorry. It is all my fault.'

It was not her fault at all. Their son, Shozo, had declined an executive position in his father's firm and had gone to Hokkaido

178

to work on a farm, only because he would not work cheek-by-jowl with Yuki's bastard who already held a senior position in the firm.

For the rest of the evening Mrs Itoh kept on taking the blame for everything that her husband found fault with. She even had to apologize for the anti-mosquito incense that made him sneeze. Under any other circumstances the guests would have enjoyed the pleasant after-dinner languor, sitting on the terrace, wordlessly fanning themselves with large round Chinese fans with the lights turned off in the room behind them, but the host's boorish behaviour had completely spoilt the evening and in a short time the Shinodas rose to go, a cue immediately taken up by the Masudas. As the goodbyes faded away, Kana ran upstairs to collect her rehearsal clothes, script and notebooks and put them in an old mountaineering knapsack of Shozo's that she was to borrow for the mud road. Remembering Wood Peck's instruction to bring back all the goodies she could lay her hands on, Kana went down to the kitchen and with the help of Hirano's wife filled a furoshiki with whatever edibles there were left over from the dinner. As Hirano took her knapsack and loot to the car, Kana went back to say a final good night to her uncle and aunt.

The light was still turned off in the front rooms and on the terrace. Except for the brittle crackling noise of the bamboo leaves it was quiet, and the air was sultry with burning incense. Kana glided softly over the tatami floor towards the terrace that glowed in a faint pale reflection of the sky, and then beyond some scattered silk cushions she saw them.

A grisly sight. Kana stood wide-eyed with horror, feeling not only her hair but her skin and nails all stand on end.

Her dear aunt lay sideways across him with an amorphous abandon like a drowned body, with her sleeves, her disturbed kimono and her untied obi billowing all round her. Her left arm limply lolled round Mr Itoh's neck, her right hand held upright the large Chinese fan. Her eyes were squeezed shut, her lips pursed askew and there was a furrow of strain on her brow. As she let out a strange throttled 'Ah', her body writhed

179

and coiled to a further submission in his arms, and her Chinese fan tilted low.

Kana saw that her uncle's thick red arm was thrust right into the folds of her aunt's kimono. She took a jolting step backward; their eyes leapt up. Her uncle squared his shoulders, his thick lips wet, his eyes bloodshot, and gasped audibly. Defiantly, he kept his hand where it was. Her aunt – perhaps in Kana's wishful eyes – seemed almost totally oblivious of the fact that her large fan no longer hid her but lay beside their grotesque bodies.

'Good night, I'm going.' Kana bowed and turned on her heel.

'Stop! Watch your arse!' The music of Kana's summer of '59: Otani cracking his voice and banging at his head. 'Slug! Don't waddle out of the chair as if your tail got stuck. Hand your lyre to Melita, what's a slave for? And, Clea, when you rise, rise like an iris, not like a sack of potatoes. Once more from the top!'

'Stand by.' Myshkin opened his arms wide apart. The 30-degree centigrade afternoon was sizzling, glueing Kana's fingers to the papier-mâché lyre and her poreless acetate rehearsal robe against her legs.

'Go!' Myshkin's palms slammed into each other. Bobchin, dressed in a white undershirt and an old sheet pleated and belted round the waist, ushered in Rudo for the fifth time and, showing no sign of weariness or irritation, went through the business of introducing to his wife the handsome captain from Athens.

'Honour your guest, woman. Wash his feet in scented oil,' he ordered Kana, who got up, and hardly had she taken a step, before the scene flopped again like a torn kite.

'Clea! Spine!' Otani seized the rickety desk before him and shook it, cigarette ends and ashes spurting out of old tin lids. 'Spine! How often must I tell you, dumb clod, you're only as beautiful as your spine. Look at you, Balloon, you're so tentative, so puny, so earth-bound, an egg dropped on the floor! Come on, believe beautiful, soar beautiful, and let go. And one more thing, pull up your anus as close to your navel as possible; where they meet beings life. OK?'

Once again, 'Stand by, go!' and Myshkin's red-hot palms

180

clashed together. Bobchin gave the cue and Kana crossed the stage to fetch her basin and oil props. As soon as the men had seated themselves, Rudo delivered his bravura speech. He was confident, slick, expansive and enjoying every reverberating sound of his own voice. Everyone watched the scene with renewed interest. Sta-san stood up to be ready for his entrance, and Kana, holding an aluminium bucket and an empty soya sauce bottle, sailed back into the scene and knelt before Rudo.

'No! No! No!' That odious, too-familiar cry jerked the players out of their sweaty Stanislavskian concentration. They remained in position, blinking at each other, wondering what had gone wrong this time. How fervently Kana prayed that she would not be the cause this time, only her ancestors in the world beyond would know. Otani violently slumped back into his chair: 'Bah-lloo-oon!'

Rudo clicked his tongue. The rest of the cast waiting for their entrances behind the makeshift set groaned. They had not set a foot on stage all morning. Otani dropped his head into his hands and gazed at Kana with a defeated look. The intense black of his pupils seemed to recede further inward against the flashing white of the eyes. Kana could count the pearls of perspiration trickling down the inner sides of her thighs.

Eventually Otani spoke, beginning in an ominously low voice: 'Clea is a woman. A woman, every milligram of her is a musky ripe effusion of a twenty-nine-year-old woman. Shove that into your head first, then the fact that she's been married for eight years to Xantos, a painted cardboard of a man, some twenty years her senior. So, think, what it would mean to her to meet a handsome young captain from Athens. She couldn't possibly just sit there looking like an ad for teen-age sanitary pads! It's no use your giving me Clea in bits and pieces, Balloon. I want to see Clea as a whole person. I've asked you a hundred times to delve into Clea and find yourself in her. . . . Oh, hell, not those tears again!'

Large salty blobs were flooding out of Kana's eyes, but what could she do? Unblinking, she just stared at Otani. Balloon's loose tear ducts, they called the phenomenon, and by now no one paid any more attention to it than to a bee buzzing in a fig tree.

'That's enough. We've wasted enough of everyone's time. OK, Mysh, let's go on.' Otani lit a cigarette.

Sunflowers in the overgrown back yard stood perpendicular, it was long after lunchtime, but the rehearsal went on relentlessly.

'Now, tell me, Clea, what's your pahspektiboo?'*

'Ahm . . . transcending my class,' said Kana and saw Otani gesture to Bobchin and Rudo to sit down on the floor; so Kana tried again. 'Transcending . . . her . . . class?'

'You don't know what the hell you're talking about,' came his verdict. 'You can't cheat me with that dead cliché. Try again in your own words.'

'In my own words? Pahspektiboo. . . .' Her mind in a frayed stupor, Kana stared in front of her for minutes on end, but nothing stirred in her head. Kana could hear Wood Peck mumbling: 'Sadist! This isn't rehearsal, it's a persecution. Poor Balloon!'

Myshkin exchanged a few words with Otani and to everyone's relief clapped his hands. 'Break for lunch. Be back at four under the elm for chorus.'

'Ethiopia!' Otani shouted. 'Get three curry-and-rice. Balloon and Mysh stay with me, we'll work.'

'No, not for me, thank you! I mean curry-and-rice, I don't feel like. . . .' Kana gathered up her long sticky skirt in panic. She hated curry.

'Three curry-and-rice!' Otani threw his two 100-yen notes at Ethiopia.

'Curry doesn't agree with me, especially in summer.'

'Don't listen to her, Otani-san!' Wood Peck shoved herself forward. 'Make her eat something serious; shake her and you'll hear the bones rattle.'

'Right, Wood Peck. Get three bean cakes as well, Ethiopia.'

Otani held up to Kana an illustration from a book on Greek sculpture. 'See how voluptuous this Aphrodite is? You must begin expanding, Balloon.'

* 'Perspective'.

182

That evening, in the swirling smoke from an anti-mosquito ring, Wood Peck washing her hair in the kitchen sink humming 'Kachusha', Kana wrote in her Excelsior diary:

Phew! I have survived another day of monstrous humiliation and torture and again I have come out of it feeling elated, cleaner and simpler. Getting thinner; couldn't be more pleased. It is my personal protest against carnal rot and indulgence. Only I see a summer-long battle with Otani-san who force-feeds me just as Mother used to do during my entrance-exam hell.

A sultry, debilitating evening. Beret took Kana to the air-conditioned Eleven Potatoes. He looked drawn and shrivelled with black bags under his eyes.

'I hear,' he said, 'you have fallen prey to unprecedented Draconianism. I really must find time to come up to Science Hill, but as you can imagine with such gadfly assistants as Denim and Single Cell, I can't afford to leave the HQ even for half an hour. Single Cell is getting more and more involved with the campaign against a missile base on Niijima Island. She has the fanatic look of "the chosen" when she extols the virtues of this live-in protest on the island. I keep on telling her that those poverty-stricken islanders may very well prefer cash to their hopelessly barren land and that they might resent the know-all students from Tokyo pontificating and meddling with their affairs. I don't get any answer but that stony chosen look from her. As for Denim, most nights of the week she is out singing with the Waseda High Society Jazz Orchestra at student dance parties at smart downtown hotels. What's left of her during the day isn't much, she's either cat-napping or sneaking off to Science Hill to keep a glutinous watch on Otani.'

Kana took a 'arge lump of ice out of her lemonade glass and stuffed it into her mouth and crunched it to pieces. The cold that pierced to the roots of her teeth turned to pain and her eyes swelled with fresh tears. Kana just managed to ask him: 'Why didn't he give Clea to Denim, if that is the case . . . ?'

'He's not that kind of a man,' Beret said simply and it killed Kana that he went on sipping his beer and smoking as if nothing in the world had gone wrong.

Rehearsal hours sprawled longer and longer into the night till green-winged insects swarmed so densely round the only electric bulb in the room that Otani could hardly see his actors. His curses and abuse raged with increasing venom, tearing Kana to shreds, daring her, maddening her, and roasting her in every hell fire he could think of. Kana's tear ducts were now almost continually open and she put lanolin on the reddish rims of her eyes before going to sleep.

With only three days to go before the dress rehearsal, Single Cell had the nerve to leave for Niijima Island without so much as a goodbye to Beret, let alone asking his permission.

'Seduction of the extreme.' Beret was being philosophical about it, but when twenty-four hours later he lost his second assistant he was in a state of panic. Denim had suddenly announced that she was leaving with the High Society Jazz Orchestra on a beach and resort tour. Kana treated Beret to a beer after the rehearsal.

'Just think of the amount of correspondence I now have to conduct on my own, with provincial organizers, inn-keepers, university dormitories, railway freight idiots, union big potatoes. ... and all in longhand, with three carbon copies! Oh, I don't know, I just don't know. ...'

'What a bitch to let you down like this,' Kana said severely. 'Couldn't resist the lure of money, I suppose.'

'It wasn't that.' Beret threw a few pep pills into his mouth and washed them down with beer. 'A woman's wrath, my dear. Denim proposed that she should be taken on the mud road as my assistant, but the proposition was vetoed by the Executive Committee. Being a resourceful lady, she then suggested that perhaps the director needed an assistant. He turned her down flat, and you know the rest. But, don't worry, I'll survive somehow.'

'Of course, you'll survive, of course!' Kana treated him to another glass of Asahi beer and herself to a monumental mess of chocolate and banana and whipped cream.

After the final run through at the Okuma Theatre, Tamiko came round to the girls' dressing room.

'What a metamorphosis,' she said and with a glinting smile of connivance dropped a square white envelope between Kana's hair brush and a pot of cold cream. Before Kana realized what was in the envelope Abe's flounder-flat face turned up in her mirror, wreathed in a big smile.

'A veritable case of a minnow into a rainbow trout. And we all thought Otani had gone completely off his rocker when he gave you the part!'

'But the way he's done it would make your hair stand on end, Abe-san,' Wood Peck piped up from the other side of the dressing table, as Otani walked in, shouting back into the corridor, 'Right, dye all the white costumes in weak tea to kill the glare from the lighting.'

'Bravo, Otani, a splendid job and the cast have surpassed themselves.'

'Don't be too optimistic, Abe, they haven't had an audience yet. Listen, Clea, what the hell did you think you were doing when. . . .' he went on, just as usual, and everyone in the room burst into incongruous, hilarious laughter, except for Kana who sat there petrified like a frog, face to face with a snake's red tongue.

4

At Tokyo station the road ahead seemed to glow with resplendent technicolour promises; all the Free Stagers who lived in Tokyo came to see the mud-roaders off, sang the Circle song and thrice cheered Banzai as the train pulled out. The gleaming Diesel greyhound was clean, comfortable, uncrowded and for two hours and a half they sang their way lustily along, sustained by beer, green tea and supper boxes.

But the picture changed brutally at Takada junction where they had to transfer to a branch line. The third-class night train was already jam-packed when it arrived.

'Scramble, settle anywhere, and try to sleep. This is mud road, kids!' Beret yelled and the troupe scrambled. When the train began to move, Bobchin, Tonton and Oka were found squatting on the iron footplates above the buffers, marinated in the engine's smoke and smuts, saying they preferred the intermittent blasts of fresh air to the sickening heat inside the coach. Kana sat back with Wood Peck on a couple of dimmer boxes piled against the lavatory wall. Rudo had conveniently perched himself on a wash basin in the outer compartment of the lavatory, and Otani, Beret and Myshkin were trying to sleep in the corridor of the next coach with newspapers spread out as sleeping mats.

'Elegy for a third-class night train,' Rudo was shouting, banging the lavatory door with his foot. An insomniac, as strikingly spoilt and selfish as he was handsome, he was worried to distraction about losing his voice from lack of sleep. 'You ailing failing centipedes of woeful countenance, let me out of your piss-reeking clammy womb!'

The train suddenly jerked to a halt in the middle of nowhere.

'A driver stealing water melon or something?'

'Peeing zestfully into a cricket colony, more likely.'

'I bet Rudo has thrown himself under the wheels. Couldn't stand the shitty train,' yelled Bobchin from the footplate.

'Thanks, I'm in a piss-house stinking and wide awake but not dead yet!' came a roar from the wash basin.

Fellow passengers complained about the young hooligans' raising such a din and blocking the passage; a young apprentice conductor came to deliver a homily, but the poor boy, barely eighteen, fidgeting with his new cap, was so intimidated by the mass of unsavoury-looking types that when Ethiopia, looking weirder than ever in his US Army camouflage jacket and a battered Waikiki straw hat, menacingly blew on his harmonica a hysterical cock-a-doodle-doo, then 'La Marseillaise', he beat a quick retreat.

Seeing the total futility of struggling to sleep under these circumstances, those perched on the buffers or huddled round the lavatory, roused themselves to join in.

'*Marchons, marchons!*' they sang. Ethiopia burst his lungs on every crescendo and went on to play 'Lake Baykal'.

'Let me take care of the next stanza, listen!' Rudo screamed from behind the lavatory door and sang:

> One morning maiden let's forswear
> this pissy messy ugh-ugh everyday
> and I'll paint a hammer and sickle in
> twenty-two carat gold on your pink behind
> on the shore of Lake Baykal . . .

Cheers and clapping, but a raucous yell put an end to their jubilation.

'Stop! What filth, how dare you mouth such muck! This is a public lavatory and you, young man, have no right to sit there. Get out and let me in.'

A portly middle-aged man, having taken off his suit to look fresh on arrival, stripped to the waist with a towel round his red neck, his long beige underpants making him look like a trapeze artist, towered over Rudo, whose legs blocked the entry into the lavatory. The latter lifted his knees up to his chin with his bottom still securely planted in the basin and said with cordial impudence: 'Pass, my dear sir.'

This aggravated the portly gentleman's anger even more; he exploded: 'Shame on you! Coming as you do from our highest educational institution, you have no right to behave like a bunch of foul-mouthed hooligans. I'd like to meet the parents who brought you up like this. No respect for authority or the law of the land. I bet you don't worship the Emperor and are glad we lost the war, you muck of the earth!'

Rudo suddenly jumped from the basin, stood as erect as a bayonet and with a stiff military salute began howling:

> In the sea I'll fight till I'm drowned corpse,
> On land let me be at the bottom of the pile of my dead
> battle-field brothers . . .

The most cherished of all wartime songs. The boys joined Rudo in a wailing chorus. The effect on the man of this song was incredible: he stood at attention, his face tightly puckered in ecstacy, his eyes glazed, and his stomach so tightly pulled in that his body trembled under the strain. When the boys finished the first refrain in a dramatic rallentando, his tautened body immediately collapsed into its former sweaty flabbiness. He pressed his eyes with the end of the towel, gasping half in laughter and half in sobs.

'Well, well . . . fancy . . . youngsters . . . Well, that was nice. Brings everything back. Now, excuse me . . . .'

Rudo, taken aback, moved politely out of the way and the man closed the lavatory door behind him. No derisive reaction, not even a snigger from the boys who had sung. Embarrassed and somewhat touched as well, they glanced at each other.

The train made a stumbling move. As it gathered speed, more air cum soot. Beret lurched his way to their coach and ceremoniously took out a piece of paper from inside his greasy beret.

'Are you ready, comrades? I'm going to read you the slogan I've just composed for our hand-painted poster outside the theatre.'

'Bravo, maestro, let's hear it!'

'Right, here we go. "Despite the daunting road Free Stage has come to entertain, enlighten and enthrall you!" How's that?'

'What? Oh, no, Beret!' Oka slapped at his own forehead in disgust.

'Sounds shamelessly like a cheap version of *Vu Narod*,' Wood Peck quipped. 'We're not touring in Siberia or the Ukraine, you know, Beret-san.'

'Thank you, thank you for your ungracious comments.' Beret raised his arms imperiously. 'Two hours of my nocturnal concentration has been spent on this and I'm not going to waste it. After all we can't carry a Voltaire-like aphorism to the kind of audience we are to face. Bang out our zeal and devotion, touch them with our youthfulity, grab their confidence and carry them forward with us, zoom! Isn't that the right style for mud road?'

'Hear, hear!' The imperialist had come out of the lavatory, his face and chest washed and scrubbed to inflamed red. 'Young man, I'm with you. That's what I'd call the true Kamikaze spirit. Good luck to you.' He stumbled off.

Rudo, back to his wash-basin seat, hailed: 'There you are, Beret, the Kamikaze spirit, that's your new image.'

They all laughed, with all the mud road magic and abandon they laughed and when they relapsed into an exhausted silence Kana was not the only person whose eyes were blurred with tears and whose heart was blown up till it ached with affection for one another.

The heat was appalling; eggs could truly have been fried on Toyama's scorching pavements. At 3 p.m. in a makeshift dressing room at the Town Hall the August sun beat down through the bare window, setting white fire to everything it hit upon. Bobchin and Kana sat on the cement floor to get what coolness they could from it.

Kana wanted to have a nose like the Venus de Milo and kept a photograph of it next to her mirror, but her many attempts to mould its likeness resulted only in a squelchy misshapen mess.

'I'll have to go on without a Greek nose. Oh, damn, damn!' She peeled off the latest disaster and threw it into a jar.

'No use getting hysterical about it, Clea. Now, look.' Bobchin who had finished his own nose picked up a fresh ball of plasticine and rolled it between his creamed forefinger and thumb. 'Mould it to just the right emolliency, certainly not too runny in this heat, yet not too inflexible either. The false nose has to be supple enough to dance with your facial choreography, understand?' He felt the tip of Kana's nose.

'Dry it, our friend won't stick to a sweaty nose. That's better.' He slapped down the plasticine between her eyes, then peering askance beyond the obstructively high bridge of his own false nose, he caressed, pinched and gently manipulated the limp dough. After what seemed an eternity he handed Kana a mirror. She took one look and her eyes boggled. There was a nose-shaped scoop of vanilla ice cream, glistening irreconcilably against the pink flesh of her own skin.

'Structurally, you couldn't do better.' Bobchin was pleased with his work. 'All you need now is a thick make-up.'

After a layer of pore-choking grease paint, lavender smear on eyelids, pink blush on cheeks, blue-black lining for eyes, suddenly every feature fused into one grotesquely beautiful face with every individual part clamouring for prominence.

'What a screaming loud face,' Kana marvelled.

'It'll look perfect under the stage lighting. Now, exercise it a bit. Make faces.'

'Feels awfully ticklish under the nose, Bobchin-san.'

'Wait, wait, I'm coming to that.' Bobchin tossed back his head and showed Kana his two and a half nostrils.

'Drainage,' he said. 'Take a match stick, moisten it and stick it up along the ridge of your own nose. Don't be vain, make it fairly large. After all it's got to drain away quite an amount of perspiration. Audience won't see it.'

Rudo, whom nature had endowed with a highly sculptured nose – people often mistook him for a Eurasian – studied the sudden protuberances on Bobchin's and Kana's faces.

'No offence to your handiwork, Bobchin, but why is it that one piece of fake flesh makes your whole being so false? Blame your false nose, if I steal the show tonight.'

Kana's nose was one thing but Ethiopia's 'ebony skin' was quite another horror story: he had to spread black make-up all over his raw-boned body except for the small area that was to be covered by a gold lamé loincloth. He blinked his exotic white-rimmed eyes and wailed: 'Think of the risk I'm taking. Haven't you read about the strip-tease artiste who died from skin suffocation by painting her whole body in gold powder?'

'Quiet, Ethiopia.' Myshkin was at the doorway. 'To be on the mud road is a privilege worth risking your life for. Now get on with it. You still have both legs to paint. Ten minutes to go, everyone!'

190

Beret, his khaki shorts and white cotton socks in ridiculous contrast to his woollen beret, rushed in, shaking his right arm towards the auditorium. 'You hear? You hear the earth quaking under the blessed feet of our spectators?'

'How full, Beret?' Bobchin's head emerged from the voluminous toga which Dre-Ma had just heaped over him.

'Jam-packed, bursting. The fruit-canning factory sent all their girls. The whole place is one big pink giggle.'

Otani entered the dressing room in khaki trousers and rubber-soled shoes, his white shirt sleeves tucked up and with the look of a doctor inspecting an epidemic ward prowled around, keeping the necessary critical distance from his actors.

'I want Ethiopia's hair teased till every hair stands on end.' Ethiopia raised a tearing yodel of protest but was instantly seized in Dre-Ma's fat grip.

'And you.' Otani turned on Kana. 'What are those bulges doing there, may I ask?' His eyes were set on her breasts where Dre-Ma had buried half a dozen pairs of old nylon stockings.

'Where?' Kana blurted out, and the boys raised rude guffaws.

'There, you fool, you can't grow a pumpkin on a celery stalk. Take them out one by one till I say stop.'

Eventually he let Kana keep one stocking in each side.

'Hell, hell, hell!' screamed Sta-san, who had been working hard on a magnificent giant wart of plasticine on his forehead over his scotch-taped right eye, 'Hell, oh, hell, my sweat shirt! I'll never get it off. It'll take half an hour at least to re-do this monster make-up!'

His slave costume was only a burlap round his middle, and he had completely forgotten to remove his tight round-neck vest.

'But, Sta-san, we're about to go up!' Myshkin turned white looking at his watch.

'And the house is bursting full.' Beret made an emphatic gesture at the auditorium.

'Cut it open, what's the matter with you all?' Otani was already behind Sta-san with a pair of scissors snatched from Dre-Ma's sewing box. Sta-san gave only a whimper as Otani ripped his vest from top to bottom.

'Here, Dre-Ma, a present for Asano. He's always short of rags. Now, everyone, on stage!'

Halfway through the second act, the full house now sizzling in the nineties, the husband and wife's reunion was being consummated in a theatrical embrace, while Aesop spat out his tirade downstage. Xantos and Clea were hugging each other on a dais upstage and since Kana loathed any form of close bodily contact she kept her cheek at least an inch away from Bobchin's and shut her eyes tight.

'Clea, my nose has come loose!' Xantos whispered in panicked urgency. Kana opened her eyes and saw a glistening object hinged from Bobchin's sweat-spangled forehead, undulating irresolutely like an open car bonnet.

She tried to push it back into place with her upstage hand but Bobchin's skin was too wet.

'I can't, it won't stay. What do we do now?' Kana whispered.

'Don't panic. Just stay where you are.' Bobchin, without waiting for his cue, tore himself from the embrace and, clutching at his nose, dashed into the wings, from where he proceeded to bellow his lines when his cue came. Mercifully, the audience did not seem to mind Xantos' inexplicable scuttle and Kana bravely lashed her lines into the wings, till Bobchin reappeared beaming contentedly with his nose secured.

During the interval Otani checked Xantos' and Clea's sweat drains himself and forbade the cast to drink any liquid till the end of the performance.

As the last act was drawing to its close, Takada who was operating the follow spot at the back of the balcony dozed off in the numbing heat, and what was supposed to be a romantic moonlit scene was scorched by a blazing shaft of pink-gold. But no one was in a pernickety mood; the dusty curtains opened and closed again and again to rapturous applause. The audience, mostly in their late teens, sat on the edge of the hard wooden benches and clapped their hands high above their heads. The house lights were switched on; the exit doors were opened; but the applause continued unflaggingly. When the curtains reopened yet again, Beret, his flying-saucer eyes wet and red, stepped forward, thanked them for the generous reception and invited as many of them as wished to do so to stay for the symposium.

'Symposium ... er, a sort of discussion,' he reiterated to a nonplussed crowd.

Then, arm in arm, the cast swayed to the left and then to the right as their Circle song echoed through the hushed house. All the pent-up emotions of those gruelling weeks of rehearsal in Tokyo were sluiced open in gratitude and exultation towards the good people who were no longer to them just words like 'masses' or 'public', but responding and lovable human beings.

Beret was ecstatic. 'What a communion, what a staggering beauty! This mud road! I must make a speech . . .'

'No, you don't. Not here on the stage,' Asano hissed in Beret's direction from the row behind. 'We've got to load the scenery by ten o'clock.'

The curtains were drawn for the last time.

'Right, clear the stage quickly for his lordship!' Beret said sulkily. 'And keep your make-up on, that's an essential attraction of the symposium. Get some toilet paper from Mysh and mop up your perspiration before you go out front.'

A big turn-out for the symposium, some eighty people. The fruit-canning factory girls led by their union officials were the largest group. The girls, with fuzzy peach complexions, were hardly sixteen; they stared at Rudo and emitted breathy giggles whenever he happened to look in their direction. Businessmen and town officials bowed at each other: some were accompanied by their wives, to whom shopkeepers rushed up with small steps bowing deeply. Farmers with tanned faces sat with their eyes shut.

Kana gazed at the rows of hard-working, abstemious, polite, frugal, cautious, authority-fearing people, young and old, of earth, factory and shop-front, sitting on their accustomed haunches. They were the people whom she was now determined to love, to share with and to work for.

The discussion got off to a sticky start. When the mimeographed leaflets on ANPO were passed round, the audience took a

193

cursory glance at the headlines: 'Why alienate Japan from the Asian community by signing the security treaty with the USA?' and promptly used the leaflets to fan themselves. Beret, the MC, did his best to encourage an intelligent discussion, but no, they did not want to know about ANPO, or about missile bases, Okinawa or Hiroshima. Desperate to break the stagnant silence, Beret pinned a last hope on a group of unsmiling keen-eyed high-school boys.

'Now, any question from you boys?'

'How much a month would it cost to live and study in Tokyo?' the first boy asked, making way for a deluge of questions entirely confirmed to their own selfish futures. 'Does Waseda have a better Agricultural Department than Nippon?' or 'In order to get a job in a government office is it essential to be a Tokyo University graduate?'

'Time is running short. Can we come back to the most vital question of ANPO?' Beret pleaded, but the audience at once began fanning themselves more urgently than ever; and their attention was now being distracted by the activities behind the curtain, where Asano and his crew were breaking down the set and dragging flats and properties off-stage with less and less restraint.

Beret finally spied a scrawny bespectacled man who had been wringing his hands like Lady Macbeth in patient exasperation.

'Honoured Students from Tokyo,' the man began, 'I'm sure you haven't come here prepared only to preach to the converted. So, I hope you won't be offended if I tell you frankly what I think of ANPO. I for one believe ANPO is a providential gift, just as I believed fifteen years ago that the American occupation was a blessing from our ancestors. If there had to be a foreign occupation, we were fortunate that it was America-san. General MacArthur, I'm sure you all agree, did more good to this country than any rulers of our own. Since the so-called Peace Constitution denies us the possibility of rearmament, I declare I am glad America-san is to defend our democracy and freedom; and besides we've never had it so good as we do now and it's going to get better each year. I see no point in wrecking this good life, do you? However, I like your play and I'll chew on it like a patient cow and think about it for a long time to come. We don't often get to see plays round here. Thank you.' The man smiled apologetically for having spoken for so long. The students simply gawked at him. Even Beret remained speechless for a moment, like a hen that had swallowed a ping-pong ball.

Asano poked his rude head through the curtains.

'Please don't let me break up your chit-chat, but we're off to the station.'

Asano's interruption gave the symposium its quietus. With a sheepish fixed smile, Beret declared the symposium over and with tentative bows all round the audience quickly melted away.

At 10.30 the company returned to their inn from the Town Hall and Asano and his assistants from the station. The innkeeper had gone to bed drunk but his wife and daughters waited up to give them supper.

'Sit near us, Balloon.' Asano winked at Kana, then below his breath, 'If you're not going to eat your rice . . .OK?'

Otani clapped his hands for silence. 'Well done, everyone. As the first performance on the road goes it was almost too good to be true. I have some minor performance notes but they can wait till tomorrow. What won't wait is your health. We haven't any understudies or substitutes in any department. Please, every one of you, look after yourself. Turn in early, get all the sleep you can, and even if you have no appetite, force yourself to eat.'

As Kana fidgeted with two almond chocolate bars inside her yukata sleeves, she saw Wood Peck on the other side of the table shake her fist at her.

'As to the symposium tonight, don't be discouraged. We learned a good lesson. The last thing we students from Tokyo should do is to pontificate with "Why alienate Japan, blah-blah". This is a remote thunderstorm beyond many mountains to them, whereas if we said instead "Because of ANPO one day probably your son may be fighting in the Cambodian jungle" it would jolt them out of their smug skins. We'll have to have a completely new approach that will meet them face to face in the mud of their rice paddies, so to speak, or on the conveyor belts of their factories.'

'Meet - me - in - the - rice - paddies - when - the - moon - is -low-ow-ow,' Rudo yelled. 'Ugh, so much sickening corn, Otani, spare my appetite, please!'

Before Otani could retort, Myshkin cut in quickly: 'Here is the bathing order: the three girls first, then sets of three boys in turns and last but not least Ethiopia and Sta-san because of their heavy body make-up. Each group to follow the other with minimum delay, please. And no clothes washing tonight. We have to be up and away by half-past-six tomorrow morning.'

Golden hair powder still itching behind her ears, Kana lay awake on a thin sleeping mat. Although numbed by exhaustion, the taste of forbidden chocolate and the anti-mosquito smoke was magic to her senses. Wood Peck and Dre-Ma were already snoring gently; crickets concussed the quiet of the night and the wind was rising. When the day comes when I can no longer understand how I found such bliss in all this, I'll be very old, thought Kana.

As the Free Stagers moved along the coast of the Japan Sea from Toyama to Kanazawa and then to Fukui and to Toyooka, local papers were headlining the highest recorded temperatures since the first Emperor Jinmu. Each day began with Myshkin waking the company at six o'clock or even earlier. His harrying and shepherding of the company was so masterful that they managed never to miss a train nor to leave anything behind, not even one of the many plastic bags full of personal washing still damp after such a short humid night's sojourn.

The ride to the next town on a slow stopping train was followed by a nap for the cast and a gruelling get-in and fit-up for the staff in the white heat of the afternoon. In every town they had so far visited the symposium had seemed to demand much more energy and nerve from the actors than the performance itself and by the time the whole company had supped and taken a bath, usually past midnight, none of them had the strength even to say good night; they simply fell to the floor.

With the exception of the first night in Toyama the inns Beret had booked the company into did not help ameliorate the already none-to-agreeable living conditions on the road.

'How the hell, Beret, did you manage to find such a down-and-out dump as this?' Even Bobchin who had been through the mud road hardship before could not get over it. Usually the only toilet was a mud hole, its nauseating presence evident even from the farthest guest room. The bathroom was either non-existent or out of order or without enough water; so the company often had to walk to the public bath, still in half-removed make-up. The floors of the rooms they were given either sloped to one side or sagged into a valley in the middle and the boys who had to sleep six in a small room complained that they often found themselves in the morning gravitated to the room's lowest point like autumn leaves into a ditch.

Like a fig, the fruit of her month of birth, Kana suffered quickly from the heat. She began to feel faint whenever she had to deliver a long speech; she could force down very little serious food; every stitch of her clothing became a torture, rubbing and worsening her heat rash; she had to give up wearing the bra into which Wood Peck had sewed a secret purse and now wore only clouds of talcum powder; her complexion had a bruised-apple look and her hair fell out in alarming quantities. It was not surprising that now not only Wood Peck but almost the whole company began worrying about her.

On the 8th of August, Otani at breakfast proposed a silent prayer for the atom bomb victims of Hiroshima. At the end of the two-minute prayer Kana was quietly sliding her rice bowl down to Asano, when Wood Peck let out a yell: 'Watch, Otani-san, what Balloon's doing!'

Blue veins stood out on Otani's temple. He pounded on her with a rigour that stunned everyone into a silent chewing.

'But even if I tried,' Kana protested in tears, 'I couldn't possibly swallow a raw egg mixed in cold rice. Soya sauce doesn't kill the slimy egg taste ... I just couldn't!'

'Shut up, you're becoming a bore and burden to the company!' Otani raged.

'Listen, Otani.' It was Beret coming to Kana's defence, as always. 'It would be delicious if the rice were piping hot, cooking the egg softly round each grain. But a raw egg on cold left-over rice would revolt anyone's stomach but yours.'

The same evening after the symposium Otani handed Kana a packet of garlic and carrot tablets. 'Two after each meal. Come on, Balloon, try.'

Noticing how gaunt and tired he looked, Kana nodded and faithfully swallowed the odorous tablets after breakfast and lunch the following day. After the performance in Tsuyama Bobchin dragged Kana to Otani.

'Clea stinks,' he said, 'like Korean Kimchee pickle. As I don't intend to choke to death from holding my breath for five minutes, either she stops taking your damn pills or we cut the so-called love scene.'

'No, we certainly can't cut the scene, Bobchin-san,' Otani answered his senior and told Kana to give the pills to Myshkin who had also been visibly wilting in the heat. Good riddance, Kana rejoiced, that's the end of Otani-san's exotic medicine. But no, he persisted. Shortly after boarding the train for Kurashiki, he lurched over to Kana, his white shirt rumpled and grey.

'You know this region is famous for Chinese homeopathy?' He lifted his dull tired eyes. Kana said yes.

'Here.' A neatly tied-up parcel was presented to her. 'Entirely herbal. I've been to the oldest Chinese chemist in town. One portion after every meal. Will you promise to take it?'

She promised. After a day or two of black nutty powder three times daily she even thought she was beginning to stand up to the heat and the strain quite remarkably well.

It was not till the company reached Okayama that the horrid truth was revealed to her. Ethiopia, who had taken her aside, asking for 200 yen for cigarettes and talcum powder, could not resist dropping a hint – a very broad one.

'You mean! I'm eating . . . snake?'

'No, no, of course, not, don't misunderstand me . . .'

Ethiopia back-pedalled at once, but his impassioned denial

coming after a momentary salivating grin told everything. Finally in exchange for the 200 yen he confessed.

Delicious nutty black medicine, indeed! It was in fact a legendary stamina powder made of roasted viper, mamushi. Kana remembered that whenever she passed a famous Chinese homeopathist's show window in Kobe, she had hidden behind her mother so as not to see the glossy black viper, dried and preserved in its tall glass jar. So Otani with his dark melancholy eyes had deceived her into swallowing powder of mamushi!

The following morning the train for Hiroshima was behind schedule. After leaving her rucksack in the waiting room Kana walked out on the platform and went up to a kiosk. She knew Otani was following her, but brazenly ordered half a dozen packets of sugar wafers and almond chocolate.

'What do you think you're doing?' Otani said.

'Buying chocolate to kill a reptilian after-taste,' Kana said aggresively.

Otani shrugged his shoulders, wincing imperceptibly, but remained by the kiosk, glaring at the vendor who was wrapping up Kana's purchase in old newspapers. As she was waiting for the change, unflinching in Otani's accusatory presence, Kana spotted four paperback books by Saburo Otani: *Afternoon of Indiscretion*, *Madame Long Spring*, and *Nights of Indiscretion* I and II. Darting a glance from the books to Otani, Kana said, 'I suppose they provide the funds for my mamushi powder?'

He stared at his father's best-sellers which occupied a prominent position in the jumble of tangerines, boiled eggs, maps, tooth-brushes and other travelling necessities. Kana saw him blush gradually but thoroughly to the earlobes.

'Monkey's red ass!' he hissed and his face did not regain its customary sardonic indifference till he stretched to receive the change from the vendor. He did not hand it to Kana but pushed her behind the kiosk, where unseen by the others he banged the coins down on to her hand.

'What if they do? Blackmailing bitch. If you're trying to get back at me, OK, go ahead, go and give them a nice juicy story about my father.' He jerked his head angrily towards the waiting room.

The fact that her snide comment had found its mark and with such devastating effect frightened Kana, yet a devil inside made her lash out at him. 'No, I won't tell them, I shan't stoop to that. But never forget that I know who you are, where you come from, and what a fraud you are. If you smoke, it's Peace; when you read, hard-covers; when you drink, it's real Scotch or Asahi beer. And who pays? Your father. And when you gamble, *his* money, not yours. Your dirty mac is a costume. And why are you so bent on sneering at me in public? Because I remind you too much of yourself, a bourgeois fake!'

Oh God, I've said it! Kana took a step back and looked at him in consternation. And ... she could not believe her own eyes: on his face anger had disappeared and in its place was an ingenuous smile, an open friendly smile like the one Kana had often seen on him when he had just won or lost a good mah-jong game. His eyes shone with new curiosity. He watched Kana intently like this for at least a whole minute till she became so ill at ease that she began blushing and fidgeting.

He bent down and hitched up her chin with his forefinger. Just as the pungency of nicotine brushed past her nose, she shut her eyes, having seen how very tenderly his eyes looked at her. His lips, loosely closed, cool and crusty on the rims, rubbed against hers, till something secret, wet and tremulous crept between her lips, but then at once his body recoiled and her lips were bare, damp and left alone to cool.

He took one step back and still with that curious smile said: 'You were rude and bloody ungrateful, but as you can see I'm not really angry with you. I hope you'll keep on taking the delicious nutty black medicine.' He turned and went away. Kana picked up the chocolate parcel she had dropped and walked back to the waiting room at a snail's pace.

By the time the company, looking a washed-out remnant of what they had been at Tokyo station ten days earlier, reached Hiroshima, the stage flats and the Corinthian pillars made foldable like paper lanterns for easy transportation were no longer white or straight. Costumes that had been only spot-cleaned with lighter fuel had dulled in colour and smelt foul.

At the Hiroshima University theatre in front of a small house they gave a lack-lustre performance, followed by an uninspired symposium. At Kana's request Wood Peck went to see Otani afterwards, while Kana peeled off her Greek nose and costume. Wood Peck came back in a matter of a few minutes.

'OK,' she said. 'You may go.'

'What? How did you put it to him?'

'I said simply "The kid's father's staying at the Grand and if you didn't let her spend a night there, you'd be an unfeeling swine." That's all, and he said, "OK, let her go".'

The Hiroshima Grand Hotel was an exotic world, carpeted and air-contitioned, full of pink foreigners.

'But it's past ten! I was expecting you for dinner. Didn't Mother write you "dinner"?' Flustered out of the first and deepest stage of sleep, Kana's father paced about the room in a hotel yukata.

'Mother told me to spend the night here with bath and breakfast; dinner was never mentioned. In any case it would have been impossible, Father, for don't forget, we give performances in the evening.'

'I don't remember exactly what she told me ... Oh dear, if this was a Japanese-style inn, I could have another set of sleeping mats spread out for you in an ante-room, but here they operate on a Western system: you'd have to have a room of your own, and the place is full.'

'Don't worry, Father, I'll take this fruit and go back to the University dormitory.' Kana began putting into her rucksack the contents of a basket of fruit, a gift from the management. Mr Toda crept back into bed and studied his daughter curiously. 'I must confess I'm surprised that they let you in. You look a perfect vagabond, and those sandals! You realize you're asking for street filth and germs to make trouble? Good gracious, Kana, the fruit, yes, but *not* the knife and forks!'

After Kana had put the knife and forks back on the coffee

table, her father suddenly dropped his voice, peering at her cautiously. 'Did Mother mention anything in her letter . . . er, about Yoko? She didn't! Well, perhaps I'd better break it to you. Yoko is engaged.'

Kana stared at her father, her mouth half-opened.

'Engaged. To marry.'

'But she's only seventeen!'

'She is, but she will be eighteen by the time she graduates from Konan. Don't forget your mother was only nineteen when you were born.' Kana sat down on a sofa and listened.

Yoko's fiancé was her father's dream come true, an athlete aged twenty-six, who had climbed up the Nada-Tokyo University elite course and had smoothly landed in the banking division of the Sumitomo Concern.

'Arranged, I suppose.' Kana put a vibrant contempt into her voice.

'No, no, we didn't have a hand in it at all. A case of a perfect love at first sight. Fortunately, too, when we had a private detective check up on him, the young man turned out to have an impeccable background and record. An additional blessing for Yoko is that he has no sister to make her life difficult. Just one younger brother. No worry about the mother-in-law either. She seems quite sweet and is thrilled to have a girl in the family at last.'

Mr Toda pulled the blanket up to his chin and getting no reaction from Kana, continued: 'We hoped, Mother and I, that it wouldn't upset you too much. Although she's your little sister, you really mustn't in any way feel . . . left on the shelf. . . . You understand?'

'Oh, no, not at all, don't worry about me.'

'Good, I knew you would understand. You see, Yoko is quite different from you, makes no fuss or special demands on life, so for her everything she wants comes easily, fast and in good order.'

Kana ordered a taxi and left the hotel just half an hour after her arrival. She even forgot to take the longed-for steaming hot bath. When she got back to the dormitory, everyone was asleep.

She climbed up to the laundry balcony and ate the hotel fruit ravenously.

Have they kissed? Have they pressed against each other rubbing passion into every hollow of their lithe, firm, athletic bodies? Kana started to cry as she spat out the pips of the hot-house grapes.

Aboard a ferry from Hiroshima to Shikoku Island the washing that had begun smelling musty after days of incarceration in plastic bags was at last hung out and flaunting itself on an improvised laundry line on the boat deck. Luxuriating in the unaccustomed peace and space, the mud roaders ululated a round of their favourite songs; the three girls mended costumes and Sta-san composed haiku, counting busily on his fingers, trying to squeeze the quintessence of his summer images into seventeen syllables

'Pines green, beaches white,
peace of the sea complete.'

At last Sta-san was able to seize a brief respite in the singing to read out his haiku.

'Peace of the sea complete, my ass!' Beret, sitting across the prow of a lifeboat, howled. 'How can you even talk about peace when you've so recently visited Hiroshima? Aren't you scared? Scared not by a Harry Truman or a guy who pushed the button, but by what we, you and I, the agents of destruction, can do to the planet Earth? Given time, we'll blow the whole thing up. Now, here's mine. Listen:

As to forewarn the total
Incineration of Earth,
White dusts fall, fall in Hiroshima.'

'Desperately obvious.' Sta-san waved his arm about in the air. 'A subtler hand would have . . . .'

'Don't you talk to me about subtlety when I'm concerned with a universal holocaust!' Beret jumped off the lifeboat, snapping the laundry line; the girls screamed and rushed to pick up the fallen clothes.

'But I liked Beret-san's haiku,' Kana said to Wood Peck when they both resumed their sewing.

'So did I,' said Wood Peck and they both fell silent.

Kana could not get out of her mind the photographs she had seen at the Hiroshima Memorial Museum. One was of a child reduced by the atom bomb to a black cinder in the shape of a cross with its tiny arms open. Had it not been for the caption under it, 'Child', she would never have known what it was. Another, a lava-like object, a mother and a child charred together, and in some ways the most frightening of all, a man's oversized shadow etched on the wall by the searing heat of the atom rays. To complete the traumatic horror there were those close-up photographs of the dying, wide-eyed in complete bewilderment, with parts of their bodies melted away or swollen beyond recognition. Little had they known what the blaze in the sky meant!

'Had we not been yellow, Balloon, have you thought about that?' Wood Peck suddenly started. 'Had we not been, would they have dropped it on us? Suppose Hitler had lasted another year, could you imagine them, I mean Truman, Churchill, Stalin and the rest, dropping it on the Germans? No, never, unthinkable! But, on those yellow bastards, OK, boys, go ahead, we've got to try it out sometime on something!' Wood Peck cut the thread between her teeth with a shrill angry rasp.

In Shikoku, the smallest of the four Japanese islands, of pilgrims, puppet shows, and sleepy bays, the student actors from Tokyo were something of an event. Representatives from the local unions who had sponsored the performance came to greet them at the station with billowing red flags. The performances in both Matsuyama and Niihama were received with such enthusiasm by full houses that the entire company was thrown back into the buoyant excitement it had felt at the start of the mud road. They volunteered to give an extra matinée free of charge in the hall of the Mitsubishi electrical workers' union, where the symposium lasted over two hours. No stand-off lack of interest here; they stamped their feet and waved their outstretched arms impatiently to be allowed to ask questions.

In the dressing room Sta-san said of the young workers: 'I couldn't help thinking of the poem by Mushakoji: "I am an apple, complete and beautiful while I hang on a tree. When I drop, I leave a seed in the earth. A contented full existence." They *are* the apple from earth!'

'Your assessment of today's workers is as sentimental and outdated as the sepia-coloured photo of my mother's wedding,' Bobchin countered, but his sally was received with groans of disapproval from everyone.

'Shh! Listen, Typhoon Number Seven is heading for Southern Japan –' everyone fell silent as Rudo raised the volume of his radio – 'and is expected to hit Shikoku by the evening of the twentieth.'

'Autumn, already,' sighed Myshkin.

On the 19th they performed at the Tokushima Seamen's Club, a relic left over from the Meiji era, masses of pink and brown bricks and Gothic windows. In the torrential rain and the tempestuous wind roof-leaks got out of hand, buckets and pots and other improvised receptacles littered the foyer and the aisles. Windows rattled furiously and some loose panes fell out and crashed to the floor under the pressure of the wind. A handful of audience sat uneasily in the damp hall, listening more to the roar of the elements outside than to those on stage. The symposium was cancelled and the company bent all their energies on tearing their way back the few hundred yards to the New Moon Inn.

'Why, have you been crying? Your eyes are very red,' Wood Peck said when Kana tottered back to their room after supper.

'No, just feeling terrible.'

'Come on, bath time. I'll help you wash your hair.'

But the moment Kana had squatted and plunged her golden-powdered head under the running water, she collapsed into Wood Peck's arms. She remained in a comatose sleep without food all day on the 20th.

'Have I held up the company?' was the first thing she asked when she finally came to.

'Couldn't have been better timed, really,' Myhskin assured her. 'Even without your collapse we could never have made it to the mainland. The performance in Yokkaichi has been cancelled.'

Late on the 21st the first boat for the mainland made the crossing. On landing they learned that parts of the railway track to Wakayama were still blocked by landslide, and lacking sufficient funds the mud roaders had to spend the night in the blacked-out harbour station waiting room.

More dead than alive, after three days' delay, they arrived in Wakayama city where they gave the last performance of the mud road. They gave what was left of their best to an audience which, owing to the two day postponement, was smaller than they had so far known, and cancelling the symposium they ended by singing their beloved Circle song, their hands and their hearts knotted closely together. Kana noticed Beret and Wood Peck sobbing and sniffling but she herself felt too tired even to loosen her notorious tear ducts. She just wanted to collapse again and sleep, sleep, sleep.

Otani was gentle when, meeting her in the wings, he said, 'Clea, so this is it. This *was* the mud road for you . . . ,' then rubbed Kana's cheek with the back of his rough hand and walked away.

Myshkin tactfully waited till the conductor made the first intercom announcement of the train's arrival at Nagoya junction, then officially told Kana that she was not going back to Tokyo for after-the-road clearing up, but was to get off at the junction and catch the next train for Osaka.

'Don't send me home, I want to stay with the company till the end,' Kana pleaded.

'No, Balloon, this is the company's decision: they want you to go home and have a good rest. Now, get ready.'

Kana began gathering her books, fan and sandals into the rucksack. The sight of her mamushi powder packet was the last straw. Tears splattered and ran in streaks down her face. She went on weeping as she was more or less carried out of the train by Asano and Tonton and deposited with her belongings on a platform trolley. The whistle blew.

'Take care, look after yourself, Clea!' Kana heard Myshkin shout and many other familiar voices cried their goodbyes.

Sobbing her heart out with her face buried in the sodden warmth of a handkerchief, all Kana could manage was to wriggle the ends of her fingers in the direction of the departing train.

At home she was welcomed as if she had been a World War Two straggler who had belatedly emerged from the Borneo jungle. Her return home was drama and excitement to both her family and friends; there was a keen hush whenever she opened her mouth to begin, 'On the road . . . .'

Yoko, looking tanned, sleek, long and gleamy, asked Kana wistfully: 'Do you think I should, perhaps, go to a university in Tokyo for experience . . . ,' and invited a furious glare from her mother.

Poor child, she is so young, Kana thought tenderly of her sister.

5

In early autumn Otani formed a splinter group on the left wing of the ZGR Mainstream, naming it after a minor character from *The Possessed*, Kirilov, a Nihilist who had decided to serve the cause by offering his death whenever, for whatever purpose the cause required it. Clearly Otani's aim was to shift the anti-ANPO campaign towards a social revolutionary movement. His maiden speech at the first Kirilovist Students League meeting was incendiary stuff: 'Let us no longer ask ourselves "Could there be a revolution in Japan?" What is the point of asking or answering such a question? A revolutionary commitment must be positive to that end without promise of success or even of hope. Yes, we must conjure hope out of the ashes of a million broken hopes; we must first despair so totally, so completely that we may begin in the limpid air of no-hope, no-illusion and no-return. If you ask me yet again "Is a revolution necessary in Japan? Do we have it in us?", from the nadir of my hopeless hope I'll spit back at the question and haul you to the front line of the barricades!'

To some ears it might have sounded hysterical and even comical, but at a time when the fatty tissue of affluence was thickening daily under every young Japanese skin, smothering both moral and political integrity, what Otani said disturbed and dared and excited those who filled the Okuma Theatre. Myshkin, Sta-san, Abe and naturally the red-hot Single Cell joined the movement at once; and Single Cell appointed herself a recruiting sergeant and nagged every Free Stager to join the Kirilovists with the persistence of a wasp.

Returning from the summer holiday, Kana went to the second Kirilovist meeting at Nippon University, where Otani with savage contempt made mincemeat of the Anti Mainstream: 'Those mealy-mouthed so-called revolutionaries, who preach a gradual, non-violent, happy-go-lucky revolution, who sing the words of Lenin as if they were out of *The Merry Widow* and pride themselves on their good manners in picking up their litter after a demo, have no more revolutionary vision than a mole, they are middle-aged at twenty!'

Otani finished his speech to a tumultuous reception, and the whole place seemed drunk with the idea of revolution; the very air vibrated with the revolutionary thoughts pulsating in it. As Kana tottered out of the hall, Single Cell, her militant plaits spinning, bounded at her from behind the membership registration desk.

'Cheers, Balloon, good to see you here. Come and give us a hand. Doing wonderfully; we've got 347 paid-up members already.'

Kana was shaken by Single Cell being so strappingly sure of herself and of the Kirilovists' future, and went to look for Beret at the Eleven Potatoes.

'To tell the truth, I'm a bit shaken by the whole business myself,' Beret said, sitting at his usual corner table. 'It's not every day that a youngster of barely twenty starts up a political movement, and what is more, makes a good job of it. The way he carries on! Admirable, ridiculous, gigantic, a fraud, call it what you like, but you can't deny that he gets away with it. Maybe it's because he was born in Manchuria, he has that Continental

208

breadth of mind one finds in the Chinese but never in us Japanese. Absolutely no false pride or petty scruples about himself. Moreover, he's never had to swallow two major disillusionments, as we oldsters had to: one, that Moscow *can* and *does* do wrong; two, that the JCP is *not* after all a revolutionary force. A man who's never suffered such a double trauma can run recklessly like a horse that never broken its knees.'

In these circumstances no one in Free Stage had counted on Otani to take on a major responsibility for the autumn production; but when the Executive Committee met to decide on the play, Otani not only appeared on time but kept the Committee members till past midnight at the Sancho Noodle House, trying to bulldoze them into accepting Arthur Miller's very latest work, *The Crucible*.

'But, Otani, the Japanese translation of the play appeared only last week in *Theatre Tomorrow*. How are we going to get permission in time? And how are we to pay the license fee?' said Abe, who was pushing *Ivanov*.

'Ah, but that's why we should do it, quickly before professional companies put their sticky hands on it. The license fee we can't afford, therefore we shan't pay. Let them sue. What the hell. Call it *Witches of Salem*, and the tickets will sell as if they had wings. Don't you all agree with me, it's really strong high-protein stuff? OK! So, why not do it?'

The rest of the Committee were persuaded, but only on the condition that Minami should co-direct the play with Otani.

Beret's perverse desire to stage-manage a 'tough, brand-new show with a huge cast swarming like ants' was readily agreed to, and Myshkin was promoted to be the producer. Wood Peck was asked to design the costumes rather than Dre-Ma whose sense of colour and style was judged too florid for Puritan New England: instead she was promised the part of the Negro slave, Tituba.

When Kana applied for the part of Abigail, the ringleader of the Salem witches, she quite expected to get it, having enjoyed such generous glowing praise for her Clea in the summer. But, instead, she was given a much smaller part, Mary Warren, seventeen, 'a subversive, naive, lonely girl'. Kana could not help a pained look of surprise when she saw it was Denim who had been given Abigail. Denim, of all girls, who had reappeared amongst the Free Stagers at the beginning of September with just the same mocking insolence with which she had disappeared with the High Society Jazz Orchestra in July!

Yes, Denim was back, all right. Swaying her beer-bleached hair, alternatively mothering and queening it over the boys. During the summer she had learnt to paint the rims of her eyes with burnt match sticks; set in her smoker's turgid complexion, her Cleopatra eyes flashed like black lizards on mud.

One early October afternoon, during the preliminary study session on the effect of McCarthyism on US intellectuals, Kana witnessed how these black lizards shimmered and writhed in little private messages of intimacy as Denim handed her cigarette, wet at the filter, to Otani. Kana felt a scalding sensation run down her back and could not breathe again till Otani returned the cigarette to Denim after lighting his Peace with it.

They are ... lovers. And lovers will embrace each other. His same lips and his same mouth. For her what he had done to her lips behind the station kiosk was a spiritual experience upon which her whole being had fed and bloomed ever since. It was unthinkable to her that he should give such an experience countless times to any girl anywhere, like a bee to a field of flowers.

'What's wrong? You look deflated, Balloon,' Beret quipped after the Circle. Before Kana let go of her tear ducts, he glanced at his wrist watch and screamed: 'Hell, I've got to run. Recording at TBS studio at eight. Get mamushi powder, the delicious nutty black medicine, remember? That'll do you good.' He scuttled off. Beret, more than ever a caricature of hyperthyroid case, emaciated from ravenous eating and exhausted from the surefeit of his own energy, had been engaged to take part in a weekly late-night discussion programme on radio to represent the voice of 'liberal but not radical ZGR students'. In other words, he had sold out, but no one loved him the less for it.

Alone and ashamed of her jealousy of Denim, Kana tried to think more kindly of her aunt. Since the Star Festival night she had not been once to see Mrs Itoh, but after her return from the summer holiday she had made a point of telephoning her aunt regularly. While their conversations were as affectionate as before neither of them insisted on actually fixing a date for a visit.

Weeks of pleasant telephone chatting, avoided any embarrassment on either side. But when she heard from her mother how Yoko's engagement announcement had alarmed Aunt Sachi, making her utter, 'Poor, dear Kana! People might think there's something wrong with her,' she decided to lunch with her aunt. Kana hugged her in the middle of Ginza Street as they said goodbye, and Aunt Sachi wept. I will and must learn to think of her as a great big baby, but a baby with a 'nasty habit', Kana told herself.

Another side-effect which Yoko's engagement and Denim's return to Free Stage produced on Kana was that she began seeing Akio Masuda. Their evenings together followed a pattern as predictable as the sun's movement from east to west: a dinner at a smart new restaurant, low black ceiling, candles and a menu written in French, followed by an American film, and ending with a quick handshake through the lowered car window in front of Jardin-En. 'Thank you for a very pleasant evening,' was what Kana invariably said.

After the luncheon in Ginza Street Mrs Itoh resumed her behind-the-scenes manoeuvres. She obtained a pair of gala-opening tickets for *Solomon and Sheba* with Yul Brynner and Gina Lollobrigida, the first Technirama film shown in Japan, about which there had been much advance publicity. And she was crafty enough to send them to Akio, not to Kana.

In the morning Akio rang to say he would pick Kana up by the letter box at the foot of Science Hill at 6 p.m. After the rehearsal Kana rushed to the gymnasium changing room and put on the ensemble that had been made for Yoko's engagement dinner, a black raw silk suit with a ruffle-collared white organdy blouse. She then piled her hair up, carefully sticking in at least a dozen long pins to hold it in place, thinking if there was a thunderstorm tonight, she'd be a lightning conductor. Due to this unusually elaborate operation she reached Akio's red Triumph fifteen minutes late.

With one hand on the Triumph door to steady herself, Kana took off her dusty canvas shoes and began putting on a pair of black patent-leather pumps, when to her horror she saw Otani coming down the hill with Myshkin. Akio was saying something to her, but she stood petrified with one foot in an evening shoe and the other tiptoe on the pavement. As he loped down the road towards Kana, Otani, tall and solid and slim, seemed to soar even taller, solider and gaunter, his mackintosh flying about him like wings.

If he tells me to come away, I'll go with him now! The thought pierced her from ear to ear. She stood stock still holding her breath. He did not stop, he did not slacken his pace, he did not even cast one curious glance at her, nor at Akio. His long shadow swept past.

'Balloon, you look ... really lovely! I've never seen you dolled up like this,' Myshkin said and trotted in a circle round her before he ran to catch up with Otani.

'What a weird pair. Doesn't the other one know you?' His eyes following Otani, Akio pressed the starter.

After this Kana did not enjoy the film, the supper, and least of all Akio's company.

'Did he say that? But what does he mean? Why "sad"?' Kana shook Myshkin by the arm. 'Only because I was taken out to a movie last night by a man in an imported sports car?'

'No, it isn't that, I don't think. It's just that Otani-san is disappointed that you haven't changed after all.'

This was enough for Kana. She wrote immediately to Akio.

If I say I don't think I'll be able to see you again, it is not because of how you are or what you are, but because I don't wish to be identified any longer with the class you and I were born into, its values, ideals and mores. I cannot have it both ways, so I have decided to be on the side of the people and be one of them. I know you will say, 'Don't delude yourself.

You're born irreparably bourgeois, so why can't you reconcile yourself to this plain fact? T. S. Eliot answers the question better than I can:

> Home is where one starts from
> We must be still and still moving
> Into another intensity.

I cannot stay in an intensity I no longer find stimulating, idly enjoying the fruits of a birthright I myself haven't earned. I must go on and on into another intensity, where I will incinerate all that was preconceived in me in the soaring flames of Large Sincerity.

In reply to Kana's letter Akio sent her a big tin of assorted biscuits with horses and hunters colourfully painted on the lid. The accompanying card said on one side:

Made in England. I am a confirmed Anglophile.

and on the other:

So many 'cannots' in your letter. Good luck, yours ever,

AKIO.

A typically male, condescending gesture. Kana felt depression ooze out of her pores as she sat and nibbled the buttery biscuits in her Jardin room. She saw herself being rejected by both sides and dangling in mid-air in an appalling muddle.

At the start of rehearsal on the 21st of November, exactly a week before the 28th November demo, Minami broke the news to the Free Stagers:

'Otani has resigned. He dragooned us into putting on *The Witches of Salem*, and now he's abandoned his joint-directorship. Come December all the unions will be at their most restive, ready to strike at a drop of a hat, clamouring for large end-of-the-year bonuses. Otani is no fool. He wants to exploit this seasonal hysteria, bringing the union members en masse behind his 'Down with ANPO, Up with Kirilovists' movement.

Hasn't a second to lose, he says. For my part I find it both embarrassing and tragic to see Otani making a fool of himself, haranguing a band of sycophants, littering the streets with incomprehensible leaflets, back-slapping with the illiterate union bosses who haven't a clue what he's talking about and antagonizing the country's leading intellectuals with his rabid criticisms.'

Kana was indignant that Minami should publicly criticize Otani. 'How dare he?' she fumed.

'You can't blame a revolutionary stylist like Minami-san for not appreciating Otani-san's carryings-on, Balloon,' said Myshkin. 'He's going to go the whole hog and that means not only a lot of sweat, dirt, but a lot of compromise. Personally I find it rather moving.'

Myshkin and Kana went to a bonfire symposium the Kirilovists organized on the steps outside the Okuma Theatre. About three hundred students dutifully huddled round the fire, their eyes watering from the gust-blown smoke. Single Cell and two other girls tended to the fire, distributed leaflets and acted as claque.

A rumour had been around that Otani had been thrown out of his lodgings for having failed to pay his rent for six months and that he now moved from one friends's 'apahto' to another, but Kana, who already suspected the worst, did not bat an eyelid when the flames from the bonfire picked out Denim's striped muffler round his neck.

Overwork and strain had gutted the flesh and robbed the colour from his face. His voice, hoarse and toneless, sounded like a drum of canvas; in order to stress a point he had to jerk and gyrate his body till blue veins stood out on his neck.

As she listened to him, she believed in the coherent reality of an inevitable revolution. She found herself accepting its eventual coming as naturally as tonight's sleep. When she heard him say 'We students owe our people a revolution!' she felt she could, or rather she felt she must and therefore she did, see every *sprechchorring* mouth and every sunlit forehead of the people, Otani's people, knocking down the sick old society like a pack of cards.

But, away from Otani and Waseda campus, she was not sure at all what future she saw for the world. Chatting with the Jardin girls, driving past the Imperial Palace in her uncle's Mercedes or lunching with her Aunt Sachi at Kitcho, she saw things and society as implacably lasting and unchanging as she had been brought up to think they would be.

The morning of 28 November, Kana took the precaution of getting Miss Arashi's permission to spend the night at her aunt's.

It couldn't have been a better day for a demo. A cloudless blue sky gaped high above thousands of colourful balloons and red union flags and 28,000 demonstrators who thronged the streets of the Diet Hill sang 'Dark-Eyed Slav Boy' or 'Stenka Razin' and tirelessly *sprechchorred*.

In fact the whole scene was rather like the dress rehearsal for a grand opera. The dense lines of armoured police trucks, loudspeaker cars, hooded trucks, motorcycles and fire engines seemed only to enhance the solemn grandeur of the production. Three thousand helmeted policemen stood in reserve with the vacuous expression of sun-bathers; sentinels with walkie-talkies, planted on top of the steep slope of the lawned embankments, were silhouetted against the warm setting sun.

During one particularly uninspiring drivel of a speech by a Mainstream orator, Wood Peck, who had joined the Kirilovist Students League only the week before, suddenly appeared amongst the Free Stagers, wearing a Kirilovist yellow headband low over her eyebrows.

'How-dee, Wood Peck, you look just like a Yellow Apache in a John Ford film!' Yamada teased her.

'Never mind how I look, silly. Why are you all lurking so far back today? Come to the front.' She said briskly. 'So many of us up front are Free Stagers anyway. Do let's join up!'

'But does your Kirilovist boss want us in the front?' asked Minami.

'Of course, Otani-san sent me. He wants us to sing together.'

The Free Stagers with their *Witches of Salem* placards moved up front, to a hearty welcome from the Kirilovist group, amongst whom the most jubilant were Myshkin, Single Cell and Abe.

Sta-san conducted and with the well trained Free Stage alto and tenor singers the chorus flowed on impressively, inviting much applause from all the nearby demonstrators at the end of every number. It was during 'Kachusha' that Otani's voice through a loudspeaker suddenly blared out: 'Friends, attention . . . The Fascists . . . the Sacred Island Defenders have . . .!' The voice was abruptly cut off and Kana saw two trucks with men in black uniforms and headbands ram the open truck on which Otani was still clutching a dead microphone.

The Fascists, using wooden pikes and swords, and yelling abuse, lashed out viciously at the unarmed students, driving them cowering to the ground. Kana caught sight of Otani's mackintosh for a second, then he was lost in total chaos.

'The Fascists have got Otani-san!' Kana shouted over her shoulders to Denim; why to Denim, Kana could not think.

'No, he's all right. I saw him dash through the side gate into the Diet grounds!' Myshkin screamed, wrenching Kana's arm.

Without the provocation of the militant right-wingers the students would not have stormed the Diet grounds, some kinder critics of the event said later; while the conservative papers declared that the Kirilovist element in the ZGR had long premeditated the Diet break-in. As far as Kana could tell, it all happened quite spontaneously on the spur of the moment; from the moment she heard Myshkin shout 'Follow Otani-san! Inside the gate!' till she actually found herself inside the Diet wall, not more than five minutes had elapsed. The rank-and-file simply surged forward, for the whole purpose of forming a scrimmage was that once one was in it, one had to move forward.

In front of the Diet building, that awesome bastion of inviolable authority, the invaders *sprechchorred*, sang and zig-zagged in child-like exultation. Otani and the ZGR leaders harangued them from the top of the semi-circular balustrade that had seen the arrival of many heads of state; meanwhile the police encircled them in tight dense rows and then kept a hostile watch with their right hands gripping their truncheons.

A bun-vendor who had been flushed inside the Diet grounds with his customers sold out in no time at all and, wishing to renew his stock, the silly man went up to a policeman, asking for permission to pass through their lines. The policemen seized him by the collar of his white smock, spun him round and kicked him back into the ranks of the students.

Just after five, a small van carrying the big bosses of the People's Movement was ushered into the Diet grounds. No sooner had the Socialist Party General Secretary begun preaching respect for law and order, than the heckling and booing got so completely out of control that the crestfallen mediators decided to beat a quick retreat. One student, disgusted into a nonsensical rage, rushed up the ramp and urinated all over the main entrance, to the accompaniment of jubilant cheers.

This was excuse enough; the special Riot Task Force moved in fast, and with vengeful relish of violence. They opened up their powerful water hoses simultaneously from three directions, then using their spiked boots and truncheons fell upon the students, who, quickly demoralized, collided against each other like blind rats trapped in fire.

With the first fierce jet of water Kana tumbled out of the scrimmage. Myshkin threw away the Kirilovist banner he had been carrying and shouted: 'Run! Cover your head, run under the wisteria trellis and over the embankment . . . .'

Two boyishly young policemen, grinning, kicked Myshkin in the back of his knees and as he fell, truncheons whizzed down on his head. Wood Peck grabbed Kana by the arm and spinning her other arm like a propeller against the bumping, colliding bodies of the mob, dragged her to the top of the turfed embankment.

'Catch us, please!' she shouted to a group of students in the dark street below.

'Look, Balloon, like this!' Wood Peck jumped over the barbed-wire fence and wrapping her arms round her head, rolled down the slope and thudded into the waiting arms below. Kana followed; slid on her bottom as if on a sleigh, and made a crash landing against the three men. Wood Peck quickly pulled her up, while the men rushed to receive more falling bodies.

Wood Peck took Kana home with her and painted her bruised

buttocks and grazed limbs with tincture of iodine. Wood Peck was up early and went out for the newspapers. When she returned Kana was still clinging to her sleep. Wood Peck threw herself down on the tatami beside Kana.

'Balloon, they've arrested Otani-san! Minami-san too. Look at the headlines and there're the photos of both of them.'

Kana, her buttocks and thighs still throbbing, sat bolt upright.

'I rang Beret up at the TBS studio,' Wood Peck continued, 'thinking he might know more than what's in the paper. The gnat had already recorded his comments on last night. Regrettable escalation of violence . . . blah, blah, you know the stuff. Anyhow, according to him, Mysh, Single Cell, Sta-san and Yamada-san were arrested as well. He thinks they'll probably be released quite soon, but that Minami-san and certainly Otani-san will be held in custody for some time.'

'I'd like to join the Kirilovists.' And seeing Wood Peck smile, Kana added, 'Emotional reaction to the last night, that's what you're thinking. OK, I admit it, still . . . .'

'That's all right, but nonetheless I should think carefully, Balloon. To start with, you'll be thrown out of Jardin-En. They work round the clock, you know.'

'I'll move out of Jardin-En.'

'Well, then, your parents?'

Kana looked Wood Peck sternly in the eyes.

'All right, as long as you know what you're doing . . . . I'll take you to the HQ as soon as the police have stopped searching the place.'

Widespread searches and arrests were in progress and not only the extremist groups but even the tame Anti-Mainstream factions had the honour of being raided; the Socialist and Communist parties, smarting under severe censure from the government and the media for having failed to keep the radical students from storming the Diet grounds, decided to expel ZGR from the People's Movement.

Gloom and despondency at Science Hill was thick as gruel: on director (Minami), no producer (Myshkin), and Sta-san

(Reverend Parris) and Single Cell (the Reverend's young daughter) missing. But by the end of the day Bobchin, now in retirement from Free Stage in order finally to graduate next spring, came to the rescue and as giddy and happy as a fish back in water stood in for Sta-san; Wood Peck volunteered to fill in for Single Cell. Abe was called in to direct and Beret took the job of producer as well as the stage management.

Wood Peck sent Kana to the Kirilovist HQ, the backroom of a sweet shop two blocks away from the Tokyo University main gate. A buck-toothed, skinny high-school girl whom Kana had often seen with Single Cell gleefully took Kana's membership fee and put away her particulars in a small case for filing elsewhere in safety. She was obviously the type of person who thrived on difficulties; she grinned almost with rapture when she told Kana: 'Have you heard that the Socialist and Communist fuddie-duddies have sold us down the river?'

'No,' Kana shook her head.

'Petty bastards, just the sort of thing they'd do. Not at all important politically, but financially yes, it's a blow all right. We'll have to finance our activities entirely on our own now.' She assigned Kana to stand outside Shinjuku underground station during the morning rush hours with a collection box strung round her neck, holding a long placard tied to a bamboo pole. Each evening after Circle several Free Stagers, including Wood Peck and Kana, took a tram to the HQ, where they helped mimeograph handouts and letters pleading for financial contributions, addressed hundreds of envelopes and arranged legal assistance for those who had been arrested.

Since economy was the order of the day, the electric stove had been pawned and there was no other means of heating the draughty room. For Kana, pampered by the mild sunny winter at home, it was cripplingly cold. After long hours of desk work she felt her kidneys congealed like two ice cubes.

'A lack of protein and fat,' Wood Peck diagnosed. 'It shows in your chapped fingers and the sores inside your mouth.'

'But I feel good, Wood Peck, this is a good hard life,' Kana said, arching her chest.

219

'You know sometimes your dogged puritanical drive reminds me, strange as it may seem, of Otani-san? With you I know it's your Amen-education, but I wonder what it is with him. . . .'

'A Jesuit school in Manchuria, I bet.'

'Yes, perhaps, something like that.'

Kana was now too tired and preoccupied to bother about her appearance, and often hurried in and out of Jardin-En in coduroy trousers, a wool rubashka shirt, and dung-coloured duffel coat, which hardly fitted Miss Arashi's image of a Jardin young lady. Besides, as the awkward cross-town journey from the HQ to Nampei Hill involved a tram ride and two changes of buses, Kana could not help returning far too often at what Arashi called 'unmentionable hours'.

On one such evening, Miss Arashi, exploding under a sludge of hormone night cream, forced Kana into her Steinway sitting room and called her 'a degenerate and undisciplined little slut'. Kana did not retort, she retreated with a blank-faced silence to her room. The following morning she packed a large furoshiki bundle and walked out of the place for the last time. At noon Mrs Itoh sent Hirano to Jardin-En to complete the move.

Mrs Itoh, always thrilled to be useful in a crisis, admirably refrained from suggesting that Kana should stay on with her: instead, not only did she manage to find a respectable little apahto owned by a friend of hers who had lost her husband in Burma, but she promised to take on the task of breaking the news to Kana's mother. Kana was so grateful and touched that she rashly promised her aunt in return to invite her and her haiku-lesson friends to the first performance of *The Witches of Salem*.

Within four days Kana moved from her aunt's into a clean, new, white apahto in Mejiro with the help of Hirano, who was much impressed by the shower, literally a glass-doored standing coffin directly behind the kitchenette sink and separated by a flimsy thin wall. He had never seen a shower before.

'To take a bath standing, think of that! That's progress. But mind not to open the glass door before you're through, miss.'

He thought one filled the whole shower room with hot water up to the neck.

Myshkin, Rudo, Sta-san and Single Cell were amongst those who were released on December 14th. The Free Stagers crowded round them, touching, patting or shaking them gently as if they could not believe in their return without tactile proof.

They rehearsed till 9 p.m., then a boisterous, happy Circle. The indefatigable Beret reported that despite the general atmosphere of unrest, due to the playwright's fame the advance ticket sale had been most encouraging and that with a little extra push from Myshkin, now that he had returned to the bosom of his friends, the production costs could be expected to be recouped before the play opened. Long cheers for this good news, followed by three banzai for Mr Arthur Miller.

The first night happened to be the coldest night in eight years; but the house, almost capacity, was warm and vibrant with human calorification. The translator of the play, despite the fact the Free Stage had 'pirated' the copyright and had not paid him a penny, sent the company a stiffly cellophane-wrapped bouquet of flowers, which was placed in the foyer alongside the company's manifesto against the continued retention in custody of Otani and Minami. Mrs Itoh and her friends sent round half a dozen boxes of doughnuts and a case of beer, and the boys sang.

Two hours before the curtain went up Beret made a historic announcement: 'All members of the cast, attention please! In view of the amount of grappling, sweat and acrobatics involved in the trial scene, forget the plasticine noses and dyed hair. We'll play tonight *au naturel!*'

What relief, what bliss, the actors threw their plasticine back into a jar. The Salem girls writhed, leapt and howled, glorying to the hilt in the devilry on stage, and the audience seemed to like it immensely: the reception at the curtain call was deafening.

Mrs Itoh and her friends who had never been to the so-called 'new theatre', as opposed to kabuki, noh and bunraku classics, were flabbergasted by the argumentativeness and the lack of sentimentality; but they thoroughly enjoyed singing the Circle song, swaying amongst the young audience.

Mrs Itoh, moreover, appointed herself as Kana's press cutting agent and every time there appeared any mention of the Free Stage performance in the paper, she sent it to Kana.

The Witches of Salem being the latest work by the author of *Death of a Salesman*, two leading national papers reviewed the students' production: 'Inspiring and animated performance. Congratulation to the artistic front of the ZGR,' said the *Yomiuri* and in the *Mainichi* a veteran drama critic, G.K., picked out Tamiko, Denim, Kana and Single Cell: 'Mercifully, they have not yet turned coy and tart, a prevailing professional disease amongst our more famous actresses,' he wrote. 'These girls come on stage, move, speak, and listen as simply as a tree would stand.'

That gnawing sense of void of the day after the last performance; the world of Salem, Massachusetts, Abigail, Mary Warren and Tituba, all that hard work, lacerated ego and tearful repetitions, all over and done with. And now? Yet another holiday at home.

The day before Kana was due to take the Tokyo-Osaka bullet train home, she joined the ZGR demo against the government's bill to control mass demonstration that had just been passed at an early morning so-called 'quick draw' session, one of Mr Kishi's many dirty tricks. 'Save democracy from the Kishi Fascist regime!' they *sprechchorred*. But with every loudspeaker on every shop roof crooning Bing Crosby's 'White Christmas' and the made-in-Japan Christmas an ungodly commercial orgy of gift-wrapped Johnny Walkers, Omegas and sake barrels, with cash registers jingling and jangling everywhere, the students could not help feeling humiliated and demoralized as they trekked in cold wind to little real effect.

Kan went to say goodbye to her aunt after the dismal demo.

'Auntie, come on, let's hear your opinion on ANPO.'

'Oh, no, Uncle says I shouldn't think.'

'But, Auntie, of course you should, you should think! It's a question of your own country, your own future . . . .' There

Kana broke down. While Mrs Itoh stroked her hair, she sobbed on her aunt's silky lap with the ecstatic abandon of her romanticized patriotism and her pure hopeless passion for Otani.

6

On New Year's Day Kana and Yoko were woken up by their father clapping his hands and chanting before the family altar at six o'clock, and all day long a swarm of relatives came and went. The entire second day was spent in receiving Mr Toda's employees who lived in the region and on the third day Yoko's fiancé and his clan came to lunch. On the fourth day of the New Year Kana took to bed, saying she heard a nasty rasping noise in her lungs, and wrote to Wood Peck:

Help, Wood Peck, help! Write me with all the news. I feel so unreal, so weird here. Just picture me, dolled up in my best kimono, my hair coiffed and lacquered to look like a carnival float, and my lips painted in Shiseido's 'Young Pinkoo'!'

Bless Wood Peck and all her descendants, Kana got a reply by return:

Dear Balloon, it has been snowing heavily here and the city is a slush of sullied white and grey. Very bleak. And our morale, very low. You have heard Ambassador MacArthur* and Mr Fujiyama have finally concluded the negotiations for the renewal of ANPO? Now all that is needed is for Kishi and Ike to sign the miserable document. Once the New ANPO is signed on 19 January in Washington, Kishi will force its ratification through both houses before Buddha knows what's happening. Then, ANPO banzai! Kishi banzai! It's almost obscene how predictable it all is.

Your apahto keys have been most appreciated, by the way.

*The General's nephew.

We call it Kirilovists' Winter Palace. Two of our members from Kyoto University are staying there and we use it for meetings almost every day and night. I'm afraid all your tea, instant coffee and biscuits have disappeared.

The Police Chief is doing his desperate best to persuade the ZGR Mainstream not to cause any major disturbances before Kishi's departure for Washington and last Monday Mysh went to see Otani-san in prison, who whispered to him: 'You could still stop the signing of ANPO. Start a sit-in at Haneda Airport from the night before Kishi's departure, and next morning as the airplane is about to take off, run fast and lie down on the runway.'

'What if the pilot goes ahead?' Mysh was understandably apprehensive.

'He'll run over you. But, you'll stop the signing!' said Otani-san.

I hear Otani-san's father is pulling every possible string to arrange bail; if he succeeds and gets him out before Kishi's departure, you can be sure we'll be a bloody red carpet under a Boeing 707. Balloon, take a deep breath and listen, for when I said 'Otani-san's father' I did not mean anyone else but . . ., wait for it: 'Best-seller writer and rebel son,' was the head-line over a three-column article in the *Tokyo Evening News*, 28 December. It went on, 'Saburo Otani, the author of *Afternoon of Indiscretion*, whose last year's income tax was ranked with Mr National Electric Matsushita's, was given a short shrift by his Kirilovist leader son: "Keep out of it, Father, you don't understand!" ' Well, I never!

Denim, titillated by her vicarious proximity to fame, carries on most irksomely. Have you heard that Minami-san was released under police surveillance on New Year's Eve? Am told that he's in a poor state; emaciated but swollen in the face and hands and feet and suddenly with a massive amount of white hair.

Otani's father did not succeed: Otani was not there to lead his Kirilovists to lie on the runway. As 4,000 students watched impotently, shivering in the sleety rain outside the airport, Mr Kishi and his entourage took off for Washington, and just as Wood Peck had written, 'how obscenely predictable', the two king-pins, Eisenhower and Kishi, signed the New ANPO Treaty on the 19th of January.

Then came the unpredictable: Ike is coming!

The first visit ever of a President of the United States to Japan. Eisenhower was very popular; he was the only foreign head of state who was universally called by a nickname. Yet, to everyone the mere thought that Kishi was to be his host and would be able to exploit Ike's popularity to compensate for his own lack of it was repugnant.

So, putting on the worn-out dirty shoes, trudge-trudge-trudge, the rank-and-file Kirilovists went marching and zigzagging, feeling quite on their last legs, and threw themselves unconvincingly at the police line. Only now they were *sprechchorring:* 'Stop Ike's visit!' 'Stop ANPO ratification!'

'All so bloody inane and ineffectual,' said Myshkin with a crude bitterness that was unusual with him; 'like farting in a bathtub.'

With the national ailment of Vitamin B deficiency making their legs heavier than lead, at the end of a long trek they felt much too depressed to go straight home.

'Let's get *kaput!*' Someone would always lead the way to Shinjuku, where shochu* and Chinese dumplings were the cheapest in Tokyo. Even those who drank only coffee or fruit juice got equally maudlin, incoherent and argumentative and they talked and talked and talked.

'This is the age of talkativeness: once we stop talking we plunge into the wildest, insanest violence. So, boys and girls, let's keep on talking. . . .' Beret always uttered these famous last lines before he passed out. By then everyone knew it was Beret's professional duties rather than his committed comradeship that brought him out so diligently to every demo that threaded the Tokyo streets; he had to know his subject well to get on the

*Low-class distilled spirit.

air and comment on it. Not too savoury a motive, but in those grim wet days he supplied them with comic relief, and how badly they needed it!

At a very confused and bitterly split Free Stage General Assembly a decision was taken not to mount a spring production but to concentrate on the ANPO campaign. Beret and Abe went to see Otani at Sugamo detention ward to inform him of this. When they returned, they were surrounded by a hushed crowd in the HQ.

'We brought him cigarettes and books,' Beret said. 'We talked about everything under the sun except ANPO, naturally. And he kept on firing jokes, desperate stuff, mostly of a lavatorial order. When the time was up and we got up to go he said, "Don't come again, please. It's exhausting, isn't it for you too?" We demurred but actually couldn't agree more.'

'Did you ask him if I could come and see him? You promised you would,' Denim whined.

'Of course I did.' Beret flickered a dangerous little grin. 'And his answer was: "Oh, no, I'd rather see . . . Balloon. She and her pink nonsense would be a real sight here." '

Everyone in the room burst our laughing, including Denim and Kana. Funny at the time, but later on, sitting alone in her tiny white apahto room, Kana could not help reading a hundred different meanings into it.

From mid-April onwards, the ZGR demonstrated daily outside the Diet and their encounters with the Riot Police only aggravated the violence of hatred between them. On 26 April, 'Stop Ratification' general strike day, it culminated in the ZGR throwing stones and broken glasses at the police. The front line students then climbed over the armed trucks that blocked the road to the Diet, stripped off number plates, broke bumpers, punctured tyres and finally set fire to one of the trucks.

Kana got away with only a small cut on the head and bruised legs, but Wood Peck and Single Cell suffered from concussion and sprained ankles and were forced to hibernate in Kana's room for nearly a week. The news followed of the arrest of seventeen Mainstream leaders. Wood Peck moaned: 'Everybody who's anybody is in detention! How much longer can we go on?'

It was then at this low point that Mr Saburo Otani succeeded in bailing his son out, on the condition that his son should reside until further order of the court at his parents' house in Denen Chofu. Bail was fixed at the phenomenal sum of 150,000 yen.

When Kana finally found Beret at the Eleven Potatoes, he poked her in the head. 'You've been laying an ambush on me ever since . . . Never Mind, I'll tell you. OK, so we've been to see him. Mysh and your friend, Denim, and I. You still want to hear? Right. Picture to yourself two well-fed maids skimming over the highly polished floor, carrying trays of lemon tea, cakes and hot towels; there's a sound-proofed and air-conditioned room somewhere deep inside the house where the father churns out his next best-selling crap; a large green net in a corner of the garden where the father practices his golf swings . . . And Otani, gnashing fire between his teeth, doesn't know whether to puke or laugh. He has this bruised, mad, furious look and Mysh tactfully hardly opened his mouth and I was certainly very careful, but Denim unfortunately opened hers: "What a gorgeous de luxe home! Smells of butter. I'd give anything to live like this for a change."

'And, boy, didn't she get an icy retort from him. "You are profoundly shallow, Denim. I hope you'll live and rot in a place just like this." He stood there boring a hole in her face. Denim giggled, not knowing what to make of his reply.'

'So?' Kana pressed for more.

'So, the moral is, dear girl, never burn your fingers on a heartless man like him.' Beret's doorknob eyes were set dead still on Kana. If Kana managed to refrain from breaking into a dishwater of self-indulgent confession there and then, it was entirely because she liked Beret too much to embarrass him.

Kana read about it in the paper and saw the scene live on television, yet, even so, like millions of other Japanese on that morning of May the 20th, she was incredulous, till gradually anger and shame seeped into her with this crudest of testimonies that Japan was not fit for parliamentary democracy.

Kishi, whose political future now more and more depended on Ike's visit, got impatient with the little progress the House of Representatives was making in the ratification of the New ANPO. The slow-paced, painstaking process of democracy had never been his cup of tea and now with Ike's visit looming so imminently on June the 19th, he could not afford to let the Opposition continue to drag on with countless questions and amendments. Besides, Washington, DC, was reported to be getting nervous.

Half an hour before midnight on the 19th, Kishi ordered five hundred armed policemen into the Diet and they swiftly dragged out every single member of the Opposition. Doors were smashed; wrist watches flew; sofas were gutted; and false teeth scattered. When the last stretcher disappeared with a shrieking Socialist on it, there remained only the Government Party members left. In record time the Government motions to extend the current parliamentary session by fifty days and try to ratify the new US–Japan security treaty were both passed unanimously. Flabby bellies and double chins trembled in triumphant 'Banzai! ANPO banzai!'

With the extension of the current Diet session, under the thirty day rule of Article 61 of the constitution, without even being put to the vote in the House of Councillors, the treaty would be considered automatically ratified at midnight on June the 18th, the day before the American President was expected. Kishi could now hurrah, for who could stop time?

At this juncture, with only thirty days to reverse the course of the battle, both the ZGR and the People's Movement decided on a daily demo outside the Diet. Very few students attended classes that term; Kana met her professors chiefly in the tube, after a demo. She bowed to them and they smiled and nodded back to her, like friends.

While opinion polls showed that only twelve per cent of the population supported the Kishi regime, poor Ike was getting the backwash of the mud slung at Kishi and inevitably the ANPO campaign began to turn more and more anti-American and anti-Ike's visit.

On the second general strike day, Kana saw Otani for the first time since his release; dressed uncharacteristically in a light blue suit, he stayed on the pavement throughout the demo, to be on the safe side, looking miserable and out of place. There was another surprise on that occasion: Ethiopia had finally decided to come out and 'do a demo', as he put it, and at the end of the massive, orderly and almost festive zene sto* he confessed he had a smashing time and as was often the case with beginners became hooked on demos.

From then on he went every day to the Diet Hill and stuck himself on to the tail end of any group. On the 10th he trekked down to Haneda Airport, ignorant of the fact that the Kirilovists and Mainstream had refused to take part in this particular demo against Ike's press secretary, Mr Haggerty, for fear they might be considered 'pro-Moscow' by taking so clearly 'anti-American' a posture. Only Anti-Mainstream and some muddle-headed SOHYO members went.

The following afternoon on the Diet Hill Kana found Ethiopia in a state of panic: 'It was pathetic how this glossy white helicopter, carrying Haggerty and MacArthur, star-spangled and eagle-crested, had to hover and circle above us and finally land in a ramshackle way. It wasn't the almighty America-san I had grown up with. It was a little rich old man next door whom even I could scare by leaving a dead rat on his doorstep. A shattering experience for a staunch Americaphile like me. If I'm kicking a wall, I want to be sure it won't crumble at my feet, see? I'd zigzag and *sprechchor* so long as America-san is the invincible land of John Wayne and T-bone steaks for breakfast. But now I don't know ... I'm completely discombobulated.'

On the eve of 15 June demo the entire Free Stage company was out on Ginza Street in a so-called French-style demo, snail-paced, hand-in-hand, arms stretched out and filling the full width of the street.

*General strike.

'Oh shit!' Otani shook his arms free abruptly, leaving Beret and Wood Peck to hold their arms awkwardly in the air. 'I've had just about enough of this peaceful shit, haven't you?'

'Shush, jailbird, you pipe down or they'll take you in again, and in any case we rank-and-file no like bad lingo,' said Beret, the jester.

'OK, then let's go to Shinjuku. Much better to get *kaput*.'

Otani took Wood Peck, Beret, Myshkin and Kana to Kidney Stone, a basement snack bar in the seedy west of Shinjuku. As soon as he had left the peaceful parade he was in an unusually affable mood, almost solicitous to please. He ordered spaghetti, Asahi beer, whisky, then, remembering, added an orange juice for Kana.

'Eat serious food, Clea!' Otani clowned, and Wood Peck caricatured Otani's snoring as it used to reverberate through the paper-thin walls of the mud road inns. Nostalgia, mirth and mutual teasing rippled round the table. Otani ordered more beer, more Suntory whisky, and more orange juice.

'You've been up to no good, I hear, Balloon,' Otani kicked Kana's foot under the table. 'Giving your apahto key to every smart guy who comes along in a red sports car.'

'Not true!' Kana protested, thinking – so, he did take notice of everything!

Beret and Myshkin yelled in unison, 'True! True!'

'One morning I awake ...' Otani suddenly burst out singing with his eyes fixed on Kana, Beret and Myshkin joining in at once:

> 'To find you're gone
> Wind rustling, rustling
> in Mimosa, mimosa, mee-m-o-zah ...'

'Crazy, what rotten crap!' Wood Peck shouted; she was tipsy.

'Here's to the health of us all. May we rot and become good penicillin for our beloved old sick world!' Otani gulped down a glassful of neat whisky. 'Oh, no, look what we've done! Balloon's loosened her tear ducts again!'

230

Kana was crying open-faced as she used to do at the mud road rehearsals. Everyone looked at her, amused, but not at all worried.

'I'm crying because . . .,' Kana began in gasping efforts to speak through her tears.

'Go on. Speak up, dearie,' they heckled.

'We *sprechchor* . . .,' Kana went on, 'zigzag, stone police vans, and what's the result? Otani-san gets jailed; Mysh-san gets scurvy; Beret-san does a soft-soap radio stunt; and Wood Peck repeats time and again that the outlook is bleak but we're doing fine . . . . but really, if you look at it hard, we're so insignificant, unprepared, flatulent with hot air but nothing else. June the eighteenth midnight *will* come; ANPO *will* pass; Ike *will* come . . . all our efforts, just one large damp squib. Then, where will you and Large Sincerity be? What will you do? What will any of us do?'

'That's enough, Balloon. That's enough.' Otani bent forward and touched her on the sleeve. I'll tell you a story. My version of Don Quixote.' Myshkin and Beret groaned; they had heard it before. 'A Windmill stands there, gigantic and sinister. If Don attacks the Windmill, he'll be battered to smithereens in a second. But, no use staying put and certainly no use retreating either, for the slaughterous arms of the Windmill reach far. It's a dead-end situation. What could our Don do?

'He can eat almond chocolate while waiting for his head to be chopped off. That's one way of coping with the situation. He can lie still pretending he's dead or commit suicide or dance the samba. It's entirely up to him. But Don, with the full dreadful understanding of the situation, with no suggestion of madness, in full possession of his faculties, charges forward. The revolutionary intelligence dictates a revolutionary answer, which is, as long as there is a Windmill charge!'

'Frankly, it's not one of your best stories,' Beret said kindly as he wiped the foam of beer from his lips.

Otani laughed, tossing his head back. Kana dried her eyes with a spaghetti-smelling napkin and was smiling again. Perhaps it sufficed that Otani was alive, laughing and his talk-bag still inexhaustible.

231

They sat in silence and drank more. Precisely at a quarter to midnight Otani, with no sign of the many whiskies, got up. 'I must go.'

'What? You are mad, Otani. You're not going to that meeting!' Beret who had access to all that was going on behind the scenes grabbed Otani's arm.

'Beret. .' Otani fixed his hard, menacing eyes on Beret.

'OK, OK. You know best,' Beret dropped Otani's arm. 'But, really, Otani ...' He mimed handcuffs by putting his wrists together. Otani looked at Beret's linked hands and a warped smile came slowly on his face. Myshkin bit and chewed his nails with his eyes darting from Beret's hands to Otani.

'That Windmill stuff was a bit depressing, wasn't it?' Wood Peck said with a beery yawn after Otani left them at Shinjuku station.

'I wonder what he's trying to bulldoze through at the meeting,' Myshkin said. 'A suicidal attack on the Diet proper tomorrow? What do you think, Beret-san?'

'What do I think? I think I'll keep to the pavement tomorrow.'

On the morning of June the 15th Kana rang up Akio and asked him point-blank if he would provide an alibi.

'What makes you think I'd help your revolutionary carryings-on?' Akio was by his lights justifiably indignant.

'Oh, please. You know my aunt. I'm afraid I have already told her I'd be out with you tonight. All you have to do, if she should call, and she probably won't, is not to let me down. You'll help, won't you, please?'

'Oh, well, all right . . . . But promise me you'll be careful and won't go near the Diet Hill.'

Kana said she would keep to the pavement, but at 6 p.m. that afternoon when five hundred ZGR students cascaded into the courtyard of the Diet Building before the police could stop them, Kana was amongst them.

By 9 p.m. hard cold rain had turned to a glutinous dark mist. Kana sat in a pool of water, marinated in mud, sweat and rain-

232

diluted blood. Her denim trousers felt like cold omelette against her legs. One shoe had been lost and she had just pulled from her bare foot a small triangular piece of glass she must have stepped on while running past an upturned police truck. A long barbed-wire gash behind her ear had only half gelled; her left thigh, where a policeman's spiked boot had dug in, felt numb beyond pain.

'Just imagine,' sighed Ethiopia, with his small head wrapped in a blood-stained towel and his right eye in which a blood vein had been broken a lurid red dot, 'that somewhere outside this massive nonsense there's the order and bliss of a well-functioning world. A ten yen piece into a juke-box slot, a push on the selector button, and there he is, Thelonious Monk, tickling the ivories. . . .'

'Please, Ethiopia, that's enough.'

'Students, this is the last warning. The Diet grounds must be completely cleared by ten. At ten o'clock . . . .' The police car went on like a leaking water tap. No one bothered even to boo. Like rounded-up cattle they obstinately huddled closely, eyes shut, mouthing a selection of their usual songs. Two helicopters buzzed overhead and the solid rows of gas-masked riot police stood silently with their hands on their truncheons.

It was during the slow chorus of 'My Father was a Mail Coach Driver' that the ZGR car loudspeaker blared out.

'Friends!' shouted a voice, out-jangling all the din across the Diet courtyard. They stopped singing. Beams of light from the TV news crews criss-crossed the hushed yard expectantly.

'Friends . . . one of us, one of us . . . . has been killed about an hour ago! A girl student of nineteen. The cause of her death . . . She was battered to death by the police! Murderers! Murderers!'

Under the deep helmets the policemen's faces were black. A moment of silence while the students stared at them, then they broke into cries.

'Murderers, swallow your truncheons!'

'Take off your helmets!'

'Your helmets, murderers!'

Soon the night was reeling with a unison outcry.

'Take off, take off, take off your helmets!' they persisted, knowing fully that the police would not. Anger was not enough, it had to be frenzy, had to be madness. They wanted to go berserk, they had to go berserk.

The veteran journalists at this point opened their notebooks. The police tightened their helmet straps. The ZGR speaker jammed his microphone to his mouth.

'Let's force the front gate again and let the others in to join us. We'll occupy the Diet!'

The riot police did not give the ZGR squatters time to finish forming scrimmages; they pounced on them with lightning speed from all directions. Truncheons flew up into jaws and hissed down on skulls. Spiked boots crashed knee-caps and thudded into recoiling abdomens, and high-pressure water hoses were opened.

When Kana saw a policeman hauling Single Cell away with a grip on her long plaits, fright jerked her battered limbs into action. She ground her teeth hard so as not to bite her tongue and lifting her senseless left thigh with both hands limped towards the lawned embankment she remembered from the time before. But hardly had she gone a few steps, before truncheons fell on her. As she covered her head, the knuckles on her left hand were flattened. Just then, a fierce sprawl of water hit her on the chest and she was blown up against a red ZGR armband, who picked her up and threw her into another set of arms, then to another . . . .

When Kana came to, she was staring at a clock which said 1.45, in a white hospital room. The doctor's cold finger with a stinging odour of disinfectant pushed Kana's head down on the pillow.

'Let me out of here!' Kana raised her body, felt faint at once, covered her face and groaned. The numbness in her left thigh had turned to pounding pain. Her left hand in thick taut bandages throbbed as if it were being hammered by hot iron.

'See? Now, let us get it over with. Your name? Address? Name and telephone number to contact?'

234

A tearing siren outside. Another ambulance. Running foot-steps of hospital workers. Kana groaned again and gave Akio's telephone number.

Kana's parents arrived in Tokyo by noon on the 16th. Fearing that the hospital report might lead to a police interrogation and even arrest, they decided that Kana should leave the hospital at once and be nursed at her aunt's. Mrs Itoh called the manager of the Isetan department store, and being a good customer, after much blandishment and wheedling she managed to have a Western bed delivered that same afternoon. It was installed in the drawing room with its gruesomely ornate furniture, as it was the only Western style room in the house. Kana lay speechless at the centre of the solicitous bustle. Her one consolation was that her uncle was away in Hakodate where he was building a new tanker.

'Where did I go wrong with you?' her mother kept weeping and moping, till Kana was forced to say, 'Oh, Mother, please! You haven't gone wrong, I haven't gone wrong, no one's gone wrong.'

Her father, on the other hand, was ruthlessly unsentimental about the whole affair: 'Indigestion of too much liberalism. I'll have to disown you if you get involved with the ZGR nonsense again. It's better you learned now rather than later that you can't have it both ways. Either conform to my capitalistic way of life and benefit from it – who's ever heard of a Communist student with 20,000 yen monthly allowance? – or go to a kolkhoz in Siberia or where you will. One or the other, understand? Meanwhile, I'll have your apahto cleared out.'

Mrs Toda nearly fainted at the mention of 'disowning the brat' and begged Kana not to provoke her father. 'For I promise you, he will do it. He will. A streak of samurai brutality runs in his family and how well I know it!'

For the first time in her life Kana was really frightened of her father, or rather of what he could take away from her. Stripped to nothing but herself and Large Sincerity . . . no address, no bathroom, no frame of reference, no security. Could I give up all that for. . . . There Kana caught her breath. For what? For Large Sincerity? For the Kirilovist cause? But, really, what *was* Large Sincerity? She could not answer. What had once been so real now slipped out of her grasp like vapour.

Myshkin, Single Cell, Bobchin, Oka and Tonton, but not Otani, were on the list of the 174 arrested. Wood Peck had been taken home by her parents. Several students and one professor lost their eyesight from point-blank tear-gas shots.

Before the new rain washed away the bloodstains of the night before, endless lines of marchers with black mourning bands across their banners demonstrated round Diet Hill. Flowers were thrown for the late Miss Michiko Kamba at the barbed-wire barricade that blocked the South Gate.

Mrs Itoh brought a TV set into Kana's room and she woke up every hour on the hour to watch the news.

The 18th of June came, the fatal thirtieth day for the automatic ratification. Rumours had been rife that the ZGR would attempt a kamikaze-type attack on the Diet at midnight, but the ZGR students sat on the Hill, most of the time in glum silence, hardly *sprechchorring* or singing; even deliberate right-wing provocation produced no reaction out of them.

The minute hand slid on to the hour hand on the large illuminated face of the Diet clock. The formal ratification of the new ANPO was now history.

As the TV camera panned and showed the street-cleaners making bonfires of abandoned leaflets and banners, Kana could no longer hold the tears back. She sobbed and sobbed till her bed shook.

The day after it was announced that the Emperor had signed and sealed the new ANPO, Kana asked for the television to be taken away, had her windows wide open and watched the green mottled light on the walls and ceilings reflected from the leafy trees in the garden. Mr Itoh was back at home and Kana determined she would go back to Rokko Hills the following week with her father.

Beret's letter arrived by the afternoon post:

I'm glad, Balloon, you weren't there to see it all. As you may have heard, the final demo was a most ghastly flop; it had no stuffing in it from the word go. At the ZGR extraordinary meeting in the afternoon of the 18th Otani led a fierce campaign advocating a final and total break-in into the Diet, but no one, not a single solitary voice supported him. They just sat there looking embarrassed. He was alone, disinherited, if you like. Despite the fact that in the circumstances I thought him making a wretched fool of himself, my heart bled for him.

'What the hell are you doing here then? You never did believe in . . .' he mumbled without fire or dignity. We left the meeting together, drank whisky at Kidney Stone and went to Diet Hill.

I sat on my inflatable plastic cushion and Otani on his mac. Midnight came. Why we didn't go home then, I'll never know. We curled up and fell asleep. A warm moist June night. He slept like a stone, and I only fitfully as usual. Just after sunrise I saw two plain clothes policemen holding out a scrap of paper.

'Must be a mistake. We've just slept here, done nothing else!' I protested. But it wasn't a mistake, as it turned out. The charge against Otani was related to the 4 June and 15 June demos which he had master-minded, and the police had caught up with him.

Yawning and sneezing, without any of the expected vociferation or scuffle, he was taken away. All he said to me was 'Thanks.' I think he was muddled and thought he had spent the night in my digs.

Am very tired and more goggle-eyed than usual. Get well and strong. How one needs an iron constitution to withstand the devastation within.

7

You are walking or taking a book from the shelf, when suddenly you remember; in a flash it comes back – all those hideous and glorious moments that are no more. What can you do but shudder and say, Ouch! Then, screwing up your face, biting your lips, you walk faster, perhaps run, or throw the book on the floor and flee. Flee from the memories and from yourself.

The whole summer Kana was fleeing. She tied up the three volumes of her Excelsior diary, wrapped them in a plastic bag and put it away in her lockable wardrobe. She did not write to anyone; no one wrote to her.

In mid-May her Faith friend Emiko had got engaged to a jovial squat young man who ran a successful chain of steak houses called Texas Tavern in the Osaka–Kobe area. An arranged marriage; his father was the sixth-generation owner of a famous inn in Atami and was remotely related to Emiko's mother. He called Emiko—as plump, vivacious and quick on the uptake as ever—'Cushion', and they seemed to glow in each other's adoration.

By August Kana was completely recovered and had no excuse not to attend their wedding reception. As she had dreaded, there in the vast ballroom of the Osaka Royal Grand Hotel were congregated practically all the old friends from the Faith, perfumed, powdered and covering their mouths coyly with lace handkerchiefs whenever they laughed. They nibbled the party food as if they had only one front tooth. Some paraded their bashfully grinning husbands and some both their husbands and swollen tummies; everyone knew the position and status of everyone else's father or husband and much acquaintance-making for the sake of business was conducted. Men talked about their golf and women traded secrets about their kimono-makers.

Her old friends said Kana looked pale but lovely in her white lace dress, and meeting her silent blank stare they ventured: 'I'm sure to a Tokyo intellectual like you life here is very dull.' Since Kana replied to all such sallies with the same indifferent stare, they soon drifted away from her.

'Don't sulk and scowl like that at my wedding reception, you rat!' Emiko, having changed from the white kimono that weighed tons into a Western-style wedding dress complete with a veil and imitation orange blossoms, hissed into Kana's ear. 'I'm sure you're despising and cursing us all and wishing to get the hell out of here or something disgraceful like that?'

'Yes, something disgraceful like that . . .' Kana puckered her mouth, for she was going to cry otherwise. Emiko's round tiny hand quickly picked up Kana's wrist. Her beady quick eyes were full of affectionate banter. 'Come on, grow up, Kana. I had a chat with your mother the other day. She's very worried about you and who isn't? You have become such a pointless arrogant creature, I mean really! I wouldn't employ you as a nanny, not even as a waitress, you'd incite a strike or worse; besides you'd make a lousy waitress. Don't look so hopeless. When we come back from our honeymoon, we'll see what we can do with you.' She spoke blithely in the conjugal 'we'.

That same evening Kana told her father that she would accept his ultimatum: that she should be allowed to return to Waseda on the condition that she should take no more part in ZGR activities and that she should become a paying guest with friends of the Itohs who lived only a few doors down the same street.

'Why, suddenly?' Mr Toda looked benignly curious.

Kana did not answer his question but watched him finish cutting his fingernails on a freshly laundered handkerchief.

'Why do you spread the handkerchief?' she asked.

'Why . . . I don't know. Perhaps I want to count them.'

'But, you know you have ten nails?'

'I know I do, but that isn't the point, is it?' He now lined up ten cut-off nails in a row. 'Well, it's just the way I have always done things.'

'I'm very unhappy,' Kana said suddenly.

Mr Toda looked at her as if she had declared she was from Mars. Unhappy people to him were strange.

'I don't know what to do with myself, my life or with anything. I wake up in the middle of the night in a cold sweat and hear myself scream inside, *I must accomplish!*'

'Accomplish what?'

Kana shrugged and gazed at the ten neat exhibits.

'I'm afraid, Kana, that's one thing you've got to work out for yourself. But, I want you to know that when I gave you the ultimatum, if you had decided to go whole-hog as a revolutionary, I'd have respected your decision and hoped my daughter would make a damn good job of it.'

Kana blushed, deeply ashamed.

Come September, and the first typhoon of the year blew open a hole in the sultry summer, and autumn roared in. By then every bookshop in every city was stacked with books recapturing, analyzing, summing up, and giving judgements on the ANPO period that now seemed light-years old; one of them was by Beret, a spokesman for the New Liberalism, titled *Beyond the 15th of June*. He had finally put an end to his eternal student's life and now had his own TV panel discussion programme in which his gargoyle-like looks and droll sense of humour had made his name a household word, and he was affectionately known as 'that funny little goggle-eyed man'.

'Dissipation of golden youth . . . I have interviewed most of the 117 students who are still awaiting trial. The tragedy of those ex-ANPO heroes, in my view . . . ,' Beret would say with a suitably wistful grimace at the camera. His old Free Stage friends spurned him and called him 'oily tongue', but it was not only Beret who had managed an oily smooth about-face; many others had shaken off Free Stage and university life altogether as easily as brushing dandruff from their shoulders: Rudo had a small part in a popular lunch-time drama on television; Ethiopia had abandoned Oriental Philosophy and now, his long hair dyed a startling copper-red, sang a Charles Trenet-style repertoire of songs nightly at the Chanson Café de Ginza; Asano had joined the Nichigeki Music Hall as production manager and was currently building a reproduction of the Taj Mahal and a stairway made of pink velvet and mirrors; Denim had quit the university and become a stewardess with All Nippon Airways, a much-coveted job amongst educated young girls; and Wood Peck, that hardiest, most unsinkable spirit, had also given in. After being more or less house-arrested by her parents for three months, she had agreed to the marriage proposal of a widower surgeon, fourteen years her senior.

No wedding as such, wrote Wood Peck to Kana in October. He is a fine man; I like his six year-old boy and we get on well. Why did I do it? You know how it is, a sudden forest-fire of insecurity, out of all proportion and reason, flared up in me, and just then came this proposition on a silver platter. 'The doctor has been offered a three-year exchange fellowship at Harvard University, America,' said my mother and that did it, I think. To be able to get out of Japan! That did it.

By entering into his life mid-journey, I'll be spared all that appalling struggle to find out what I want or should or can do. The scene is set, the cast's on stage, all I have to do is get on and play. Opted out, you might say, but, Balloon, think of it: I can get away from it all and make a fresh start, in Beret's florid language, 'beyond the 15th of June ashes'.

Kana understood every word Wood Peck had written in her letter and was truly glad for her friend's sake and sent a light warm blanket as a wedding gift.

While many, like Kana, went docilely back to the routine of loudspeakered lectures, overcrowded buses, mah-jong houses, exams, kaffeeklatsch, *arbeit* and hoola hoops, a handful of the old ZGR activists turned fanatics. Single Cell for one. She swore that as soon as the Juvenile Court made up their rotten mind, she would go underground and start a guerrilla troop. 'Small, silent and religiously obedient. I'm sick to death of vote-taking, persuading, and co-operating, aren't you? Democracy is a bore,' she said when Kana chanced upon her at a bus stop.

There was a notice on the Free Stage HQ door that had been firmly shut since the end of June:

We are not finished yet. Come back. May have good news soon, very soon. Come back!

Months passed by and no news of any kind seemed to be forthcoming and the notice turned yellow and frayed.

Otani, Myshkin, Tonton, Bobchin and Oka, still awaiting their trials, spent the New Year in their cells. Wood Peck, her doctor husband, and the little boy flew to New York on the 3rd of January. Beret, Ethiopia, Denim and a few others went to see them off; Kana was dutifully spending the holiday in Rokko Hills.

By April, the graduation month, most of the ex-Free Stagers who had earlier vilified Beret for his oily volte-face were singing a different tune:

'One can't be a revolutionary for ever. There comes a moment when one must start *gagner le biftek*,' whined Sta-san apologetically. He was now working for the D. Agency which handled the promotion and public relations of some of the country's largest and most spectacularly capitalistic corporations.

'Don't say *one* must. Say *I* must. It's *you* and *you* alone who made the decision!' snapped Yamada self-righteously. He was one of the very few Free Stagers who still actively worked for the reorganization of ZGR, now split into varying factions each wrapped up in fratricidal hatred against the other.

Abe, having failed to get into the National Broadcasting Corporation, became a muck-raking gossip-writer for the popular weekly magazine *Ladies Own;* Kubo and Dre-Ma married and started a boutique called 'Three Loves' selling dresses, shoes and accessories; and the rest entered the world of the staid nine-to-six white-collar employees, only allowing themselves to remember their dear old mad old ANPO days when they got drunk on Saturday evenings after work.

The new Prime Minister was almost as rotten as Kishi. Elvis and Pat Boone were fading out, Paul Anka was lingering on. More butter, milk and beef were consumed. Cars and traffic jams and pollution became the norm. Pamphlets were circulated on planned parenthood and more jobs were available than ever, thus bringing an inevitable labour shortage. No more home-delivery of hot noodles. The era of instant coffee, the washing machine and supermarket was on the way. The opinion polls showed that the fifty per cent of the young people's ideal in life was 'a home of my own, a car of my own, and a wife and two children'. It had taken less than a year for the ANPO generation to mature into a 'my home' generation.

Another summer; two years since the mud road.

Just before she left for home, Kana received a letter from Tamiko in Karuizawa, a fashionable resort east of Tokyo where poor Minami had been confined in a sanatorium with the complications of kidney trouble and tuberculosis. Tamiko had taken a room near him and divided her time between looking after him and her French translation *arbeit*.

Feeling punctured, Balloon? I am. Today I feel a mother compared with the child I was before 15 June. Think what a preposterous amount of energy we used to spend in pretending, pretending above all else to believe. Believe in what? You may well ask! But, god, how bloody sincere we were about it!

Our life here is bound up in times past: we read and discuss only up to the end of the eighteenth century, dare not go any further. Walks, listening to birds, hot-water bottles ... it is as if we have reached a married state that would be normal for those who have spent half a century together. No doubt our old friends of Free Stage will condemn us for leading the lives of comfy pampered recluses on our parents' money. I don't care. Let's face it, Balloon, it is an unfair world. Take Otani-san, for example, why did he get that seven-month sentence, while others who were far less responsible got twelve to eighteen months. I find it hard to swallow that Tonton, that athletic, simple, devoted disciple of Asano-san – and you and I know what political views Asano-san held! – after being locked up for six months waiting for trial, got twelve months. And it was only the second time Tonton had joined a demo. But, of course, his father wasn't Saburo Otani. We both wrote to Otani-san but got no answer. Bobchin after his acquittal came to see us here, but refused to discuss Otani-san. If you get any news, do write.

Tamiko

Myshkin was acquitted.

'Bad luck,' he sighed when he came to see Kana at her lodging. 'Now, out and free, I don't know what to do. The "my home my car" world isn't for me.'

The next time Kana saw him, it was to see him off at Tokyo station. He was to join a Buddhist commune in Yamashina near Kyoto where he would have to give all his material possessions to the commune and live in prayer, service to others and self-effacement.

'Will you have to shave your head?' Kana sobbed.

'No, I don't think so. It's not compulsory.'

'Will you beg in the street with an empty rice bowl?'

'Yes.'

Kana sobbed louder.

The train pulled in. They stood watching the crowd jostle at the doors.

'You saw Otani-san?'

'Just once when I went to tell him I was joining the commune and becoming a sort of a monk. He gave me a send-off present.'

'What?'

'Bought me a woman.' He blushed furiously but kept his sweet clear eyes on Kana. There was a touching pride and impudence; like a young brother standing up to his sister, declaring his immunity. Kana couldn't help smiling. She handed him a basket of oranges and apples.

'This is for your journey.'

He took her gloved hand and squeezed it once.

'Thanks, Balloon. Thanks for many things.'

After his train had left, she sat on a station bench, wiped her tears away and shut her eyes. An idea was taking shape.

On a day of Great Felicity in September Yoko got married in

Kyoto. Mr Toda had prayed to his ancestors for fine weather every morning and evening since the wedding announcement. After the morning mist had cleared, the sky turned as high and blue as if the celestial limits had been blown off.

When Yoko was led out by the matchmaker, she looked glittering, shimmering all over in the limpid sun. Her shoulders bore the enormous weight of her multi-layered kimono, white on white on white, and with a huge wig wrapped in pure white silk, she looked holier by far than the priests in their gold and rust brocade robes. Mrs Itoh stood agape with tears streaming down her cheeks, for it was her wedding kimono that Yoko was wearing, and Mrs Toda also wept as she had done almost every day during the wedding preparations at the thought of how she had had to barter hers for fish to the peasants in Shitsukawa during the war.

Kana could hardly look at the young couple. It downright offended her that they both appeared so cocksure of their youth, beauty and the right to everlasting happiness.

After the ceremony Mr Toda had arranged the wedding luncheon for some two hundred guests at Emiko's parents' restaurant. Emiko herself, six months pregnant and already the shape of a sake barrel, was one of the guests.

'Honestly, Kana, it's great fun being a mother-to-be.'

'Nonsense, you look grotesque, I'm sure you *feel* grotesque.'

'I feel beautiful! And you, stop sniping like an eternal spinster. What's this, sponge or cotton-ball?' Emiko flipped her finger lightly at Kana's breasts and they giggled together.

After the twelve-course luncheon which lasted four hours, Yoko and her husband changed and bowing in all directions slowly made their way through the line of guests and left on their honeymoon trip to Kyushu.

In the car returning home, Mr Toda was snoring lightly and Mrs Toda rubbed her temples wearily as she said, 'Nine out of ten guests asked me, when is it going to be your turn, Kana.'

'Ugh!' snorted Kana, measuring the density and volume of her insulted small breasts.

Shortly after Yoko's wedding, Akio broke his shoulder bone

in a car accident. Mrs Itoh insisted on taking Kana to see him at Keio University Hospital.

Looking clean and new like a baby in his hospital bed, Akio grinned bashfully at Kana and something private and gentle heaved in her.

'Your Triumph . . .' she said for the sake of saying something.

'Smashed.'

'Will you buy another?'

'Alfa Romeo, I think.'

'Never heard of it. Fast?'

'Of course. Very.'

'Incorrigible.'

How short-sentenced and easy her conversation with him always was. Mrs Itoh arranged the flowers they had brought, made the nurse brew tea, opened a box of choux-à-la-crème and they remained happily chatting till the visiting was over. Kana promised to come again. As she and her aunt rolled sideways in the wide back of the Mercedes on their way home, Kana thought darkly: I suppose I'll end up Mrs Masuda junior. Like moving from a chair to a sofa, as lazy and easy as that. I must see him, see Otani-san.

Kana telephoned Beret at his new de luxe apahto in Shibuya. He sounded truly delighted to hear from her and suggested a luncheon. 'Sunday after next, OK? I'm booked up till then.' He then went back, as always, to the good old days. 'I shall never get over my Free Stage days, never! A blatantly retrogressive sentimentalism, I know, but what can I do? *Konminto*, mud road, *The Witches of Salem*, oh, Balloon, I swear I'll never be as happy again.'

Beret went on to insist that now that Yamada had got Free Stage going again Kana should apply for the part of Jessica, a scatter-brained coquette, in the autumn production of *Les Mains Sales*.

'I know for a fact Yamada wants you. God have mercy, Balloon, you're the *grand dame* of the company with all the old battle-axes gone! Listen, I'll come to the rehearsals, I'll review the damn thing and call you a genius, I'll even sell tickets for you, how's that?' He went on, but Kana did not tell him of the pact that she had made with her father which did not allow her to return to Free Stage, besides she did not want to.

'Beret-san', she said, 'do you by any chance know where I can find Otani-san?'

A choked silence, Beret cleared his throat and said slowly. 'No, Balloon. No.'

'Why not?'

'No. Don't see him.' Beret was firm.

'Don't be silly, I want to send him a New Year card . . . or something. That's all.'

'Liar.' Kana heard him strike a match and exhale smoke with a low groan. 'I don't know exactly what devilry you're up to, but I know it will bode no good. What do you want of him?'

'An end, I suppose,' Kana answered honestly. 'I want to finish.'

'But my dear girl, how can you finish something that never started in the first place? There was nothing!'

'And everything!' Kana said and it was almost a cry. 'Please, Beret-san, please tell me.' A long silence while Beret went on smoking.

'He's with his parents again. Their ex-directory number is 771-2995.'

A young maid answered the phone. 'I'll see if he is up.' It was a quarter past noon.

Kana was surprised that her heart was so still, without one missed beat, when she said to his heavy early-morning breath: 'This is Balloon Top. Could I see you? Today . . . oh, any time.'

He considered, then after a long pause said, 'Five at Chat Gris in Roppongi.'

Before going downtown Kana called in on her aunt and told her she was going to a play in which a girl friend of hers had a small part.

Mrs Itoh was always thrilled to see Kana nicely turned out and she thought her niece looked particularly lovely in her lemon-yellow wool crêpe dress and its matching coat with a mandarin collar. The black patent-leather shoes with bows were perfect. Only perhaps the bag was too sporty and big, too much like a suitcase, she thought, but said nothing.

Kana arrived ten minute late. Chat Gris was as usual full. Otani sat in the corner by a huge palmetto with his long legs sprawling under the table right up to the wall. As Kana reached him, he uncrossed his arms and with an unintelligible mumble shifted his legs as a token of greeting.

It was well over a year since she had seen him and she now faced a young man, slovenly but expensively dressed. A navy blue blazer, a white shirt unbuttoned at the neck, and grey flannel trousers. Whilst he no longer seemed gaunt, he was still slim and under his eyes she detected a blueish yellow flabbiness, not yet bags but a noticeable mark of young debauchery. His lips undulated sensuously, discrediting the rest of his face which, chiselled with stoic clarity and strength, could have been Kirilov's; Kana saw how the strong manly neck spread roots into the strong shoulders, how the large-boned hand made white misty marks on the glass-topped table, and how his trousers clung tautly round his long thighs.

I could – even at this late stage – not go through with it. I could turn round and walk out. I still could . . . . The thought flashed across her mind but her body fell into a chair. He said something about drinks but she paid no attention.

'Ken-chan!' she said and saw a rush of colour rise in him. He drew back his hand on the table. Kana cleared her throat. It was as horrendous a single act as to deliver a baby through her mouth. 'Would you, please, deflower me tonight?' She had looked for the right verb in the dictionary, compared and tested many possibilities, and this was the one she had chosen.

Otani slapped his flat opened hand on his forehead, kept the hand there and began shaking with laughter.

A determinedly unco-operative waitress drifted over to Kana. 'I'd like some lemon tea,' said Kana. Otani was swaying to and fro in laughter, his hand still over his face.

'What tea?' asked the waitress.

'Tea with lemon, please.'

'Not milk?'

'No, no milk.'

'One lemon tea . . . .'

Otani slowly widened the aperture between his fingers, peered through it when the waitress went away. He stared at Kana for some time with eyes that glistened with wonder and mockery.

I could still get out of it as a bad joke, Kana was thinking. Otani laughed, his face bare, sitting up in his chair

'You are . . . you really are such a *non sequitur* . . . .'

Without further pursuing the subject, he began telling her about his car, a Jaguar; Kana listened with a politeness that would have frosted the Sahara.

'You aren't interested in cars!' said Otani suddenly.

'No.'

'Interested in *me*, in the Jaguar?'

'Not really. Otani-san, you've become very boring,' she exclaimed with no needles meant.

'Oh, very,' responded Otani light-heartedly. 'That's because I spend much of my time with women, doing the most predictable things which blight my imagination to a grievous degree.'

'Then I'm not asking any extraordinary favour of you.'

'Don't go on about that . . . you're embarrassing me.'

Otani raised his arm and asked for the bill.

'Where do you want to go?' he asked as they left Chat Gris.

'The sea.' Kana said the first thing that came to her head.

'Right.'

He drove her at a frightful speed on the new highway to Yokohama.

'This isn't the sea I had in mind. . . . It's not at all like the Inland Sea,' Kana moaned as she climbed up the ramp of the waterfront. Mother was right; they make a mess of everything in the East. The Bay of Tokyo was an oil-spewed, inanimate liquid kept in shape by a concrete embankment. No white sand, no green pines. 'It's a slop pail!'

'Ingrate! I've driven you fifty kilometers to satisfy your whim.' Otani, standing right behind her, gave a slap on her back and his hand stayed there with a timid light touch.

Kana flung her head round. Otani looked down at her. Even in the sickening yellow lamplight they saw each other blush. Something lurched inside. A frenzy of hesitation like the first few flickers on a fluorescent light. Otani, looking away, slipped his hand into his trousers pocket. Kana was appalled by the implausibility of the evening. A physical intimacy, however elementary, had never been what her passion for Otani had meant. So, how could they suddenly, now?

He took her to China Town for dinner. He drank whisky on top of 'Old Chinese Wine'. He did most of the talking, small talk. Otani filling ttme with small talk! Kana listened with her head tilted, her eyes skulking somewhere amongst the unclean legs of the chairs and the tables. When he paid the bill Kana glimpsed the thick wad of 1000-yen notes in his black morocco purse.

Strolling back to the car Otani slanted his wrist watch towards a lighted café window. 'It's twenty past eight. When must you be home?'

Kana quickly stepped away from him; she had almost said, 'Ken-chan, I didn't mean that it had to be tonight.' She sat on the fender of his car. A Chinese song as unctuous and slippery as a Peking duck's fat reeled from under the paper lanterns of the café. People, laughing and cooing, sauntered past her. Odours of salt pork and fried vegetables steamed everywhere. Kana had always disliked the queasy-making lustfulness of China Town.

'Is it – ' Otani stood in front of her, balancing himself on the edge of the curb – 'a kind of revenge, because I was not what you'd thought I should be?'

'No, it's just cheap and nasty, simply a body matter.'

'Don't, Balloon. It's not like you.'

He lit a cigarette, puffed at it fitfully, and kept on swaying on the curb. Suddenly Kana turned red down to the nape.

'You couldn't ... bring yourself, I mean, couldn't face it with me, because I'm ...' Emiko always called me vegetable, Kana thought, and teased my skimpy breasts.

'Oh, Balloon. . . .' Otani breathed her name with a tenderness and desire that made her feel like crying. He bent down and blew away a strand of hair that fell over her left ear.

'When was your last period?'

Of all questions! How crude, how obscene! Kana hadn't the remotest idea what he was driving at.

'Balloon, answer,' he pleaded.

'Not now!'

'OK, but when was it last?' he insisted, his breath burning her ear.

'Just finished. Just.'

'When?'

'The day before ... or anyway just finished,' she said grudgingly.

He nipped her ear lobe.

Midway up the hill, screeching the tyres, Otani pulled up in front of a stealthily lit hotel.

> Overnight: 1,500 yen
> Rest: 950 yen
> Sunken bath and fridge in every room

He got out first, opened the car door for her and played with the bunch of keys till Kana got out of the car, shielding her face with her bag. While he registered, a quick, silent, matter-of-fact procedure, Kana stayed away from Otani as if she did not know him and mentally went over the list of toilet items she had packed in her black bag.

A sullen middle-aged woman with her eyes perpetually cast at about the height of her clients' knees, led the way through a winding dimly lit corridor. Their room was named Harbour Light.

A small red refrigerator was working with a soft rumble and the dressing table was equipped with a comb, hairpins, a box of tissues, two toothbrushes and a tube of toothpaste. Beyond a pair of glass sliding doors, hot water purled constantly into a pebble-laid sunken bath.

What the billboard outside had not mentioned was the already spread sleeping mats that occupied three-quarters of the whole room. The fluffy thick eiderdown had a synthetic crêpe cover of flamboyant peony and peacock pattern.

'The door is lockable,' the woman whispered and left.

They sat facing each other across the massive embarrassment.

'Take a bath?' Otani said listlessly.

'No, not with you!' Kana said in alarm.

'Come on, Balloon.' Otani shook his head smiling, resigned. 'I want you to be honest. Wouldn't you rather we called it a day? I don't want to . . . .'

Kana jerked to her feet and began unbuttoning her coat. Otani closed his mouth, looked away, then swivelled himself entirely towards the window and watched the criss-cross of lights over Yokohama Harbour.

Kana slipped into a yukata that was laid on top of one of the two pillows, brushed her teeth with her own toothbrush and paste, walked into the bathroom and did not take off her yukata till she was literally above the hot water.

He waited till she came out and went to take his bath. Kana sat erect, feeling very naked. The yukata, starched and ironed paper-crisp, stood like a large house far outside her. Cradling her petrified small breasts she listened to the downtown Yokohama purr and groan from satisfied pleasures – drunken, over-eaten and over-stimulated. With not a thought breathing in her head, she sat there, till suddenly with a shudder she turned round.

Otani was standing at the far end of the room. How inglorious he looked without his red armband and soiled mac, his long red limbs unmanageably sticking out of the hotel-sized yukata. He stood lost, gazing at Kana; so deeply lost that even after she turned to him, he still stood gazing in a stupor at her. When he came to, he dropped the towel and like a baby who had just learnt to walk towards the encouraging arms of his mother, walked up to her, stepping on the airy thick eiderdown like a clown on a trampoline.

For goodness' sake – Kana was so ashamed for him that she

had to look away. A baby, a waddling baby!

He flumped down all over her and clasped her recoiling waist in both his arms. As he buried his face in her lap, he drilled his head greedily into her belly and catching one of her hands, placed it on his head.

'Haven't I always looked after you, watched over you?' His breath scorched her thighs as he spoke. 'Damn it, Balloon, it's too perverse. It's like asking your own father to eat you.'

He dug his head even more urgently into her.

'Nine months in the cell, I wasn't a Nechayev . . . nor a Kirilov, just a pig. No, a pig would be offended by the simile. An amoeba, more like it, reduced to an existence of the basest survival instincts: eat, excrete and sleep. I threw away letters without opening them, didn't feel like conversing with my fellow inmates, I was past caring, way, way past everything. Something must have snapped. For a long time I couldn't string a long sentence together, couldn't walk straight, kept on stumbling. Only cerebral function I could boast was lusting . . . but even that, after a time, palled on me and I got to the point where the perverse and the impossible alone could stimulate me. Can you guess what was one of such ultimate images?'

'No.'

'Guess.'

'Can't'

'You.'

She was dumb.

'Because you were . . . you. I'd never thought you possible. You were Balloon, small, ridiculous, defenceless, who needed protecting. Perhaps you're one of the very few things I've ever held dear.'

Her hand placed like an ice bag on his hot nape, Kana listened, incredulous – bad timing, bungled chances, good intentions derailed, and here we are, Ken and I, a couple of comics, closing a dismal flop without having even opened! *Tout casse, tout passe, tout lasse*: he'll decay, I'll decay. Like dear old Japan we'll accumulate, fatten, slacken, and decompose. Oh, Mother, what's virginity worth when everywhere else I'm impure?

With Misa, it was different, Saint Misa, she was pure everywhere –

'Ken-chan.' Kana applied her lips on his ear and whispered as if it were a useful piece of advice she was parting with, 'You will commit suicide?'

'No!' Emitting a cry of fierce hopelessness, he lifted his shoulders, his face sodden with tears and perspiration, and looked down at her. 'You bitch!'

His ten fingers forked into her flesh, he felled her. Sinking to the unknown depth of the sleeping mats, Kana shut her eyes slowly.

'Poor dear, poor poor darling . . . .'

Kana heard him whisper in short urgent gasps as he kissed her all over her face and neck and behind her ears, 'My little tiny Balloon. . . .'

Stupid. Painful. Painful.

With a sizzle of agony through her clenched teeth, her eyes shut so desperately as to turn the lashes inward, Kana writhed, shamed and defeated by the knowledge of how alone she was. And how very alone he was too.

If only I could cry like a river! She couldn't. Her notorious loose tear ducts for once were dry. It was stupid, painful, and painful.

He suddenly flew above her, quaking ... then, very still, he cried His tears and perspiration rained on her And he can cry!

Crying out nonsensical little words of wonder and pleasure, he gently lay on her, warmer, heavier and wetter. His caress, no longer selfish, quietly cherished her, grateful that she was close to him. Kana clung to him for fear of bearing the sense of total futility by herself. With her eyes still shut, she hid her head inside his armpit. She felt feverish, cold and bruised.

'Don't cry,' he repeated. 'Don't cry, darling.'

But she was not crying. She despised him for his dreamy contented smugness afterwards. She snapped her legs closed and threw him out of her with the cruel finality of secateurs on a tulip stem. He whimpered, lost and very sweet.

'Don't leave me,' he said very softly. Kana opened her eyes. Ken was beautiful, long, slim, flushed and gleamy.

'I was selfish, I was frightened and it hurt you,' he said. 'But next time I'll give you so much more pleasure. So much more. I will. . . .'

Kana shook her head and suddenly tears gushed and flooded out of her wide eyes. To think once she would have died for just a nod from him! Kana gave a resolute push, rolled away. She heard him call her name. So much possessive love was in his cry that she couldn't help looking back. His arms were stretched out for her and just by his half-raised body on the lower sheets she saw a splash of red, red, red. Kana, horrified, looked away.

'I'm sorry . . .' She covered her body with a corner of the eiderdown. 'I . . . hadn't thought. . . .'

'Why sorry, little one?' Otani took her back in his arms murmuring silly sweet things. She read desire in his voice, in his hands and in his entwining legs.

'Let me go!' She shook him off violently and sat up, no longer bothering to cover her nakedness.

'Will you see me again?'

'No.'

'Why not?' he asked, crudely betraying his surprise. 'You know I. . . .'

'No!' She jumped to her feet and ran into the bathroom where she scrubbed and washed herself in scalding hot water and quickly got dressed.

Just before they were to leave the room, she sat correctly on the tatami floor and bowed to him.

'Thank you, Ken-chan, thank you.'

She was going to go beyond him.

255

About the Author

Born in Shiya, Japan, Nobuko Albery studied at Kobe College and then in the dramatic arts department at Waseda University in Tokyo. In 1960 she came to New York, where she earned a degree in drama at New York University.

As the U.S. and European representative of TOHO, Japan's largest film and theatre company, Nobuko Albery brought many Western plays and musicals to Japan, including the first stage production of *Gone with the Wind*. She has lectured throughout the United States and now lives and works in London, where she is married to Sir Donald Albery.

Nobuko Albery worships Mozart, plays the piano, and is a champion Scrabble player.